SHADES OF REDEMPTION

Chuck Hoyle

iUniverse, Inc.
Bloomington

Shades of Redemption

iUniverse books may be ordered through booksellers or by contacting:

iUniverse
1663 Liberty Drive
Bloomington, IN 47403
www.iuniverse.com
1-800-Authors (1-800-288-4677)

ISBN: 978-1-4620-4286-9 (sc)
ISBN: 978-1-4620-4287-6 (ebk)

Printed in the United States of America

iUniverse rev. date: 08/19/2011

CHAPTER ONE

The great hall was silent, all waiting for their lord on his throne perch to speak. For the people below, the old man held in his eyes the wisdom and control of one hundred lesser men. In these, his final hours, he would pass with dignity. An heir would stand ready. For this, the old king would move into his eternal sleep with hope. Everyone in the room felt the gravity and labor which rested on the old man's shoulders, yet not all shared his ability to hope.

The adjutant general to the king was ushered in between the huge swinging doors of the throne room. Probably the second most powerful man in the empire, the magnitude of his duty was weighing heavily upon him. He looked at the crowd lining the red carpeted and pillared walk and imagined them forming the banks of a stream upon which he was the only navigator. Wise and powerful men of all stations of the domain were paying their final respects to each other and especially to the beloved leader. The thudding boots of the general were the only noise. All heads, on either side, turned solemnly toward the strutting military man hoping desperately some miracle was in the works. He had none to offer. The look on their faces, reflecting his own, told the general they also knew it was irreparable. Why waste the words?

1

He knelt before the steps leading to the throne. The king looked on his faithful servant with a placid smile. The fact this proud man of arms had so dutifully carried out his command without hesitation or protest filled the old leader with calm. It was evidence, he thought, he had been a good leader, to raise such duty in the face of adversity. "Rise and look at me my child," the king said raising a hand, palm out, toward the General. "What tidings do you bring to your king?"

The General had done his duty in a state of numb fidelity. Anger at what he had done festered in his gut. On the walk back from the command center he had twice stopped to consider the possibility, however remote, of what would happen if he were to mutiny. It took great effort to think such things. The General was like his countrymen and loathed standing out from the norm; his duty was his raison d'être. It spoke to the seriousness of the times he was able to even think the thought. He knelt pondering his thoughts, new and radical. As he raised his eyes and looked into his master's serene face the pain of fidelity was washed away leaving only a residue of shame at having questioned filial duty. It was the king who had the most to lose; why would the General try and dilute this thought with his own, silly pride?

The pause engaged between the two caused the wise men to stir with false anticipation. A titter broke on the moment causing the entire room to swell with hope. The general felt the shift in the crowd and forced open his mouth to quickly quell the spark. "All is done as you commanded my lord."

He could feel the spirits break around him, shattering like brittle glass without sound, and then melting into the tile as hope sank out of existence. It was done. It was finished. He felt as if the massive consequences deserved a more eloquent eulogy. But he supposed no words could now convey the heartbreak around him. There was not a single gasp of despair. All air had simply frozen stiff as each entity in the tall hall separated themselves from the crowd in the ultimate existential act the realization of certain death brings.

The old man rose from his chair. How he stood un-shaking in the storm brewing around him no-one knew. His radiance lit the room. It was not the light of hope or strength, but the energy acceptance brings and doing so with dignity. Stretching out his arms he parted his lips and said, "So be it. Go my friends, my faithful servants, beloved children of the empire. Go and find those things which you hold dear and kiss them good-bye. I am no longer in need of your loving patronage. In the end it will be yourself who answers to the living God. Go and prepare yourselves for him, for I am no more.

"Faithful General the task is at hand. Go and do your duty."

One by one the Ministers, Counselors, Politicians, and wise men backed out of the room in bowed reverence to their beloved leader. Some cried, trying to stifle their tears in deference to the strength offered by the old man. The great, adorned doors of the hall stood open until all had passed out save the general. The doors were closed and the final pact made. The last functions of state passed between the general and king to solidify the details of a secret pact; the last secrets of the planetary empire known as Bren. As the business became final the hardened, tall and lean general felt a tear roll down his cheek. The king smiled, "Cry not for an old man who has lived a full life, oh faithful general, my friend Pestia. Save your tears for when all hope is gone. Save your tears if our plan fails. Until then, my last command to you is to have strength."

With the final words he would ever hear from the king, the general too backed out of the hall. He stood watching the proud king until he disappeared between the cracks of the shutting doors. Out-side the hall, in the corridor running perpendicular, the men of power were wandering aimlessly, already lost. They didn't have long to complete their task and Pestia was rightly disturbed. "Show your colors men," he shouted at the mass, "time is going. There is less than an hour now. Find your loved ones and kiss them good-bye. Listen to the last words of our lord and be done with it."

One of the counselors began losing his nerve. He was one of the younger and wanted his life. "It is fine for you to talk of strength Pestia. You are the one chosen to live."

The general snarled around cocking the man's head sideways with the flat of his palm. Pulling out his pistol he shoved it into the man's face. "Hear me counselor," he hissed, "one more word out of you to tip those wretches as to plans made and I'll not allow you the privilege of seeing your loved ones once again. Is it better to die in peace or live in hell? Who among you will risk the dungeons of Ranson? Who here is up to the task? I will gladly change my station with any."

"Forgive him," said an older Minister, who had on a crisp red robe. He stepped between the two, and said, "Pestia, lower your weapon. He is young. You cannot deny him his want for life. He will say nothing."

The younger counselor hung his head sobbing quietly. "Your secret is safe," he said. "I will miss my wife and children. I will say nothing."

"Our secret counselor," the General glowered, "our secret. You have my sympathy."

Pestia entered the control room, the doors decorated on either side with a saluting guard in honor dress. Officers from every service were running back and forth with data and reports, others glued to their terminals. The room was graduated like an amphitheater with the entrance at the highest and, for a moment, Pestia imagined he was only watching a play. After all, the men were running about only on a script now and for no real purpose. The five huge screens, below on the opposite wall flickered evilly with the advancing fleet. He stared for a while at the five, three-dimensional portraits of his planet to gain his own conclusion, and then rhetorically summoned his intelligence officer. "Corporal! Report!"

The stiff, handsome, young coordinator of intelligence swung around in his chair. "They are advancing on all latitudes twenty to one-sixty. There is little time to activate our municipal screens. Time might be already past to activate outer . . ."

"I'm not asking for conjecture corporal. I only want your report. The orders from his highness stand." He could see the glances being exchanged around the room. And these were the most loyal of men. Though he understood their mutinous thoughts, he banished them from his own mind and shouted again, "The last orders of his highness stand. As you will obey my last. No defense is to be offered. No reason shall be given to the butchers to fire."

As the general turned his corporal met him face to face. "Sir, permission to ask for the terms of our surrender."

The general looked into the sharp focused eyes of the proud young man and nearly broke. The thought of his charges being humiliated by the invading scum without a fight sapped his resolve. These, the finest troops of the empire, will suffer the greatest humiliation. They will become the severest object of excoriation, not only from the attackers but also from their own people.

"What terms are there to unconditional surrender corporal?" he said softly. "Stay and do your duty. I need you just for a bit longer."

The general turned toward his desk and the young coordinator side-stepped to be meeting the general face to face. "General," he said with more defiance, "Is there no plan? You are to run and die in your painless booth while we all live to suffer. What is the purpose . . ."

"Lieutenant," the general retorted snapping up straighter showing indignation, "I still have the right to shoot traitors." The corporal grew cold and stood back. Pestia could only feel for the man and continued in a softer tone. "Live without your pride for a while."

"Then there is a plan?"

The General suddenly paled. He thought he had said too much. He felt like cutting out his own tongue. How would it be possible, if even he had slipped, to keep those one-hundred other fools from tipping half the populace before pulling their plug? The general leaned forward close to the lieutenant's face whose eyes were suddenly glowing with hope. The general said loud and as resolute as he could muster, "Lieutenant Fornin, the plan is unconditional surrender."

The Lieutenant stood back questioning. Something in the general's face remained unconvincing to the proud young man. The Lieutenant shook his head knowingly with a small smile. "Yes sir," he said and returned to his station.

The General had been steeling himself for this little bit of treachery since the plan was first spawned. He was to act cavalier to the situation at hand, but nothing he did seemed convincing. He felt rigid and cold. He tried his best to fend off his own true sentiments. He became morose. Every face he stared into seemed to see right through his ruse and into his inner thoughts. With thoughts of failing the lord roaring through his head, he felt the sooner he finished his task the better. Towards the end of his task he was not even convincing himself.

The general insured dozens of people watch him go into the door-less corridor which housed the euthanizer. This was good. People would be needed to testify he had entered the facility. The fact the sentry had abandoned his post at the waist-high Iron Gate that stood for the registry seemed insignificant at this point in time. Pestia leaned into the small booth and signed the book. The design of the long rounded hall, of a beautiful bluish hue which radiated joy and vivacity, seemed so ironic to the general. Had he designed the thing it would have been located in a dusty little corner next to the city dump—such was the man's idea of the dignity of running away from life.

Down the passageway Pestia found a lone figure to greet him. It was an old friend he had left far behind in rank from the military academy but never far from his heart. The sight of his friend infuriated him. He wondered how his friend knew he was coming here. The dutiful general wondered what he would have to do to his friend now he was here as a witness. Pestia stopped and let his friend come toward him. "Pestia," the friend said with water in his eyes. "They told me you and all the rest were to be euthanized today. Is there no hope?"

The General embraced his friend with a hardy hug. "Where there is hope my friend there is folly. Come breathe with me my last few breaths."

His old friend suddenly laughed. "Well, Pestia, how many war games did we fight together to come to this?

Surrender. I know you are doing the wishes of the Lord. He is rightly saving what would be a slaughter. But . . ."

"I know," said the general, "it is ignominious. Let's not talk of things bad right now my old friend. We have but a few moments. They know where we are and will be coming soon. They have already demanded our sensors off. We don't know how close they are."

Pestia's mind was racing now. This was one last obstacle flung at him he hadn't needed. How would he plug this leak in intelligence? "Who told I was coming here?" he asked his friend.

"Your Lieutenant Fornin, but don't worry; he knows it's a state secret. He told me that too." The friend then laughed. "I believe, as he does, there is no need of state secrets anymore."

They made their way down the corridor well past the small, now unguarded, gate. At the end of the long blue hall the corridor turned to whitish marble which contrasted drastically with the monolithic black door of the chamber which sat in the center of the forward wall. One bewildered orderly, standing next to a group of sheeted bodies, stared blankly at the new arrivals. Pestia went to the attendant and asked sternly, "Why aren't these cremated yet? You're behind schedule."

The orderly shook his head saying, "Some were late; very late."

"What is the count?" demanded the general.

The orderly began flipping through the leaves of paper he held in his hand only to begin shaking his head again and sob out, "Too many."

The General gave him an icy stare. Through clenched teeth, the words came one at a time. "What . . . is . . . the . . . count?" he growled.

The young man collected himself and made through the list. "You sir are the last. Eighty-eight in all, you shall make eighty nine, and our lord . . ." he broke off swallowing hard.

"Yes, and he shall be ninety. Yet he will do his duty in the great hall." The general walked to the orderly's desk and picked up the phone. He twitched only once at what he was about to do, then proceeded. The computers of the complex recognized his voice and sent him to security. "This is General Pestia. You must hurry to intelligence before the invaders arrive. There you will find lieutenant Fornin. Shoot him on sight. He is a traitor. Leave him not alive to soak in the glory of this treachery."

The general turned to his friend who was shaking his head in disbelief. "A traitor? How? I know this young man. He is not a traitor."

The answer never came. The building suddenly shuddered under a blast. The rumbling went up and down the halls. The invaders had arrived. Pestia knew at once they had blown the security doors. The confusion would make his job easier. The invaders had rightly guessed the secrets of the empire were dying here in the capital. They had come to pluck them before they passed into silence in order to wring the last bit of life out of the conquered. There was much left for the general to do.

"Pestia, I won't forget you," yelled the old friend over a second roar, now closer.

"Forgive me my friend;" yelled Pestia in return, "no-one must see what I have come to do." Thereby he withdrew his pistol and with a marksman's aim shot his life-long friend between the eyes. Turning to the pale, quivering orderly quickly, before he regained enough sense to fly, he emptied his magazine. He stooped over the bloody man clutching the list in his hands. He had fallen propped partially by the wall. His white face was now nearly the color of his white smock, contrasting starkly with the spreading puddle of blood. People could testify to his entry, but no-one must be there to testify to his disappearance.

Shouting could be heard outside the hall. Suddenly bursts of gunfire echoed against the hard marble, then footsteps. Pestia pulled open the heavy black door with haste. His last view of the world outside was that of the twisted body of his friend lying on the polished rock. It was an image which would haunt him until he too passed into eternity. The door shut with a thud.

It was a door thick enough to withstand any prying, but the invaders wouldn't dally long before blasting it open. Pestia fumbled for the key and noticed his hands were shaking uncontrollably. The black marble interior was just large enough for the slab. It was there to lie on when one had decided this life had offered enough. The room would grant a painless death, yet the disposal of the corpse was a different affair. The orderlies were supposed to take care of this detail, but today would be different. He fought to slip the key in the slot which would, normally, begin the sequence of a painless passing. His hands were betraying him. The building shook fiercely under another blast. He stuck the key in and, before it turned, he wished the room would do its job and kill him. Yet, as he knew, and almost no-one else, this wasn't the right key for death. The key went over and nothing seemed to happen. A panic gripped him. Had the plan failed at such an early stage? He wiggled the key furiously in the little slot. The sound of bullets popping against the granite walls could be heard outside. He jammed it in hard with the palm of his hand. He knew he only had moments now. Every ruinous scenario rushed through his mind. What if the planners had gone to the wrong chamber? Had the one-time switch been accidently tripped by someone else earlier in the day? One more twist and he felt the lock go further. Pestia found himself panting and tried to calm his breathing. The slab rose from the ground until a slot big enough to crawl into appeared underneath. He pulled out the key and moved quickly to wedge himself into the slot when another blast knocked him to the opposite wall exposing the seams of the door with smoke and fire. He fought to his feet. The alter began to lower on its pre-timed sequence. One more lunge and the general slid into the narrowing gap and the slab lowered totally, swallowing the General into the floor. An instant later the black monolith shattered.

CHAPTER TWO

Sergeant Lenning stared at his screens in disgust. It had been two months since the invasion and he had yet to smell the air of victory. The people on the ground had tortured him with the images thoroughly. Scenes of the one-hundred mile long parade which had wrapped through the capitol of the conquered. Images of the huge parties and fireworks and shows which lit up the nights were sent by people to taunt him by showing him what he was missing. Each eight hours, his fellow comrades would beam him the glorious news direct on the Military Information Network. Lenning would watch the messages even though he had no real desire to see all the fun going on without him.

The small ship he and his despised commander inhabited was an old style sensor ship which was about as low as one could go and still be a part of the Trans-Solar Elite Force. The newer sensor ships were all automatic and this one was only automatic enough to make the station incredibly boring. If it weren't boring enough, he was on a geosynchronous orbit over one of the deadest fly zones on the planet. The glamour of the fleet, after all, was to monitor the heavier traffic with the new automatic equipment. The two times his station perimeter had been alerted in the two months he had been on duty it had only been the monthly system check and nothing else.

He knew the news on his screen was, thankfully, drawing to a close. They always placed one of those insipid human interest stories on the end and it stuck out like a sore thumb. This one had been especially annoying to the Sergeant. It was a spread on school children who were designing something the government called "Liberty Pamphlets." The children of the Union were to impart to the children of the former monarchy of Bren how to live in freedom within the greater Republic. "Gone is the single head that once thought for the billions below," crooned the cheesy reporter, "and what is left are the sweet faces of young children reaching out to other sweet faces an entire orbit away . . . Tamos Redik, reporting for the M. I. Network." Click. The screen went off. The sergeant groaned then actually spit on the screen.

It was perfectly silent in the little craft. There was no hum from an engine or gyroscopes, no hiss of air-locks, not even the artificial electronic beeps and buzzes which so often accompany complicated computer equipment: nothing at all. He unbuckled himself from the chair and floated into the back to get his ration of tobacco. As he passed his partner, asleep in a wall mount, he feigned punching him in the mouth. "Puritanical bastard," Lenning thought to himself, "of all the whoring, boozing, obstreperous rejects left in Sensor Corps I have to get stuck with the one pasty-faced religious freak that could make my life even more miserable." Even worse than his religious views, from Lenning's point of view, was this mollycoddle was his boss—a full Lieutenant. "Butt-sucking, ass-holes always get promoted over competence," Lenning mumbled to himself while sticking a cartridge into his smoker. As he loaded the little machine he looked at the Lieutenant and remembered how he had wrestled his precious smoker away from the "little prick" just before it had been jettisoned towards the atmosphere. He had been too late to save his magazines and bottles of contraband booze. And, in saving his smoker with all zeal he, in the heat of the moment, had slapped the uppity Lieutenant with the back of his hand sending him bouncing across the control panel in the zero gravity; thereby he received an official reprimand based on the Lieutenant's version of events. This report guaranteed his absence of shore leave. "I should've strangled the bastard," the good Sergeant mused firing up his smoker. "Fucking puritanicals seem to be everywhere these days."

The priority message bell brought him back from being lost in his smoker. One glance at his watch and he knew what it was. Every day two fellow sergeants of the Elite who were lucky enough to be posted land-side would send up a priority message which would contain only two numbers. Lenning pulled himself into the control room to buckle in for the message. If it weren't answered in thirty seconds the priority message alarm would go off with transmissions to headquarters and wake the "little weasel" of the lieutenant.

Lenning took one more long drag off the smoker and exhaled slowly back. "They better stop this shit," he mumbled in exasperation. It was a violation of the martial law statutes to use the priority system for private use—with some big consequences. He fantasized about letting the alarm go off too long just to teach them a lesson but reached up to tap the priority button just in time. The two numbers fading onto the message screen in succession were 15 and 2. The first represented the bottles of alcoholic beverages consumed in the last day by each man and the second the number of women they had sex with—either by force or persuasion. Today was special, however, and the numbers were followed by an alternating red and green flashing statement reading "EAT SHIT LENNING". "Bastards!"

the sergeant mumbled out-loud, "one of these days the little prick is going to be awake and he'll see this and we'll all catch hell."

Suddenly the alarm went off. WA, WA, WA, WA, it roared until Lenning instinctively hit the override. He had, of course, thought it some consequence of the message he had received and had rushed to cover it up. But in a quick review of events it couldn't have been. He had taken the message in plenty of time.

The thin voice of the Lieutenant could be heard as he pulled himself out of his sack to come forward. "What? What? Report Thargeant."

Lenning reinstated the sensors only to find everything normal. "Jesus," he thought in a chilling scenario, "what if this had been the monthly? Oh fuck! The monthly check and I over-road the signal to ignore it."

"Wha . . . Thargeant, report now!" The thin pale Lieutenant was now panting stupidly next to him. Just what was Lenning going to report? "Wath it our monthly already? Where ith the rethponthe?"

Normally, the Sergeant would ignore the lisping little wimp to the limits of insubordination. But today, he had to think fast. "Well, by-damnit sir I uh . . ."

"Thargeant, you will watch your language on duty."

"Oh yeah, yes sir." The sergeant tried to give his superior eye contact for the big lie but the little soft face was spewing out a morning time halitosis forcing his head back toward the screen. "I think it was a, uh . . ."

"Well, thargeant? Report now!"

Quickly the sergeant mulled over all of his electronics training for some loophole in the Intruder Alarm system. "It must have been a, uh, generator flux sir . . ."

"Impothible, thargeant. Thith craft hath been equipped with the flux thurprether. The . . ." He stopped and suddenly got a startled look on his face. "Thmoking on duty thargeant? How ith thith pothible?"

The skinny fingers of one hand grabbed the meaty forearm of the sergeant and pulled the smoker, up for inspection. At the same time the priority alarm went off diverting both men's attention toward the message screen—the sergeant was thankful for a reason to turn his head away from the nauseating exhalations. He reached up and tapped the message button.

Who came on the screen shocked both men equally, yet frightened only the sergeant deeply. It was Premier Matan, chief of Liberation Intelligence. Premier Matan was the most feared man of several planets for the direction of his brutal interrogation squads and ruthless information gathering tactics. His plump, avuncular looks belied the bloodthirsty interior. Even now he was smiling pleasantly when both men knew he would only make personal contact in order to crush one of them either figuratively or literally—the sergeant knew which of the two he was looking for.

The Lieutenant began ingratiating himself immediately. "It ith indeed a plethure to have you call uth Premier. What can . . ."

"Silence good and faithful warriors," the Premiere began in an even tone chilling the sergeant's blood. "I come to you tonight for some special information I hope you can impart to me." The pleasant tone hardened and the smile narrowed along with the eyes, "I certainly hope, you can impart to me."

Lenning could feel his breath become short and all the color drained from his face.

"Forgive me Lieutenant," the Premiere went on, "but I must disrupt protocol for a moment in order to talk to your good and faithful sergeant. Do I have the honor?"

"Oh, yeth thir." The Lieutenant was somewhat deflated by not being the interlocutor to such an important visage, and yet was doubly relieved the bloodthirsty Premiere was searching for other quarry than he—even though he knew cognitively there was no reason he should be searched out.

"Dear Sergeant," the Premier intoned in a sweet manner betrayed only by his reputation, "a few moments ago we were tracking an un-authorized flight of a Bren ship. When we relied on your sensors to give us information about this ship our Intruder Alarm Network was manually overridden. Can you give me any reason as to why you overrode an inquiry of the Liberation Intelligence?"

The Sergeant felt faint. "It was a serious mistake sir. I thought, um . . . I don't really know why."

The Premiere's face suddenly hardened and took on a ghoulish fringe. "Let me rephrase the question Sergeant," the sweet voice went, "there is an L.I. transport near your sector which is on its way to see you. Is there any reason why it should not bring you in for interrogation?"

The tough old sergeant was suddenly shrill, "Please, sir, there is no reason for that." On the adjacent screen he could see the ship approaching. "It was only a mistake. I have some friends who have been playing tricks on me."

"Yes, yes, we will have time to discuss all of this. sergeant." crooned out the avuncular image. "Lieutenant see that your companion makes it on the craft."

"Yeth thir," the skinny commander responded.

"It will be your responsibility to see to it the sergeant makes it into the transport. Is this clear?"

"Yeth . . . thir."

"Do see he makes it on this transport. We don't, as of yet, have a reason to bring you in too. Priority message out."

If there was one constant within the entire Union, it was the horror the word "interrogation" inspired within the populace. It inspired such terror it had become common practice to take one's life before the interrogators got their fingers inside of you. The obvious implication of the Premiere's directive to the Lieutenant was to insure the Sergeant did nothing to himself prior the arrival of the transport—or the Lieutenant himself would be next.

The Lieutenant had yet never had such responsibility. He had been, as the sergeant assumed, nothing better than a kiss-ass in uniform. The invasion had been responsibility enough though he had no direct contact with the enemy. But to deliver his comrade in arms to such horror was too much. The poor lisping Lieutenant looked at the pale countenance of the Sergeant. He ran his tongue over his lips trying to feel what his companion felt at this moment. He knew the Sergeant hated his guts, but deep down he really didn't blame him. He knew he was a reject among men and his sternness toward the Sergeant stemmed half from his jealousy of the Sergeant's ability to cope.

The Lieutenant put his hand on the sergeant's shoulder. "Lenning," he started slowly, "I don't know what to thay."

The sergeant stared at the screen in silence.

"What did you do thargeant?"

Lenning didn't turn, yet tears began to crawl out of his eyes. He knew what was going to happen to him. He had guffawed a thousand times at the reports intelligence let 'leak' for the regular guy in uniform; a leak cruelly designed to let the common man in on what was in store upon a trip to Intelligence. Eviscerations, flaming genitals, lobotomies, rapes, septic tank swims with maggots crawling in your sores, nothing was past the sadistic animals in intelligence. The quivering sergeant wondered how had he participated in such demonic revelry and laughing at such horror. The humor of other's horror now escaped him.

Lenning looked up into the eyes of his Lieutenant. "Let me go," he said in desperation, "and I'll tell intelligence I conked you on the head. Or something just like that. They won't blame you. My identity slate will have my measurements. They'll know I'm capable of doing so."

The Lieutenant backed off from his partner a bit to reach for a cabinet which would respond only to the touch of the ship commander; which he officially was. The door of the cabinet swung open just in time for the sergeant to realize what was happening. He knew instantly what the Lieutenant was doing. He fought to unbuckle himself from his chair just as assuredly as the Lieutenant fought with the cupboard holding the pacification gun. The sergeant floated free and the Lieutenant swung the gun around to fire once, twice, both shots going wide. The Sergeant flung his smoker in desperation at the little man and screamed, "Goddamn you!" Then a shot found its mark.

The Sergeant hung pale in the air, motionless. The Lieutenant began to sob. Outside he could hear the airlock of the docking ship. The airlock over his head opened and the faithful Lieutenant addressed an intelligence officer who was poking his head through the hatch.

"I had to thubdue him thir," he said while pointing at the sergeant.

The intelligence officer was a young, pale, man with heavily lidded eyes. His black dress and vapid countenance added to the evil of his bearing. He gave the lieutenant a look of disgust and then glanced at the weapon in the lieutenant's hand saying, "Are you forgetting it is a crime to point a pacification gun at a member of intelligence?"

The lieutenant's whole body twitched at the word 'crime' and fumbled to put the gun back into its holder as fast as he could. "Thorry, thir," he said smiling, "I wathn't thinking."

The intelligence officer made a slight motion towards someone up and into the cabin of his ship. A set of manacles were sent down and he placed them on the slumbering sergeant. The lieutenant attempted to help yet backed off when the officer gave him a most disapproving glare. The intelligence officer guided the sergeant towards the hole where a hand came out and hauled the body in by the hair.

"I guess thith meanth I thould petition for a reathinement," the lieutenant said.

The officer continued to stare at him with his heavily lidded eyes which were half closed. The look on his face was half disdain and half boredom. Perhaps the overtime put in interrogating thousands of the conquered was actually taking his enthusiasm away. Or, perhaps, he knew Premier Matan found too much enthusiasm suspicious. Without any further display of emotion he drew his own pacification pistol from its holster and fired into the convulsing body of the young lieutenant. When the body stopped twitching, he pulled another set of manacles from the mother ship and fastened them tightly to the hands around the back of the pale lieutenant.

C HAPTER THREE

In the dark of space there is no sound, no aberration of atmosphere to twinkle and humanize the stars, only a sharpness of vision piercing the soul with a billion points of light whose appearance of more is only predicated upon your determination to stare into the blackness—to stare into the blackness until madness creeps upon you. With your orbs stretched to their utmost ability of light gathering power, as if your soul had yawned open with them to be bared naked for the oracles of eternity to freeze with their gaze, you stare into infinity. Silence and dim light from distant suns are now the only two constants of your universe.

Face the hollow void of space alone and the receivers of your vessel would find very little left of you. Face it alone without the aide of modern science to cushion the blow, with its state of suspended animation, and all they would find of you is enough of a former being to scrape off the walls. Frothing mad, gnawing on its own flesh, screeching for death to take it away from the loneliness of infinity, this creature would yearn for ultimate demise but lacking sense enough to do the job itself.

Pestia saw the darkness and felt its madness creep up on his back. Like a demon sitting on his shoulders it grabbed his face, twisted his neck upward and forced the head into the void to stare. The light of infinity entered his eyes and he wondered. He wondered about all those things so recently transpired: The destruction of his world; the inhumanity he knew which would be forced upon his family. The distant lights forced him to wonder how many of his friends were now in the dungeons of Ranson who he might not ever see again. He could only feel their pain; their pain and the madness which was forcing him to stare.

There would come a time better than this, thought Pestia. There must be better times ahead of this void or he could not continue. How they had gotten so far puzzled him. He had expected it all to end in a painless flash of light long before they had reached free space. Sensor ships were everywhere and missiles an instant beyond them. Maybe the God he prayed to every day was listening to him; maybe this deity had listened to the prayers of the king before his passing. Something had surely helped them through.

The ship was nothing but a small tube built for two. It was a sleeper transport once used by diplomats on their shuttles to Ranson and back; diplomatic ships were now no longer necessary. Cramped and unadorned they were not designed to stay awake in. However, in the last few hours, Pestia had wanted to take in what he had believed to be his final moments. He hadn't imagined success. He had not imagined getting to the ship with his precious cargo. He had not imagined achieving a launch and actually reaching deep space.

And now was time for sleep. Yet, he stared. His face was pressed into the small porthole wondering if it had all been a dream. It would be a dream from which he would wake after the induced sleep and see his friends and family in the parks of his home town. They would all be laughing and drinking wine like they had always done on holidays and feasts. The air would be warm and fresh with the smell of garden flowers; flowers grown in gardens with care. There would be song and smiles and his friends would slap him on the back laughing at the terrible nightmare which had forced its way into his imagination to ruin his sleep.

Across the tube, he looked at the young man sleeping; the son of the Lord, and the heir to the throne of Bren. Would the invaders really believe the prince had been cremated with the others? In what sort of nightmare would this poor, young man awaken? He looked over to his own chamber which would house him in his suspended animation. By the time they reached their sanctuary they would already be a faded memory to the people of Bren. By the time they chanced to return they would only be a rusty, battered legend with no real meaning at all.

Pestia knew how long thirty years were. He had lived every minute of them plus ten. If the preposterous notion of returning upon arrival came to pass, it would be sixty years since the indoctrination of his people had begun. Where was the hope? He looked one last time into the handsome face of the young man. Here, he thought, was the only hope.

CHAPTER FOUR

Two orbs circumnavigate the same light, both of similar size, bluish hue and composition. When viewed as a picture, from high above, each appeared quiet and motionless. Their albedo, which made them visible in the dark, reflected the life giving energy from a common sun. Without the shared use of this fusion fueled object, both of these planets would be frozen spheres. Yet, the commonality of the solar system seemed lost on both worlds. Two worlds which were in the same solar system, made from the same cloud of collapsed gas. The serenity of the picture of the two silent orbs masked the horror and turmoil taking place in microscopic fashion on the surface below. Pictures of the whole do not reveal, perhaps, the detail of what actually is.

The two planets, built from the materials forged in a great furnace of some ferocious explosion beyond a time imaginable by mortals, coalesced from the space-time void in due turn after the ignition of their common star. Their youth a fiery demolition of falling debris; molten surfaces cooled and melted again with massive impacts vaporizing the hardest stones. And time passed. Slowly the objects encountering the conduct of their ellipse began to diminish. Probability began to fall in favor of the cooling masses and collisions became rare. With the cooling came chemicals which were compatible with the ambient temperatures. Free radicals, in a burst of chemical energy, associated to form larger compounds and these larger compounds reacted in another flash to form in the steam of creation the precursor of life. The steam cooled and condensed and a life-giving fluid was created. Torrents of hot water roared across flat, black, lifeless plains carving, mixing, and shaping the inanimate mass into the forms life would come to know. Huge pools of warm water, filled with the solutes offered by the land, grew and connected and constructed massive oceans roaring to and fro in ferocious storms; storms created with only a whisper of the energy given to them by the element creating super-nova from countless eons ago.

And somewhere within this new chemical solution a miracle takes place. Directed by the physical laws of existence or orchestrated to exist by an omniscient being it is a miracle in either case. Somehow, and in someway, life is born and starts its insatiable need for order and complexity as if to mock the expanding chaos and disorder around it. Life, the fragile mockery of the inexorable march of existence itself, climbs from the muck to find being, awareness, and consciousness and shows itself to the entire universe as a symbol of divergence from the unfeeling laws of physics from which it was spawned.

And so it has. Through billions of years of evolution to the pinnacle upon which we stand we are the product of a trek whose origins are now forgotten. Through the eras, over the eras, and upon countless generations we have come. Here we have come to arrive to all this. As the spirit of life, inculcated into our being in this magnificent progression of nature through heliotropism, kinesis, telesis, thought, and purpose, has created the magnificent self aware beings of human kind. What has this zenith of achievement done?

It created people bent on using all their miraculous skills of being, awareness, and thought and focused it in on the hatred of their own kind; as life is a poetic mockery to the forces which made living things, so too is the sentient being a poetic mockery of the life that produced it.

C HAPTER FIVE

In a radar tracking station on the remote atoll of Kwajalein, in the far western Pacific, a top secret message was urgently sent to American air defense head quarters there. In a span of only three or four minutes the entire network of phased array radar assemblages, communication bunkers, hot-lines and military personnel became focused on one small object entering the atmosphere. Its trajectory indicated it was either coming from out of the earth's atmosphere, or it was the trajectory of an object re-entering from the outer edges of that atmosphere. If it was a re-entering object, its direction indicated an origin of eastern Siberia.

The panic might have been greater had the object, in any other way besides direction, actually resembled an inter-continental ballistic missile. The speed of the thing resembled more of a meteor than a missile. And, much more intriguing to the technicians doing the tracking, the thing seemed to shift tack away from oncoming objects—which, towards the end of its journey, had multiplied from a few happenstance air-liners to a whole host of air force interceptors.

Yet, its speed proved to be tremendous, which made it frustratingly elusive to those trying to track it. The object had velocity far beyond the maximum speed of the interceptors. The object had a velocity which made these super-sonic aircraft looking like they had become propeller driven aircraft. In a space of less than thirty minutes after the object had come up on radar screens in Kwajalein, it disappeared somewhere in eastern California. The tracking had been definitive until somewhere northeast of Los Angeles. At this point the trail became more sketchy. Ferocious sonic booms were reported on the ground, indicating that the object had suddenly swerved north; but all radar contact was mysteriously lost prior to its course change. Moreover, the sonic booms themselves disappeared somewhere over the China Lake Naval Weapons Center—as if to ridicule the military's ability to track the object. The deceleration of the object seemed nearly as remarkable as its original speed. The trackers assumed the object had crashed, yet no impact was observed, indicating the object had done its deceleration while in flight and not upon contact with the earth.

By this time, in a space less than thirty minutes, the White House itself was being notified and a whole host of lesser entities were crawling over the top of themselves in order to get to the truth. Civilian bureaucracies are often faulted by a vitriolic and skeptical public as harboring waste and abuse. Yet civilian bureaucracies are, rightly so, under the glare of the public and this waste takes place in-spite of such accountability. One can only imagine, therefore, the waste and abuse that goes on in a bureaucracy hidden under the secrecy necessitated by national security and without the indignation of a frugal public to force reform. One should have observed the waste and SNAFU's of conflicting regimens, equipment, and egos employed by the military to find the UFO, if only to document the waste or at least to wring humor out of the situation. Naval centers were threatening to shoot down air force planes that over-flew the base on orders from their commanders.

Marines were demanding all ground search personnel using marine vehicles be marines themselves. Commanders were screeching orders for no other apparent reason than to hear their own bombast. Every general in the region wanted his name next to the headlines in Stars and Stripes reading, "UFO Found By . . ." Each and every branch of the armed forces had just enough personnel resembling the other branch—marines with planes, sailors with trucks, air men with troops—that each believed itself the sole proprietor of, and best suited for, the search. By the time the dust had settled, the furor over who had jurisdiction to carry out the search probably outweighed the gravity of the search itself.

Yet the patience of humans is short. The patience of an inanimate object is remarkable. Minute by minute, hour upon hour, day by day, week by week, and months strung together until the whole of this aggregate of time brings year upon year until thirty have completed their passing. All the while pieces of metal and plastic along with valves and circuitry have bided their time through the void of space. They felt no compunction to scream with boredom, become jittery, or prematurely do their duty. When it comes time to function they move into place as if they had been waiting to snap to attention for only a moment, without hesitation, sleepiness, aching joints, bleary eyes or loss of idea. There is no conflict of interest or ego or want of recognition between the parts. For thirty years a little craft, slung-shot around a medium sized star, traveled the void of the space-time continuum waiting for the moment to land. And when the moment came, as if launched an hour before, it had clicked and buzzed and whirred into action setting its precious cargo down without fault, with a modicum of privacy. For every second men had argued the proper way to search, it was to the gain of the purposeful little craft and its passengers. It performed its duties to the end with faultless fidelity. And, after the passengers had been woken, instructions and supplies given, the small and honorable spaceship waited for its cargo to get free, flew south, and then blew itself to smithereens; suddenly, the search was over.

An air force pilot, one of twenty still in on the search some five hours after initial engagement, reported a large cloud of dust rising off the floor of the southern Saline Valley—a full eighty miles to the north of the last sighting and past the northern edge of the search grid. The cacophony of men and machines that roared to the area was impressive. Within minutes, at least a dozen helicopters were on the ground and forty to fifty vehicles were on the way by land—a coordinator still did not exist. In the roar of men and machines to the area, miles from the explosion itself, the greatest clue to the origin of the craft was blown to the wind by chopper blade and plowed into the ground by spinning wheels; two sets of footprints were lost forever on the desert floor.

To the credit of the military, it became embarrassed by the events rather quickly. The Joint Chiefs of Staff reigned in their regional generals and their differences, and appointed a forensic specialist drawn from the ranks of the army. He would be given full autonomy over the investigation and whatever personnel or equipment requested. The captain in charge stood a stocky five foot seven. His head was bald and his dark features carried with him a constant expression of worry whether he worried or not. The good captain was a career military man who despised military politics and career enhancing shenanigans. He was a quiet man who shied away from self-aggrandizement and was repelled by sensationalism. Because of his reputation for a no-nonsense approach the top brass was even more astounded by his conclusion. Captain Gregaris concluded, in only two short weeks, beyond reasonable doubt, in a report thick with scientific reference and little opinion, that this craft had come from another world.

The reputable captain knew a firestorm would break-out from his conclusion. But he, having little to do with the political realm, knew nothing of the vicious personal attacks which would be forthcoming. He sat with a rigid attitude in the general's guest chair; his worried expression now lying upon a foundation of defensiveness. The hefty, white haired general paced back and forth behind the desk running a hand through his white locks.

"Captain Gregaris," the general began solemnly with a sidelong look at the intelligence attaché who was also present for the grilling, "what sort of frame of mind do you find yourself in, while reporting something like this?"

Gregaris was not looking at the general but at the pernicious smirk of the intelligence officer. "Sir," he said clearing his throat, "my frame of mind is lucid. I realize that . . ."

"Captain," the general interrupted, "I don't think you realize much of anything at this point. For two, goddamned weeks we have bent over backwards to your every request. Every man, in every branch of the service, has been kissing your pretty butt and been giving you anything you need. And what in the living hell does our good captain do to thank his United States Army for all the help? He makes them the living laughing stock of anyone with a security clearance and a brain. Why you miserable little, stinkin' rat. I'm gonna . . ."

"General," the intelligence officer interrupted raising his hand, "let me have a go at this." The general acquiesced by yanking out his chair and plopping into it. "Captain Gregaris," the officer continued, "we understand that there are a lot of extenuating circumstances around this case. I think what the general is trying to ask is if you have considered, fully, other possible explanations prior to racing into something, so . . . well, so blatantly sensational."

Captain Gregaris tried to hide his contempt of the intelligence man in his response. "Sir," he began first looking at the officer then turning to the general, "I have tried, seriously, to find other scientific explanations. The case does, indeed, need further study. But, from the speed, the apparent stealth technology, right down to the composite fragments from the explosion, this object did not come from . . ."

At this point the general smacked his hand flat on his desk and jumped to his feet yelling, "Don't you say it again, goddamn it. Don't you say it again or I'm gonna make you eat this report page by page or shove it up that shinny butt of yours everybody has been kissing. You hear me?" The general caught hold of his emotions and sat back down. His red face began fading into pale. Rubbing his face with both hands he groaned, "Just what the hell am I going to tell the joint chiefs tomorrow? Tomorrow, I'm flying to Washington to tell the Joint Chiefs of Staff that my crack expert, who was brought out of his belfry on my strong recommendation, is telling me he believes in little green men; Little goddamned green men!" The general smacked his hand back down on the desk again shook a fist. "Gregaris, I'm gonna take you down with me. So help me god."

Several more meetings were held, none less acrimonious than the first. Captain Gregaris was privy to his skinning at the first couple, the last of which he was taken off the case and barred from further inquiry. Later meetings decided to form a committee in order to work late into the night re-writing the report into a less conclusive form. The need for "further study" was sprinkled around the document like salt in a stew to lessen the bitter conclusion of inconclusiveness. The joint chiefs were not impressed.

In three months Captain Gregaris was up for re-enlistment. He let the papers sit on his desk an entire week. He had been ridiculed, disgraced and belittled. At every turn of his job he found fresh faces to do the ridiculing, all energetically condescending. He was indignant at their lack of knowledge on the subject at hand and discouraged by their willingness to draw conclusions without fact. He was disconsolate because he had only done his job, and he felt strongly he had done his job well. People were supposed to be rewarded for doing good work. He wasn't wet behind the ears; he knew the world didn't need to be fair. Yet, this was beyond the pale. The order and structure and relative impartiality offered by the military, attributes craved by the forensics expert, were now fading into the background of a pernicious, political railroading. George's re-enlistment papers ended up in the trash and Captain Gregaris out of the army. He would leave his beloved life in the military. But never the mystery of the Saline Valley would ever leave him.

CHAPTER SIX

Hope is an amazing thing. One small grain of it is as contagious to the spirit of a people as dry kindling to a small flame. In a place of absolute blackness, one small ray of hope can light a massive space. Rising high enough, this same small source of hope can be seen for miles around. As it is seen it ignites a burning desire in others and, where before there was only a sullen gloom, there is now a glow of optimism and resistance to returning to the dark. The weakness of evil darkness is it must be absolute to quench the spirit of a defiant populace. If an oppressor lets one small spark of hope escape, for even a moment, then the darkness begins to recede under the advancing will of all who want to be free.

From the dungeons of Ranson came a rumor. One so secretive that its utterance meant death. But catching a ray of hope is like holding onto the wind. The rumor came and with it the hope of a people subjugated by a force beyond their will. From these dungeons, through the evil of torture, came a story very distressing to the conquering power. From the wife of a young advisor to the king came the story of a plan leaked to this poor woman out of frustration of the advisor, her husband, as to the purpose of the plan itself. He was to die, he lamented to his wife, yet someone else was to live: a general, and the heir to the throne.

As soon as the tortured woman had convulsed out the story the kindling caught fire. A guard present at the interrogation told another guard and he told another. The underground gossip continued and spread until the story found itself traversing millions of miles to another planet where a spark of hope found an entire world ready to be consumed in its fire. The cowardly whining of a man doomed to die, exposing his own wife to torture and the last hope of his planet to failure, had ignited a furor of optimism which could not be quenched. Each and every attempt to quench the flames only fueled the inferno of defiance and the resistance. The careless gossip of a lowly guard had given birth to the demise of Ranson.

Whispers of an heir were everywhere; there might be a savior for the people of Bren.

Soon, everyone was looking for the young prince. The people of Bren thought of him to have him lead them from bondage and the conquerors thought of him to offer his head to the vanquished. As the resistance grew the intelligence of Bren grew until they were attaining some of the deepest secrets of Ranson. A single ship had escaped the fleet. Of all the thousands of vessels sitting on the ground only one made the attempt and only one made the escape. Racing along at the outer edge of speed attainable and out of range of ordnance that could blow it up it escaped. Yet, it could be tracked. And tracked it was. It was making its way toward a planet discovered by its radio transmissions some fifteen light years away. With this information the hope became a brilliant glare and the occupation of Ranson untenable.

Ranson poured men and materials into the planet at its maximum rate. The opposition of Bren gobbled them as if they were being poured down a vortex. It was easy to vanquish an enemy when the enemy had no local support and no means of being supported. When many of the forces of Ranson became intertwined and friendly with the guerrilla forces of Bren, the task of maintaining the occupation became Herculean. Supply ships vanished in a flash sabotaged to take out half a fleet when they did. Whole regiments succumbed to nerve gasses planted without remorse by children of the resistance. Tactics were of no concern to a people who had watched their mothers raped and fathers tortured. And, as the suppression of Bren took on a more vicious tone, so did the insurrection take on a face so horrible those involved could not recount to others what had been done. The whole world burned.

As soon as there was, hope the conquest became hopeless. The seemingly senseless gamble of an old man, whose wisdom was questioned by all, was paying off. Through the black days people had cursed his name. He was a traitor. A fool. A disgrace to the entire planet of Bren. Yet, now he was the most revered strategist of recorded time and his son the probable savior of billions.

The little ship had, at first, not been followed. At the time it seemed useless. Here it was spinning off into the void on a course that seemed to tell everyone they were never to return; the craft had no ability to turn around and the planet it was headed toward had no interstellar technology to aid them. Later, as the problem of the escape presented itself to the conquerors, a plan to go after it was spawned. It was reasoned that it was futile to block the glaring and growing light of hope, yet it might be possible to extinguish the source. In the early days of the insurrection the plan was ridiculed by officers of Ranson as a sort of capitulation. They saw this notion as an indication of the weakness of the occupying force. When it became apparent that the insurrection of Bren was real, growing and not going away, the plan was put into action.

Premier Matan had recently escaped an assassin's bullet. The would be executioner had leapt boldly off the roof of a building right past the Premier's Liberation Intelligence Guard. On raising his weapon the assassin screeched out, "The king lives," and fired point blank into the stomach of the hated Premier before being gunned down himself. Except for a severe bruise, the protective jacket had shielded Matan and done its job. What the bullet had damaged, more than the person, was the confidence of an arrogant man who had thought himself omnipotent. An irreparable wound had been inflicted on someone who should have been the most secure person in the Union.

The words 'the king lives' haunted the deadly Premier and he became obsessed with stamping out the hope of the resistance. Not only would he try and see this ray of optimism extinguished, he would go and try to snuff it out himself. Not one year after complete victory had been presumed there was now a titanic struggle for maintaining control and the repercussions of insurrection had reached out and touched the Premier himself. The vicious and calculating Matan knew what was stoking the fires of rebellion, and he would be the one to remove the fuel.

It was argued to Premier Matan that he was needed more in the crisis at hand. It was argued that in the space of thirty years, any crisis would have played itself to its fullest and war would be either won or lost by the time any assassination could be brought about. To these arguments, the evil Premier thought he knew better. He knew what fed the spirit of living beings and he knew how to break this spirit—he had done it thousands of times. If the insurrection could be inflated on a promise a long time from being fulfilled, so too, Matan reasoned, it could be flattened by a threat yet to be realized.

He would go himself. He and a companion chosen from the ranks of the most elite. The Premier would go and with him a killing machine of a man and every device necessary to do the job. The chase would be well publicized. The networks would croon about the loss of all hope of eventual survival of an heir. It was useless to pretend that the heir did not exist, reasoned the Premier. Admit his existence, and then admit your determination to exterminate it.

The advisors had been correct. The efficient Matan would have been better used at home. While the strategy of the Premier held water, it lacked the personnel to be effective. The implementation of the psychological punch was critical and only the Premier had the cunning and will to do so. The psychological benefits of the assassin's plan were quickly squandered by the bungling of subordinates. The short term advances of the plan were quickly over-run with a new reinvigoration within the resistance. The snake had lost its head and the invasion force became direction-less. Infighting took over the command. Loyalties shifted from one fiefdom of political control to another within the enormous intelligence structure. Inefficiency and mistrust spread through the ranks. Some officers turned on each other, sending those who lost the struggle to the dungeons of which they had been the vanguard. When the machine of terror collapsed, the average fighting man had nothing left with which to cow the populace. With the ability to control the conquered removed, the average military man's will and loyalty toward the republic began to strain. Without the dreaded intelligence leaning over every man, as it became consumed with a crisis within, the soldiers began to desert in droves.

Official news in Ranson had always been up-beat. It had to be. Premier Matan and the government always made sure it was. A reporter, daring to tell the truth in contravention to prescribed shibboleths, would invariably be speaking his final words. Yet, there came a time when the people saw through the lies and ambiguity. In the mood of public perception, the realization came in an instant.

One day, one show, one hour, something precipitated the transformation. The change was immediate, sharp, and clear being catalyzed with the buried suspicion things were not always as wonderful as they were told. If the war had been won, why was it that everyone knew a family with a casualty? If the people of Bren were thankful for their liberation, why was there an insurrection? If the insurrection were small, why were the hospitals of Ranson packed with critically wounded? The ultimate epiphany of public realization, that lodestar of mistrust, came in a blinding flash of light in the largest city on the planet. A hospital ship, loaded with more than a thousand critically wounded, was several hundred yards from landing when it went off. A nuclear warhead, planted by the resistance, was the first taste of war for Ranson on the home front.

Suddenly public suspicion turned to paranoia. Instantly, nothing the government told the people was true. Every family with a loved one who had perished became polarized from the populace at large. Their passions on the need to continue or discontinue the fight came to the fore. Alternative news sources, all of them clandestine, began to show up; some of them legitimate, most of them charlatans. With the under-ground news came an under-ground resistance. Soon, the ruler of the solar system, the imposer of will, Ranson the mighty was fighting a war of survival on two fronts; one millions of miles away and the other at home.

Four years after a whimpering surrender, three years after the departure of the evil Matan, the occupying army surrendered. The people of Bren suffered much in the last days. The retreating army committed pogrom and genocide out of vindictiveness. In turn, the last exodus of troops, flying in fear of retribution, endured a great slaughter. Troop transports were blasted out of the sky by the thousands. Pieces of rotting carcass dotted the landscape by the millions. Horded into strongholds, deprived of materials and food, the armada of the grand army of Ranson collapsed.

Evil takes many forms. Some of it is evil of circumstance; forces of inertia can compel people by excuse of authority or timing to perpetrate an atrocity on another living being. So it was with the military men of Ranson. They were following the laws and rules and dictates of power hungry men with authority above them. Another form of evil has a mind of its own. It is not compelled by circumstance but creates the circumstance and seizes the opportunity to be evil. A truly vengeful and hateful being needs no excuse, inertia, or particular reason to be evil. For thirty years a seed of hate was making its way towards its destination. Upon arrival this germinating seed of enmity knew the cause was lost and the mission futile. Messages of conciliation and reconciliation were backed up on the recorder; both sides begging for a halt. Some even suggested the Premier's larger and more capable ship be used to return the prince to his throne in return for a certain degree of clemency to be offered to the former interrogator. But the hatred in Matan's mind ruled him. The evil he had always used at his own discretion now dictated his actions beyond reason. Premier Matan, once the most feared person on two planets, was now only a fugitive. He would never return to face the charges which surely awaited him. He would never rest until his final mission was complete.

CHAPTER SEVEN

Coming home had always been hard enough for Barbara Cerasoli. There were plenty of built in tensions, misunderstandings and suspicions. But now, with the added pressure of a new job, one that highlighted the philosophical differences between her and her parents, home had become nearly un-bearable. Her father was the main instigator of trouble—coming with the constant nipping, yipping and yapping of disapproval. Yet, at times, the bald faced yipping and yapping seemed a refreshing breeze as compared to her mother's sighs and groans. Her mother whimpered in a way designed to let Barbara know how 'long-suffering' she was as to allow her daughter have an 'attitude', while giving the pretention of tolerance.

This week-end had been exceptionally bad. It always was worse when her father drank too much. When he drank he felt more compelled to criticize and his wife more compelled to give out her mewling groans and sighs. Between the wheezing and rolling eyes of her mother and sharp tongue of her mordant, sardonic and drunken father it had been three long days of indigestion. On Monday morning, preparing to go to her apartment, readying for her first day of work on Tuesday, Barbara was raring to go.

Her father met her in the hall, with his ruddy complexion, sweat already visible under the arms on his white t-shirt.

"So where you going to meet these goddamned bums?" he said scratching at his sizable beer belly.

Barbara wanted, sometimes, to see her father's point of view. A blue collar worker like him, who scraped to get by his whole life, would look down on social services. But Barbara was content, at this point in the week-end, to see her own point of view and keep it to herself. "I gave mom the address," she said slinging her bag onto one shoulder. "The phone number is there and everything."

Her father wasn't about to be dissuaded by her outward calm. "These people ain't crazy," he went on. "If they was crazy they'd be working for a living, nothing but stinking bums. And one of them is going to hurt you. You mark my words. You're going to bend backwards to help the stinking, filthy little bums and, when they get their first chance, they're going to get you."

Barbara held her tongue while staring at the diminutive, pudgy, man standing in front of her, telling herself just to walk away. He had seemed so much more of a commanding figure in her youth and wanted to remember him from earlier impressions. She wanted to turn and walk, but her feet stood fast. He stared back gauging the contempt on her face. "Every young person thinks they know it all," he went on, "I'm just telling you what you're going to learn in a few years. And you would learn it now if you weren't such a spoiled shit and would listen to good advice."

Barbara's mother had been eavesdropping from the other room and came rushing into the hall to try and ameliorate the situation; which always had the effect of exacerbating it for Barbara. Like a fighter who feels more compelled to try and pick a fight when there is someone there to hold them back, Barbara's father was always more vicious when her mother came to act as intermediary. "Now, dad," the mother said, letting out a gasp of air that irritated Barbara more than her father's previous statements, "she's doing what she thinks is best."

"What the hell does this little snot know about best," he said directing his comment to his wife. "She ain't gave a thought about what was best in twenty-two years. All she cares about is pissing off her parents. Here she is going down to the scummy parts of town to give money to people who wouldn't lift a finger to help themselves instead of having them get a real job that paid something. You might think that she would care about what we thought. You might think she would care about what anybody thought about people who would go down and give government handouts to filthy niggers and wet-backs."

Her father was getting into old, muddy waters. He believed, out of some fantasy, he had put Barbara through college and could, therefore, tell her what she should be doing with her degree. Barbara had worked her own way through school and was paying off her own student loans. The only time her father became interested in her education was when she graduated. He then, in his infinite wisdom, pronounced her an 'idiot' for having got a social services degree.

This last comment was too much and the feet began to move. Her mother reached out grabbed her around the shoulders from behind. "He just loves you so much Barb," she soothed wheezing again right in Barbara's ear.

Barbara shrugged loose her mother as gently as possible and opened the door. "Thanks for the hospitality mom," she said looking down and away. "Take care dad." And she was on her way.

She navigated the old car out of the middle class neighborhood with her stomach in knots. After a scene like this it was hard for her to not look at all the big houses with a sort of contempt. She knew, though, when she was in a less emotional state, there would be no reason to blame these denizens for her parent's attitude. She halted the car at a stop sign that fed the main road. The tears in her eyes began to roll down her cheeks. She felt around under the big old bench seat for her box of tissues and found one to wipe her eyes.

Family matters were always the hardest to deal with for Barbara. The closeness and intimacy of the verbal blows thrown always made any contention that much more lethal. Barbara understood filial duty and valued the commodity of respect. Yet the pull and push of family matters was tearing her apart. The good, in these situations of good and bad, had forced her to childhood fantasy. Maybe next time she could get them to come to her place, she thought. It always seemed better when she could get them to a neutral corner.

Behind the car, she heard a horn honk. It was a late model BMW. From the rear view mirror, the honking driver looked like a business man in an expensive looking suit. Barbara leaned out the window, made eye contact with the driver, raised up a middle finger and yelled, "Blow it out your ass!"

Tuesday morning came in a whirl of scenes and emotions which began with a raucous alarm clock. Boxes were littered around the apartment, yet to be un-packed from the move. Barbara had given up trying to put the bed frame together and had plopped the mattress on the floor and slept with a couple of beach towels for blankets and a pair of jeans for a pillow—the bedding accoutrements were still lost, somewhere in one of the many boxes. The sound of the alarm made the day leap out at her like a hungry carnivore emerging from a cave. She had found solace the night before on the telephone with a friend and in a bottle of wine; the same bottle of wine which was now muddling her thoughts. She stumbled around the small apartment having to search for everything; one shoe was here and another way over there. The ensemble of clothing flung itself together just in time to run out the door.

She looked fine for her first day of work, but, to Barbara, she looked and felt like a rat's nest of confusion and un-professionalism. She checked her appearance in the rearview mirror at least ten times on the drive in. Her contact was a large black man named Jeremy Brown. He had a friendly smile showing between a scraggly black beard. The foul insults from her father played over in her mind as she talked to him. She found it ironic that her father, such a crude and pompous man, could refer to someone as nice and professional as Jeremy with words like "stinking nigger." She felt a little uncomfortable even thinking the words, though they never would have entered her head under her own volition.

The office was in a part of town bordering on the financial district. On one side of the cramped quarters were the convention centers, hotels, high rise office buildings, and all those things that go into making a vibrant center of commerce. On the other side were the slums, housing projects of good intentions gone awry, crime and all those things which seem, anymore, part and parcel of what is considered vibrant commerce. As if a physical and metaphorical buffer between the two, her social services office sat on the battle front between the haves and have not's. It was undersized, chaotic and in bad need of maintenance. People of all types were pushing their way around desks and cubicles loaded with computer terminals, files, stacks of paper and office paraphernalia. Clients, some filthy and stinking of urine, some on the road to apparent recovery, followed their case workers to station after station.

Jeremy sat down in the chair at his cubicle, opposite Barbara. His enjoyable, rubbery, and pleasant features seemed out of place in the stressful surroundings. He stroked his bristly little beard for a moment then said, "Well Barbara, welcome to the jungle. Any questions?"

Barbara didn't feel competent enough to ask questions but figured it was polite to do so. She felt the tenderfoot, an awkward rookie, very small, weak and vulnerable. She looked at the stack of files on Jeremy's desk and made the attempt at being polite, "How many open cases do you have?"

Jeremy looked puzzled at the question. Barbara saw the expression and became embarrassed. "Was that a stupid question?" she asked.

"No, no," Jeremy said waving a long-fingered, flat palm in the air and shaking his head. "I guess it's just that . . . well, I've kind of lost count. Maybe, a hundred. I'm not sure. They come in faster than I can deal with and leave slower than I want them to." He finished by letting loose a giggle.

Barbara looked around the office trying to hide her shock. It was all fairly overwhelming at this point to a young woman from the suburbs: the smells, the confusion, the security guard, and the graffiti on the outside. She felt positively silly having bothered to put on make-up and having worried about not meticulously doing her hair. She bit her lip and tried to think of something else to say.

Jeremy continued, "Look Barbara. We used to have a person in charge of training. But they took off. Training got dumped on me because . . . well, that doesn't sound so good, 'dumped', but I think you know what I mean. I don't really have a set program. Actually you're a god send to me. During your training you'll be working some of my cases. I'm supposed to supervise you during this time, but I'll be honest. It's a baptism by fire out here. The cases I give you in training will most likely become your permanent cases, unless, of course, you don't work out. Which is damn near impossible. Down here we just need bodies."

Jeremy paused seeing Barbara looked somewhat offended at the thought of being a shoo-in. He leaned back and adjusted his tie. He had never been a supervisor before and hadn't had to gauge the honesty of his comments. What would he say to someone who hadn't yet been in this meat zoo of human waste before? That this is a place where screeching, vomiting, derelicts with AIDS raise nary an eyebrow. Fasten your seatbelt? Hang on? "Hey Barbara," he started again, "It's nothing personal. I didn't mean you won't be a wonderful employee. It's just going to be a rough ride. C'mon, let's get started meeting some of your clients."

They took Jeremy's car, an older model, not in much better shape than Barbara's, down to the house of a client. Jeremy was looking for one of his clients he found most interesting. Since this client had never exhibited any violent tendencies, Jeremy felt he would be a good person to start Barbara out with. On the ride he tried to explain the young and odd client to the young and fresh social worker.

"It might be better to start you out on someone a little more classifiable. But you should see it isn't necessarily ugly out here. This guy is really kind of clever; chronic alcoholic, but really harmless and funny and not necessarily hopeless. We're trying to keep him in a treatment center. He's been picked up by the cops at least four times and the judge is getting tired of seeing him. He's got an uncle who helps with his bills. He can't keep a job longer than a week or two.

"I used to think he was schizophrenic. But now I don't know what to think. When I first took him on he looked kind of palsy. Real strange. His background is in the file." Jeremy pulled a particularly fat file out of the box sitting between the two of them on the dusty bench seat and stated the obvious, "It's huge."

Barbara flipped through some of the papers looking at arrest reports, court orders, and the like. As she read, she struggled to keep the papers assembled from the effect of the open window.

"One of the funniest things about the guy," Jeremy continued, "is the alcoholic deliriums he has. When he's really fucked . . . uh . . . messed up." Jeremy glanced at Barbara apologetically. "You might as well get used to it. Everybody down here has the foulest mouth you've ever heard, not the least of which are the clients. Anyway, when he's really gassed he thinks he's a prince. You want to know where from? From another planet."

Barbara shook her head. "Wow," she said, "another planet. How hilarious. Does he believe this when he's sober?"

"Nope, just when he's trashed, when he's sober he's just real confused. Here's his house."

Jeremy swung the car into the lane of a white, run-down looking little dwelling with a green, asphalt shingle roof. The car heaved over the cracks in the drive. It was an older style drive with the grass in the center, grass that was brown and un-mown. He put the car in park and let out a sigh. "You wouldn't believe how much this guy has improved. I really think he has a chance. You won't find that very often. This will be a good place for you to start."

Jeremy knocked long and patiently at the door. Paint fell off in large, oxidized flakes from his rapping onto the faded blue wooden porch. Peering in the two barred windows, one at either side of the door, Jeremy looked for some clue as to the client's whereabouts. Jeremy found his evidence, stood up from the window and said, "Here he comes."

The door opened.

"Good morning Mark," Jeremy said, "How's it going? I'd like you to meet Barbara. She's going to be your caseworker from here on out."

CHAPTER EIGHT

Nearly nine-months after his discharge Captain George Gregaris felt an emptiness he could not fill. His grousing and un-willingness to find a job had driven his wife into a reluctant separation. One year ago such a separation would have been un-thinkable to George. He would have chased her down, soothed her nerves and been the loving husband he had always been. But something fundamental in George had changed. Ever since his assignment to the Saline Valley case he had not been the same.

George knew his analysis had been correct. Perhaps, he thought, his natural distaste for the politics surrounding the issue had blinded him to his ability of using the fractured nature of the military to his advantage. The fractional realities of the upper echelon irritated him greatly though and he could not bring himself to exploit these proprietary imbeciles. Maybe it was more honorable that he had ignored the partisanship. It might not have done any good anyway and then he would have been sullied with the stench of having participated in the political games he hated. Why couldn't they take the information on merit alone? The craft, beyond all reasonable doubt, had come from another place than this earth; from the metallic-carbon-like composite fragments, to the speed, to the physics of its escape, right down to the thoroughness of the obliteration of the object when it exploded. Everything pointed to a technology well beyond our own. The idea the Russians were behind this, especially in this post cold-war era, was rightly laughable to George. And the aggravation stuck.

It ate at Captain Gregaris day and night. The idea something or someone from another planet had come to this earth without him proving it chewed on his guts relentlessly. The concept of being so close to real interstellar contact gripped his attention. To be so close to such an historical event tantalized his every sense. This wasn't some tabloid crap or farce. This was real and he knew it.

There had been contact with another being from another place right under his nose. The thought he might have missed a piece of the puzzle or not solved some riddle making contact with an extraterrestrial palpable drove at him persistently.

For nine months the former officer had been spinning the investigation around in his head. His sharp acumen chewed on each piece of the mystery scanning for possible clues. From hard data and circumstance, drawn from every possible angle, he digested the investigation over and over. Some questions went unanswered. Some questions came with answers boiling up out of the wellspring of reason as obvious to Gregaris as the existence of the object itself. Why had the craft foiled our radar so successfully then so thoroughly blown itself to bits in a huge, easily detectable fireball? George correctly reasoned the fireball was a distraction; one which was to draw attention away from the true mission of the object. Fire and light from the explosion were to camouflage something much more precious than the craft itself. In George's mind, as sharp and rational a mind as there might be found, he was convinced, without a doubt, that the distraction of the explosion was meant for passengers of the vessel to wander free without detection. The great military machine had let extra-terrestrials slip between their fingers to wander free on the planet earth.

This was the third time he had returned to the desert. Now, in the summer time, the heat was unbearable. Sweat had just enough time to emerge from the skin before drying salty, crusty white and the perspiration from the forehead dripped into and stung the eyes. Why he kept coming and what he was looking for he was not sure. He did not expect to find any clues, especially one year after the event from a quarry who had so deftly eluded detection at the time. All clues, he reasoned, had been laid out before him nearly a year ago. Perhaps returning, he thought, was only an attempt to ameliorate the frustration which was trying to find a way out of his soul.

He had driven the four wheel drive up the dusty path until it petered out. He could have continued but felt compelled to get out and walk. After so much time out in the clear air and wide open spaces, he was beginning to appreciate the subtle beauty of the desert. Colors of the earth ranged from chocolate brown dirt to flour white alkali. Some plants managed, in between their tenacious struggle for survival, to show a graceful and delicate side with small flowers and a particular hue. The walk would do him good anyway.

It was near dusk and the heat had begun to subside yet was still potent enough for a large, straw sun hat. Prior to the hat, binoculars were slung over one shoulder and a canteen over the other, their straps resembling crisscrossing bandoleers. Every object was hot to the touch; anything black and metal was prohibitively so. Phlegm coated the inside of his mouth pasty thick. No amount of the warm, stale water from the canteen seemed to sate the instant need for more. Any piece of flesh exposed was parched any confined behind clothing was soaking wet. The back of his shirt, against the driver's seat of his vehicle, was drenched until he stood. He then got about two minutes of cooling until the garment was devoid of moisture. The high, leather military boots he wore felt as if they had filled with sweat. Cooler shoes, however, would be foolhardy in a country so filled with snakes—one of the only animals which happened to thrive in these undue conditions. George thought about the snakes and how they seemed a perfect match for the desert. Both were slow and patient. Neither respected any life which was weak; compassion was not in them.

A low ridge in front of him, nearly barren of everything but brown dirt and small rocks, rose several hundred feet above where his truck sat. It was amazing to the good captain that anything survived out here. The northern and much less known cousin of Death Valley, the Saline Valley was as barren and desolate as anything the world had to offer. A valley, though, it really was not. It was more like a broad sauce pan of alkali; a broad and shallow baking dish, fueled by unrelenting solar energy. At the top of the ridge the pure desert air allowed Gregaris to see far to the low, brown mountains on the other side—brought deceivingly close in a dangerous perception that has been the death of many trying to cross such a plain. The clarity of the air and lack of obstruction on the valley floor makes it seem like only a day's walk to the other side when indeed it is much further. The absolute command of the landscape made it seem as if it were being observed from an airplane and not a hill only a couple of hundred feet above the valley floor.

George scanned the broad alkali flat with his binoculars from one end to the other. At one point he fantasized he could make out the point of explosion far to the south. Yet he knew the desert wind would have long covered traces to be seen from so far away. He licked his dry lips and tilted back the khaki, cloth covered canteen. Sitting down on a formation of sandstone which rose a foot or two above the brown monotony, George scratched at the back of his sweaty neck. He rested and took time to wonder just what the hell was he doing there.

As the darkness came he tried to convince himself to hurry back to the truck in order to get out before nightfall. After darkness fell the hazards of the desert would multiply. The cool nighttime, in the summer, allowed the reptiles to slither out of their holes. The simmering heat of the day forced snakes and the like to go underground and with the absence of the sun they soon would be coming out. Even so, there was no such thing as hurry in George's mind. He felt as if he should simply perish in this place and fade into the dusty brown as part of the great unknown. It was dangerous at night and the idea of this danger only fuelled his resolve to stay in that self-destructive mood which accompanies great depression. The sky lit fire in crimsons and oranges near the horizon, and faded in succession from turquoise to blue to purple at the zenith. The huge red ball, shining into the valley from the west, grew distorted and dropped with speed. Stars followed the setting sun in progression from the east. They appeared in singles and pairs at first, then in handfuls and whole splashes of specks across the heavens. There were more stars this evening than George had ever remembered seeing. Only a sliver of a rising moon coming in the east kept the blackness on the ground from being complete. The earth's albedo illuminated the dark side giving away the illusion of missing parts of the sphere. There was no sound. No wind, crickets, or rustle of grass.

His ears strained to hear a sound. His eyes worked to see light.

George leaned over, putting his face in his hands hearing himself murmur, "Why am I here?"

Suddenly, something hissed from high to low on a pronounced Doppler effect diminishing quickly in intensity. Captain Gregaris bounded to his feet looking around above him. The noise had scared him nearly into panic. From absolute silence to a loud whirring hiss, whatever it was diminished to silence again in less than five seconds. As he stood in the silence his heart beat so hard he could feel the vibration against his shirt. He tried to keep from breathing so hard so he could better listen. After a while, his breathing calmed and he put his binoculars to his eyes straining off in the direction he presumed the object had gone. He strained and cursed the lack of light. He alternated between using and not using the binoculars, wondering which would be the most effective. Nearly an hour passed and he still was frantically scanning the bottom of the valley. At two hours, the silence began to betray his resolve. Seeds of doubt could not help but work their way into his mind. Deserts were famous for illusion, but visual not audio. Fighting through his apprehension, Gregaris resolved not to leave for any reason until he had found something, anything.

About three hours after the noise, George thought he made out an object that could not be attributed to the normal shape of the valley floor. The moon was a little higher now and more forgiving in the light it cast. He would try and get closer. It would be a hike of several miles in the dark just too significantly increase his observation power. The effort might prove fruitless, yet he felt he must try.

He worked his way down the small hill twisting his ankles this way and that on small unforeseen rocks. The only sounds were his sliding boots and harsh breath. He did not want to use his small flash-light for two reasons. First, he did not want to reveal his position to anyone who might be watching, and second he might need to save the batteries for a later emergency. He continued to survey the area as he went. The night air settled in on a chill. As he came closer to the suspicious object, his enthusiasm began to wane. He became surer and surer his supposed object was nothing more than a shadow of a depression in the valley floor. Out of desperation he scanned the whole valley. He glanced at his watch, now five and a half hours after the noise. About five miles now separated him from his truck. That is, if he were able to make a direct path back to it in the dark. The canteen felt light. He put the binoculars back to his face.

Far to his left, toward the northern end of the sauce pan, George found something amazing. Something he wasn't quite sure of at first, but became convinced by apparent movement. It wasn't what he was looking for but it filled him with as much satisfaction as any space-ship: there were men out there. More than one certainly but how many he wasn't sure. Three? Four? Maybe there were only two. His pulse began to pick up again. They were at least five to six miles away working their way up the ridge George had just come down. The former captain stumbled as fast as he could back up the hill ignoring the pain of his falls and thick, dry mouth. As he again neared the top of the ridge the men—now supposed as only two—had rounded out of sight somewhere in a nook on the ridge.

George wanted to get back to his four wheel drive vehicle and cut cross country with the lights out. He stopped on the top of the ridge heaving from the effort and could make out his vehicle in the blackness—still at least a half mile away. He took his last drink of water and stock of his situation. They would hear him coming in the truck, he reasoned, and if they didn't want to be found there was no way he would be able to find them in this blackness. It was twelve miles back to the main road. Anyone determined could make it there before light and, with luck, find other transportation. He would have to find them tonight. He was in no position to run anyone down by foot, he thought, so he would have to try the truck—as difficult as that might prove.

He took several steps toward the vehicle when the hissing started again. It was very faint yet unmistakable. George spun around trying to determine the location. It was coming from the northern end, in the same general location as where the two men had come from. A dull red glow appeared and began to rise along with the intensity of the hiss. A cylindrical object, now discernable beneath the glow, rose in a ramp-like trajectory past a transfixed George towards the south, gaining in speed as it went. Perhaps a dozen miles later the object faded significantly and appeared to dip. Over the spot of George's last visual contact there came a great flash of brilliant, white-light. Blinded, as if with a flash bulb at close range, George stood mesmerized, filled with awe and revelation, as if he had seen the second coming of Christ himself.

It took him a while to gather his senses, let alone regain his eyesight; echoes from the blast rung in his ears. The thoughts surrounding the flash clouded his mind as surely as the white spot dominated his damaged retinas. George walked to his truck, almost feeling his way along in the dark. Arriving at the truck, and having retrieved most of his eyesight and senses, he noticed a flurry of air traffic appearing some fourteen miles or so to the south. The same thing had happened one year ago, he thought. They had been looking in the wrong place. The decoy of the blast had been miles from where our visitors disembarked, leaving them far from discovery. The simplicity of the ploy seemed rather elegant to the Captain. Not only once had this deception been spectacularly successful, but now twice.

He climbed into his truck, leaving his thoughts of a year ago for the present, and wondered the best way to seek out the current visitors. He knew the general direction and could estimate the distance. But did they want to be found? Were they armed? Were they dangerous? Would he be able to communicate with them? There was plenty of time, he reasoned, so he shouldn't rush. He was in a vehicle and them on foot. Leaning his head out of the open window he strained into the night. Glancing at the stars above he reveled in the enormity of the events. Finding these people would not only vindicate him in the eyes of the army, but be an historical event without parallel. An event of which he could be the lynch pin. Fear was a luxury not permitted a man so obsessed with an event. There was no question that he was going to try and contact them. Anything less would be tantamount to throwing away the last chance to set his life straight.

A plan befitting the military man's penchant for strategy was put into place. Rather than estimate their course and extrapolate a direct route toward them, he would exit the desert directly toward the road. He would exit with the lights of his truck on their high beams showing the two travelers there had, indeed, been someone in a relatively close proximity. He would have given away his position had he moved toward them anyway. It was better, he reasoned, to give away his position moving away from them and, perhaps, convey a false impression of intent. He would continue all the way to the highway where he would turn north. Driving the estimated distance to be in-line with the travelers, he would turn off his lights and re-enter the desert on a course head-on with them. He would move in only so far as to take up a suitable position with which to observe the entire desert. The only thing left to do would be to wait.

The contour of the land was forgiving to Gregaris. A small knoll, a lump on the flanks of the sloping hills, provided an excellent observation point. Anyone coming from the east would not be able to see the truck and it put him in an excellent position to see all comers, though it was dim enough to not be able to command an entire vista. The dim star-light and faint moon-light played tricks on his eyes as he stared across the sloping desert.

While the direction south was clear for miles to his direct view, only two miles to the north a gentle ridge obscured anything past it. After an hour or so of silence, Gregaris began to wonder if he had grossly underestimated his drive north. If they were beyond the ridge they could get all the way to the road without him ever seeing them. He crept back to the truck to re-check the odometer. It correlated with what he had estimated and decided to hold his position. He walked back to the height and lay on his stomach over the top of a large, flat rock where he could continue his surveillance. He took stock of his small cache of tools: a flash-light, pistol, canteen and binoculars, and tried to imagine how they would help him. The binoculars scanned the horizon once more. He looked at his watch and scanned again. They were there.

They had come much closer than he had anticipated first encountering them. The black night had obscured them in their dark clothing well closer than he had thought possible. They were probably no more than a half mile away. Chills ran over his body in the cool night air. His pulse quickened again and his mind raced. The reality of what he was doing plopped onto him like a wet blanket. Just what the hell was he going to do now? Would he try to stop them? Would he simply follow them? What if they were violent? How could he subdue them? He rolled the chambers of his small twenty-two caliber pistol around in full circle insuring a bullet in each. If they were from an advanced civilization, he thought, this little pea shooter might be a kid's toy compared to what they were packing. The sight of it might cause them to fire first. He set it back down into its old leather holster. His in-experience at the coming event became immediately apparent and weighed on him.

The realization of what he must do came slowly but in an unstoppable wave. He must gather the courage to meet them. Stepping out of a shadow he would confront them. This was personal now. He alone, on the entire planet, knew of their presence. They had come before and left his life shattered. They had come again and would now provide answers. One way or another, friend or foe be damned, Captain George Gregaris was going to meet his fate. These two beings were going to reveal to him great truths or gun him down where he stood—to hell with it.

The courageous captain was so lost in his final resolve that he didn't hear the soft footsteps coming from behind. Reckoning with fate was consuming the normally careful man. He was just beginning to move from the knoll down to a small ravine which ran in front of the two on-comers—now only several hundred yards away—when the bolt of a rifle clicked into place while the barrel of that same rifle came to rest simultaneously on the back of his skull.

"OK, mother-fucker," came the odd, whispering voice, "I don't know who you are but if you make a noise I'm going to scatter your brains all over this desert. Put your hands behind you."

Gregaris swallowed hard, realizing all at once how dry his mouth was. He set the binoculars down carefully and complied with the request, placing his hands slowly behind his back—there wasn't much choice. His two wrists were quickly cinched with a belt, and then the end of the gun came to his temple. "Remember, not a word. Not a sound. Don't make me kill you." The dark shape grabbed him by the feet and slowly drug him down some twenty feet from the crest, across the rocks and dirt, toward the truck. Once there, a crude gag, probably a t-shirt, came around his mouth forcing him to breathe heavily from his nose.

Gregaris lay with his face in the dirt for several seconds before granting himself a small peek back up the gentle slope. The large dark figure crept towards the same spot he had been using as an observation point. He squat down with the rifle across his knees and waited. After some minutes he raised himself slightly to one knee and brought the rifle to his shoulder aiming it into the night. George was stunned. Did this man realize who he was killing? Why? How did someone else know these interstellar visitors were out here?

Profound indignance came over George. To be so close to finding a solution and having it yanked away tore into his pride. He must save them, at least try to save them, these were his only thoughts. Even at the risk of his own life he must try to save them. These were true extra-terrestrials, beings which had come across the void of space. No matter the reasons behind this man wanting them dead, Gregaris thought urgently, it would be a tragedy to have these visitors snuffed out. If not for the loss of their existence, then for the loss of answers they might provide a broken man.

The dark shape was calm and rigid in its firing pose. There couldn't be much time now. They must be close. As carefully as he could George brought a knee up under his chest keeping an eye on his subduer. He pulled his torso off the ground shaking from nervousness and the intensity of the effort. The marksman kept his pose. The problem was now what to do. Gregaris looked to the truck. It was no more than ten paces away. On one great effort he leapt to his feet and ran to the truck not looking behind him. He dove through the open window landing face first on the bench seat. He rotated his torso jabbing his elbow onto the horn. It rang out in the silent desert night like an air-raid siren. Only a couple of seconds later he was yanked out of the window by his feet, slamming hard onto the desert scrabble. As he rolled over he saw the butt of a rifle coming for his head and then remembered nothing more.

C HAPTER NINE

Only two months on the job and Barbara Cerasoli felt like a long-time veteran. In sixty short days she had been threatened with a knife, vomited on, lied to on occasion beyond enumeration, and leered at by every disgusting male imaginable. The heat of the summer, the filth, the foul language all added up to one giant head-ache every evening. Ironically, she had her father to thank for not going into despair. Like a boyfriend and girlfriend who are driven closer by the disapproval of the parents, Barbara clung closer to her job the more she was expected to fail.

Her first two paychecks went to clothes which made her look as dyke as possible. She cut her silky black hair short and stopped wearing make-up the first week. Anything showing her shapely contour never made it to work. These men needed no provocation at all to be idiotically horny. The drunker or higher they were the worse it was. Plucked eyebrows grew thick and nothing resembling a perfume touched anything she might even think about wearing to work. She had not yet worked up the fear about her clients to buy a gun, but pepper spray and a whistle were her constant companion. She had tried coming to the job trusting and relaxed and this strategy hadn't seemed to work at all; nor had it lasted more than a day or two. Tense and cynical would have to do—and this was even when the majority of her clients were women.

She received most of the female clients in her sector from her boss by the reasoning a woman would be less intimidated by and better understand another woman. This was of little solace to Barbara. She had about as much in common with some of these large, hard, minority women as she had in common with a sumo wrestler; one was big and aggressive, another small and intimidated. Oftentimes she feared her female clients more than the male. The males were infinitely more predictable: totally hormone driven. The females, however, lashed out at the strangest things. They seemed to have a chip on their shoulder at random intervals, one moment gentle and conciliatory, the next a bulwark of snarling defensiveness.

Jeremy was a good mentor and confidant. Though his time was precious, he always took moments to guide the rookie through all pitfalls. She felt much more at ease around Jeremy than the other men at the office. He was happily married and the sticky issue of sex never came around to muddy the waters as it did with all of the single and some of the other married men. He never made her feel stupid even after some classic, neophyte pratfalls. She admired his calm in adversity. His advice was followed to the letter and never seemed to fail. Her cubicle was right across the hall from his and she took every opportunity to seek his council. Some of the other workers put on airs of veteran superiority. She didn't much blame them for doing so. A few years down here could make anyone hard. The attitude of the others only made Jeremy stand out that much more from the pack.

The phone on Barbara's desk had a spot for three incoming lines and sometimes they would all light up at once. This morning, head already pounding, she let the phone ring and reached into the desk to grab a couple of aspirin. She picked up the receiver and tapped the hold button, then repeated the procedure twice more to lock up all three lines. Reclining her office chair all the way back, Barbara stared at the ceiling. Tiles were stained in patches from water and generally discolored from smoke, though still probably the cleanest part of the office. She was working on a couple of particular problems which just didn't add up. She glanced through the file on her lap then over to the cubicle across the hall. She wanted to be weaned from Jeremy but the temptation was just too strong. Taking the file with her she walked to the opening of Jeremy's cubicle. He was on the phone. Pictures of family and children rimmed the desk. Papers, in singles and bunches, littered any open space and were tacked to the wall.

"Yeah," he said into the phone waving for Barbara to take a seat, "yeah that's right . . . No, no family contacts at all . . . His last address? Jersey . . . . No, sorry, nothing more specific. Only Jersey . . . . O.K., thank you."

Jeremy hung up the phone rubbing his temples with one large hand. A big sigh puffed out of his rubbery cheeks. "It never gets easier," he said to Barbara. "You remember Herrigan?"

Barbara shook her head up and down indicating she had remembered. He was a pudgy, vanilla ice-cream white fellow with more drug addictions than most street gangs could boast in aggregate. Supposedly he had been doing fairly well.

"Dead," Jeremy spit out plainly. "They found him in a dumpster this morning all cut up. Looks like a drug deal gone bad. Fuckin' bull-shit." Jeremy threw his pencil into a stack of papers.

"Sorry," Barbara said.

Barbara could see some real pain come across his face as he leaned back in the creaking, old office chair. Then, as quickly as it had spread, it eased away into that stoic look carried by most everyone at the office. It wasn't OK to feel too much. Time was precious and the living took precedent. "That's OK," he said as flavorless as possible. "What's on your mind?"

Barbara felt pretty silly at this point in the conversation. Her relatively unimportant concerns stuck in her throat and she deferred to say, "Oh nothing really. Can I do something to help?"

Pain forced its way back onto his face, into the corners of his wincing eyes. "Yeah," he said, trying to push the ache back down under the hard lines of his professional code. "Let's go out to lunch. Then you can tell me what's on your mind so I can forget what's on mine."

In a corner sandwich shop the two sat at a table near the window looking out onto the busy boulevard. The hoards of cars passed on cued intervals as determined by the stop-light. They represented a fair cross section of the opposing neighborhoods in jalopies, low-riders, executive town cars and vehicles of commerce. Their sandwiches were wrapped in white paper sitting in little red, plastic baskets. It was crowded and the little ceiling fans were not adequately dissipating the steam rising from the clientele. Barbara started into her sandwich to mollify her noisy stomach—forever hungry, Barbara was blessed with a very forgiving metabolism. Jeremy sat staring out the window as if he had forgotten there was food in front of him, the top button of his shirt undone and his tie loosened. Barbara took notice and put down her sandwich.

Remembering his earlier request of helping him take his mind off of current problems, she jumped right into her prior concerns saying, "I've got a few questions if you don't mind."

"Yes, please," responded Jeremy, turning his sandwich tray this way and that with a disinterested gaze.

"Well, you remember Courtney House, don't you?"

"Uh, let me guess," said Jeremy with a sneer. "Someone broke into the office and took all the meds."

Barbara laughed. "This is usual?"

"About twice a month. I can't believe someone could be so hard up for psychotropic medication. Kind of a weird thing to be in demand for out on the street—I think so anyway. But somebody's got a market for it. I hope you kicked some butt."

"I was going to see what you had to say first. I started the complaint but they were so damn belligerent I didn't know what to think. I was going to pursue it, but I thought maybe they knew something I didn't. So I laid off a little."

After a giggle, which seemed to put Jeremy at ease he said, "Yeah, they know something. They know they're guilty as hell. If we had any other place for the price we'd put our clients there. But at that cost, shit, we could lose the meds ten times a month and still be thousands under target. It's just too good of a deal. But kick some ass anyway. Raise hell from bottom to top. Don't let the fuckers think we have a reason to be soft or they might really start disappearing ten times a month. What else you got?"

"One more thing, it's about your loner, Mark."

Jeremy leaned forward whispering, "Which Mark?"

The confidentiality of the patients required the social service people only use first names in public. Barbara leaned forward and mouthed out, "Johnson."

Jeremy shook his head, "Who?"

"Men can't do that, can they? Read lips. It was the first guy you introduced me to last May."

"Oh yeah. that guy."

"Yeah, Mark has been developing rather rapidly—like you indicated. But he's really taken a strange turn. He's acting very paranoid. I dropped by yesterday and I caught him packing his bags. He said he was moving right away. Any idea where I can get a hold of his uncle? There's no street address on the checks. No phone number in the file, any ideas so that I can confirm this move?"

Jeremy shook his head. "Nope. Boy that Mark is one weird, fuckin' duck." He paused, and then burst out laughing. "Maybe he's on his way back to planet Zorcon. God I hope the hell so. Then we can stop worrying about the young prince or king or whatever the hell he thinks he is now." Jeremy looked at his watch then took an uninterested bite of his sandwich. "Hell," he went on, "after lunch I'll go over there with you. I kind of miss the little weirdo. Him and his laser-green eyes." Jeremy bulged out his eyes trying to imitate his former client.

"Yeah," agreed Barbara, "those eyeballs are pretty intense. I've never seen anything like them."

"His uncle has got the same kind. They aren't quite as potent as Mark's, but still kind of scary looking. Makes you think he might really be from someplace else."

Jeremy's old, dilapidated sedan shook thunderously on the huge pot-holes of the neighborhood forcing him to cruise under the speed limit. Mark lived in a community deemed by fellow workers as falling somewhere between the worst and not-so-bad. It was behind a row of businesses and machine shops not far from the office. Some of the houses along the route kept an air of respectability with mown lawns, clipped hedges and painted trim. The civic pride, however, was rather haphazard and one average looking dwelling could border a battered crate with rusting hulks of former automobiles in the front. Mark's house, as was with his neighborhood, stood somewhere between a battered crate and decent living quarters.

They pulled into the drive and Jeremy yanked on his door handle only to have it snap off in his hand. He gave Barbara a disgusted look, tossed the handle out the window and reached for the latch on the outside of the door. They climbed out of the car to the thump, thump, thump bass beat of a ghetto blaster emanating from a lowered cruiser nearly a block away. The community was mainly Hispanic but it tolerated, without much tension, a smattering of other backgrounds. Everything seemed in order from the outside and Jeremy took to his persistent rapping on the door. After a period of time, even suitable for Mark to answer the door, Jeremy went around to peer in the windows. At the bedroom window he turned to Barbara.

"Looks like our boy has flown the coop," he said. "His dresser is emptied and suitcase gone. Oh, well. Better get with his parole officer and see if he checked in."

Upon returning to the office, with the usual swarm of activity, the problem of Mark went to the back burner. Crises surrounding work seemed to crawl on top of each other with every one of them seeking precedence. Each and every client, co-worker or supervisor believed his or her own 'crisis' took the lead no matter what other business had been presented to her prior in the day. And, each and every client, co-worker, and supervisor would take it personal if their event was not on her front-burner at any particular moment.

With the help of Jeremy, Barbara had developed a strategy commensurate to the situation. In the beginning she tried doing everyone's request. Yet it was quickly apparent actually doing everything expected of her was impossible. Her next tack was to prioritize events based loosely on authority from highest boss, to lowest client. This quickly caved in, however, since each person on the hierarchy refused to acknowledge the superiority of the other. And, often times, actually doing the job wasn't sufficient to placate their concerns anyway, as nothing she did seemed good enough. She finally settled for the most efficient method: that of lying about what she had done. As sixty percent or more of all requests were superfluous, she simply ignored them and when it came time to answer for them she would make the fib. She then had just enough time to spend on the forty percent of meaningful work requests of merit and general duties. "Of course I read the memo's on the new value adjustments," she would say to sooth a supervisor when she hadn't even seen them. "I signed the bottom. Didn't I?" Or to a client over the phone, "Yes, yes, I'm working very hard on seeing if you can get funding for your brother-in-law's second marriage. In fact, I'm going to a meeting with my supervisor right now about it. Call back tomorrow, why don't ya?" With that, the storm around her went from untenable to mere hurricane status. Life in the office as it was, she didn't get a chance to check her voice mail until the very end of the day.

At fifteen minutes past five almost half the office had gone home. The other half, those who felt enough energy on that particular day to spend extra time trying to stay afloat, were winding down to a dull roar of activity. Barbara strained to remember her key code to the voice mail and had to punch it in three different times to get it right. The first six messages were of the normal tenor; those of the gimme, gimme, gimme variety which no longer shocked her with their audaciousness on asking for what were essentially a hand-out. She scribbled small notes to herself on the desk pad for those messages she actually felt like responding to. The seventh message caught her attention for who it was. It was Mark.

The tone of his voice had changed so much that it was hard to recognize. It seemed, somehow, more dignified, loftier, and more lucid. "Barbara, this is Mark Johnson," the voice went. "I am going to need a little help. I believe that my uncle is in dire trouble. I will contact you at the office tomorrow. Please set aside some time to meet me, but not at my house. It is most urgent."

It was the last message on the recorder and Barbara put down the phone shaking her head. The eloquence of the phrasing threw her from her normal thoughts. "Most urgent?" she thought, "dire trouble?" This sure didn't sound like the shaky drunk she had been counseling and cajoling to represent himself at AA meetings to fulfill a parole violation. She shook here head again, this time as if rousing herself from sleep. Oh well, she thought, the abnormal is normal around here. Worry about it tomorrow.

CHAPTER TEN

The flight had gone well for the prince and Pestia. The approach and landing had not been perfect, but well enough for its purpose. And, when considering the lack of information, and ad-hoc equipment, things could have gone much worse. They were safe, and undetected, who could ask for more?

All things considered, the earth had not been the first choice for the navigators of the long distance voyagers for several reasons. Earth was not united. It was much more violent than others. It had no previous or regular contact with other interstellar travelers, possibly rendering an interstellar visit, at best, a global curiosity. Worse, the planet had periodic global conflicts which seemed to endanger almost everyone. But an inordinate weight had been given to this place due to its close proximity to Bren relative to others. The weighting had been given by one whose opinion mattered: the King. It lay nearly ten light-years closer than the next nearest alternative and, therefore, this particular planet was chosen. The king believed the ability to retrieve the escapees quickly might prove more important than other considerations. Besides, the King argued, any planet with regular interstellar contact would be more likely to be aware of their arrival and of the situation between Ranson and Bren. Thereby, it fell to the king's reason that people with other world contacts would be more likely to tip their hand as to the presence of visitors, purposely or not. Advisors had argued strongly against the choice. They believed the return of the heir might lie one hundred years or more hence, making the proximity irrelevant. They thought it better to take into account such things as safety and civility. The old King would have none of the argument, however. The king, perhaps, knew better.

The nation selected for Pestia to live with the prince on this un-unified planet, was named the United States—chosen simply because there were vastly more radio transmissions emanating from it and, therefore, they knew more about it than any other nation on earth. From these garbled and intermittent radio signals the language, customs, rights and wrongs, and do's and don'ts were put together piece by piece by the linguists and sociologists of Bren. It was not an easy task formulating a picture from the words. No visual transmissions made it across the trillions of miles of space intact enough to be of use—the higher frequencies of television transmission translated through the void with greater difficulty than the much longer wavelengths of radio.

It was deduced from this stream of information that earthlings, at least some Americans, resembled the men and women of Bren. They gathered there were different colors of people on earth and that people of all colors lived in the United States. This was regarded as a positive development since it would reduce the chances that the color of a person of Bren might prove awkward—shades and hues are not easily deduced from radio transmissions alone. There was always the chance they would stick out like a gorilla among macaques, but the scientists of Bren were convinced, due to linguistic similarities and other clues, they were anatomically very similar.

The people of earth appeared to love sports, music, and be fiercely political over the smallest of events. There were religions of sorts, based primarily on a single deity, brotherly love, and the giving of money. It was deemed a 'religion of sorts' since many of the religious leaders seemed too fiercely political over current issues and it was never clear whether the religiosity was farcical, a splinter, or simply a political tool. There was little discourse in the area of real science or philosophy, so it was presumed such dialogue took place on the visual frequencies. The earth was, after all, advanced enough to necessitate philosophical conflict and drama of all types. Missing this information was considered a major gap in their intelligence.

It was clear the United States lie in the northern hemisphere, in the mid-latitudes, but wholly unclear as to the point of longitude since there would be no specific reference point without better visual contact or specific point of radio emission. It was necessary then for the craft to find its own reference point as it came close to the earth. Entering on a course toward the United States it would embark on a series of preprogrammed maneuvers depending entirely on the reaction, or non-reaction of the people on the ground. The radio transmissions were, after all, at best, fifteen years old. The course was as exact as it could be. Fifteen years was a long time for developing a course into such a dynamic society. What seemed friendly and peaceful now could be hostile and warring forty-five years later—fifteen for the message to reach Bren, and thirty for the ship to reach earth. With the earth's discovery of nuclear missiles, there was the risk it might not be inhabitable at all.

Advisors had pleaded with the king to send the Prince away earlier but the king felt it necessary to wait until the last moment, not wanting to provoke the aggressors. Yet both the king and military advisors had grossly underestimated the speed and ferocity of the attack. Caught under surveillance long before planned, the military men watched in horror as one of their interstellar craft was blasted from the sky while trying to re-enter Bren's orbit. It had been the morning of the original planned escape. Further contingencies were now needed. Secrecy became stricter and plans for a covert launch, probably one under occupation, were hatched.

The craft itself was much less than had been hoped for by the Bren under-ground. The original craft in the plan had been confiscated. Every ship with landing\ take-off, trans-planetary technology had been pronounced a threat to the home of the invading army, registered, then disabled. Quick thinking technicians saved one small, older, trans-planetary craft with landing but not take-off technology. They brought it up to date with the fastest engines available and all the necessary computer equipment. The ship would go, but never return. It was a time of desperation; this would have to do. The engineers and technicians in the silo that finally launched the ship watched, with absolute exhilaration, as it escaped the web of Ranson. They gathered together in the control room hugging and crying with joy, throwing their hats into the air with shrieks of happiness. They formed one large circle, held hands, sang the anthem of Bren and, as a final precaution, blew themselves and the silo to bits. They were all doomed to the dungeons of Ranson anyway; they would meet their maker with hope alive.

As the ship entered the atmosphere of earth, a program of hostile intent took over the helm. There were armed interceptors everywhere. From the reaction of military forces on the ground, this kind of space entry was obviously considered antagonistic. It was feasible for the small ship to cloak itself from the eyes of the simple radar, but to do so and still probe the ground for information was almost impossible. Therefore, a superiority of speed was employed to dodge the attackers while time was gained to decide on a specific landing point and how to do so helping the passengers elude detection.

After sufficient information—mapping, current technology, landing point, etc . . . had been collected, the cloak came on and the little ship landed. The two groggy passengers were given their supplies and a summary of current events on the planet. The explosion of the craft was a text-book case of trans-planetary spy tactics, taken from the pages of ancient lore. If there were no focal point, the reasoning went then the search parties would look everywhere. If, however, there were a focus to the search, it would be limited to that point. An eye focused on a point, it was reasoned, is much less dangerous than a wandering one. And it worked like a charm just as it had ages ago. It duped the technologically handicapped earthlings into believing, not only they were looking in the right place, but also that the explosion had ended the search by destroying all contents.

This strategy, so it happened, would be employed successfully not once, but twice, thereby showing the utter ignorance of earthlings in matters of interstellar cloak and dagger.

Though the ship performed well, through no fault of the ship itself, the cargo had not fared as nicely. Something was wrong with the Prince. Pestia had seen it before on some diplomats who had undergone the same procedure. The surgery done on the language portion of the brain of the prince had not been completely successful. Though new to Bren, the practice of neuro-translation was widely employed on other planets, especially if there were great differences in noises made in order to speak the target language. Often times sounds are learned from birth and exceedingly difficult to mimic as an adult. Neuro-translation helped mitigate this difficulty, let alone the time of learning.

The prince was having no difficulty hearing and understanding the new language, but he was having great trouble speaking it. The muscles in his mouth were not responding to the words he wanted to say causing his jaw and facial muscles to flex and twist spasmodically. Pestia did not fear for the young man's life. The condition was not known to be fatal. What caused the general concern was the fact it was going to make assimilation much more difficult. As he had seen it before, time and practice alone were not enough to help match the tones and verbalizing to the muscle movement. To keep the strain on the muscles and, more importantly, on the verbal portion of the brain to a minimum, it was advisable to have the patient use a particular muscle and cerebral relaxant. The relaxant of choice, lacking surgical intervention, was ethanol.

The flaws in the surgery also seemed to make the prince weak and lethargic; of all times to be weak and indifferent, thought Pestia. One more damned head-ache to be dealt with. Soon he would be walking around a foreign planet, deemed hostile to outsiders, with a weak, indifferent, spasmodic who had to drink gallons of alcohol in order to improve.

Pestia yanked the poor, floundering, young man around as fast as he could. They put on the clothes designed to be as neutral, ubiquitous, and as historically constant as possible to their new host country. A white shirt, tie, and blue jacket came on with black shoes. Pestia led the stumbling, poor prince outside pulling on his tie as if he were leading a horse to water. He felt as if he were taking part in a great, childish hoax. Play-acting as one child might pretend he were a fire chief if he had the proper hat, they were play-acting earthling in these silly clothes. It was difficult, here on the ground, to maintain the proper weighting to the task at hand. Pestia had never been anywhere near fifteen light-years away from his home and the distance seemed to diminish the urgency and importance—not to mention having his charge act like a dopey child himself.

Outside it was dusk. Pestia was impressed with the heat and dryness. The color of the sky was nearly the same as Bren. Data readings before landing gave him a compass course and distance to the nearest settlement, twelve miles, and nearest road, almost ten. A peculiar unit the mile, Pestia thought, five-thousand, two-hundred and eighty units of a large man's pedestal. Yet he was used to measuring distances in many different units from planet to planet and took this one to heart quickly. He put a pack of supplies on the stooping prince, having to yank him upright to keep him from falling several times. He put on his own pack and pulled the young man forward by one hand. The Prince shook and tottered groaning out some unintelligible complaint, his jaw twisting back and forth in a painful sight.

"Oh, forgive the ignominy of circumstance my good Prince," Pestia said with a sigh. "I have no patience for this either."

They stumbled for several hours towards, then up a small ridge of barren hills, the prince falling several times, tearing his trousers and bloodying one knee. Pestia surveyed the now dark landscape. He realized this planet had plenty of vegetation and other living things but, standing in this empty landscape, not a blade of grass to be seen, it was easy to imagine himself and the Prince the only, lonely living things on the surface of the entire sphere. They were up off the desert floor several hundred feet now and it offered a good vantage point for observation. Pestia decided to rest here. He glanced at his watch. It was almost time for the show, anyway.

Several minutes passed before the little, loyal craft glowed to life. It had become obscured by darkness but now was easily visible as the engines glowed with heat. As it lifted off the salty plain Pestia winced at how audible the hiss of the drivers were. Anyone within miles would be able to hear, look, and then see the origin of the ship. It mounted its trajectory without question to its final purpose, going, going, until it slowed and descended to its last moment. The flash of light entered Pestia's eyes and tore something loose inside. It was the passing of the last connection to home. They were both now adrift, completely separated from their former world. A great depression settled over him as the distant thunder reached his ears. As if to echo the rumble, the prince let out a long tearful groan, he too sensing the solemnity of the event.

To the east, when his eyes became re-accustomed to the dark, Pestia noticed a large, yellow-orange glow not previously there. It grew in intensity as did his cause for concern. Was this some kind of search party illuminating the horizon? It seemed too large and distant, however, to be coming specifically toward them. The rim of an orb appeared on the horizon as if a dull sun. Pestia then laughed, letting his depression give way to a moment of frivolous wonderment. He was seeing his very first moon-rise. Neither Bren nor Ranson had a substantial, gravitational partner—Bren having nothing and Ranson one miserable little comet of a moon which barely outshone a bright star. He had been informed of the huge partner, but had never before envisioned its appearance. Pestia leaned back on his hands, sitting with legs crossed, and watched the gigantic satellite rise in the sky, smiling and tapping a foot as if to a celestial tune.

The moon had not only helped their spirits, but its fullness helped illuminate a path without having to use lights which might give away their position. Pestia stopped several times in their march to monitor the air traffic to the south with a passive sensor retrieved from his pack. The aircraft seemed intent on monitoring nothing but the blast site; everything was going according to plan. The ground became more forgiving in its texture for hiking and more flat the further they went. A highway slowly came into view; its lighted vehicles, moving north to south and south to north, showed its position across their westward path. Behind the highway could be seen white peaks of substantial mountains standing purple and majestic. They made their way toward a stationary set of lights, presumed correctly by Pestia to be a small, permanent settlement. Several hours later they were near the edge of the roadway.

There were a total of three buildings in the settlement and it sat on the opposite side of the highway from the two travelers. Pestia placed the poor, fumbling prince behind a rock, down below the road out of sight. Crouching above the rock, on the slope of the shoulder, Pestia could observe vehicles passing the settlement and, more importantly, the actions of those who chose to enter. His first profound observation was that Earthlings were indeed anatomically similar. The second was that they were not the same color; at least the first few were not. He noticed the vehicles looked very similar to those on Bren excepting they worked on liquid fuel and required a key to operate. One of the buildings dispensed this petrol from small, automated kiosks. A second building was dark. At the third, goods were sold using paper money and coinage—Bren had long ago gone to universal debit cards issued at birth. Pestia was very interested in obtaining two things: one, a place to have shelter from the coming heat of the day and, two, just such paper money and coinage to pay for it.

The human inside the store was spending much time counting this paper money from inside a small machine. It was much to Pestia's relief that humans looked very close to the people of Bren in feature and height—or at least this female did. (Pestia's faith in the scientific interpretation of earth's radio data went as far as he could prove it. He did not have much faith in his scientific comrades) Much to Pestia's consternation, however, this female was also not of the same color as he. Everyone on Bren and Ranson was, not only of the same color but, of nearly the same hue; a very comfortable, bland, landscape of uniform people. Seeing a different colored person made him feel very uncomfortable. He looked down at his own skin and back to hers several times wondering how she would judge his skin tone, and of how close he was to people of other colors from around this country.

The autos roared by too fast and dark to glimpse the passengers and judge their appearance. Soon, however, a smaller styled vehicle came up to the front of the establishment. Much to Pestia's relief, this human, an apparent male, was of a color closer to his own, not an exact match, but of a tone he regarded close enough. He was much smaller than Pestia and dressed radically different;

but never-mind. Pestia was most concerned with color. For all he knew, humans were purple. The man took one small rectangular box out of a dispenser and handed it to the female. He then pulled a small pouch out of a pocket on the rear of his body and opened it. From his vantage point, Pestia could see inside the pouch. Pestia could see plenty of the green currency he was supposed to need. It was time to move.

Running across the road Pestia crouched at the rear of the diminutive vehicle. The highway was momentarily quiet. Steadying himself with his right he reached his left hand into an inner pocket and pulled out his pacification gun. The man returned and opened the door of the vehicle. As he swung his legs inside Pestia leaned out from around the back-end and fired one shot into his back. The gun popped and hissed. The man grunted, twitched, then fell flat, back onto the ground. Pestia picked him up and shoved him to the far seat. He would be out for about six hours. The woman inside could not see the auto from where it was parked. Pestia took the opportunity to circle back to the prince, making sure to arc out of view of the female and other vehicles. The poor Prince was beginning to deteriorate. He had begun to wander and it took Pestia several anxious moments to find him. Grabbing him angrily by the arm he drug him across the road to their new found transportation. The former general found it necessary to forgo politeness for efficiency. Finding a handle that raised the driver's seat forward, he roughly stuffed the babbling monarch into a seat located in the rear.

The human male was out like a light, snoring gently. Pestia reached into the back pocket of the human and found the small pouch. He removed the currency and tossed the pouch to the floor of the vehicle. The prince began to groan. Pestia implored him to be quiet, but it was apparent the prince had drifted into a state beyond communication. The general looked to the store and the variety of items viewable through the window. Maybe, he thought, they had some ethanol.

CHAPTER ELEVEN

Annie was bored. So bored she wanted to die. At least she said she wanted to die a thousand times. No-one was going to tell her what to do. She would fight any command with all her might, but getting into trouble up here, in this desolation, was nearly impossible. It was a cruel joke to send her to this god forsaken place; nothing but dust and heat. For Annie this place was like hell, or worst than hell; perhaps hell's goddamned sewer. Hell's goddamned sewer with stupid, dull, provincial assholes.

Sent to live with relatives from the San Fernando Valley, the Mecca of the young, restless and spoiled, Annie was ready to explode. She just didn't know how to do it yet. One month out of high school where she had left the most stupendous moments of her life, running loose on the whole city, boyfriends, parties, sirens and lights, here she was, stuck in an all night convenience store owned by her ass-wipe cousin, three hundred miles from the nearest beach. She was going to show her parents. She was going to show them all. She'll find a way to raise hell, one way or the other. The opportunity just hadn't presented itself yet.

Annie sipped on a stale cup of coffee and puffed manically on a cigarette. At five o'clock in the morning she felt hard and worldly. She imagined herself a whore on the rainy streets of some European capitol. Seeking her next trick, tired and indifferent to the lust of her Johns, she was only looking for the one with the most money. High heels and lace stuck out from under the tight, leather mini-skirt. She was now much taller and thinner and more worthy of lust. Ironically, she imagined being put off by her salubrious benefactor, looking lethargically to the ceiling as her young, handsome trick pumped away his fifty dollars in less than five minutes. She would tell him he was great, hoping for a tip, while secretly despising him from behind a smile in complete control of her feelings, the surroundings, everything.

If there were anyway to steal from the ratty little store without getting caught, she really believed she would do it. She looked up at the security camera and stuck out her tongue. The entry buzzer shook her out of her fantasy.

He was at least six-three, maybe six four, lean and muscular, a gorgeous hunk. His attire was like something she had never seen. A bright blue jacket, no collar, a black tie wrapped around the neck in a granny knot. The pants fit tight to the ankle, like a star trek episode and bagged seductively, she thought, around the crotch. Even in the funky clothes, however, there was an aristocratic air about him which just melted her. He looked like he was lost, or surveying the place. Maybe he was a mugger. Maybe he was a rock star. Maybe he was high on something. As he turned his back she allowed herself to stare generously. He turned again and walked to the counter. Annie tried to act disinterested, but her pulse elevated.

"Good-evening," he said in an odd way, "do you have any ethanol?"

Annie looked up into his eyes. Catching her off guard, his bright, dreamy green eyes pulled her out of her act of disinterest into a longing stare. Feeling awkward, suddenly young and inexperienced she said, "Huh?" which made her face blush.

"Excuse me," repeated Pestia. "Do you have any ethanol?"

Annie tried to make up for her awkward state, recovering to puff on her cigarette. "You mean," she said blowing smoke out to the side, jostling to a non-existent beat, "like in the gas."

"Gas?" Pestia asked, beginning to worry. He was not communicating nearly as well as he should be. It wouldn't be prudent to leave a memorable scene so close to the touchdown point. He tried again saying, "It is a beverage that you drink."

"Oh, you mean, like, alcohol? Yeah, there's plenty. Over there. I like your jacket. It's cool. Where're you from?"

Pestia pondered for a second, then said, "From the north," and began walking toward the area she had indicated.

She talked to him as he searched. "Are you from Canada? I hear Canada is so cool in the summer time. Its light twenty-four hours a day and you can have the most incredible parties all the time. I'm going to Canada next month; just to get out of this hell hole."

Pestia tried to concentrate on looking and listening, doing neither very well. He suddenly felt very tired, and confused. He scanned the items on the shelf until he saw a bottle that read, "Alcohol, forty percent by volume." He took the bottle in hand. The brown liquid looked much like the liquor of home and he felt confident as to its contents.

"You know," the small female continued as he walked to the counter, "we don't get many of you guys in this part of the country. You need to be careful. There's plenty of red-neck assholes up here. You know what I mean?"

The term, "you guys," set the wheels of paranoia turning in Pestia's weary mind. "You guys?" he asked setting the bottle on the counter, "what do you mean, 'You guys'?"

"You know," she said in a confident, cocky tone only available to youth and fools, "blacks. I mean African-Americans. You're the second one tonight. One guy just left."

Pestia looked down at his brown, creamy skin. Black? He thought. The idiots at the language department must have screwed up again. "Is this true?" he asked, now growing more confident in his communication skills. "There are not many black people here?"

"Are you kidding? Not with all these ass-holes around here. They're real red-necks. Are you a singer? Why are you here all the way from Canada?"

Pestia ignored her question to pursue information. "Where is it, in this country, that there are many other black people?"

"You don't know anything about California. Do you?" she asked in a teasing manner. "That's OK. I don't know anything about Canada either. They're all over L.A. I mean in the places you want to visit like Venice, and stuff. Of course there's plenty in Compton and like that. But you don't want to go there."

Pestia made a note of the places and said, "Thank you. How much currency do you need for the eth . . . alcohol?"

Annie scratched her head suddenly remembering something. "Oh wow," she said, "I can't sell that to you now. Not before six o'clock. That's a California law. Can you buy alcohol anytime in Canada? That would be cool. Party all night."

"Six o'clock," Pestia reiterated. He looked at the clock on the wall. It was five thirty. "Surely, it is close enough.

No-one is around to see you. I would really appreciate you doing this for me."

Annie mistook his cajoling as playfulness and was both flattered and excited. "Well," she said leaning closer across the counter, "what's wrong with staying here and talking to me for a little while?"

There seemed, to Pestia, at least on the two planets he had visited, to be a universal body language of the humanoids when it came to sexuality. He recognized this female's lust rather quickly. He looked at her white skin. It looked nearly translucent and slimy to him.

"Oh come on," she coaxed, taking his delay and roaming eyes as another sportive ploy. "You can talk. It won't hurt you." She then reached out and playfully tapped the back of his hand which was resting on the counter.

The touch caused his skin to crawl. He half expected the white flesh to leave behind some sort of foul residue. Pestia recoiled at the thought of what sort of sexual apparatuses might lay under the primitive garments. "I'm sorry," he said finally, "I must be leaving."

Annie shrugged her shoulders. "Whatever," she said hurt, and again trying to act disinterested. "You can buy it now. I don't care."

The owner of the vehicle was pushed out onto the parking lot. It didn't take Pestia long to figure out how to operate the vehicle and what P, R, N, D, 1 and 2 stood for. The error coming closest to critical came in the beginning when he found which pedal operated the throttle and which the brake. Soon, however, he was deciphering road signs and feeling fairly comfortable. He liked the way the lights and windows made him invisible to the outside world. It gave him a good sense of security. He decided to move south as a map found in a compartment indicated a large metropolis with the name Los Angeles was there. Not finding any place named Ell A, he made the connection between Los Angeles and its acronym used by the white earthling. After a few hours on the road the sun started to rise and with it Pestia's eyes began to droop.

The prince was dutifully sucking on his bottle, nearly passed out. Though his speech had become clearer as he drank, his thoughts were completely muddled. "Whar ahr we," he croaked, and then slumped to sleep, not a twitch or spasm in his face.

Sunshine caused Pestia's eyes to droop more with each passing minute. In a small town, he saw a hotel and decided to try and figure out how to get a room. It was eight o'clock.

The proprietor had a skin tone close to Pestia, which made him feel more comfortable, but features sharper and leaner. He had a large, graying beard and a cloth wrapped around his head. "Yes, please sir," he said, "how may I hallup you?"

Pestia was growing in confidence. It appeared every person on this planet was radically different from the other and allowances were given by each for dissimilar looks and behavior. Discovery by acting different seemed un-likely. It was very different from his own planet where individualism was not prized, and often ridiculed. "I need a place to sleep for two individuals," he said calmly.

"Two beds?" the bearded man asked.

"No," replied Pestia, "only one apiece."

The proprietor gave him an odd glare saying, "Sorry sir. We have only one room with two beds."

Pestia agreed, paid for the room with cash and asked for directions to it.

The skinny, bearded man pointed one thin digit towards a door saying, "You go through the brown door. It will be on your right side. It is number one fourteen."

Pestia pointed to the same door. "Do you mean this black door here?"

CHAPTER TWELVE

Somewhere past the mist there was a way around all this pain, he thought. Things were blurry and the light way too bright. The eye went back closed. A closed eye brought the dark and with it depression, hopelessness. Why and where? Why and where what? Where did this depression come from and why was it here in the mist? The people were going to die; those people. Who wanted them dead? Did they die? Suddenly he pictured the man with the gun. He was going to kill the visitors.

The remembrance of the event brought on the gush of adrenaline necessary to bring Gregaris out of his stupor. This time the one eye opened and focused. The other eye was bandaged shut. It was a false ceiling, with white, square tiles he was looking at. Beside him was a bottle with a tube which ran to the back of his left hand. He tried to raise his right hand to check the extent of the bandage covering his right eye. To his surprise, it was hand-cuffed to the bed. He tried to remember more.

An orderly walked in with some bedding, saw that George was awake, and turned to walk out. "Hey," George called out half-heartedly after the young man. "Hey!" The orderly ignored him and continued out the door with a designed purpose. The good captain yanked at the short chain on his wrist a couple of times to convince himself it was real. Silver and hard, the manacle was the realest thing in the room to the groggy patient. The door opened again and in walked a sheriff in a green uniform, hat tucked under one arm. Teardrop sunglasses were hooked in the v of his open shirt and his leather shoes creaked against the tile. He was a pudgy man with huge, hairy arms jutting out from under the short sleeved shirt, crooked like the front legs of a crab.

He stood at the end of the bed tapping on the wide brim of his hat with two thick, short fingers. The face was stern, deeply tanned and looking at George suspiciously. After a heavy sigh, as if sizing up the right words, he said, "Morning Mr. Gregaris. How are you feeling?"

Since the tone of the sheriff's voice and bearing didn't match the niceties verbalized, George answered by only shaking his sore head back and forth. Suspicions and caution began clearing the painful cobwebs out of George's head, eventually leading to sharper thought.

The sheriff set his starched hat down on the end of the bed and pulled out a note-pad. "You mind answering a few questions for me?" the sheriff inquired gruffly, snapping the cover of the pad open like an oversized cigarette lighter.

George took a full breath and blinked his one good eye. He was obviously not in good graces with the large fellow. It was best to try and figure out what was going on before he implicated himself in something. "You mind doing something for me first," He asked.

The sheriff looked perturbed by the request but answered anyway. "Depends. Depends on what it is."

"Why not tell me where I am?"

The big, hairy man took on a cock-eyed smile, as if one of strange satisfaction. "Does it bother you, Gregaris," he said with mordant tone, "that you don't know where you are?"

The usually calm and collected captain took an indignant turn at the sheriff's belligerence. Normally George would be very cooperative, but he felt himself in a corner. He felt like the sheriff was trying to bully him and George had known for a long time it was unwise to ever back down from a bully. Backing down would only be a gracious invitation for more of the same. "Listen to me, deputy dog," he snapped pointing at the interrogator, "You had better tell me where the hell I am, and why the hell I'm handcuffed to this bed. And if I'm charged with something I sure don't remember getting my rights."

The sheriff's gaze narrowed on George and his dark, tanned face took on a red flush. "You aren't charged with anything. Nothing yet."

"If I'm not charged with anything and you want me to answer questions," George said, rattling the handcuff against the bed's rail, "Then take this stinking thing off of me."

In slow, stiff, deliberate steps, the sheriff came around to the side of the bed the handcuff was on, not taking his steady eyes off of George. He hovered over the spot for a moment, then un-hooked a bundle of keys from his big, black, leather belt. Inserting the correct key, he paused to stare and say, "We just took a precaution so you didn't go no-where. We don't take too kindly to torture and killing in this part of the country Mr. Gregaris." The handcuff snapped off and he walked back to the end of the bed.

George turned his head from the green goon and tried to think. Had this rifle man shot those two poor visitors, tortured them, and implicated him?

The sheriff saw George puzzling and tried to turn up the heat. "All we're waiting for is the lab result Mr. Gregaris," he said bouncing confidently on the balls of his feet. "You care to tell me anything before those results come back?"

The captain rubbed his wrist with the needled hand. Beyond the harassment, George also hated people who danced around the point of a conversation. He always felt it incumbent on himself to be as succinct and precise as possible and expected the same of others. "Could you tell me what the hell is going on? Where am I?"

"You're in the hospital, but that ain't important now boy," the sheriff said, letting his professional tone drop to a more country twang. "Seems the L.A. zoo looses a baby gorilla and you show up here the same night. You want to tell me that's a coincidence? Am I gettin' warm?"

The door to the room opened and a second, younger, thinner and taller deputy with a gawking Adams apple walked in. The two sheriffs exchanged some kind of body language and the younger man answered by shaking his head 'no'. Then he took his place at the end of the bed. Meanwhile, Gregaris was flustered. A baby Gorilla? He thought in a state of complete confusion.

The bigger sheriff returned to Gregaris, "Well? Coincidence or not? L.A.P.D. is gonna be here in a little while and they ain't nice like me. They get their answers."

This last bit of machismo didn't set well with George. "What are they going to do," he snapped, "get out the rubber hose? Jesus. Would you just tell me what is going on."

"Alright," the big sheriff said with the same cock-eyed smile, "let me see if any of this sounds familiar to you. There seems to be some sick-o going around doing animal sacrifices. Dogs, sheep, and all kinds of zoo animals. Seems this sick-o steals animals just to cut them up in some kind of sick-o ritual. Then it seems that we find this fellow, you that is, knocked out in a truck with animal blood all over the seat. We know that baby gorillas is awful strong. Maybe this poor little thing gets scared by bein' cut. Maybe this defenseless little animal picks up something while it's bein' tortured and knocks that guy doin' the torturing on the head—whoever that might be. Am I getting warmer Mr. Gregaris?" The big sheriff paused and reached down with his two crab claws to adjust his gun belt for dramatic effect, then continued, "You see, all we got to do is find out if that blood all over your seat there is gorilla blood or not. You see, the lab already knows it ain't human blood. And they say it looks like it came from something damn near close to being human. Why don't you tell me, Mr. Gregaris, what it is that is damn close to being human that bled all over your truck?"

The forensics expert began to put together the pieces. Blood from something other than a human-being was on his seat. Gregaris let out a laugh. "I could tell you, but you wouldn't believe me if I did."

"Oh, yeah?" the big sheriff said leaning over the bed with his caustic grin, "try me."

"Alright, how about a spaceman?"

Red flushed the angered officer's face. He stood up straight and dropped the smirking smile. "You go on," he growled, "you go on makin' jokes. We'll be laughing in about four hours when that lab report comes on in." The big man turned to the skinny one grabbing him by the shirt. "You watch him. You watch him good. If he tries to get out of that bed you give them doctors reason to stitch up that other eyeball. You hear me?"

The young man swallowed hard sending his Adam's apple gyrating. "Yes sir sergeant," he said.

Strutting strongly, the big man stalked to the door and exited. The younger one, standing still, turned on George with a determined stare as if the captain would disappear if he blinked. George rubbed his sore head and stifled a laugh at the gangly deputy's resolve.

"So where's this baby gorilla now?" George asked coolly.

The young man tried to screw up a vicious stare but only succeeded in pushing up his cheeks to make half-moons out of his eyes. "We ain't found him yet," he said. "But we will. He can't of gone far with all that blood. Don't you worry. We'll find him."

George scratched at the back of his needled hand, raw and irritated around the entry point, wondering about the fate of the visitors. It must be their blood on the seat; they would have matched, what he presumed to be, the human blood of the rifleman right away. Yet, he wondered how their blood got inside his truck. He ran his tongue slowly, back and forth across his cracked, chapped lips. If they didn't find any corpse, at least one of them was still alive, he reasoned. Maybe both of them, with one wounded. But then, where did the guy with the rifle go? Had his horn alarm worked well enough and simply scared him away? Then, how was one of the visitors injured? Had the visitors deposed of the rifleman after one of them had been shot?

George wasn't worried about being charged with any gorilla killing. Their case would fall flat when the blood test came back negative. What he was worried about was how to explain this strange blood all over his seat and as to why he was knocked on the head way out in the middle of the desert. Should he tell them the truth? George pondered this for a second or two, considered the absurdity of the story, and decided it would be better to plead amnesia. With their lack of evidence, and the big lump on his head, they would have to swallow the lie.

"Hey," George said to the two glaring, half orbs with the quivering ball underneath. "Can you tell me where the hell I am?"

The deputy licked his thin lips nervously not sure if talking to the prisoner was contrary to orders or not. "You're in Barstow Community Hospital," he said sending his lump vibrating.

"Barstow?" George asked. "Don't you mean Bishop?"

The narrow man stood up straighter slapping his hat on. "I know what I mean," He said in a determined tone, "I said Barstow. That ain't Bishop. I know where the hell we are; yer the one who don't know where they're at."

Chills started to run over George in waves. Bishop was less than forty miles from his last known position. He was now one hundred fifty miles away from where he had started. Someone had put him into his truck and driven him one hundred fifty miles, a wounded someone no less. He had been riding in a car with an alien. He had been touched, handled and delivered by an extra-terrestrial. Why did they drive all the way to Barstow before dumping him and where were they now? Were there bodies rotting in the desert? Moving him had been fortuitous, George concluded. Any evidence left at the scene would not be tampered with by the police and, hopefully, by no-one yet.

CHAPTER THIRTEEN

Barbara felt uncomfortable going to meet a client at a new location. Mark hadn't wanted to come into the office—too paranoid about something—and hadn't wanted to go back to his house. Instead, he wanted to meet at a place called the Lucky Forty. When Barbara found out it was a bar she said no. There was no possible way she would go to some dark, seedy bar to meet any client, let alone a male client, even one as polite as Mark. She suggested a more accessible place: the public Library near his house. It took some convincing but he finally said yes.

Jeremy was very busy. Barbara wished she could have asked him about the visit since it was, to date, unprecedented. She watched her big, black friend shuffle papers with the receiver tucked under his chin, balanced against his shoulder, and decided to expedite her weaning process. He was always giving but she knew she was beginning to push the limits of his patience. And she did not blame him for beginning to act put out.

Riding along in her old jalopy she felt silly all of a sudden having let one of her clients dictate the terms on which they would meet, to meet in order to let her give him help. After three months on the job Barbara had expected to be surer of herself than this. Perhaps she should have consulted Jeremy. She had blown off other clients for less garbage than a change of venue and started wondering why she was going out of her way to help this particular one. He had seemed so different on the phone; maybe she was going more out of curiosity than anything else. At least she hoped it was more curiosity and less letting a client lead her around by the nose telling her how to do her job.

She stayed in the car in the parking lot long enough to review the folder in her briefcase. Not much of a trend to help in the diagnosis of this fellow, she thought; certainly not in diagnosing paranoia, at least not before the last couple of days. Besides the now diminished palsy, and drunken hallucinations of other-world grandeur, the only pattern of Mark was that of being based in reality; which might seem odd to someone out of the field of social services—considering someone who thought himself a prince from another planet when he was drunk as being fairly based in reality. But as compared to other clients he was a true model of rationality. Polite, sensible, and fairly bright, the only thing missing on Mark Johnson was a comprehensive background—which was a very common thing to be missing among clients. She looked into all the mirrors on the car, visually inspecting the area for safety's sake. On the corner there were four Hispanic men, she presumed as illegal aliens, drinking beer about thirty feet away. Other than that it was clear and, since she had never had any trouble with illegals, she made her way into the graffiti scarred library.

He was sitting inside, near the entrance, on one of a row of chairs by the water cooler. He sat, as always, in his rigid, stiff back position, holding himself in what Barbara thought as a most pretentious manner. His hands were folded gracefully on his lap, feet flat on the floor. It always seemed to Barbara Mark went out of his way to look unassuming and to try and blend into his surroundings. He seemed to be trying so hard to be unobtrusive, in her mind, it had the opposite effect. It caused people to be suspicious as to why such a large, athletic-looking, handsome young man would need to blend in. The air around his pronounced Negroid features was dignified; which must have been very much so to have Barbara notice—it was easy to overlook the positive traits of a client when barraged every day by the negative. Today his large, walnut shaped eyes, green as an emerald sea, were hidden behind some cheap sun-glasses. The t-shirt and baggy sweat pants drooped on his angular, wiry frame. For a drunk, Barbara thought, the young man had a terrific build. Muscles thick and dense rippled everywhere skin exposed itself, suggesting great amounts of exercise. But she knew of no exercise he performed regularly other than lifting a bottle to his lips. To her surprise, he had shaved his head. His hair had been black, limp and straight as any Anglo's. Coupling the green eyes with the straight hair told Barbara, as her grandmother would say, Mark had a 'whitey in the wood-pile.' When he saw her coming he stretched himself to his full six feet, three inches with a pleasant smile. "Thank you for coming Barbara," he said in his odd accent with a small dip of the head. He then glanced furtively both ways while watching the glass door she had entered shut.

Barbara took his exaggerated scans behind her as further evidence of his paranoid state. She stepped up to the point immediately, foregoing any pleasantries. "I'm not at all pleased with you demanding that I come to some filthy, little bar to see you," she said in a flat, professional tone. "You better tell me where you're living now, and remember you're not supposed to leave the county until you've finished your treatment and probation. You got that?"

Mark sat back down in his easy, controlled fashion. It was almost effeminate, to Barbara, the way he moved. She thought he might be a homosexual. She had never asked. But if he was gay, he was not a particularly stereotypical homosexual. He was just so different. And she rightly thought it to be none of her business anyway.

"Yes, I am terribly sorry for bringing you here," he said. "But I do not feel it is safe for me to go home. I know you think me paranoid; that is your job. But you need to trust me. I cannot, right now, go home." His tone was calm and serene, nearly dream-like, which caused Barbara to be all the more surprised when a tear rolled down from under the glasses. "I believe that my Uncle," he continued, "is dead, and that those same people who killed him, want me dead too. It is important . . ."

"Look Mark," interrupted Barbara sitting down in an adjacent chair, letting her briefcase separate them, "when did you start believing that someone was out to kill you?"

Ignoring her question he continued, "I need to get some information from you and to give you some. I need to know what the consequences of leaving the county are, my chances of being caught, what means will they use to track me, and what resources are available to do so. Also . . ."

Barbara was not used to such brazen activity from her clients. On the one hand it was admirable that he wasn't lying to her, like everyone else. Yet, this was unacceptable. "I don't think you heard me Mark," she interrupted again. "Look. I'm a busy person. I've got a hundred other clients who want my time. Can you please tell me why I need to help you do a damn thing? If you don't give me an address right now, I'm turning you and your intent to leave over to the parole people. Got it?"

Mark rubbed a long, thin fingered hand across his shaved head. Continuing, his voice didn't change, "If you can promise me that you will not tell anyone, or write it down, I will tell you where I am staying."

Barbara lowered her head into her hand, pinching her temples with the middle finger and thumb as if she were keeping the two halves of her cranium from splitting. She let out a low and theatric groan. "Oh shit," she mumbled, "yeah, sure, I promise. I promise not to tell anyone."

"I am living at the Wayside Hotel. It is on . . ."

"I know where it is. Mark, I'm really busy. You need to try and stay focused with me for a little while. No-one, and I mean no-one, is out to kill you. You can't leave the county anyway, so you're going to have to make the best of it. Why don't we get in contact with your uncle and ask him? We'll get in touch with him during our next visit on Friday. You do know how to get in contact with your uncle, don't you?"

Mark shook his head slowly and calmly to the negative, letting another tear roll down his cheek.

Barbara started to feel something for him. He was not an ordinary client. Besides the fact he was very handsome and striking looking, he showed so much potential. So many of the others were manipulators, drug addicts or just plain hopeless for no distinct reason other than the fact they were. Before she let herself feel too much she steeled herself against it. I'll be damned, she thought, if I let this guy get to me. It was Jeremy's first rule of survival: feel for no-one but yourself.

Pulling her briefcase up on her lap, she opened the leather case and looked into Mark's file. "Alright," she said with professional resolve, looking for a suitable conclusion. "It says you've got an AA meeting tomorrow night at seven.

You get there. You settle down. You will see that people aren't out to get you. OK? When you calm down we'll get in contact with your uncle. Now I've got to go. OK? Is there any problem with that? No? Good."

She closed her briefcase and stood to leave. Mark stood with her. "Remember," he said, "you promised to tell no-one my address."

"Don't worry about that," she said already starting to walk. "Like I said. I promise."

On her way to the car she paused in the blinding light to reach into the briefcase to put on her sunglasses. She raised her head back up to see one of the drunken men from the corner interrupting her path. He had been waiting behind the library sign. She had not noticed his heavy boots protruding there. When she came to an abrupt halt she could hear the jeers and exhortations of his fellow comrades. His approach had obviously been planned. He faced her close, his breath heavy with alcohol. His face was covered in sweat dripping into a thin beard, eyes barely holding any sense of cognition. Barbara tried to sidestep one way and he followed. She tried the other way and he followed again. He then smiled with inquiring eyes and flicked his chin upward in a motion well known for, 'how about it?'

Barbara slipped the hand free of the briefcase into her pocket to retrieve the pepper spray as he began to laugh in a slow, staccato grunt. In a blaze of surprise, some of which must have escaped to animate her face, she found the pepper spray wasn't there. A picture came to her startled and frightened mind. The scene was the bench seat of her car, and on the passenger side sat the small aerosol tube of pepper spray, where she had placed it this morning. The dismay of not having her weapon almost caused her to give away her vulnerable position to the confronting man. It was time to be strong, she thought. No-one is vulnerable except a victim. "Get the hell out of my way," she said in a determined voice.

As if an echo to what she had said the other men let off a roar of laughter and further comment; some telling him to let her pass, others telling him to 'get her'. A dull smile spread out on his face from under glassy eyes. "Yeah, white bitch," he said in a thick accent, exhaling noxious vapors, "you want me."

Barbara tried again to step around him, this time quickly.

The man responded by pushing her back in a way strong enough to deter another try. Adrenaline was starting to flow. Her nerve was beginning to fail her. As if reading her fear he stepped closer poking his chest out more. "I said," Barbara yelled in one last attempt at being brave, "leave me the fuck alone."

The man reached out faster than she could react and pinched the nipple of her left breast as hard as he could. Barbara jumped back. Tears of embarrassment, pain and anger sprung to her eyes. Looking at his greasy smile, feeling the pain on her breast, in what was almost an involuntary action, her hand came out and slapped him hard, stinging the palm of her hand. The hoots from his cohorts became a roar and his face twisted with anger. Swinging a hairy, meaty, calloused hand, with the force meant for a stronger foe, he smashed the side of her cheek with a closed fist.

Barbara spun around and fell nearly face first on the side walk. The pain in her cheek left her breathless, dazed and only semi-conscious. The hot cement burned the palms of her hands and one side of her face. The world seemed distorted as the interval between vertical and horizontal had been lost and suddenly everything had been turned sideways. She could hear the coarse laughter and yells of juvenile delight.

"Vamanos negra," one voice went, followed quickly by a biting splat of flesh on flesh. The laughter turned to menacing howls. Someone yanked her to her feet nearly dislocating an arm. It was Mark.

"Come on Barbara," he whispered urgently, "we need to leave quickly. Give me your keys."

She felt for her keys and handed them to the large man. Still spinning and groggy from the blow, the eyes would not focus properly. She saw the three other men coming toward them. On the ground was her attacker. His jawbone was grotesquely dislocated, twisted until the bone looked as if it would rip through the skin. He wasn't moving. One of the men coming closer brandished a gun, another a knife, the third wielding his bottle. Mark pushed Barbara against the hood for support and reached into a garbage can which was chained to the lamp post beside the car. Out of it he pulled a wine bottle. He slung it at the attacker holding the gun, grunting from the effort given. As if on a wire the bottle smashed squarely in the face underneath a hand rising to defend the blow. The bottle shattered with such savagery against his forehead the other two men, on either side, recoiled from the flying shards. The gunman lurched backward from the force of the impact leaving his feet, landing limp on the white cement, red blood gushing from his wounds to form a puddle.

Barbara was lifted off her feet by the powerful defender. When the door opened she was slung like a sack of potatoes toward the far side of the bench seat, smacking her sore head against the passenger window. With her face pressed against the window she watched in a daze as one of the men stooped to pull the weapon out of the hand of the wounded gunman, the gunman's face now hidden in a mask of liquid crimson. Drifting towards unconsciousness everything became slow motion. Irrelevant facts presented themselves as the focus of attention: The low viscosity of the red fluid surprised her, running with ease off the side-walk into the gutter; the man holding the gun was pudgy and had a tattoo of a naked woman on the forearm of the hand holding the gun; the face of the armed attacker had fear, not anger. As the car sped from the scene, Barbara heard the weapon fire once. It seemed to have no effect. Her field of view slowly spun to the left moving the man out of sight. A huge hand grabbed her hair and yanked it toward the floor yelling, "Get down!" There were gunshots, broken glass, and then nothing more.

CHAPTER FOURTEEN

He shoved the hand into the homemade sling with all the care due the shoulder it was attached to. Another swig of whiskey went down the throat from a half finished fifth. The pain was more than he had imagined a gunshot wound would be. Blood caked that portion of the sling next to his body. The bleeding had pretty much come to a halt and only restarted when he was forced to move suddenly. A foul odor came from the dark, stained bandage. It was placed high on the right shoulder to cover the oozing wound. His right hand felt cold to the touch; he knew the circulation was not good.

A cool and welcome breeze swept under the small culvert. Heat from the dry, summer afternoon had nearly beaten his will into submission. Dark was coming and none too soon. Another swig and a small stream of the burning liquid dribbled off his chin. He heard a vehicle approaching. It was a large truck. Noise from the vehicle began to crescendo as if in the bow shock of an advancing earthquake. The weight of the truck shook the bridge; dust and bird droppings sprinkled down from ledges and crevices and stuck to the sweat of his tortured body. As the noise reached its apex, reverberating off the slanted, cement walls, Pestia let out a roar of pain and frustration, a scream fully drowned out by the noise of huge machine above. The noise and vibrations receded leaving him panting in the heat.

Stalks of fox-tails, that existed in one small line in the lowest part of the culvert, long since burnt brown from the heat, waved back and forth in the forgiving draft of air and invited him to venture lower to seek relief. He scooted down into the gully on his backside using his two legs and one arm to make the journey as smooth as possible. Sweat stood out in beads on his brown, shirt-less body, burning his eyes and leaving a taste of salt in his mouth. Flies, which had swarmed ferociously in the full heat of the day around the bloody wound, now found a resting place for the late afternoon and early evening with only one or two left behind to remind him of the day's torment. As horrible as it was, he was thankful he was still alive.

There had been times in the past year when he had unabashedly wished for death, something and anything, to take him from his mental torment. The memory of having to shoot his best friend callously between the eyes haunted him. The fact he ordered the death of a fine officer, and had sneaked around as a coward as the rape of his planet began sent him into a place of the blackest frost. When he woke from his journey, the respite from his despondency was short lived. Energy received from his new task quickly faded to languor as he obtained news from back home. The message recorder dutifully spit out the information backed up on it during the thirty years of sleep. At first, there were only the ominous threats from the attacking fleet. Then messages from an underground bearing news of hope for the planet, yet of personal tragedy for Pestia. His family had been taken to the dungeons of Ranson; their prognosis was not good. As the news of the resistance grew more promising it only pained the soldier. He wished to be in on the fight to pay the bastards back himself. There was nothing he could do. For twenty-seven years his people had been free and celebrating while he slept. It would have done no good for the victors to wake them. Once the momentum of the craft was set forward it was impossible to slow for a return. Like time itself, the only choice was to move ahead.

The one thing that had kept a fire burning in his guts for the last year was the knowledge the crown prince of bastards, the devil himself, was on his way. He counted the minutes, ready and eager to give the filthy scum an easy way out. A way out much easier than he had given to millions of his victims. Pestia stayed awake at nights fantasizing about the moment. Standing over the squealing coward with a boot on the throat, he would squeeze out his last breath as one might stomp a rat. But now, this vision was gone too.

He struggled to his feet fighting the vertigo from his lost blood. After another swig the pain seemed to be farther away. Pestia spit a thick lump of phlegm on the ground wiping his mouth with the back of the hand holding the bottle. He began mumbling out-loud to himself. "I should have broken the little bastard's neck. Of all the cowardly beings on this planet I have to find the one with a little bit of nerve."

Matan and his henchman had taken decisive action to the alarming horn. Pestia didn't believe he was dealing with fools and saved his life by acting quickly in turn. He knew the element of surprise had been his only hope with two against one in such an open field of battle. Now that his position was known, and theirs lost, he had to retreat. They came around both sides of the knoll keeping low to the ground, weapons drawn. The delay taken to shove Gregaris into the truck was his only tactical mistake. It allowed them just enough time to take the shot that wounded him. Why had he taken time to save the little man? Perhaps he was moved by George's bravery. Maybe he just didn't want another being to suffer the fate of the Premier's expertise, as he surely would have. How he would now sacrifice one thousand Georges to have one more chance to rid the universe of such filth. The Premier, the personification of all evil in Ranson, had been within his grasp. Why hadn't he saved one pellet from a pacification gun? Why hadn't he just snapped the little man's neck? Why had he taken such a risk?

It was a blessing Matan and his companion responded with conventional weapons; perhaps their one tactical mistake. Had he been hit with a pacification gun he would now be suffering the sort of torture endured by thousands of his countrymen—a justifiable notion to Pestia, since he had abandoned his family to such a fate. But duty called and it was for the sake of duty he thanked the lucky fates. The bullet struck him in the upper, right shoulder knocking him against the truck. The truck was pointed in the direction the shot had come from and he reached in and turned on the lights. They illuminated a lone figure, perhaps the Premier, who dropped to the ground for cover. Climbing into the truck, Pestia fired with one arm at the other shape moving in from the opposite side, sending this silhouette to the ground too. With any luck he was hit, though probably not. In the seconds that remained for escape, he started the truck and roared it toward the prone figure. Pestia screamed in pain at each bounce of the vehicle which jostled the injured arm. The silhouette dodged and dove out of sight. Whether he had hit him or not Pestia did not know. Whoever it was, was very close and the trail very rough.

When he came back from the bitter memories, Pestia pulled what was left of a shirt out of his back pocket to wipe his face and the back of his neck. A canteen filled with water lay at his feet. He knew he should keep fluids in him and especially since he was drinking to dull the pain. He picked up the canteen only to sprinkle some water on his head, then retrieved his bottle of whiskey.

Since reading that the revolution had succeeded it all seemed so ridiculous. A chess game was to be played whose outcome was already known; the only reason to play the game was to determine those pieces to be lost in victory. He could have, in all probability, hidden successfully for those three years more it would take to receive the rescue fleet. Yet, all of Bren would have admonished him had he not tried to exterminate the filth. All that was important now was to not lead Matan to the prince and, perhaps, if fate is kind, to live for one more chance at finishing the job.

He would miss his knot-headed, young charge; the only other being within fifteen light years who shared his beliefs and culture. The young man had such good humor and was a faithful companion. The Prince was heir to the throne but never haughty. A worthy occupant to the seat of his father. Further contact was out of the question. There would be no risking leading Matan to him. Pestia could never see him again and could only pray the young Prince vindicates his decision to try and kill Matan by living until the fleet arrives. Pestia would miss him dearly.

He had foolishly let the truck run out of gas. Half blind with pain the thought of filling the vehicle with petrol had not crossed his mind; he wasn't in any shape to stop and gain the fuel without drawing much attention to himself anyway. He stumbled off into the twilight of morning until he was confident that no-one could have followed his trail, walking on pavement or stepping from rock to rock to not leave a print. The ache was horrible. How he had fought through the pain without passing out he did not know. Respect grew in his mind for the soldiers of old who had stayed in the field with wounds worse than this in order to win the day. He must stay in the field now. He must win the day.

Pestia knew, after a time, he was not going to die—at least not immediately. Originally, part of his motivation for finding a secluded place was the fact he thought he might die. If he were to do so in plain sight it would inevitably lead to the discovery he was of a different species. Even these dullards, he thought, have the chemistry to determine such a basic thing. That being resolved, the knowledge of the presence of aliens would spark a witch hunt like the world had never seen. He knew how this intrusive country could latch on in frenzy to rumors. It would not be safe for the prince in a country determined to find aliens.

George's truck had been nicely supplied: a bottle of whiskey under the seat, a small blue, first-aid kit in the glove compartment, and a canteen of water. George's wallet was well supplied with several hundred dollars in currency. These pathetic green papers would come in handy. Money talked, walked and paved the way on this planet. Pestia had bandaged his injured shoulder in the truck cab, stuffed George's money in his pocket, slung the rifle over the one good shoulder, and made his way to his present location.

Standing in the twilight, in the culvert under the dusty bridge, he reflected on the past year. He imagined how the good subjects of Bren would react to hearing all the details of it. How they would laugh, he thought, hearing about the poor Prince sucking on wine bottles to relieve the spasms of his failed surgery. They would roar with delight at the story of how the good prince got loose from him one night. How he had wandered out the front door in a stupor and ended up on a street corner confused and drunk enough to mistake a group of black Americans for his subjects of Bren. What a comedy when the Prince lectured the local authorities as to his majesty and proper lineage while they were arresting him for being a nuisance. A nuisance! The king of billions, an entire planet, soon perhaps two planets, being treated as a common drunk and a nuisance. Pestia laughed a little then hung his head at his culpability in the affair. "I am not a fucking wet nurse," he said aloud, defending himself to no-one, "I am a general."

Spirits sank with the sun. It was cool enough to sleep but somewhere in the attempt to anesthetize the pain Pestia became defiant as to what he needed to do. He swigged at the bottle clumsily, stumbling with dizziness as he tilted his head back. He should rest and plan action yet felt like doing neither. A black depression at the events, past and present, fell on him with the growing gloom. Standing in the shadows, which were disappearing to black, no thought could enter his mind. For a long time he stared as a blank slate opening himself again to the stars, the stars of taunting wonder. His breath was heavy. Staggering to the center of the culvert Pestia crashed to his knees. He glanced at the half empty bottle mumbling, "Save some you fool. Morning will bring more pain. It is time for rest. Save some you fool."

CHAPTER FIFTEEN

The dreams were long and unsettling. Every one of them had to do with a dentist drilling mercilessly, or yanking a tooth without anesthesia, or placing huge, silver metal contraptions into her cheek for no apparent reason other than to make it hurt. When she finally did wake she had full recognition of the sore side of her face. She woke more peeved than groggy, angry at the dentist, the orthodontist and every dental hygienist she could ever remember meeting. Her jaw on the left side throbbed. The true events of the afternoon came back slowly without surprise, only intensifying her anger. Instead of fearing what had transpired, the memories created more indignation at having been accosted and a sense of relief in having not been hurt worse.

She had, somehow, expected to wake up in a strange place and the unfamiliar surroundings didn't disconcert her at all. This kind of certitude could be interpreted as either being brave or foolhardy. The determining factors she had in her mind deciding whether she was showing courage or being an idiot was, to her, circumstantial. In this case, as in most cases of valor, it was a little of both. The room she was in was a hotel room. She rightly guessed it as the inside of the Wayfarer—her clarity of thought, considering the circumstances, was much more amazing than her bravery.

She sat up on the bed and found an old, brown, analog radio/alarm clock whose digits rotated on cards like the update of an airport terminal. It creaked, shook a little and flipped two cards over to thirty, and preceded by a six.

"Six-thirty," said Barbara noticing a difficulty in speaking.

Across the end of the queen-sized bed was a paste-board, veneer dresser with a mirror on top. There, staring at her, was a frazzled, injured looking version of her self. She looked like half a chipmunk, bulging out on the left side only. The cheek wasn't as badly swollen as it felt—which felt three feet wide—but significantly pronounced nonetheless with a purplish coloring already present, extending clear up to the lower corner of the left eye. Her head hurt too but not nearly as much as the side of her face. A bathroom door, to the right of the dresser, hand-prints staining the old paint around the knob, was open which showed no-one else was present.

She kicked herself for not having the pepper spray handy. She had dutifully carried the little spray bottle for months and never had occasion to use it. It was so typical for Barbara that the only time she forgot to put it in her pocket was the time she could have used it. She reflected on how lucky she had been encountering such unsavories with someone as big and strong as Mark around to defend her. Then she reflected on how she would not have been at the library at all had it not been for the big idiot and blamed Mark anyway. Still, he had acted heroically and had it been anyone of her other male clients they would have done most anything to violate her person after she had fallen unconscious. As if to second guess this thought, Barbara felt around her clothes and crotch area. Everything seemed to be in order, and nothing particularly sore.

Time to strategize, Barbara concluded. It was too late to check in at work. If anyone had noticed her having missed appointments it would be a miracle anyway. She remembered shots were fired and hoped Mark was alright; though she reasoned if he had been seriously wounded he would not have made it back to the hotel at all. This was not going to help his paranoia, she thought, letting out a small laugh. There was no phone in the room. She could go out and check the damage to the car and find a pay phone.

The lock of the door rattled and Mark appeared. He had on a baseball cap pulled low and was wearing different clothes than earlier and new, cheap sun-glasses. He was carrying a paper bag from a local liquor store and set it on the flimsy dresser. "How are you Barbara?" he inquired politely. "I brought you something to eat if you are hungry."

"That's nice Mark," Barbara said, gingerly rubbing her cheek. "But I don't think I want to chew on anything right now." She watched him move nervously around the room for a moment then continued. "You, uh, didn't happen to call my work and tell them what happened did you?"

Mark sat gracefully in a dirty, old, cloth-covered, stuffed chair, the only other piece of furniture besides the bed and dresser in the shabby room. He shook his head no. "I have something rather shocking to tell you."

Barbara let out another laugh. "You mean after this afternoon there's something left to be shocking? Did you call the police?"

"That is what might prove to be slightly shocking." Mark removed his grey cap and set it in his lap. "I cannot call the police. The man I struck, in order to rescue you, is dead. His friend, it seems, is close to death."

The picture of the grotesquely twisted face jumped back into Barbara's mind with increased gravity, more graphically than before. "Dead? How do you know?"

"I heard it on the radio. They also say I am wanted for questioning. They called it 'bizarre circumstances'."

Barbara stood up from the bed feeling very odd about the situation, heavily aware of her own presence inside the scenario which had been played out. Events seemed all at once serious and trivial, as if she were greatly removed from what had happened; like she had seen it in a movie, yet intertwined deeply with a glare of reality. "Now we really have to call the cops," Barbara heard herself say without much conviction. Mark shook his head no with increased emphasis. "Look Mark," she said trying to act stern, "it's obviously self defense. You came to someone's rescue. They'll know that."

"Oh yes," Mark agreed, "they are already calling me an 'unknown hero'."

"Well, there you go. Let's call."

Barbara moved toward the door. Mark quickly jumped to his feet and came between Barbara and the exit. He seemed very anxious. Barbara took on her social-worker demeanor and pointed an index finger up into his chest—he was nearly a foot taller. "You listen to me damn-it," she said opening her mouth wide to the discomfort of her cheek. "Get out of my way. I'm calling the police. That's what we need to do and that's what we're going to do."

Mark uncharacteristically stood his ground. He was usually rather sheepish when it came to orders. "I am terribly sorry. But I cannot let you do that right now, Ms. Cerasoli. You must listen for a while first."

Barbara continued treating him as a client. "You are going to get out of my way and stop this inappropriate behavior right now. Move over or . . ."

At this point she was interrupted by Mark reaching out with both hands to lift her gently and effortlessly off the ground to set her back on the bed. Barbara was taken aback by his strength and sat on the bed with her sore mouth cocked open in amazement. Mark stood back up tall saying, "I am very sorry Ms. Cerasoli."

Barbara bobbed her head up and down and crossed her arms. "OK . . . OK," she said, "We can discuss this. But not too long. I'm supposed to be home right now and there's people waiting for me. So don't take too long."

Mark sat down on the dresser. "Thank you very much," he said in all earnest. "I cannot, right now, let you call the police. This event is proving to be a story of a magnitude as to necessitate being in the papers. And, most likely, it will also be on the television."

Barbara continued to bob her head drawing her arms tighter. She felt silly and vulnerable inside, amazed at the huge man's capabilities, but tried to keep up the hard resolve on the outside. "OK . . . OK," she responded tersely.

"If it is well publicized," Mark continued in a logic and tone more befitting a college professor than a client, "it is reasonable to assume that my picture will accompany the story. Perhaps even interviews. Do you suppose me correct?"

"Yeah, yeah, sounds reasonable. So?"

"Barbara, there are people looking for me who must not find me. If my picture is readily accessible to the media it will make their job very easy. Are you understanding now?"

Barbara stopped bouncing her head and loosened her arms a bit. The truth of what he was saying started to shine through her layers of suspicion, though not totally. She sat thinking. Mark continued, "Now, you need not be my prisoner. I am not considering such a thing. What I am asking is you indicate to the authorities that you do not know who this person, the person who saved you is."

The last vestiges of Barbara's work attitude held on. "That would be lying, Mark. I can't do that."

"Very well," Mark said. "As you are fond of the truth, and so am I, I must tell you I am leaving the county. I must. Regardless of your decision, I must anyway. You could, perhaps, circumstances being as they are, help or hinder me in my flight."

Barbara stood up. "Mark," she said definitively, "you are not going anywhere. What you need to do . . ."

"Barbara," Mark interrupted, "I might have saved your life this afternoon. I certainly risked my own. Do you have no appreciation for this?"

Barbara felt deflated at the truth and candor in his voice. She sat down feeling embarrassed at not having thanked him for his actions before. He had risked his own life for hers. "Yes you did," she said, "and yes I am. I appreciate it very much."

"If you cannot find it in your heart to lie for me," Mark continued, "then please do not hinder me. Please allow me sufficient time to go before telling the truth."

Her embarrassment turned to shame. She looked in the mirror again imagining what she would have looked like, and where she would be now, had Mark not stepped in. "OK Mark," she started, "you can have your time. I, uh, won't tell anybody it was you. I'll tell them that I don't know who it was."

"Thank you. This is all I am asking for."

Still feeling a little guilty at her former attitude she volunteered more. "You asked some questions earlier. Nobody is going to know you're gone for about five weeks, if then. If I don't notify the parole board—which I won't—it won't come up for a long time. We don't have the resources to find our own janitor let alone a parolee who jumped out of paying for something as trivial as a drunk and disorderly." Barbara stood up. "You got my keys?"

Mark pulled her keys out of a ratty looking pair of jeans and handed them to her. "Thank you very much Barbara," he said.

Barbara took the keys and offered Mark her hand. "Thanks again Mark for your, well, I guess I could call it intervention. Good luck wherever you might be going. I sure hope I don't fry for this. But I guess I do owe you one."

Her car was parked only a few feet from the door of the room. In the U shaped parking lot of the old hotel, grass growing in every crack, there were only two other cars, both in worse shape than hers. Bottles, soup cans, crack vials, homeless blankets and cardboard were strewn around in front of a background of gang-land graffiti. It was an exceptionally filthy corner of a filthy part of town. No one would blink at a shot-up automobile here.

The driver's side window of Barbara's car had been blown out and only fragments of the sugared glass remained in the edges of the guide. Most of the shattered pieces had landed inside leaving what looked like a pile of crushed ice on the floorboard. When she closed the door more pieces of the shattered glass shook loose and scattered and rattled off the sheet metal of the door. On the passenger's side there was a bullet hole in the trim below the window. She leaned back to the missing window, eying the bullet hole, trying to estimate the trajectory of the shot. It had come very close to both of them. A set of goose bumps came over her arms and legs. It was *very* close. Seeing how close of a call it had been only firmed her resolve to help Mark. Anyone willing to brave a bullet to save her deserved something in return. Despite of what her social work training told her to do deciphering whether his agitated state was paranoia or reality would no longer be her concern. She would follow his wishes.

C HAPTER SIXTEEN

Barbara wasn't in any hurry to get home. She cruised around the neighborhood at half speed periodically tapping gently at the sore cheek and checking it in the mirror. The lackadaisical return was as if she were already trying to give mark a head start on his getaway; though she figured it would be several weeks before anyone started looking anyway. It was a naive assumption. Perhaps she was trying to fool herself into believing this lie for Mark was going to be relatively easy—believing that she could separate Mark from the scene. Maybe she actually believed it would be easy. A clue as to the ferocity of the man-hunt ensuing came when she stopped at a small bar near her house to have a cocktail.

It was a plain, typically decorated place, trying to be 'hip' as if 'hip' came in a can. These kind are so common in southern California, constructed with cost as the absolute guiding light and all the personality of a sack of flour. It was prim, proper, quiet and clean and sanitized, the kind of establishment in which your average east-coast bar-hopper would gladly vomit on the carpet. A waitress, with whom Barbara shared a casual friendship, told Barbara she had seen the story of her assault on television and tried to pump her for information. Barbara was stunned to find out this story was grist for the television. Several other people at the bar also recognized her picture from the television—a work file photo making her look washed out and cross-eyed—and offered comments of all type, also grilling her for details. It was her first indication of how hard it was going to be to sequester the truth. When the bartender offered to call the police, since the news story said she hadn't yet been found, Barbara politely declined, left her half finished cocktail and drove home.

Barbara had not realized how easy it would be for the police to glue her and her client together to the same scene. Guilelessly and stupidly she didn't think, in a place where death seemed so common, the police would bother taking time to follow up on a couple of killings. It had been obvious to the library employees she was a social worker. Such a nicely dressed white woman would normally have no other purpose in their part of town. Police called the office and from the description the personnel chief knew instantly who it had been. Her day-timer brought confirmation of the meeting at the library and also told them who she was scheduled to meet. The person seen driving from the scene matched the description of the person on the agenda: Mark Johnson. In less than twenty-five minutes on the scene, the police had made their first call to her apartment and were on their way to Mark's house.

The answering machine in Barbara's apartment was backed up with eleven different messages. Even her parents had been contacted by the police and the voice of her mother sobbing on the other end made her almost nauseous. "Baby, my baby," the voice went, "why didn't you listen to your father. Those people aren't like us. Oh my baby . . ." It was merciful the recorder limited messages to thirty seconds. Barbara rode through the call only to get to the other waiting messages. She felt sympathy for her mother, yet the tone of the call made her think mom felt more sorry for herself than for her. The police left three messages; each a perfunctory request to have her contact them as soon as she arrived. There were several calls from radio and television stations each asking for an interview in a most demanding way. Barbara refused to let the attention fluster her. Barbara should have been flabbergasted at the attention. She should have realized how ridiculous the notion was to try and separate Mark from events. Consequences and their relation to actions, however, are usually only apparent in twenty-twenty hind sight.

Jeremy was on the recorder twice and seemed to have the most sincere concern for her person. She would answer him first. "We're sure worried about you Barbara," his voice went. "Call anytime you get in."

It was only seven forty-five, not even dark. She flipped through the little phone index and found Jeremy's number. The familiar sights of her apartment wrapped around her and seemed so much more relaxing and secure than they had at anytime before. She sat down in her favorite chair, an old overstuffed cloth thing with floral print, and pulled her feet up under one side of her buttocks. The phone rang once, twice . . .

"Hello?"

"Hi Jeremy, it's Barbara."

"Jesus Christ, holy fuck, am I glad to hear your little voice. Where are you? What happened? My god, are you OK?"

The conversation continued until Jeremy was satisfied she was fine. He related how the police had come to the office on the tip that the lone Anglo woman was a social worker. They took her work photograph, biography, address and description. Less than ten minutes after the police a camera crew came wanting the same information. It was turning into a circus. Jeremy insisted on coming over with Sharon, his wife, to bring some home-made stew and commiserate. Barbara felt more like being alone, but when the issue of the police came up she acquiesced.

"At least let me come over to see what the police have to say about all this." Jeremy pleaded. "I could offer some moral support. Those guys can be kind of pushy."

Barbara thought about moral support and said yes. She called the police to notify them of her presence and the phone rang again as soon as it was hung up. She reached to the outlet and pulled the plug.

Jeremy, Sharon, and the police arrived almost simultaneously. She could hear Jeremy explaining his presence on the way up the tiered cement stairs to her second floor apartment. She opened the door before they knocked. Two detectives, both looking remarkably similar in appearance and dress, identified themselves while Jeremy, giving a wide, silly grin, stood behind them. The police were both about five-feet, ten-inches tall, a touch pudgy, middle aged, slightly balding, and in dress pants with a white shirt, tie and jacket. Sharon, a nice looking woman about Barbara's height, leaned against the metal rail of the second floor walkway, arms folded, looking uncomfortable.

The four of them entered and Jeremy gave her a one armed hug saying, "Jesus, we were so worried. We didn't know what the hell happened. Oh my god, look at this bruised up face. How are you feeling?"

"It's not bad," Barbara said giving a half smile in a way which crooked up and away from the bruising. "How are you Sharon?"

Sharon responded by shrugging her shoulders and looked to the ceiling. The dynamics between Sharon and her husband seemed strained so Barbara continued. "You didn't need to come over. I'm going to be OK."

One of the two, nearly cloned, officers spoke up in a bored tone. "I'm sergeant Jablonski, homicide, this is sergeant Espinoza, just a few questions if you feel like it Ms. Cerasoli." He didn't wait for a response. "Is it true you were on your way to meet a client?"

"Yeah. You mind if I sit down?"

The officer nodded and Jeremy stepped in. "Sir, can this wait until tomorrow?" he implored. "It's been one hell of a day for this poor young lady." Sharon could be seen by Barbara rolling her eyes in the background.

The officer not doing the questioning, officer Espinoza, took a step in Jeremy's direction offering a look somewhere between disdain and aggression. "Do you mind?" he sneered. Sharon motioned indignantly that Jeremy should stand back.

Officer Jablonski continued as Barbara re-took her favorite chair, again pulling up her feet. He started again, acting almost disinterested, folding his hands in front of him. He asked if she had sought medical treatment and whether she needed any or not. He then asked, "Did you meet a client named Mark Johnson at the Library?"

Barbara delayed just long enough to foment a small amount of suspicion with the response. "No," she said, the word forcing its way out.

"Really?" the officer asked raising one eyebrow. "You didn't meet this, uh, Mark Johnson at the library."

Barbara licked her lips and shook her head more emphatically. "Nope. He wasn't there."

The two officers exchanged glances, and Jablonski continued. "We're asking because the man you were seen leaving the scene with matches a rough description of Mr. Johnson."

"That might be, but he wasn't there. I didn't meet him."

The officer began referring to a note pad as he continued. "You were seen talking to a large, African-American male, approximately six-feet, five-inches tall, two-hundred pounds, shaved head. You're telling us that this wasn't your client."

"It wasn't."

"Any idea who it was?"

"I don't know." Barbara glanced at Jeremy, his mouth was open and his brow knit hard in disbelief. She turned away from his accusatory glare.

"Ms. Cerasoli," the officer continued, "can you please tell us why you were talking to this man and not your client?"

"I was asking him if he knew where Mark was."

The officers exchanged another glance. Jablonski continued, "Any idea, then, why this man risked his life to give you assistance?"

"None whatsoever. Good Samaritan, I guess." Barbara's statements were growing more terse and less believable by the moment.

"Yeah, I see," Jablonski said scratching his head while looking intently into his note pad. "Can you tell us anything more, then, about this, uh, man that you were talking to."

"No, I don't know him. He was big and polite. That's about it."

The officer blew air out from puffed cheeks in a long sigh. "Are you aware that this man is wanted for questioning in the death of two individuals?" he asked. The words 'two individuals' caused Barbara's head to twitch. She paused, then took a deep breath and pushed her lips together tightly. "You were seen leaving the scene with this man. Why is it that you can't tell us anything further about him?"

"Easy," Barbara said in a futile attempt to sound flippant, "I don't remember leaving the scene."

"I see. And what do you remember about the last, oh, four hours or so?"

"I, uh, just . . ." Barbara waved a hand in the air searching for words. "I, just came home and took a nap."

The officer rolled his eyes and lolled his tongue around in his mouth. "A nap?" he reiterated.

"Yes, a nap."

"Here in this apartment?"

"Yes, here," Barbara snapped now trying to sound agitated at the questioning.

The officer rubbed a hand over his face letting out a tired sigh. "Are you aware, Ms. Cerasoli that we came to look for you, here, at this apartment?"

Barbara shrugged, now trying to appear disinterested. "I guess I didn't answer the door. I was tired; hurt and tired."

"You guess." Jablonski asked, now looking very interested for a change.

"I know. I didn't answer the door. Do I look like I want to be entertaining people?" Barbara was growing defensive and losing even more credibility.

"Are you aware, Ms. Cerasoli, that your apartment manager allowed us into the premises to have a look around?"

Barbara's face flushed bright red. "Well . . . well, I, uh, I guess I don't remember what I did this afternoon. Look, I got my head smacked. I'm a little rattled. Why don't you leave me alone? I'll probably make more sense in the morning."

"All right, Ms. Cerasoli. Just one more question."

"OK."

"Is there any reason that you would not want us to talk to the man who came to your rescue? You do realize that he isn't, yet, going to be charged with anything."

Barbara was no longer looking into the eyes of the officer but at his feet. "I realize that," she said. "I just don't know who he is."

"And any reason you wouldn't want us to talk to him?"

"No, none."

"OK. That'll be all for now Ms. Cerasoli. We'll be in touch." Jablonski's small notepad snapped shut.

The officers departed without another word, both of them shaking their heads. Jeremy was still standing with his mouth drooped open in disbelief, looking like a paralyzed perch. He hadn't moved and his brow still revealed his consternation.

Sharon came up to tug on his arm. "Let's go honey," she said, "Barbara needs her rest."

Still staring at Barbara, without turning, he said, "Wait for me a minute outside baby."

"Goodnight Barbara," said Sharon.

"Goodnight Sharon," responded Barbara, "thanks for coming." Sharon closed the door and Barbara turned to Jeremy. "What's up?"

"I think," he said, finally changing expression, "you know 'what's up' better than I do. What's in this for you? Mark ain't in trouble. Hell. They're gonna make him a hero. This might be really good for him. What's going on?"

Barbara averted her eyes and could no longer look at him. "I'm really tired Jeremy," she said standing. "It's really great of you to come over. I'll see you tomorrow."

"Somehow," Jeremy said shaking a large digit at her, "you're going to get in a lot of trouble lying like this. You better think twice. You better be sure of what you're doing."

She gave a lop-sided smile. "Thanks. I know what I'm doing."

Barbara took a long hot shower trying to scrub away a nervous sweat. She put on her soft, blue felt pajamas. Even though it was too warm to be wearing such heavy sleep-ware she liked the way she looked in the mirror with them on. The pliable blue cloth made her feel young and silly, innocent of larger things. Huge pillows with decorative covers topped a bed covered with a deep blue, quilted spread. She turned on a fan and turned off the light. For a moment, in the late summer's twilight, she could think of nothing but rest. Like an explosion without the crack of noise the twisted remains outside the library exploded into her mind and illuminated her conscious. The body had a spasm under the stark glare of death. She sat up, breathing hard, a nervous sweat again taking over. Barbara tried to be angry at the man who had hit her, trying to convince herself he had deserved it. But she knew it was a consequence beyond reasonable. Death was beyond what he had done by a huge margin. The blood, pooling wet on the hot, grey sidewalk, made her empty stomach roil. It became a long and lonely night.

CHAPTER SEVENTEEN

Financial house in disarray, months, if not weeks from bankruptcy, wife gone, and under a cloud of police suspicion for the first time in his life, George should have been depressed. But he was elated. Every minute seemed a new challenge. He felt young and vibrant for the first time in years. The events of a week ago had lifted a weight off of him. The film of doubt which had coated everything he had done or thought in the last year had been scrubbed away for a fresh, clean start. There was no longer a sour taste in his mouth every time he thought of the space ship. There would be no more obsessive wandering through the desert, aimlessly, without lead or clue. It was here and now. George, if it took the rest of his life, would try and find them. He had his raison d'être. At the age of forty-two, George had found his purpose. Everything revolved around the single goal: find the aliens.

The starting point in his adventure was obvious. He must go and collect clues from the desert. He set up a base in a road-side motel called the "Come Right Inn" whose majority of income seemed to come from a seedy little lounge. It obviously didn't depend on repeat business for the hotel as service and clean sheets were non-existent. It was cheap enough, though, and removed enough from the nearest town to exempt George from the odd, gossipy dynamics a rural community reserved for strangers who asked a lot of questions. He arrived at the hotel in the early evening. Barstow sheriffs had nothing to say just as soon as the doctor gave the discharge—the blood tests were negative. George bid them a smiling, "Good-bye," then he wished them all speed in finding the real "sick-o."

The night before making his way back into the desert George was as anxious as a little boy going to his first circus. He spent the evening pacing the floor. He woke before dawn and was on his way out the door before looking at his watch and realizing it wouldn't be light for another hour. It didn't stop him. He let the truck warm for a long time. In the rearview mirror, using the soft yellow glow of the dome-light he inspected the white bandage over the eight stitches on his brow. The eye was still greenish, purple and puffy. The wound, for some reason, made the adventure seem all that much more real. This tangible wound connected him to the events of a week ago. A tap on the gas lowered the automatic choke to a more reasonable idle. The seat he was sitting on was now different. It had come from a junk yard just outside Barstow. The former bench had reeked of blood and had been liberally assaulted by the good sheriff for lab samples, leaving huge holes through the foam all the way to the springs. The parking lot was as quiet as a sound stage except for the low rumble of George's truck moving to the highway.

When he reached the point where he was to depart the main road into the desert track it was still dark. Up the road a couple of miles from the motel he had passed a convenience store and decided to turn around and go there, get a cup of coffee, and watch the sunrise. The clerk was a man about George's age with drooping jowls and squishy beer belly. His face was noticeably un-tanned for living in the desert, attesting to how often he had ventured outside. His black hair was greased back slick on his head, not out of any fashion trend of today, but rather looking like it had never changed from the original style of years ago. He eyed George suspiciously as he poured his coffee.

There were several small shops and houses equal distant from the place he had last observed the aliens, stretched along the highway. This was just the only one open all night. It was close to the same time now as when his quarry escaped him the previous week. George had originally planned to wait and ask questions after his work in the desert—then having a better bearing on what kind of questions to ask. But now was as good a time as any. This, after all, might be the same clerk who had been on duty last Saturday. He dallied around the cream and sugar musing to himself what to say. He felt childish, excited, silly, and about everything else in the world one could feel pretending to be someone he wasn't for the first time in his adult life.

"Hi," George said to the proprietor who was eying him suspiciously.

George's delay at the coffee counter had made the man more wary. He didn't respond to the salutation and only rang up the coffee. "Ninety cents," he said.

George threw down a dollar and, feeling the peak of his multiplicity of emotions, dove into his act. "Yeah buddy," George said trying to act casual, "I'm, uh, looking for a couple of guys. Big guys. They were around here last week. Last Saturday."

The man looked at George queerly. "What the hell you mean?" he asked. "Lots a people come through here."

"Well, these guys would probably seem, well, real different," George said feeling more odd then ever.

"Niggers?"

"What?"

"Was they niggers?" the clerk said with a sneer.

George had spent twenty years indoctrinating young, idiot soldiers not to use this filthy word and it infuriated him. He nearly picked up his coffee and left, yet this wasn't the army now and he needed information. He might as well play along.

"Maybe," said George and he sipped on his coffee.

"Was they or wasn't they?"

"Well, I didn't get a good look at them."

"Well, if it was niggers, two of them come in here last week and robbed the place. Scared the livin' hell out of my cousin. Least-wise it was her excuse not to work nights no more. Just a young, little girl. First year of college but acts like the first year of grammar school. One big old buck and another about my age, plump like. If you're lookin' for them I hope you're lookin' to shoot the mother-fuckers."

George's mind raced with possibilities, though he cognitively discounted the probability of a correlation. "Did she get a good look at them?"

"Why the hell you lookin'?"

George took another sip of coffee trying to remain cool, though his hand shook a little with anticipation. "Because they robbed me too, down around Barstow. Somebody said they were coming this way." Part of what he said was true. Whoever it was who had dumped him in Barstow had emptied his wallet. "I got nothing else to do. I'm retired. You know the cops aren't going to do anything about a robbery anymore. So I'm going to."

"They do that to you?" the clerk said pointing at George's eye.

"Yeah. So, is there any way I can talk to your cousin and get a description?"

"Hell, not at this hour. She'll be working the eight to four. You can come in then. Don't expect much though. Seems they got her by surprise too. Besides, she's a little goofy. Police think they knocked her out with a taser or something like it. I got a security camera but that didn't see nothin' neither. Stinkin' thing stopped workin' for some reason. They give you that nice eyeball, huh?"

George shook his head up and down at the comment. He was less excited than he had started at the apparent lack of description. "I'll come back later," he said, "what's your cousin's name?"

"Her name's Annie. Kind of a little weirdo really. Don't really fit in around here but you can try and talk to her. I used to have some locals that would come around. Hell, no more. She scared every one of 'em away. Had to put her on graveyard. Figured she would cause less harm that way. I'm gonna have to fire the little shit pretty soon. You can try and talk to her if you want."

"Thanks," the former captain said and started out the door.

"Hey," called the pudgy, white clerk after Gregaris, "if you corner them boys and need some help you just give me a call." The clerk stuck a hand under the counter and pulled up a shotgun. "Me and my old friend here will be more than willing to help."

"Oh yeah, sure," George said disingenuously. He walked out the door thinking to himself 'If I need some help containing some huge, dangerous man I'm certainly not going to call some fat-assed, pin-head like you.'

Mr. Gregaris watched the sun rise in the East at the departure point. The tracks from last week were easily visible in the gaining light. He parked at least fifty yards from the base of the little knoll not wanting to disturb any possible evidence. He got out of his truck while putting on his large, straw sun hat that had, somehow, made the unconscious trip with him to Barstow. Before the hat, however, went on the crisscrossed straps of a canteen, camera, and a leather satchel containing various items to further his investigation. As he came closer he slowed and made sweeping observations, walking this way and that, looking for any possible disturbance. When he was close enough, he could see the items he had left behind up on the rise: binoculars, flashlight, twenty-two pistol and canteen.

George followed the old tire tracks until they twisted to the south behind the knoll where he had parked the truck. There, the tracks dug deep, indicating a sudden departure. Right beside where the tire tracks dug deepest there appeared several small, dark stains he presumed to be his own blood from the cut. He took a picture of the spot then, just to be certain, George took the leather satchel off his shoulder and took out a small scooper and several vials. He collected a little of each spot, carefully labeling each vial and noting the position of each. George was in forensic heaven.

At the top of the knoll he measured his boot against one footprint, then found another distinctly different. He took a picture of the different print with a ruler beside it. He then took careful measurement of the depth of each print. This would be used to later estimate the mass of the rifleman by gauging how deep his print was as opposed to the other. Pulling out a pad he drew a rough sketch as to the tread marks, trying to note anything that might be unique to that particular shoe. On it went, slowly, methodically, and with all tedious endeavor. He swept around for loose hair which might someday be matched to the assassin. He drew maps of where the footprints had come from and where they had ended up. He scoured the grounds for a rifle shell to no avail. He collected, searched, photographed and drew just about everything in the area before moving on to his real intrigue. As if paying dues for the fun he was about to have, George had taken care of the samples of less intrigue first. Now it was time to move out into the area where the aliens had last been seen.

George tipped back the canteen taking a large draught. It was eight o'clock and already hot enough in the exposed landscape to be uncomfortable. He surveyed the distortion of heat waves already coming off the desert plain in the distance. Something was wrong. The old scientist in George was eating at him. He had been so anxious to get to the evidence further out he suddenly felt he was overlooking something. He didn't know what it was yet, but the notion ate at him. There was a piece to the puzzle which hadn't jumped out at him yet. Something he had previously assumed was not fitting into the present scene. This annoyed George terribly and, as if to punish himself, he refused to go out further until the piece had fallen into place.

He squat down on the ground and doodled with one finger in the dust. He drew a circle for the rifleman and an X for himself with a small box for the truck. Rifleman, him, truck, he went over in his mind; Rifleman, him, truck. All of a sudden it hit him. If it was alien blood on the seat, why were there only the footprints of him and the rifleman near the vehicle? Unless . . . George stood up in wonder. He then thought, 'Unless the rifleman too was an alien'.

It had been too simple. His assumption had clouded his mind. He was assuming the rifleman was terrestrial since he hadn't come from the particular ship he had observed. But what if he had come before, nearly one year before? Why was this other visitor trying to kill these current arrivals? This must mean the visitors had been ready and willing to defend themselves; it was the rifleman who had been injured. George's mind raced as he took to a strong walk toward the tracks of his truck from a week ago.

There was one possibility left. Perhaps the aliens gained entry to the truck later. He followed the tire marks for fifty or sixty yards until they suddenly veered south. The spray of gravel suggested a relatively high rate of speed. On one side of the track George found a set of footprints. They were in a wide stride as if running. On the other side of the tire marks they continued, medium stride as if resuming a walk. The rifleman had not only tried to shoot them but had also tried to run one of them over. Since the prints continued George knew this individual had not entered the truck. There were, now, at least three aliens on our planet, at least one of which intent on murder.

He followed the footsteps for another hundred yards or so. They weren't easy to follow since the hard, desert scrabble at times resembled more solid rock than soil. But his keen eye kept him on track until they met up with another set of prints. These were huge; at least a size seventeen or better. Even without a measurement George could see how much further they sank into the ground than his own or of the other individual. One of the two recent aliens was a very large individual indeed.

George followed the large prints, which appeared to be loping on long, running strides, back to the far side of the knoll until they were united with the smaller set as they came from the craft. It was just about where he estimated last seeing the two shapes before being drug down the hill and, therefore, near to where they would have heard the horn honk. To his surprise, they diverged from each other on a run. There was no indication they had tried to hide by laying down or change course together. Instead, they fanned out around either side of the small hill in what appeared to be an attacking maneuver. The visitors, the captain concluded, were either expecting an ambush or damn well trained to deal with one.

George continued to scour the region with the skill he had developed for years. He wanted to follow the tracks of the two aliens all the way back to their ship but it was getting towards the afternoon and prohibitively hot. If nothing else, George thought, the fact he had established the existence of another alien had justified today's search. Tomorrow he would also follow the tracks of the rifleman that went out of sight in a direction toward the road. He returned to the truck-side of the knoll by following the running steps of the smaller visitor and then the tire tracks to where it had been parked. In the dirt, kicked up by the spinning wheels he saw the slightest glint of metal. There he found a shell, a 30.06. George had always imagined aliens using much more sophisticated weapons than this. The position of the shell indicated that it was fired by the rifleman. Probably, but not absolutely, it had been fired toward the large individual. Yet, it was the rifleman who was injured. There just might be another shell casing in that direction. A shell manufactured on another planet. There was ample rationalization to continue tomorrow.

George was so consumed ruminating through his fresh data he didn't remember he was supposed to revisit the convenience store until he had driven past it. He was anxious to get back to the room to lay out all the collected information and do calculations so he debated whether to stop or not. After driving another mile he reluctantly found a wide spot in which to turn around.

There was no-one else in the store even though the nearby gas station was buzzing with activity. George could see the woman through the glass. It was hard not to notice her as she was lying on the counter, her head propped up on a stack of newspapers with one leg crossed over a bent knee. A cloud of smoke hovered over her face as she puffed lackadaisically on a cigarette. George pushed open the door expecting her to rouse a little, but she didn't even turn her head. The tie-dye shirt, torn jeans and limp hair seemed right out of George's past and he felt comfortable with them; though the nose ring she sported would never seem normal to this former military man. He advanced on the counter until he was standing only a foot or so from the supine body. The shapely young body on the counter, clothed as it was, caused George to flash back to a similarly dressed and supine body in much different circumstance from years ago. He glanced up from the young, motionless and disengaged female to a mirror behind the counter. There he saw his balding head, dark lines and weather worn skin. George suddenly felt very old.

"Excuse me," George said, leaving the old memory behind.

The young woman smacked her lips and said, "I suppose you want to *buy* something," leaning on the word buy in a most sarcastic manner.

George nearly laughed. She had about the same attitude toward work he had had at her age. "Nope," George responded, "I'm actually looking for someone named Annie. Are you Annie?"

Annie threw her legs onto the floor on the opposite side of the counter. She was peeved to be shaken out of her reminiscing. She had been musing over her first few college parties and the boys, those wonderful boys. She couldn't wait to get back to school and out of her perceived hell hole. Her cousin, she thought, was too stupid to fire her so she pushed insubordination to the limit. She rubbed her cigarette into a full ashtray she had purposely balanced over the 'no smoking' sign. "Annie? What a funny name," she said trying to look drained of life. "I guess I'm the one."

"Yeah," George went on feeling odd at his sudden recognition of the age difference between them, "I talked to your cousin early this morning. He said you'd be working today."

Annie took out another cigarette and tapped the end on the counter, stuck it in her loose lips and lit it. "And what does the *blob* have to say?" she said puffing out a white cloud.

"He said you were robbed last Saturday by two men." Annie shrugged her shoulders apathetically then plopped one elbow down on the counter and supported her chin with a palm. George continued, "Can you tell me anything about them. Did you get a good look at them? Did they say anything?"

Annie sighed, puffed again, then said, "And why, pray tell, are you looking for these men? Private Eye? Disgruntled Citizen?"

The novelty of talking to a younger person had worn off and was wearing thin. He began suppressing an urge to slap her. "I guess," continued the captain trying to keep an even tone to his voice, "you could label me as a disgruntled citizen."

"Aren't . . . we . . . all," said Annie with a slight smirk. George's hand twitched.

"Well, I can see this going nowhere fast," he said, "I'll see you later." George figured he could get her description from the police report anyway.

At the same time the bell rang on the door and in walked a red-eyed 'blob' carrying several boxes of stock. Annie stiffened and quickly put out her cigarette. Her cousin set the boxes down at the door and walked past George to the counter. Picking up the ashtray he dumped the contents into a wastebasket near the coffee counter and re-exited the door. One step outside he flung the glass ashtray across the road where it shattered against a rock.

Coming back in he said, "If I catch you smoking in this place one more time you're history. Then you can find your own damn work. Or sit around doin' nothin' in this *hell hole*." On the words 'hell hole' he had elevated the tone of his voice to a falsetto to imitate hers and shook his hips back and forth. Annie glowered at the ground. He turned to George offering a hand. "This little thing answering your questions," he asked, "or is she being typical?"

George looked at Annie before answering who shot a vicious sidelong glance at him. George shook the hand and smiled. "Typical," he said.

The greasy fat man stepped up to the counter. "Why can't you do nothin' without actin' like some precious little idget? Answer the man's goddamned questions. You hear me?"

Annie, back to glowering at the ground, went into a quick monotone of the story. "There was two of them. One a lot bigger than the other. They waited around outside. I could see the face of the big one. He had straight black hair and big green eyes. That's all. Didn't notice them beyond that."

"No, that ain't all," the cousin snapped. "You ain't told him about how they knocked you cold, ripped apart the cash register and all that. Well? Go ahead."

"Sounds like you're doing a fine job," Annie mumbled.

"Don't get smart now." The pudgy clerk yelled, "Tell the man."

"They knocked you cold?" George asked. "Did they hit you?"

"No," Annie said, shrugging her shoulders again and now looking to the ceiling.

"Well?" the cousin said continuing his browbeating, "why don't you show the man where they shot you; seems like you showed every goddamned sheriff between here and the Nevada border." He turned to George. "They shot her with somethin' that made a purple burn mark right on the ass. Then she goes around droppin' her pants, barin' her butt to show every young sheriff that came along, all grins and giggles. Whatever it was it knocked her cold as a six-pack. Then they tore my register to livin' shit. They ripped the drawer right out of it breakin' the locks and twistin' it all to hell." In a back room a phone began ringing. He talked as he walked as he went to answer the call. "Go on," he said, "tell the man. And hang out your ass again for all I care."

George turned to Annie. "Is that all?" he asked kindly.

Annie didn't respond. She flopped into a plastic chair which was behind her and folded her arms tightly around the middle.

George tried again. "Can you add anything to that?"

Annie shrugged again.

"Yes sirrreee," came a hoot from the back room. The rotund man came out with a big smile on his face. "Seems like you don't got to look no more mister. They got one of them. One of them coons. All they need is for little fussbudget here to go down and identify him.

"Go on. I'll watch the store for a little bit. And I'll actually sell somethin' for a change. Go on. They're down at the station waiting for you." Annie didn't need to be told twice and was on her way out the door. After the door shut the soft, little man continued. "That nigger's goddamned

144

lucky they got him before me and my old buddy caught up with him. They bagged him down at the grocery store this morning. Sure wish I would've been there to teach him a lesson or two."

George thanked the man for his time but left thoroughly disgusted by his racist demeanor. George wished the soft, craven man had been down at the grocery store also, to meet the large, hard criminal. Perhaps he would have gotten a pair of fat lips to match his fat mouth. The squeaky clean captain had no patience for criminals, or lawlessness, but probably had less for idle boasts. Fat mouthed, jack-asses were always the first ones to grab a gun when forced to back up their boasts.

Since one of the thieves had been caught, George figured it rendered more remote the possibility of an association between them and the aliens. Though he was intrigued by the description of 'one large and one small man', as his evidence pointed to from the desert, he reasoned anyone stupid enough to hang around the scene of a crime couldn't possibly be an advanced extra-terrestrial; especially if he were stupid enough to continue to hang around this place. And black? Try as he might, George just could not envision a black space man.

CHAPTER EIGHTEEN

It was a most insecure feeling. Sitting inside a cage like a bird with two cats roaming somewhere outside waiting to get their claws on him. It made him feel terribly exposed. Sheriffs walked past the barred cell from time to time reading reports, munching on apples or only swinging their arms. Each time Pestia heard the noise of footsteps echoing on the painted cement he imagined his adversaries coming around the corner, guns drawn and ready to finish the job. Being trapped was a hopeless feeling.

Pestia had recognized the little female. She was the first earthling he had spoken to on the planet and would remember this fact. She, however, did not recognize him. And she was truthful enough to not identify him as her assailant. Pestia was beginning to wonder about the truthfulness of white humans when it came to people of his skin color. Their quick trigger indictments seemed as if they were able to delude themselves into believing anything negative about him. Take these sheriffs for example. Here he had been cleared of the charges by this woman, but they still insisted on holding him because he wouldn't tell them how he had injured his shoulder. He told them it was none of their business; which it wasn't, but that true fact only infuriated them. They wanted to examine it. He refused.

He knew a bullet wound would be of special interest to the police. They held their ground and he stayed in jail.

Pestia was also sick to death of the sneers and cold glares offered every time he walked into an all white room. A commander of a space fleet which could turn the surface of this orb molten in less than a day should not have to suffer the ignominy of brutish prejudice, he thought. Out here in the country it was much worse. It seemed everyone had a smart-assed comment. Young boys in their pickup trucks would roar by screaming out filth while exposing the middle-finger insult. It was amazing to Pestia these things happened without provocation. He wished he could transport some of these morons back to Bren for a while to let them endure the glares and stares and disapproving sneers they would surely get looking so out of place. As if he didn't need enough to control his own disgust at their slimy white skin, these soft white beings looked to him as if they had been boiled and peeled.

Another set of footsteps came down the hall and Pestia tensed up. He knew who had really robbed the store and he was sure that they knew who had tried to ambush them. These facts lent credibility to his paranoia of being confined and fed it. Though there was no guarantee his would be killers were still in the area, Pestia found it palpable enough to have a high degree of anxiety. The footsteps were another sheriff and this one stopped to talk. He seemed, to Pestia, the most reasonable of the bunch. He was younger and obviously better educated than most of the others.

The name on his shirt was Henderson and he was, as Pestia presumed, better educated than the others. He was the only sheriff in the station with a college degree and was, therefore, given precinct command by default—a move which most of the other sheriffs greatly resented. Sheriff

Henderson decided to take on this case himself since he knew the attitude of the others toward a black man. He wanted to believe the prisoner, and he wanted to turn him loose. But nothing the large man said added up right down to his fake sounding name: Frank Johnson. Where on the whole planet was there a black man named Frank? There was a driver's license that checked out, but no social security number and no other identification at all. Because of the prisoner's strange accent, lack of identification and lack of general knowledge of the country, Henderson decided he must be an illegal alien from some place in Africa. He debated calling immigration but relented at the last second reasoning their hands were full enough. There was nothing left to do but turn him loose.

Henderson eyed the large black man whose odd, green eyes stared back at him with a strained suspicion. He found the prisoner's muscle build incredible. As the prisoner put an arm behind his head it revealed knotted biceps and triceps connected to the shoulders with sinuous tissue. And yet he was old. Old, that is, for Henderson. It was unfortunate the prisoner matched the description from the robbery so well. Henderson knew the arresting officers weren't anywhere near polite and it was too bad to have any innocent man go through this sort of treatment. Definitely hard, strong, and apparently of a proud past, these were things the sheriff trusted in any man, one of color or not. Henderson wanted the prisoner to be what he appeared to be: an erudite African-American beyond the red-neck stereotype. Perhaps, he thought, he was giving this man a break beyond what would be considered normal simply because he were black—maybe to give a small amount of balance to the incivility most blacks endured here in the county. In any case, the prisoner was going to go free.

"All right Johnson," Henderson said, "let's go. We've got no reason to hold you. We're cutting you loose."

Pestia continued to lie on the bed until the door was wide open. As un-reasonable as he felt his seizure had been, he felt his release was now just as astounding. It came too sudden for his oppressed mood. He glanced each way at the opening, half expecting some sort of trap.

"Come on," Henderson said, "let's go. Pick up your belongings at the desk."

Pestia picked up his belongings dutifully, avoiding the repellent gaze of the corpulent clerk. The young sheriff stayed in the vicinity of the large black man until he left the station. He did so to insure a cessation of snide and racist comments. The silence among the older sheriffs was thick.

Outside Pestia slipped on his sunglasses. It was late afternoon, stinging hot and blinding bright. His old car, purchased in Barstow with cash, ran and that was about it. It coughed, shook, sputtered and blew out a blue cloud upon starting. His shoulder ached. It had been nearly eight days since the shooting and, at times, it hurt as bad now as when it first happened, or maybe worse. He laid the right hand across his lap. The shoulder was still swollen and he could not lift the arm over his head. He hoped there was no permanent damage, only time would tell. Though he felt an urgency to chase the assassins, there was no longer a need for the desperation of a week ago. He had landed on his feet rather nicely after such dire circumstances. After a year of being down and out, dealing with welfare agencies, social workers and—perhaps the most useful source of information—other people down and out, he had become accustomed to a hobo's existence, knowing always how and where to get free meals, beds and emergency support. He found the bad side of town friendlier in many ways than the good side. Though it was decidedly more dangerous, people never looked down their nose at you if you did not look right. Police were a lot less likely to stop a suspicious person and interrogate them against a background of many other suspicious looking persons. Institutions designed to help the less fortunate were there. And people on the bad side of town were not prone to asking difficult questions, which would make his injury much less conspicuous.

Social welfare ended up becoming the lesser of the two evils for Pestia, thievery being the other option. Thievery had started out of necessity; obtaining currency had been quickly recognized as essential to life in the United States. Later, thievery merely became convenient, much more convenient than work. He tried working as a janitor for a school but found the tasks degrading and the supervisor overbearing. The general of millions was not yet ready for the stain of scrubbing toilets whether duty required it or not.

In and around this time he was also dealing with severe depression, an out of control charge, and culture shock. It all was a bit overwhelming and a radical departure from skills he had been honing his entire life. The psychology of tolerance isn't a natural one to a military man and the whole bent of individualism was foreign to his upbringing. Tasks he was doing now he would have seen as well beneath him, culturally alienating, and simplistic on his home planet.

It further aggravated him he didn't have the patience to persist with the cultural items, foreign to him, which he saw as ignorant. Chores such as making small talk, shaking hands and having to offer opinions were all such idiosyncratic requirements for the socialization of earthlings. Earthlings seemed such a loud and raucous people to Pestia. Always shouting, hooting, and wanting to talk and talk. And he refused to admit to himself he didn't have the forbearance to persevere. Yet truly, he didn't have the patience, the tolerance, the ease of motion in a new place, or the ability to change his behavior to accommodate such a new environment. Being an individual was taxing to a man who had spent his life learning how to conform. Being different was devastating to a person who had been taught individual value was largely determined with how well one could blend in with the surroundings. Walking around in Anglo neighborhoods he felt as if he were a flashing beacon of neon color noticed by all. Guiding himself through black sections of town he felt maladroit with the assumptions of African Americans with how he should talk, walk and think. Being able to deal with being awkward, a rookie, and swallowing pride were skills largely out of reach of him. Less than he was absolutely incapable and more from the fact all of this went counter to who he was. He was well aware of other cultures in his region of space, but he had never had to fit into one before. And it was sometimes nearly too much for him.

Stealing had been both a way of clandestine support and a way to secretly snub his new and often inhospitable host planet. It was comical he should be indignant for being arrested for burglary. He hadn't performed this particular act he was accused of, but there were dozens of others he was fully guilty of. In the wonderful and sometimes tragic way the brain can separate things he was able to rationalize his petty crimes as going toward a higher cause. Though he was, Pestia never thought of himself as a thief.

The pacification gun was the easiest method; used on dark streets on unsuspecting victims, it worked wonderfully until the pellets ran out. When guilt began to cloud his motives, Pestia moved from random victims to what he believed more deserving targets. As knowledge of the neighborhood he was living in grew, he became aware of a whole underground of illicit activity in the form of drug sales. He had worked for a police force on Bren when he was a young man and had little tolerance for these swaggering punks. Less than half his age the little illiterate bastards commanded power well beyond what they should. Another advantage of hitting the drug dealers, besides the moral fig leaf, was the fact they always had wads of cash. It wasn't necessary to strike more than one a month or so. He resisted the temptation to kill them; he reserved a small amount of hope one or two were reform able. He would usually only break a limb or two and leave just enough evidence behind to suggest a rival dealer or gang—he would let them do the killing.

Pestia was surprised by how much weaker the average human was. They hadn't the weight, strength or size of the average person of Bren. Even those his size in stature and larger in girth proved to be vastly weaker and much more fragile. Pestia, especially early in the year, enjoyed the combat. Out of it he drew a catharsis for all his frustrations. He preferred savaging African-American drug dealers since he could then pretend it was one of the scoundrel traitors of Ranson and take his time, sadistically pounding them into submission. Here was a broken arm for ransacking his home. There was a shattered jaw for burning the palace. He took chances beyond what were reasonable—though of inferior strength and speed they all carried weapons. Yet, at the time, Pestia was not altogether balanced. The thought of his family rotting in the jails of his sworn enemy being degraded, raped tortured, perhaps some still being interrogated, tore into his ability to focus on the greater good.

He looked back at the early part of his stay with mixed emotions. Measuring it on the standard of his military commission, standing before the high court of Bren, there were times he had clearly been derelict in duty. This, however, would not be a fair measure of circumstance. He was trillions of miles from home and he was not a machine. Public opinion would probably be less kind. Yet Pestia knew there were people whose opinion he valued and they would judge him less harshly.

Eventually he took time to be more careful. He figured out how to get the sort of social welfare to exist—automatic on his planet—health care, subsistence money, etc . . . This was both more benevolent than battering humans and more prudent to the task of being the prince's benefactor. Regardless of his early actions, the die was now cast. The prince was on his own. The subjects of Bren could judge him however they pleased. Pestia's only focus now was to kill the Premier before he killed the prince.

The hot air slapped against his face through the open window. He had lost valuable time with this arrest. The advantage he possessed by having local knowledge diminished each day. He must spring on the bastards while they are floundering in this new place. He knew how vulnerable he and the prince had been a year ago and meant to capitalize on the fact with the new arrivals. The heat sucked moisture from his body. Ahead there was a motel with what appeared to be a restaurant. Pestia decided to get some refreshment.

Pestia felt uncomfortable in an area so sparse of African-Americans. He found himself wishing for the small bit anonymity the similar colored crowds of Los Angeles brought. It was the main reason he had chosen to live in the big city rather than a safer suburb. Being the only black man in a rural area made him feel a torch of brown in a sea of bland white. These insecurities further exaggerated his perception as to the tensions between the two colors. Everywhere he went he could feel the eyes upon him. Friendly or not, the mere fact they were always looking, judging, peering at the differences put him on edge. He could sense the unnatural tones in their voices and feel the change in body language every time they addressed him. Some were patronizingly friendly, some cold and distant, both responses were annoying to Pestia.

At the hotel the road grew close enough to the moisture filled mountains to actually have some flora. Around the buildings there were some trees with welcome shade. Pestia parked the clunker under the shade of one such tree in the gravel courtyard of the lounge. Across the parking area was a row of white, stucco rooms for the motel. There was only one vehicle parked there.

With a flash of anger the image entered his mind. He sat in his erstwhile truck wondering what to do, trying not to be rash, wanting not to make a serious mistake. Without a doubt, it was the same truck he had commandeered in his escape. It was the truck of the man who had foiled his ambush. Who was this persistent, white jackass? Why had he been in his way to begin with and why was he here now? Pestia's first inclination was to plan to kill him, but more rational thoughts took hold as he realized how vulnerable he was. He decided, instead, to wait long enough to calm down then investigate.

If the little bastard were a local, Pestia reasoned, he need not be staying in a motel. He would be in his local residence. The diminutive fool had come to this place a week ago and then returned for a purpose. But what was the purpose? Perhaps he was looking for someone. If someone had bashed my head and dumped me one-hundred miles away from my starting point, thought the general, I might want to find that person too. But what had brought him into such a remote region of the desert in the first place? Was it coincidence? Not likely.

Pestia walked to the truck making sure no-one was observing him. Inside the locked doors he could see papers stacked on the passenger seat. The top sketch was of a foot-print with the words, 'R-man, top of hill,' scribbled below. On the dash was a small note pad, inverted to be open to a particular page. It read, 'V1, V2 alive . . . R-man?'

Pestia pulled his white golf cap low on his brow. Being arrested had revitalized his strategy. He realized his eyes and straight hair were the two most distinctive traits separating him from the average American black. He should have taken more care in distinguishing himself from the new arrivals. Yet, prior to last Saturday he had imagined too often vanquishing them to believe in alternative plans. After he was shot, there had been no time to pay attention to details. Sitting in a jail cell gives one time to think. A long term strategy was going to be necessary and it would start with this annoying little human. It was time, he thought, to look the little bastard in the face, and walked into the lounge.

It was dark enough in the lounge to make sunglasses conspicuous but he kept them on anyway. As his eyes became accustomed to the dark he saw his nemesis at the bar, the rancid little twerp of a human who had spoiled everything. The bartender was talking to this thing. Pestia tried to be philosophical about the events but still felt like walking up to introduce himself by twisting the man's head right off his soft, squishy, pale neck. He advanced and took a seat at the bar several stools removed from Gregaris. Conversation had stopped when he entered. Pestia was used to this treatment by now. It was apparent in the first few seconds as to the attitude of the patron and bartender towards a black man entering an ostensible white establishment. The bartender, a skinny old man with the bright red beak of an alcoholic, could not hide his contempt.

The old bartender tapped on the bar in front of George a couple of times to officially pause the conversation and said, "Just a second." He walked to Pestia and asked, "Yeah? What-cha need?"

"Anything on tap," Pestia said, coolly turning to look down the bar at George; he exchanged a dip of the head with the good captain in a pleasant acknowledgment of each other's presence.

The bartender set the beer in front of Pestia and returned to his former conversation. "Nope," he said, "can't say I've seen anything weird in the last week or so. Usually nobody but locals come in here. You been up to the that all-night store yet? They get some weird stuff. Like last week. They got robbed by a couple of . . . well . . ." The bartender and George both looked down the counter to Pestia. Pestia returned the glance, smiled and dipped his head once again.

"I've already talked to them," George said.

"Well partner, that's about as different as it gets around here," the bartender continued. "Sometimes, in the day-time, we get people on their way to Mammoth or Mono stopping in. But they usually don't stay more than a beer. You said you were in the service?"

"Yes sir, twenty years."

"What was you in?"

"I was a specialist in forensics."

"Ferrr-sensics. Don't that beat all? I couldn't do that shit, lookin' at dead people all blowed up and smelly and all that other crap. I was in artillery. Two twenty-second light. It's why I'm damn near deaf now."

George laughed. "Well' I didn't have to pick up the body parts or anything like that. All I did was to go to the site and collect information. Doctors had to deal with the body. Not me."

The old man rubbed his face thinking. "You need another soda?" he asked. George shook his head, the old man continued. "So you can't quit that information collecting stuff, huh? These two guys robbed you so you're after them." The old bar tender paused and rubbed his grizzled chin. "You know, you're lookin' for one big guy and a littler guy; you sure it wasn't them two uh . . . boys that mugged the store."

"Nope," George shook his head resolute.

"Well, shit-howdy. Seems like one hell of a coincidence, a big guy and a little guy comin' north and we ain't had a robbery here in, Jesus, eight years. How come you're so sure?"

"The guys that robbed me weren't black," said George, then paused to review in his mind the sentence he had just said.

"I thought you didn't get a good look at 'em?"

"I didn't . . . but . . ." George suddenly felt awkward. Why couldn't they be black he thought?

"You see?" said the old man, standing upright, and reading George's face. "I bet them two was it. It don't take no ferrr-sensics specialist to see that." The bartender pointed his index finger at George for emphasis, gave an exaggerated wink then walked into the back room to attend to some business.

George sat scratching his head wondering why he had so naturally excluded the possibility of their color. He looked down the bar at the large black man sitting there with his hat pulled intriguingly low, his eyes meeting the dark sunglasses resting on the man's nose. The big man leaned back to quaff the last of his brew, put some money on the table and stood to exit. George noticed how the right arm hung funny, as if it were injured. The large fellow took notice of George's stare, dipped his head pleasantly one more time, and made the exit. Suddenly George got a creepy feeling in his gut.

CHAPTER NINETEEN

The heat was on. The more she tried to avoid questions the more they came at her. Reporters seemed to multiply in front of her eyes like cells going through meiosis, all of them creatures with too much hair spray, a big mouth, and a microphone for an appendage which was jabbed toward her face. Spawned from the same master cell that had begun the infection they all resembled one another, but only to a point. Each had cleverly mutated a separate identity in order to elude a general inoculation. Like a body succumbing to a growing sepsis, there came a time in her mind when she figured there was no use in fighting on. Trying to sequester the story was having the effect of blowing it up to proportions beyond reason. Her reluctance to talk had become the small amount of compression necessary to turn a fission chain-reaction from a nuclear fizzle into an atomic blast. Barbara was in a phase of a media frenzy, seemingly interminable, to let her believe she was just being hounded.

Reporters slept in vans in her parking lot. Cameras met her every morning. Crews lugging lights, cameras, microphones and battery packs tried to push their way into the front door of the office. Fifty or more raps on the door came every evening. Clients of hers were getting wealthy saying all sorts of horrible things to any reporter with the cash, and without the scruples, to offer money for answered questions. Those reporters who slipped into the office undetected would rifle her files and sort through things on her desk. Each in their turn, upon discovery, were run off in an angry cloud of obscenity by Barbara—obscenity duly reported by the reporter as aggression on her part.

The very first stories had been the ones closest to the truth; the earliest speculation had been nearest the mark. The original media, those professionals first at the location, described only what witnesses had seen. Some of them, after the initial facts, theorized correctly she was covering for a client who had suddenly disappeared. Fact and measured speculation, though, quickly turned to innuendo, which turned to hyperbole, which turned into an intoxicating rocket fuel which fed into the veins of every profit minded editor. In two short days, Mark had transformed from being just another social-welfare case to become everything from a Nubian, ninja warrior to a lost African prince. Some tabloids picked up on the fact he had had delusions of being an extra-terrestrial and brandished them as fact on huge headlines. Moment after moment new and intriguing facts kept leaking to fan the flames of the media bon fire. Yet the facts and rumors were not enough to clear the matrix of ambiguity and anonymity fostering such public attraction; Mark had no family, no friends, and no place of origin. Just enough information came dribbling out to keep the pack of reporters on the scent. It was intriguing. It was a story pushing just enough buttons of public interest to reach critical mass. Barbara and the 'mystery hero' were a hot story in the City of the Angels.

After all the articles, all the attention and harassment, the only time her father contacted her was when one tabloid printed rumors Mark and her were lovers. Her father called to disown her and to scream racial epithets and obscenities into the answering machine. Barbara was beginning to feel very alone.

Her supervisor at work, an older, Anglo man with baggy eyes and a constant, hounded expression on his pasty white face, began to exert pressure on her to settle the matter. One day, after fighting through a crush of supporters to get into his office, he stopped at her cubicle. He suggested a vacation. When she told him she hadn't yet accrued vacation time, he still insisted. It would be leave without pay until things settled down, or another job.

Jeremy stood at the entrance of Barbara's cubicle with a long face as she packed up some necessities. She looked small and forlorn to him, the left cheek still swollen, purplish and black. She had a box and a briefcase to fill. In it would go anything she didn't want strangers pawing through, which was about everything on or in her desk. Someone had already lifted the picture of her and her friend toasting drinks in Mazatlan which had been on the divider of her cubicle. She suspected a co-worker in this particular heist. But who could blame them? These media people were paying top dollar for anything.

Finished packing the last bits of personal belongings she looked up to Jeremy who forced out a smile. "All finished?" he asked rhetorically.

Barbara started to reply when tears came instead. She put a hand over her eyes and leaned onto the desk away from Jeremy. "Hey, hey," Jeremy soothed coming to put a hand on her shoulder. "Don't let the mother-fuckers get to you."

She held her position over the desk saying, "This is becoming such a pain in the ass. Does anybody remember that I was a victim here? For Christ's sake."

Jeremy wanted to feel sorry for her but was more puzzled instead. He was nearly as interested as to why she wouldn't come clean on the subject of Mark as the tabloids, but much too much of a friend to ask. "Yeah, it must be hard," he said disingenuously. "Do you need some help carrying this stuff out?"

Barbara sighed, grabbed a tissue, blew her nose and said, "Sure. Please. I'm going to need someone to help fend off the hoard anyway. Oh fuck, Jeremy, what am I going to do?"

"Take a long drive," Jeremy replied trying to act chipper. "Just fill up the car and drive until all those ass-holes stop following you. Then park at the nearest bar and get gassed. Then call a friend. Call me if you want." Barbara turned and slumped in her chair. Jeremy squat down to get at eye level. "Look Barbara," he said more seriously, "not everybody around here is pulling for you. But there's enough of us who aren't going to get rich out of this that it should show you how we feel. You've got your reasons you did what you did. I'm not going to second guess you. And for god's sake don't tell me now. I'm too poor to be burdened with that kind of responsibility. You catch my drift?"

Barbara didn't really know what he was getting at. It seemed more like a lecture than a pep-talk to her. But she figured he meant best and stood up. "OK," she said, "let's get this over with."

They moved out the swinging glass door taking the reporters lounging there by surprise. The sun was bright, reflecting off the white cement. The difference in temperature between the dark, air-conditioned office and the blistering afternoon made the light seem more dazzling. In the second or two delay it took the mass of reporters to respond, Barbara and Jeremy walked briskly toward the parking lot. The crowd gathered, and then surged in on the two would be escapees. It came as a mass of feet and arms jostling the two of them and each other for position, surging in from one side then enveloping them. Questions started flying out of the pack as it cinched its human noose tighter and tighter with each step, the jostling now taking place for an advantage of inches. Questions came flying out: "Where's Mark Johnson?" "Who was it at the library?" "Can you tell us anything about Johnson?" "Why are you hiding the 'East-Side Hero'?" "Are you two in a relationship?" They came on and on, one right on top of another, two and three at a time. "No comment," mumbled Barbara with twenty microphones pushed in front of her, some bouncing off her head. "Client confidentiality. I don't know who the hero is."

The group was clustered hard enough around the two of them to now be determining the pace, which had slowed considerably. Barbara put a forearm across her head, looked down and made her way by following the white lines of the lot, one hand tightly gripping her briefcase. Jeremy was tall enough to be able to peer over the crowd and fought his way toward the car becoming further and further separated from the short female who was being swallowed by poles, wires, cameras and microphones.

At the car door Barbara fiddled with her keys. She wanted to scream. She wanted to whirl around and kick the first guy she saw in the balls as hard as she could. She wanted to fall down on the ground crying, and beg for them to leave her alone. The right key finally went in and the door opened. Jeremy shoved his way forward and emerged through the crowd stumbling. He fell holding the box with both hands and smacked his head against the rain gutter of the old car.

"Goddamn, fuck!" Jeremy yelled standing upright. The crowd let out a laugh. As he turned on the crowd angrily the twenty microphones around him were all he saw. A wave of embarrassment came over him and he spun back toward Barbara. "Here," he said handing Barbara the box. "Good-luck. See you soon." He closed the door and fought back into the crowd yelling, "Give her some room to get out. Give her some room."

It was stifling hot in the car but Barbara left the windows up. They muffled the sound of the crowd. Here, in the car, she could look down toward the worn, dirty gold carpet and shut it all out. She took a couple of deep breaths. She was home free, she thought. One quick stop at the house to grab some things and she would be home free. Where would she go? Maybe into the desert, some lonely campsite a hundred miles from anyone. Maybe to the mountains, it would be cooler there anyway. She just needed to go somewhere where no-one knew her. She shoved the key in and turned it over. The engine clicked and nothing more. A dead battery.

Barbara leaned her face into the steering wheel groaning, "What the hell do I do now?"

CHAPTER TWENTY

The afternoon sun was merciless. Wavy lines of distortion dominated the horizon to the point of giving a mirage of water in the distance. One could not think clearly in such an inferno, Pestia thought. He would have to miss another day. The evidence in the desert would have to wait. He knew one more day would put him farther behind the curve in tracking his nemesis but the heat, tied to the increasing agony in his wound put rest ahead of his eagerness.

He turned around the smoking little car just about where he remembered where the entrance to the adversaries was. He squinted out into the hot, dusty brown plain as if he would be able to decipher something from the distance. He licked his lips, dry and cracked. It was time to rest, get something to drink, relax, and think. It wasn't good he was showing so much of himself. If they were near they would have no trouble finding him. He would have to design some sort of strategy to bring them out before they found him. What the strategy was, though, he hadn't a clue. The old motor rattled and pinged up a small rise.

He needed a room to sleep in. He would go into town, buy some supplies and hole-up in a room until a plan was mapped. It could only cause harm the way he was wandering without purpose. It was going to take some long term planning. Pestia was just beginning to realize what a long and drawn out task this was. He was just beginning to realize the size of the tragedy which had transpired last week. If only he could have that moment back. If only he had squeezed the trigger an instant earlier. His index finger twitched at the thought.

"That wretched little beast," the general said out-loud. "That filthy, little worm does not know the harm he has caused."

Pestia thought about the little man and who he might actually be searching for. Gregaris had been a military forensics expert, if what he said in the bar was true. Had he been in the desert by coincidence? Or did he have some sort of military intelligence leading him to the spot where their craft landed? Pestia knew the fellow must have been in the desert that night because he was looking for Matan and his henchman. But why? And how did he know they were coming? Was he a recruit, a spy for Ranson? This didn't seem likely as Ranson had no investment in this planet prior to the Prince's travel to it. It seemed to Pestia more and more this little man had interest beyond the current landing. Perhaps, he concluded correctly, the former forensics expert had been in on a search for two other visitors a year earlier.

The drive to the nearest place to stay seemed interminable. Thirst and pain taxed his energy causing both irritability and apathy. The wound, he thought, was worse than he hoped. There was no time for convalescing though. He must seize the moment while the moment existed. A small, independent grocery store came up on the right. The car rocked into the parking lot shaking his shoulder causing an extra twinge of pain. He sat in the car thinking about his position. Whether it was the heat or his wound he felt weak and feverish. Nutrition, he thought, food and water were what he needed, maybe a bit of liquor to kill the pain.

Food on the planet earth was not cuisine to Pestia. He had started out his stay losing quite a bit of weight. Nothing about the texture, taste, or color of the comestibles seemed correct. For weeks it became a struggle to gag down anything. Ground flesh pressed between slices of baked dough and drizzled with a bloody looking sauce tightened his throat and invoked a heaving reflex. Mountains of pale strings, stacked onto his plate, looking like subterranean worms, this time drizzled with a chunky, sanguinary sauce, made his mouth dry with nausea. Then there was watching an earthling eat the mess, the strings slapping back and forth against the cheeks of the sucking, white pig, leaving streaks of red against the white background, it became impossible for Pestia to swallow. Gradually though, he found some items increasingly palatable. It began with un-processed vegetables and fruits, some of which resembled fruits and vegetables of home. He graduated onto some bakery items, bland breads and crackers, in order to maintain his strength. Bit by bit, over the weeks and months, many other items came into his repertoire. There was one item, however, that would never pass his lips. It was a cut up, fried, two legged creature which resembled the size and shape of a particularly vile rodent of home. The mere sight of a greasy faced human ripping the flesh from the bones of this thing stopped any appetite.

The idea Pestia and the prince might be missing a vital amino-acid in their diet had occurred to the health technicians of Bren. They just didn't really know what to do about it. If such an amino-acid did not occur naturally, and could not therefore be supplemented by ingestion, the scientists had no recourse. In the desperation of the moment the group solved the problem in the tried and true method of all committees pressed by time: they ignored it. In a move which was, perhaps, an attempt to mollify a guilty conscious they added a six-month supply of supplementary vitamin tablets. The earthly diet, however, when properly maintained beyond simple repugnance to do so, proved adequate.

Pestia stood in the cool air of the freezer section until he felt stronger. His cap and sunglasses made him feel more secure even though the country people shopping in the store continued to stare. He pushed the wobbly basket up and down the aisles looking for those relatively few items he found appetizing. Walking down the back aisle he kept his head turned to one side as the meat counter was on the other—he still grew shaky at the sight of any of those plucked, quasi-rodents. Past this section was the dairy section, where the only truly disgusting thing to Pestia was the eggs. The thought of putting in one's mouth what had exited the womb of a rodent made him twitch.

He picked out a loaf of plain, white bread, some apples and pears, two cans of refried beans, bottled water and a quart of chocolate milk. Not the items your average American might be selecting in concert but a fairly balanced diet nonetheless. He pushed the cart keeping the thumb of his right hand hooked through the belt-loop of his jeans trying to keep it as immobile and inconspicuous as possible. Standing in the check-out line, behind two customers who were eying him as suspiciously as any rural whites do a black man they are not accustomed to, his eyes began to wander around the displays. Licorice, red and black stood in tall plastic jars next to a row of similarly displayed jerky. Boxes of candy, tops pulled back, sat side by side in the wire rack, so many kinds which, after inspection, one box of candy seemed indiscernible from the other. Then there were the magazines, large, over-sized papers never quite standing straight in the holder. Pestia remembered with a smile the first time he had been taken aback by the head-line, 'Space Aliens Kidnapped My Dog'. It had actually caused him to wonder for a moment whether there were or were not other visitors. Pestia had both feared the thought and been exhilarated by it. He feared it because they might know something about the conflict between Bren and Ranson and impart this knowledge to the Earthlings. And he was exhilarated since it might provide an opportunity to find an alternate route home or to go out to meet the advancing fleet. But the creatures in the picture were so unlike any he had seen, and any he knew existed, the story was quickly taken for the chicanery it was.

His eyes rolled over the new crop of screaming headlines, things about losing weight, more space aliens, someone named Elvis, and . . . He let out an involuntary scream. "Ah," he yelled his whole body twitching, pain shooting down his arm. There, on one of the magazines with color pictures, was a photo of the Prince! Right under the headline, "Hero Spaceman on the Run," there it was: a three by five color photo of the heir of Bren. And beneath the photo it read, "Ninja Superman Flees Attention, See What His Lover Has to Say."

The two people in front of him, along with the clerk had turned and were staring at him, the clerk with a kind of mean sneer. The clerk leaned over the counter to get a better look at Pestia and pointedly asked, "What's wrong?"

The former general found himself pointing at the magazine, panting, with his mouth agape. Thinking quickly he recovered and shook himself out of his shock. "It's my shoulder," he gasped. "Sometimes it causes me a sharp pain.

I am sorry I yelled." The explanation seemed to appease the curiosity of the three, just enough so that they slowly turned back to their own business.

What had this young fool done? Pestia thought frantically. The picture Pestia recognized as the Prince's booking photo from the time he had been arrested for public drunkenness. He pulled the magazine, named 'The Inquiry', out of its rack and with his one good arm pulled it open to the page of the story. There, in black and white, were two more pictures. One was the booking photo reproduced again, the other a computer generated photo of how he would look with his head shaved, as they believed it to be now. The story read: Los Angeles: Presumed lover of the East Side Hero is still denying reports that the African Ninja Warrior who saved her life by crushing and killing two attackers is her client Mark Johnson. Police, however, say Johnson is the likely candidate as he matches the eyewitness description closely and has since disappeared. *Inquiry* psychology expert, Joan Merder PhD, suggests Johnson has a split personality. 'From previous reports he believed he was a prince from outer-space,' Dr. Merder reports, 'to his actions of heroism beyond his normal demeanor, strongly supports a theory that this man has a deep psychosis.' Dr. Merder further theorizes complicity to this twin personality by social-worker\lover Barbara Cerasoli. 'Ms. Cerasoli is obviously in on the delusion from the very start,' Ms. Merder concludes, 'It would be hard to imagine Mr. Johnson acting out his psychosis to such a degree had Ms. Cerasoli not participated in the fantasies.' Cerasoli has declined all interviews and has recently been dismissed without pay from her job pending an investigation of the rumors surrounding her bizarre conduct with a client.

"Hey," came a voice from far away, "HEY!" Pestia looked up from the magazine breathing hard, his knees weak. "Hey," the young clerk said again, "are you all right? You gonna buy that?"

Pestia dropped the magazine into the basket saying, "Oh yes, I intend to buy it."

The clerk looked him over one more time. "Are you sure you're OK?"

Pestia shook his head back and forth growing pale and weaker.

"You want me to call an ambulance?"

Pestia shook his head 'no' one more time. There was no-one behind him in line and he moved back. "No, I don't need an ambulance," he said, "I just need some medicine." He walked toward a shelf full of bottles. Off of it he selected the biggest bottle of whiskey he could find and returned to the cashier. Smacking the bottle down on the counter he said, "This will do for now."

Back in the car the old general mustered his courage. He knew the pain killer would have to wait. No matter how flustered and blind with pain he was he had to figure, now, seconds might be significant. He needed to think. He needed to think fast. Nothing came to him. Perhaps he should drive back to Los Angeles as fast as he could and pick up the trail of the young Prince as those two bastards most assuredly already have done. If they found him first, the name of the general would go down throughout the living history of Bren as an utter disgrace. What was left of his family would curse his name every day until they passed into the beyond. Pestia felt on the edge of a precipice, inches from failure.

If only he had played it safe. He began to question his motives for his actions of last week. Had he tried to kill

171

Matan for the glory it would bring to him? Had missing out on the battle to liberate his planet compelled him into trying foolish and petty revenge? His sole purpose for being alive was to protect the Prince and he was not there when the Prince had needed him most. How vehemently would he be condemned by his own people if the prince should not return in the days of triumph?

With great effort the general cleared his mind of anxiety and pain to concentrate on the problem. He listed the facts for himself in a battle stress environment coming to a quick conclusion. He was wounded and either getting worse or staying the same; he was not improving. In his present state he was in no physical shape to hunt a fiend as clever as Matan. What was, even now, still his main advantage? It was the fact he knew this place, this country, better than his adversary. Time, though, was on the side of the assassins. Every day they would learn to blend in a little bit more. How was he going to use this advantage to his greatest benefit? Pestia realized what he must do. Perhaps it had been foolish not to have done so before. Yet, trust is a commodity given out freely in a new place only by imbeciles. One must be canny and dole out trust either over time or through necessity; the necessity had just presented itself through a superfluous, little magazine: Pestia must recruit a friend.

He waited until evening in the parking lot of the disheveled motel. The dusty horizon shone red and orange in a light show even Pestia had to admit rivaled the sunsets of his home. Crickets began their chirp as the first stars appeared. He grabbed the paper bag containing the half gallon of whiskey and stood up into the cool night from the sweaty seat of the car. A slight breeze chilled the damp parts of his back and legs. The bottle, he thought, could both serve as a present or, if need be, a weapon. He wished he had more time to collect information on the little fellow but it had to happen now. He had to force the issue. If this little man was only curious, he would fill his curiosity in exchange for help. If the ex-military man had an agenda of exposure or hate, he would feed him the bottle, glass and all, through his clenched teeth and continue alone to Los Angeles this night in the same dire position he had started in. In Pestia's mind, there was now nothing to lose.

The light was on in the room; George's truck parked out front. Pestia peered into the crack between the drawn curtains. There were papers scattered around on a small table pushed against the window. The television was on and Gregaris was lying across the bed, shoes off, sipping a glass of some beverage. Pestia went to the door. Listening to the crickets he wondered what he could say to make this little man understand. Would he help? Was he treacherous? Would he even be sympathetic? He banged on the door with the bottom of the bottle.

From inside he could hear George yell, "Who is it?"

Pestia, waiting not-so-patiently, ran the words 'who is it' over in his head. Of all the stupid things humans say, he thought, this was one of the worst. "Who is it," he mumbled to himself. "Open the fucking door and you will find out who it is." He pulled the bottle back and banged again, this time harder.

CHAPTER TWENTY-ONE

George had pulled off his boots far too late to save his feet the agony of the heat and the swelling feet do after being cooped up in sweaty boots all day. His eyes were tired from studying evidence and he laid down trying to rest them. He had studied the papers and figures and drawings so long none of them anymore made any sense. Though he felt driven to keep at work, he knew it was too late for today. In his younger years, he had the stamina to keep it up but not the patience. Now he had the patience and not the stamina. Groggy eyes stared at the television not registering any of the commercials or programs flashing before them. A glass of whiskey kept him company in slow, abbreviated sips.

He had actually accomplished quite a bit in going through what evidence had been collected. The data, however, had not been revealing enough for him. There was no proverbial handkerchief with initials to lead him. There was nothing definitive, no Rosetta stone of foreign invaders. George, always driven to find answers, was sorely disappointed at the lack of substance and becoming depressed at the apparent absence of further clues.

It wasn't as if George had found nothing. He had discovered plenty from nearly nothing. He found the mass of the large visitor most probably ranged between two-hundred and eighty to three-hundred and twenty pounds. By the length of his gait he had legs long enough to suggest a height somewhere around six feet, six inches to six feet, eight inches. The smaller visitor ranged between six feet and six feet, two inches in height to two-hundred and fifty to two hundred and seventy pounds. The rifle man was also relatively large, probably around six-four and two-hundred and fifty pounds—though, from the silhouette seen, he hadn't seemed that hefty. They were all rough estimates since the desert scrabble didn't give enough to allow shoes to sink in a sufficient amount for more exact measurements. George would have been tickled to know how accurate his estimates actually were.

He let out a long yawn. It was still early, barely nine o'clock. The program he was watching was inane but since the motel didn't have a remote control television he was not going to bother getting up to change it. Another long yawn and his eyes welled with tears. Tomorrow, he thought. Tomorrow I'll get another shot. There has to be something more out there.

Bang, bang, bang, went the door. George sat up startled. "Who is it?" he yelled.

There was no answer. After a pause there came another knock louder than before. The second knock piqued George's caution and he reached under the bed to pull out his little twenty-two pistol. "Who is it?" he yelled again, this time louder. George crept up to the door keeping the gun behind his back.

This clown, whoever it is, thought George, is going to play it cute. Well, let's see who it is and keep the pistol handy.

George pulled open the door cautiously with his left hand keeping the gun behind his back with the right.

George's eyes widened and seemed to bug out. It was the enormous black man he had seen in the restaurant. The sight frazzled his already muddled and swirling brain. He stepped back and the huge man stepped forward setting a paper bag down on the little table. Reaching inside the bag, the large man pulled out a bottle of whiskey; the same brand George drank. "Here," he said, "I owe you a bottle."

George looked at the bottle, then to the face, then to the bottle, then to the face, he refusing to or incapable of drawing the correct conclusion. His mouth drooped open and he took another step back catching his heel on the chair of the table. He flopped back, flat on his butt flailing both arms to catch his balance. Pestia saw the gun and took a step back holding the bottle. George saw his reaction and reflexively pushed the gun away. Though he was confused and surprised, George knew he shouldn't do anything to scare the man from the room—he obviously, from immediate contact, fit into the puzzle somehow.

The captain raised both hands in a gesture of conciliation. "I only keep it for protection," he said referring to the gun. "I'm not out to hurt anyone."

Pestia stepped warily back inside. He scanned the room suspiciously then focused to George. "Your eye is healing nicely Mr. Gregaris," he said, "though I am not sorry that I hit you. You do not realize the trouble you have caused me. May I come in and sit. I am not well."

George stayed put, flat on his butt. Fireworks were going off in his mind. In the back of his head a grand, military march was booming, drums snapping, brass blaring. His eyes followed the huge man over to the chair he had tripped on and watched him ease into the seat. Rat, tat-tat, tat, tat went the cadence; Da, da, da-da, da, went the brass.

"I've come to you for a particular purpose," Pestia continued to the starry-eyed man. "I need your help."

"Help?" Gregaris repeated stupidly. The band played on.

"Yes, I need help."

As the volume of the march came down, the large man reached up and pulled off his sunglasses. The sparkling green eyes seemed to look right through George. The music went back to a new and higher crescendo.

Pestia saw the silly earthling was reveling in his presence. The general empathized with the little fellow realizing that the first convincing contact with an alien must be pretty shocking for a being largely assured of his aloofness in the universe. Pestia turned in his chair to grab the bottle. He stuck the cap in his mouth and twisted the fat end with his one good hand until the top came loose. He spit the cap on the floor, took a big swig, and handed the bottle to the dumbfounded man on the floor.

"Here," said Pestia. "I suppose you have a lot of questions."

CHAPTER TWENTY-TWO

The apartment seemed like the only place on the planet where she could relax. The din of pack dogs outside, masquerading as professional journalists would not rest and seemed determined not to let her relax either. Every time a toe went outside her front door she felt the tempest of public scrutiny raging there. Waves of curiosity seekers, newspapers and reporters sloshed up against her apartment door as assuredly as a raging sea. Yet inside her little, one bedroom apartment, blinds lowered, portable cassette on the ears, the problems outside the door could well be on another world.

Hot cups of herbal tea soothed nerves as she sat in her favorite chair, warm and cushioned. Easy listening music, piped into her mind through the headset, calmed ears which had been ringing from too much of everything. Pictures of ridiculous fashion in a magazine, accompanied by stories of questionable wit, distracted a brain frazzled by stimulus upon incitement upon provocation. When one is in a predicament such as Barbara, one must find ways in which to adapt. Stress like this would crush a person of average endurance without a certain amount of transformation. So adapt she did.

Barbara learned quickly the tricks necessary to seal out the print and image zealots. Locking the screen door diminished the noise of the constant rapping—rapping she was determined to ignore. Plugging in the phone only when she was going to call out kept the answering machine from clicking on every few seconds. Never turn on the television to see the lies being spewed; don't open a window to have questions shouted in; refrain from keeping a regular schedule of entry and exit in order to keep the swarm from massing at the door on particular intervals. As long as she could keep the insulated box sealed it was all right to go on living.

Barbara hadn't spent much time reflecting on what she had done. Amazingly enough, having gone through so much because of her actions, she had not rehashed, questioned or evaluated what she had done. She just didn't want to think about it. Promising Mark not to say anything had blown up in both their faces so bad she felt it would only bring despair if she spent time rummaging through the facts. So she didn't. Barbara had that ability to isolate issues of trouble into certain situations and circumstances. The only time the brouhaha was on her mind was when the cameras and microphones were in her face. The skill of being able to turn off annoyances had always been with her—perhaps coming from growing up under two people who seemed determined to annoy her at all costs—but the skill had been honed to a fine edge after becoming a social worker. This capacity was a large part of what made her such a good social worker. One had to have the ability to turn off empathy and sorrow when the situation faded from view when dealing with such a volume of human suffering. Being able to turn worry and concern off also keeps it from burning out.

She pulled open the refrigerator and bent over to look, wondering what to make for lunch. There wasn't much there: a jar of pickles, yogurt past the code date, and a dozen bottles of condiments for salads, breads and lunch meats which didn't exist. The thought of fighting out to the supermarket flashed briefly, then was swept away by a flood of anxiety at having to face the mob. Order out for pizza? She thought it might be funny to see the poor delivery boy swimming through the reporters answering questions about the size, type, flavor, and number of toppings.

Standing upright she brought an imaginary microphone up to her mouth. "Did she or did she not request pizza peppers?" she said in her best journalist voice. "We had originally feared that aliens were attempting to sneak in a message to Ms. Cerasoli in the disguise of a pizza. But upon a taste test by local pizza expert Guido 'Fats' Tortini it was generally agreed that it was, indeed, a pizza pie." Barbara continued her silly commentary as she rummaged for some type of lunch. "Furthermore, it was learned first hand today, through eyewitness informants, that the grated cheese sprinkled on Ms. Cerasoli's pizza was actually Romano and not parmesan as she had previously indicated; just one more piece to the puzzle of intrigue, back to you Jim."

A light appeared behind her. She spun around seeing her front door beginning to open. She yanked off her head phones yelling, "Hey! Who is it? Stop it!"

From behind the door popped the slick, bald, wrinkled and hoary head of her apartment manager. His beady little eyes glared at her from behind bifocals. "Barbara," he croaked in a self righteous tone, "why aren't you answering your door?"

Barbara threw down her head-phones in disgust. "What the hell do you think Mr. Peterson? Why do you think I'm not answering my door? What the hell is this? Do you just come in here any damn time you want?" She walked toward the old man who had his head craned around the edge of the door, sticking out from the border like an ornamental gargoyle. "You had better have a good reason to be barging in," she continued. "I don't think it says, anywhere in my lease that you can . . ."

She was cut off as Mr. Peterson pushed open the door further. Immediately behind him were two police officers. Further back were three more who were keeping reporters at bay at the base of the stairs. One of the officers, a large, hefty, square jawed policeman with a hat pulled low stepped forward into the apartment. The only thing keeping him from being a perfect caricature of an officer from an old slapstick movie was the absence of an Irish accent. "Sorry to bother you Ms. Cerasoli," he said with an air of sincere apology. "You didn't answer your phone or door. We have to ask you some questions and it's pretty urgent."

Barbara heaved out a sigh shaking her head 'no' but letting out a truncated, "Sure." Walking toward the front room she picked up her cup of tea from the table and retreated to her favorite chair. Pulling her legs up and under her she said in a most irritated manner, "OK. I guess I'm ready, whether I am or not. Fire away."

Reporters were yelling questions to the officers near the door. When Barbara appeared for a second in the doorway from around the kitchen divider the roar escalated then receded as if they had seen a successful high-wire act. The caricatured policeman looked back at the crowd then asked, "You mind if we come in and close the door?"

Barbara motioned him in, acting thoroughly disgusted at the notion of answering more questions. She really wasn't disgusted, not in the least, a bit unnerved at having someone come through her door, but not disgusted. She felt, for some reason however, compelled to act that way. Maybe it was a leftover from having seen too many police dramas.

The second policeman closed the door and the big man continued. "Do you know a Josiah Flint, Ms. Cerasoli?"

Barbara glared repugnantly at Mr. Peterson who had slipped in with the officers—his interest in the story had been kindled too. "Do you mind, Mr. Peterson?" she said.

The little old man blushed bright red and danced from one foot to the other. "Oh, ha, ha," he mumbled, "I guess I don't need to be here. Do I?"

"That's all for now Mr. Peterson," the second officer said reopening the door.

The door snapped shut and the big man reiterated. "Well, Ms. Cerasoli? Josiah Flint, do you know him?"

She knew the name well. He was one of her male clients, an old African-American alcoholic who refused to use public toilets and, instead, frequented the back door of restaurants when they refused to give him handouts. He had been in the same AA program as Mark and had been one of the many profiting by selling what he knew to the press. Barbara had swooned the day she saw him on the television with his explanation of how she had the hot attitude for all her male clients. Though she knew him well she delayed acknowledging the fact trying to remember the exact policy on client confidentiality when it came to the police.

The two policemen exchanged glances during the pause. Barbara noticed and said, "I'm not hedging. I just don't know how I can legally answer the question. Believe me. I don't want anymore trouble from the police."

"Let me rephrase the question then," the officer said folding his hands in front of him. "Did you know that last night Mr. Flint was the victim of a homicide?"

The legalese in Barbara's brain fell flat. "He's dead? Jesus Christ. Yeah, he was a client of mine. What happened?"

"We would prefer you to come down to the station to get the details. Do you remember sergeant Jablonski? He's waiting to handle this himself." Barbara did remember the officer. She had seen his face splashed on the television at least twenty times since the initial questioning to brief the hoard of one-eyed monsters as to the progress of the investigation.

She insisted on taking her own car down to the station. Barbara felt having her own transportation was part of her independence and, even though she would never do so, it gave her the option of leaving whenever she wanted. It was nice, for a change, having an escort push through the crowd for her. She didn't get her toes stepped on once. She enjoyed the way the officers treated the reporters with disdain, shoving them to and fro as needed to produce a path. The ride was too short. She hadn't had time to collect a strategy. She knew this would tie in, somehow, to Mark, but she didn't know how. Maybe it was time to tell the truth. She thought maybe it was time to come clean. It seemed silly now, anyway, to be trying to protect the identity of a man whose picture was exploding everywhere except in the sky as a giant firework. The only real challenge in talking, telling the truth, would be to get over the inertia of having lied in the first place.

The two sergeants, again looking like bookends, a Frick and Frack of the police world, were in a small, white interrogation room. There was one chair for Barbara, a small, beat-up table, and a window with the blinds closed. Officer Espinoza was standing and nonchalantly peering behind the blinds as if peeking at something outside. Jablonski sat in the only other chair across from Barbara with the same, bland, tired expression she remembered from before. Both of them had their jackets off, ties loosened, with a gun holster strapped across the shoulder, looking like they had dropped out of one of the bad police dramas which had previously influenced her behavior.

Barbara took her seat and the two officers took no notice of her. Espinoza continued his clandestine peering and Jablonski just tapped lightly on the table with one finger while staring up at the dirty, white acoustic tiles of the ceiling. There was a folder on the desk in front of the bored looking officer. The file was titled on the border with several numbers and the name 'Flint, J. L.' Barbara waited in the suffocating silence, trying to sit up straight and keep her pretended, disgusted demeanor.

Jablonski lowered his head and took notice of Barbara as if by accident. He jostled around in his seat and glanced into the file only to re-close it. "You know, Ms. Cerasoli," he said, his dry, tired voice rolling out, "nobody likes being lied to. Even police officers don't like being lied to. One reason we don't like it is because, sometimes, there's consequences to lying. Bad consequences. Did you know one Josiah L. Flint?"

Barbara shook her head up and down dutifully.

The officer continued, "It seems that he was murdered last night. We don't know the exact time. But we do have a witness who says he saw Mr. Flint leave the scene with someone. He climbed into a car with two individuals. We didn't get much of a description on the car. Seems this witness was more interested in the occupants. They were two large, African-American males. Both had uncharacteristic green eyes and flat, straight hair. Does this remind you of someone Ms. Cerasoli?"

Barbara suddenly felt very cold inside, vulnerable as if she were a little girl who was being severely chastised by her parents.

The officer continued, pushing the file in front of Barbara. "Why don't you take a look at some of these pictures. Go on, open it up."

Barbara opened the manila folder to a set of color pictures. She flinched and turned away, closing the folder. It was a picture of the crime scene. The victim was mutilated. She looked up at Espinoza who was, for the first time, looking at her. He still kept an index finger hooked around the back of the blinds, extending them from their hanging by an inch or two, as if what was outside was still more important and that she was only a distraction. His eyes were dispassionate, tired and devoid of any sympathy.

"You think it was Mark who did this?" she said losing her pretensions.

"What do you think Ms. Cerasoli?"

"You said the witness saw flat, black hair. Mark had shaved his head."

"You mean like the man at the library?"

Barbara looked around the room. Espinoza finally devoted his full attention to the scene and let go of the blinds. "Yeah, like the man at the library," she said. "I mean, he was the man. It was Mark. But, you know that. But, he had shaved his head. He was paranoid. He thought someone was looking for him to kill him. I promised him I wouldn't tell anyone where he was since he had saved me. He was trying to disguise himself and get away."

"Away from somebody like Josiah maybe?" Espinoza asked.

"But he had shaved his head. He didn't have any hair. It couldn't be him." Barbara was loosing whatever was left of her nerve.

"You ever hear of a wig, Ms. Cerasoli?" Jablonski asked.

Barbara paused and felt weak. Had this been Mark? Had she been responsible for the death of another person? She put her face in her hands, elbows propped on the table.

"Do you have any idea," Jablonski continued, "any idea at all where we can find this Mark Johnson?"

Barbara shook her head from behind her hands.

"It's reported by your co-worker, one Jeremy Brown, that Mr. Johnson had an uncle, a Frank Johnson, with similar characteristics: same hair and eyes. Do you have any idea where we can contact him?"

She shook her head again.

"You think hard, Ms. Cerasoli. Whoever did this was a monster, a monster not worth protecting. Mr. Flint was tortured, probably for hours." He opened the file and began reading from a piece of paper. "They cut off his ears, nose, gouged out both eyes, flayed off large sections of skin from the back and chest . . . hmmm, castration, feet burned down until it exposed bone . . . you want me to continue?"

Barbara found herself crying. She didn't want to, she just was. "No, please, stop. I don't know where he is. I lied at first because I thought I was protecting him from his own paranoia. He had saved my life. I thought I owed him. Oh, fuck. Oh Jesus, fuck. I don't know where he is."

Jablonski motioned to Espinoza who left the room momentarily. He returned with a box of tissue and a tape recorder. He sat on one end of the table with his back toward Barbara. "OK, Ms. Cerasoli," Jablonski said, "let's go over what you know one more time."

The interrogation lasted several hours. Barbara dredged up every minute detail she could recall about Mark Johnson. What she had seen him eat; where she had seen him walking; what kind of clothes he had; how many times she had met with him, on and on until she couldn't think of another thing. The police were nice enough to bring her car around the back of the station so she could make a delicate exit. Though it would begin another round of media hype, Barbara felt as if she had exorcised a demon by finally telling the truth. Yet, the image of Josiah, twisted, broken and bloody, was not something so easily exorcised. The thought of some sort of culpability to such madness, such sickening horror tore her to pieces.

During the questioning she hadn't felt anything definite. She felt numb, guilty, stupid, irrational and relieved with none of them taking precedence and all of them mixing together as one might swirl a group of colors until it was nothing but an ugly, brown lump. What she felt was substantial, only confusing. Yet afterward the image ripped into her and tears came again. Tears came into eyes which seemed too despondent to blink them away. It was all so crazy.

Hunger, perhaps as a distraction from dejection, came through her emotions as a grocery store came up on the left. She decided to go in, buy out the store, go home to hibernate, and cry herself blind. Grabbing the rearview mirror she twisted it to see her red eyes. The image there seemed to peer deep inside of her to see all sorts of things she was afraid to look at. She broke loose of the delving gaze and wiped her eyes with a tissue. Then she put on some big, ugly sunglasses, a head scarf, scrawled on some gaudy, bright-red lipstick and got out to go into the store, all the while praying for anonymity.

Her crude disguise seemed to work. It was nice to be out of the house and not recognized. Though she liked the sanctuary of her home, it was a good change of pace to be somewhere else. Slowly the warmth of relaxation crept into her tense limbs. The shopping cart moved in front of her like a shield. Bright colors from fruits and vegetables went into her mind to find old, soothing memories of a time when such normalcy as shopping was taken for granted. She found herself wandering around the aisles not doing any real shopping at all, dithering over this product and that product, not greatly concerned about any. In twenty-five minutes she had dropped nothing into her basket. The aimlessness of the shopping lifted her spirits. The impersonal nature of the place relaxed her. She was just beginning to really let down her guard when she noticed him.

A short, stocky, balding man, with dark features and a white and red, floral Hawaiian shirt was standing at the end of one aisle. His shirt was open several buttons exposing a black, hairy mat of hair underneath. He was staring at her with a fretting expression. Barbara pretended not to notice and pushed her cart by him. From the intensity of his scrutiny she figured it was a tabloid reader who had identified her. They were always more acrimonious as to the importance of their recognition. It always seemed like Archimedes running down the street naked screeching 'Eureka'. They always acted like it was some sort of great intellectual triumph to have recognized her. Who knows, perhaps to these idiots it was. It was time to get out of the store anyway. Let's grab some stuff and get a move on, she thought.

While passing the little man, he spoke up. "Miss Cerasoli," he said, "I've got some information for you."

Barbara's attitude made a sudden and distinct shift. This was not the reaction of a tabloid reader. They would usually only yell out her name and repeat where they had read all about the story. They would say something like 'You're that Cerasoli girl I read about in the Inquiry. Aren't you?' Or it was a comment reminding her of something just that inane in line with the great 'gotcha' kind of mentality surging through our modern society. But this guy wasn't like these people at all. He was too definite, too sure of who she was and what he wanted to say.

He spoke up again. "I think it would do you some good to talk to me for a little while."

From the second comment, Barbara made another inference. So this little prick is a reporter, she thought. "Why don't you people get a life?" she snapped. "I'm a human being, you know. I have a right to a little privacy."

The worried looking little fellow shifted on his feet and looked around. "I'm a friend of Mark and his uncle. I need to talk to you."

Oh, sure you are, thought Barbara. This was certainly a new tactic, pretending to be a friend. Barbara was infuriated. "You listen to me," she said pointing a finger at him. "You leave me the hell alone and tell your editor to shove this type of devious horse-shit up his ass."

Barbara started her cart up the aisle with renewed vigor. The little man followed and the silly little race escalated and continued clear to the back of the store. Barbara swung around, "I'm warning you. I'm going to scream, damn it."

The little man looked surprised then blurted out, "Mark didn't kill that man last night."

Barbara dropped her accusatory finger. "What the hell do you know about this man?"

The worried looking fellow looked around one more time. "Can we go somewhere where it'll be private?"

She shook her head. "Not a chance. Not with all the crap I've been through. What is it you know about this murder?"

An old lady came around the corner with an over-loaded cart. The little man delayed until he felt she was out of ear-shot. He then leaned forward whispering. "I know who killed him."

"Who?" demanded Barbara in a full voice.

The little worrier flipped up both hands hissing. "Shhhh, not so loud. Look, Mark wasn't being paranoid. There is somebody out to kill him. They took out Josiah because he bragged that he had information on where to find him."

"Who?" demanded Barbara, this time whispering too.

"Mark. Josiah told these men that he knew where to find Mark. He didn't, of course. He thought he was going to sell another story. But these guys wanted information. And they knew how to get it."

"Look here," Barbara said re-raising the finger, "the police got a description of the two and said it looked like Mark and his uncle. How can there be two other people on the planet who look like those two." The troubled fellow looked uneasy and shifted around. "Well?" Barbara pressed.

"Easy," he said finally, "they all come from the same place. Another place. Another planet."

"Oh brother," Barbara snarled and started her cart at a brisk pace.

The little man ran behind her. "Stop, please," he pleaded, "you don't realize that, that . . ." He reached out to pull on Barbara's arm.

Barbara spun around. "I'm warning you damn it. I'm in no mood for this horse-shit."

"Look," he went on urgently, "they're after you now. The papers say, rightly or wrongly, that you know where Mark is and are hiding him. These two men will do anything to get at him. Anything. You aren't safe now. Please believe me. You must know what they did to Josiah. Do you want that?"

The last comment caught her attention and she paused. "Why didn't they come after me first then?" she said looking for holes in his argument.

"The gauntlet of reporters around your house has probably saved your life several times now. I've been trying to contact you for two days. It's not easy getting through undetected. I've seen them try. And if I could get to you alone one day, then they can too."

Barbara studied his face. He looked so reasonable she wanted to believe him; But another planet? It was too ridiculous, and yet, at the same time, too logical to ignore. Josiah was a blabber mouth about all sorts of things he knew nothing of and, if money was involved, he could manufacture facts as fast as his pickled brain would allow. Also, as far as she knew, Josiah's murder hadn't even hit the news yet further discounting the probability this little man was just some sort of publicity nut.

Barbara wavered, and then came down against believing him. "No," she said as if her pronouncement determined the verite of her argument, "this is just too weird. Besides, I don't know where Mark is anyway." She started the cart again, this time slower and more deliberate.

"That's not going to help you," he called from behind.

His words hung in the air and followed Barbara down the aisle, but she kept moving, not wanting to believe.

George, as far as he was concerned, had tried to do his moral duty. She had been warned. After all, he might be risking his own life in order to do so. The assassins didn't know he was watching them watch her, yet. And he certainly didn't want to expose this fact. Perhaps he could still intervene before they got her. In any case, he would stay close and wait for them to show themselves, and wait for the opportunity to act.

C HAPTER TWENTY-THREE

George had found himself laughing, crying, staring in awe and blubbering like a little baby, only able to drool out a nonsensical prattle in the attempt to spit out his emotions. He had surprised even himself with this reaction. The shame, anger, loneliness and bitterness, bottled up inside for an entire year burst out onto the cheap motel carpet like the dropping of an over-full water balloon. In a splash, the emotion blew out of him. He had imagined making a more dignified introduction to a being from another world upon first encounter. He had imagined a professional disposition and diplomatic language conveying the best wishes of earthlings; but it was beyond his control. Hanging his head he bawled, giggled, pounded his fist and generally made himself out to be a complete mad-man. The huge, steady foreigner seemed so patient. Staring impassively, the big fellow calmly sipped whiskey as if watching a silly television program. When embarrassment at his break-down finally supplanted the break-down itself, he pulled out his handkerchief, wiped his face, and blew his nose.

Looking up into the mysterious eyes he said, "Where are you from?"

Pestia controlled his disgust at the slimy, little, white thing, which was disgracefully displaying emotion, and replied, "If you are not familiar with star charts, telling you where I am from will not help you."

George, perhaps identifying the disgust in the tone of his visitor's voice, stood up and tried to be more dignified. He looked around the room, as if searching for something, then sat on the bed. A nearly uncontrollable urge came over him: he needed to touch the alien, as if to prove he were really there, George felt compelled to slap his hands on the big man's back, rub his hair, and pat his cheeks. He wanted to be the first human on the planet to knowingly touch an extra-terrestrial. In an internal compromise at self-control, George stood offering his hand. "My name is George Gregaris, but I guess you already knew that."

Pestia looked at the extended hand, now not being able to hide his repulsion. These creatures, he thought, always wanting to touch hands. Invariably the palms were sweaty and soft adding to his delusion white people should leave a trail of slime like so many squishy invertebrates. Still, Pestia felt a certain security now. The little man was obviously not out to cause mischief. This was a great relief. Pestia felt he could relax here for a moment. Perhaps, in some limited way, the weak, diminutive creature would prove a valuable ally. Reluctantly, he reached out his left hand, the right was too sore, and shook the sweaty, little palm.

Chills rolled down and off of George as if he were a column of dry ice effusing a fog. The hand was large and tough, cool to the touch. He held the grasp until the visitor politely pulled away. "What's your name?" George said dreamily.

The bottle went back up for another sip. Then the hand that had shaken George's wiped itself in an exaggerated fashion on the trouser leg. "On this planet," he said, "I am known as Frank Johnson. On my own planet I have a different name. I will not tell you that name. There are people around who would recognize it."

George stood there looking at Pestia as if he were a zoo creature, trying to identify and take in every subtle difference; differences which now seemed pronounced given the knowledge he was an extra-terrestrial. Pestia observed the mesmerized state and continued. He continued to tell him everything, right from the very beginning.

He told him the story of how there were two planets in his solar system capable of sustaining life, both remarkably similar. The only major difference between the two was only one planet, the planet known as Bren, had evolved intelligent life. As the technology of space-craft developed the planet known as Ranson was explored and found to be habitable. The kingdom of Bren grew and their cities became crowded, and it was a logical step they should begin colonizing the other planet—this was almost two-hundred earth-years ago.

Government programs designed to encourage settlements were very generous. People of Bren, however, were not inclined to go. Tradition and uniformity are prized assets of culture on Bren and the subjects of the monarchy found it too wrenching to make the journey. As a result, the government upped the ante and made offers which were spectacular: all costs of moving, settling and guaranteed incomes and supplies. Still there were no throngs making their way to the transport sites to take up the offer. First settlements were less than a dozen individuals, dotting a wild and unforgiving landscape, spread across vast regions of un-connected settlements, filled with feral beasts of all sorts. With government help they survived and eventually prospered. Their story inspired others to come.

Their rugged individualism, bravery and ingenuity became the stuff of lore on the parent planet. Even though Bren was a place where individuality was not prized the settlers were romanticized in the arts and literature. Children took individuals among them as heroes. Fanciful stories heartened hundreds of people to follow, soon thousands.

Tales from the new planet rubbed off on the percentage of the populace who sought a fulfillment beyond what they could experience on Bren. Most of the individuals going were those for who the pioneering tales had grown very real. They imagined themselves cast in the same mold of hardy individual. In a radical departure from heritage these individuals felt compelled to leave the flat-line norms of the home planet. Thus many of the colonizers were different by more than physical location to those they had left behind; they were also different, or at least sought to be different, in demeanor. Whatever they were they all had a common thread: they worked very hard.

Sometimes out of initiative, mostly out of necessity, they fashioned the land with arduous work eventually carving out huge, prosperous enterprises. Farms that stretched to the horizon uninterrupted by settlement were plowed. Mines were dug into veins of mother-load which had not been seen on the home planet for centuries. Of course, along with these successful endeavors came every other business which took advantage of such success and the raw materials of the pristine new world.

Later in the colonization process, the larger cities became equipped with all the luxuries of home. This opened the way to all seeking the new planet whether rugged or not. Yet, the skew of individuals going to the new homeland remained those who were more of an individual mind than those remaining on Bren. Whether disaffected with their local government, or the monarchy in general, or merely a criminal looking for a fresh start, they all were of a mindset willing to forsake tradition. Some sincere opponents, others only malefactors, they went to a place as far as they could get from the influence of the monarchy.

These new and disaffected travelers further bent public opinion away from loyalty to the crown. The sentiment of individuality grew on the newly settled planet all out of proportion to the home planet. Existential ideas of individual entities making the whole rather than the whole making the individual grew in popularity among the intellectuals and affected the entire populace through them. Merchants on Ranson began to resent the cultural differences of the home planet while engaging in commerce. While the salesman from Bren would emphasize pricing as to its effect on all those in need of the product, the merchant from Ranson would look at it in terms of the extent to which the price could rise in order to get the most profit for himself. The anxieties of Ranson were well founded as people of the home planet tended to look down on the pioneers as odd in their breaks with tradition, and could not understand ideas of profit outside the context of how it impacted all of society. They saw the pioneers as selfish, crude and barbarian. These interactions further fostered resentment between the two. People of Ranson felt a culture of compliance was being foisted on them and this inspired further indignance at any control exerted by Bren, through regulation, tax or other. People of Bren felt confused and mystified by the new ideas coming from beings they saw as one and the same.

The monarchy, being of a mind one lived for all and all lived for one reasoned Ranson should give of its wealth so the whole empire might thrive. Ranson felt provoked by the home planet. They felt it only a drag on their expanding capital. Radical groups met and openly defied the central authority of the monarchy and at first, much to their dismay, with little success. Loyalty to the throne ran deep. It was not easy for the disaffected to foment revolt and many years passed. The decisive increase in countering the crown came when a group of fantastically rich people saw disaffection as a way to spur profit.

A small group of bitter plutocrats, fat on the plentiful raw materials needed by Bren, banded together with the direct intent on forming their own power base to separate from the sovereign. Separation would mean prices they could set and taxes they could ignore. Dividing the empire meant prerogative they could wield without interference. A plan was formed.

Percentages of profits from each financial empire were channeled into massive media events extolling the virtues of independence and the failings of the monarchy. Propaganda against the empire became ubiquitous on Ranson. It became ether one had to swim through in order to live on the new planet. Employees of the massive conglomerates inspiring the hatred were compelled to attend rallies, carry banners, and, during company time, solicit support from communities at large. Even the most loyal and sincere of minds were affected by it. Those individuals who voiced support for the crown were vilified across the planet and encouraged by monetary policy to resettle in Bren behind veiled threats of what would happen if they did not. Democracy, employed only for local control on Bren, was used as the kindling to ignite the fires of individualism on Ranson. It was promised democracy would be fairly implemented from bottom to top and from top to bottom without further interference from the sovereign. The campaign and dreams of the loose federation of billionaires paid off beyond their wildest dreams. Open revolt, with a popular mandate as a fig-leaf, came quickly thereafter.

The throne did not fight the rebels. It only asked for a formal referendum, which came, and backed away. After all, it was by referendum the monarchs resided on their throne. No-one on the planet Bren was compelled by any means to love the lineage of the king. Why should anyone on another planet millions of miles away be forced to? The crown believed it was not important to hold onto a possession as a matter of expanding an empire. And they did not fear a new companion of different ilk in the solar system. They, after all, were made of the same stuff. Independence, with the friendly competition it could spur, might be good for both planets. Bren, the monarchy reasoned, was rich enough and did not need the taxes from Ranson and, therefore, would not force a leveling of income. They had no desire to dominate for domination's sake. The king controlled the one world; there was plenty of room for rebels on another planet. But this vision was not to be.

The group of plutocrats owned the democratic process. Candidates of their choosing found huge amounts of money waiting at the door for campaigns which roared over opposition. Any poor soul who had sincerely believed the rhetoric coming from the media factories, and decided to run against a handpicked nominee, found themselves suddenly an enemy of the people. Ravaged by the press, character obliterated by hosts of innuendo, often times the would-be office holder would join the exodus back to Bren. It was all too simple for the elite.

They found their new power intoxicating. Money bought elections and steamrolled populists under mountains of literature, advertising, false accusations, and outright vote buying. The group at the top shared power between them peaceably, each taking their turn as figure-head—real decisions were made by consensus behind closed doors. And the workers below cared little for the political process. As long as they remained fairly comfortable everything coming out of the mouths of people corrupt on power mattered little at all. They believed anything their leaders told them as long as the paychecks were fat. And as long as the workers were happy the plutocracy's relations with the home planet stayed cordial—the relations stayed cordial in-spite of the monarchy's realization it was a sham of democracy perpetuated by the plutocrats. Taxes to the home planet had ended. Profits were soaring on prices set for Bren by the oligarchy. Excess by the rich turned preternatural in parties, parades, and in rivers of gold. It wasn't until the economy began to crumble when relations turned deadly.

The merchants of Bren found the new prices on commodities set by their independent brothers on Ranson irking. They were less inclined than the monarchy to be forgiving towards the plutocracy for their power-hungry excess. They felt it almost a matter of cultural integrity to stick a pin in their bloated egos. Stories of immoderation and indulgence amongst the elite of Ranson, funded by the purchases of the people of Bren, stuck in the throat of the temperate traders. It compounded the perception the people of Ranson had become something less. Therefore, a great drive to seek out domestic substitutes for all of Ranson's raw materials was spawned. After all, this was for the good of all of society; all of the society which had not forsaken its roots.

The competition for creating new, alternate materials spurred massive industries on the home planet. Around the finest universities great minds revolutionized enterprise. Cottage industries sprang to life to become huge corporations. Substitutes for nearly everything which had originally come from Ranson were found and used. Bren began to experience a renaissance of wealth. Splitting the empire in two had set back the home planet only temporarily and it came back with renewed vigor. Things, however, were not going so well with the pioneers.

Since the entire economy of the planet was based around exports to the home planet, things fell apart quickly. The artificially inflated prices of the patricians started a long and consistent plunge as markets turned inward. Ranson lacked the alacrity to turn away from its initial endeavors and the economy as a whole began to sink along with the prices. Along with the failing markets so too sank the political clout of the oligarchy.

Workers began to grumble, unionize and real, grassroots democracy took hold. Expensive campaigns, which used to be laughable walkovers, suddenly became close. The group in power took note, yet never wavered in their desire to keep an iron grip on power. Though the common man was hurting, there was plenty in reserve for them and they intended to keep it. There had to be a way to keep their control and the plutocracy came upon a solution: they found an enemy. Another massive public relations campaign was started. And because grains of truth lie in it the concept became easily sellable: the monarchy of Bren was the cause of all problems.

Everything became more serious. Campaigns of innuendo became outright accusation. Laws were changed to give a dutiful police force authority to do as they saw fit. Union officials disappeared. Grass-root politicians were jailed as spies. Public spending soared on a defense industry which made all employees swear allegiance to the democracy. The wealthy opened their coffers with livable wages for any who would swallow their pride and become one of them. Technical innovation followed and the military of Ranson found new and massive means of destruction.

Meanwhile, the monarchy of Bren stood passive. While they found the media and jailing of dissidents on Ranson repugnant, they would not use this to alarm their own people who had, by now, grown weary of worrying about their inter-planetary neighbor. Things were very prosperous at home now. And why should they worry? They were made of the same stuff. Problems on Ranson were bound to work themselves out without drawing Bren into it at all.

Most counselors to the king agreed, though the military build-up was alarming, they felt there was no reason to divert funds into a build-up in kind. Even if they had known the total extent of the industry, they might not have reacted anyway. (Much of the build-up on Ranson was a strict secret) Having been on a peaceful planet for more than a thousand years they had no inclination towards war. They had no inkling that someone who shared the same blood was capable of being able to spill it. Yet, they had no inclination as to the influence of money and the intoxication of power and, therefore, greatly underestimated the lure of domination and greed.

When relations were officially broken, the empire shuddered in disbelief. It was surreal, almost comical having one entity in space cleave all ties with its closest neighbor. Reason, the common man thought, would prevail and Ranson would soon be back to its senses. Those counselors who were studying the problem, however, had come to a different conclusion: Ranson meant to attack.

Inspired by the studies of the counselors the military, before largely symbolic on a peaceful planet, began to arm itself and prepare. Disbelief was still the overlying emotion.

How could this happen? The people of the monarchy were dismayed at the belligerence and could not bring themselves to think of their relatives across the void of space as enemies. They, after all, were made of the same stuff. Diplomats travelled between the two planets for nearly ten years. The monarchy continually sought out the source of irritation, talking, cajoling and offering good faith measures. The plutocracy was merely buying time; the invasion was already planned. The final, good faith emissaries sent to Ranson were executed. Events followed quickly.

Massive purges of dissenters on Ranson were driven home as sane and necessary by media hysteria. Anyone who questioned the need to destroy the monarchy was executed as a spy or tortured to keep them quiet. The dungeons of Ranson began to fill. Whole communities and businesses were bought into submission by the carrot of free slave labor from the 'traitors' and the 'stick' of the purges. The monarchy had shown great tolerance to the rebels but these latter stages were too much. After years of patience, the purges were condemned officially by the King himself. Using this denunciation as evidence, the plutocracy implied the empire supported the overthrow of the government of Ranson. The plutocracy lunged quickly like a snake on its prey. It was this condemnation which was used by Ranson as final rationale for invasion.

The invasion came. With superior force, and technology, fighting back would have only been throwing chattel into a furnace; the weapons, ships, training and size of the invading force was vastly superior. The hatred and vindictiveness of the attacker was absolute. They were to take away the monarchy and impose their system. The attackers had been brain-washed into believing they were doing the people of Bren a favor. All open sympathy to the throne was suppressed. All heirs to the throne were exterminated, except for one.

Pestia went on to tell of reports which had come later: the insurrection and eventual expulsion of the conquerors. He also told him of the pursuit. How a grandson of one of the original plutocrats, filled with self-righteous hatred, was continuing to hunt the last heir to the throne. He told him how this grandson had been the leader of the terrible purges and ruthless enforcer of planetary dogma. The grandson's name was Matan.

George asked dozens of questions. He found every one of the visitor's answers nectar filling empty holes in his soul. But it was addictive nectar he could not get enough of. It was late. The visitor was ill and tired. Finally, George offered him his help in the struggle to save the heir of the planet and his bed for the night. The whole scene seemed artificial to George as he watched the huge man slump into an uneasy sleep. He questioned the whole panorama and felt like pinching himself to see if he were awake. George was just beginning to realize he had found another reason to be.

CHAPTER TWENTY-FOUR

"That hell begotten little critter is my daughter," the old, grizzled man said about the young woman who had just passed through. "Seems like all women gets this attitude just as soon as they learn to spread their legs. They think just cuz they let some hog bounce up and down on 'em with their back flat on the ground and pelvis wide open like some goddamned, chicken wishbone they gots the whole fuckin' world figured out; one hell of a stinking mess. Sorry-assed little whore. At least she could figure out how ta get some money out-a the greasy pigs she's ballin' and leave me the hell alone."

The skinny old man reached back into the dusty, scratched cupboard to retrieve the bottle he had hidden from the young visitor. He turned back to his guest. "Cain't let none of my ill mannered little shits know I got any booze or, hell-a-ballicious, there it goes. I wouldn't mind half if they knew how to drink without turnin' into the biggest jack-asses, spawned out the ass of an alligator the world has ever seen. Give my boy one sip and he thinks he's king-fuckin'-kong, ready to beat the livin' hell out-a any thing that moves. Wouldn't be so bad if he didn't keep on tryin' to kick somebody's ass that can't be kicked. Gets all busted to bits then comes home cryin' when he really got what was comin' to him." He rubbed at the stubbly, white whiskers, pausing with the bottle at eye level as if trying to measure his rate of consumption. The bottle went bottom end up and he offered it back to his guest in a skeptical manner, wondering if it would all disappear too fast now he was sharing it with someone.

"Now consider you," he went on, hedging his bets with a compliment. "You're the polite sort-a drunk I can really get along with; polite and willin' to pitch in. Not like these gimme, gimme, gimme, old, dried-up, skanky, thrashed, ancient farts that come around tryin' to be my friend every time I get a bottle. Don't be shy. Drink on up.

"I think I might get my boy a bottle tonight and let him smart off to a big strong fellah like you." The old man slapped a skinny blue jean which let off a cloud of dust and he laughed. "Would serve the donkey, shit-for-brains, retard right to go messin' with such a nice boy. I know he would too. He don't take to coloreds. Me, I don't give a shit. It used to tear me up my girl goin' in the back seat with every black hunk-a meat that wandered round; she done it because she thought it pissed me off. No offense mind you. I just wasn't used to it. Hell, my daddy would-a cut my balls loose with a rusty razor and nailed my dick to the floor had I ever even thought the thought of lookin' at a black woman. He hated colored people. But not me. A man's a man and a good one's a good one and a bad one's a bad one. And my boy's a bad one and the daughter ain't no better. The little whore only stopped screwin' blacks cuz she realized I wasn't gettin' worked up over it; she just thought I would. Now she's after white-trash instead of black-trash. I guess I learned my lesson. Never let your kids know what rankles the piss out-a ya or they's bound and determined to do it."

Mark took a long, slow sip of the dark liquor. The caramel colored alcohol swirled around gracefully in the clear bottle as he set it back down. He felt at ease with the babbling little man, even finding him a trifle amusing. The man seemed a caricature of what Mark thought of white earthlings: polite, not very bright, strongly opinionated, self centered and mostly harmless. There was no color difference on his own planet and the idea of stereotyping according to color was quite fun to him. White people generally seemed pleasant, tolerant and un-able to understand anything beyond their world of influence. Yet, they always assumed they understood you totally, some even going so far as to make a pitiful imitation the language of African-Americans while talking to them—making a real spectacle of themselves. Though tolerant, they always acted differently toward you than their own, not always nicer, or worse, just different. The old farmer seemed better than average in this respect. He came right out and talked about the differences and the origin of his stereotypes rather than hem and haw around them.

The old man, with his suspenders, oil stained shirt, faded blue jeans and shredded boots had kind eyes he kept strained wide open. His white hair was slicked back and poorly cut. His reflexive need to hide his guest from all comers, for whatever reason it was, kept Mark from having to explain his need for anonymity; which was convenient.

The little shack they were drinking in was about as inconspicuous of a hide-out ever invented. It was a single-wide mobile home with a large chunk cut out of one end to open it into a small, barn-like structure, ostensibly as an add-on. The trailer was several hundred yards from the main road, connected by a dirt path, and hidden from view by a slight rise in the contour of the land passing around a wash. The seam between the barn and trailer gaped from one to six inches and let in the hot sun. Dirt covered every thing from the faded green carpet to the dishes piled on the table and sink. Greasy rags lie around the front room as one might expect to find dirty socks in a normal house, along with tools of all sort. The add-on structure had more tools and large pieces of machinery, all in different states of disrepair. Dust illuminated old cobwebs hanging off the oil caked machines. The one window of the barn would have been opaque with dirt had part of it not been broken out.

The two of them sat on pieces of overstuffed, yellow vinyl furniture that were cracked and torn in every corner and covered with clothes and magazines about hunting, fishing, hot-rods and women. The old man had confronted his daughter at the entrance of the barn in order to keep the privacy of his guest. She only got a look at the back of Mark's head as she swished through, asked for money, and then plaintively wondered why the old farmer hadn't fixed her car yet. She stayed until her boyfriend began honking outside and when her dad handed over a twenty. The father talked awfully about his daughter, but treated her face to face as any stern, caring father might an errant child.

Millard Russell was the name of the wizened character and Millard sat with his boots sticking out in front of him, splayed outward like a duck. He reached for the bottle once again and continued his alcohol-fueled commentary on women. "Don't know why a woman gots to get an attitude when she starts humpin'. I guess it's cuz they think they's doin' somethin' wrong. They's taught to stay a damn virgin 'till marriage while the boys get to go out and have a hell of a time. Everybody I know wants to get him a virgin. Hell, first of all, there ain't none left no more and, second of all, ain't no virgin ever gonna climb in the sack with the droolin' slobs I know.

"What you think, uh . . ."

"Sam," Mark filled in, "Sam, uh, Cerasoli."

"Yeah, Sammy, what-d'ya think about this virgin horse-shit? I never thought much about it. I mean there's nothin' to it. My boy's always talkin' about . . ." the old man raised the tone of his voice and twisted his face to mock his son, "'Gotta pop me a cherry. Gotta pop me a cherry. Hell, he seems good and attached to the sleazy-slime he's been trackin'. Don't know why he thinks he needs a virgin. Anyway, that boy's so damn stupid he'd believe they was a virgin if they told him for the third night in a row. What-d'ya think Sammy? Is virgins all that good?"

Mark was embarrassed by the question. He was required to remain chaste until taking a queen on the throne of Bren and he knew the stigma earthlings applied to males who remained so. "I really don't know," he replied politely, then reached for the bottle.

"You ain't never had one neither, huh?" the old man said scratching liberally under a sweat stained pit. "Hell, Jesus, fuck, all good girls end up with people a hell of a lot better than us. Not that I begrudge 'em none. I wouldn't wish no good girl on me nor my walkin', talkin', turd of a boy. Well, speak of the horny, little devil himself. Here he comes."

A car could be heard making its way up the long dirt path, which made its way on the flat, dessert ground by dodging large patches of cactus and tumble-weed. The old, loud, dilapidated hot-rod squealed to a stop on the hard-pan, sending a cloud of dust over the trailer and into the cracks. The dust stuck nicely to the sweaty skin and helped parch the dry mouth under the blazing sun.

"See what I mean Sammy," Millard snapped shaking his head and stomping to his feet. He returned the bottle to the little cupboard and walked down into the barn. "The little shit gots no brains and cares about nothin' but hisself."

A radio was playing country music and it amplified as the car door opened. Millard yanked open the door of the barn, homemade and splinter ridden, and stood waiting. Millard's boy walked towards the door, then retreated to sit on the hood of his car. He could tell by the look in his father's face that he wasn't welcome inside at this particular moment. The 'boy' was actually a grown man of twenty-two, larger by several inches than his father and a good deal more stout. The father, however, carried the boy's respect and his son would not transgress a perceived request; at least not more than once. One time the son pushed by Millard in a drunken rage only to get smacked in the back of the head with a shovel. When the boy came to he realized he had asked for it and nothing further was said and he hasn't crossed his father since. In an era of revenge mentality, the Russell household still showed proper respect for punishment. And for all the hollering and bitching transpiring between them, the two still had an inseparable father-son bond.

The lanky son pulled himself up onto the hood looking at his father. "What the hell you all worked up for old man?" he asked in response to his father's stern countenance.

Millard rubbed his chin again and said, "What makes you think I'm worked up?"

The son pushed his stringy, dusty, black hair to one side with one of his large, calloused hands. "Yer standin' there like I ain't supposed to do nothin'," he said plaintively. "I wasn't gonna do nothin'. I know you got a nigger in there. Clarice told me. I don't care."

"Yeah, well that ain't none of your business. Whad-ya come for?"

"You're lucky Grandpa ain't here."

"Grandpa's dead, fool," Millard said, putting his hands on his hips.

"Yeah, well he's spinnin' in his grave knowin' there's a nigger in the house." He then spit on the ground.

"Your grandpa cares a whole lot more for the worms crawlin' in and out-a his ass right now than who the hell's in the house. Whad-ya come for?"

"I need gas."

"Booze more like it."

"I got to go to Bakersfield to talk about a job. Look at the gauge; it's suckin' fumes now."

Millard turned back into the dwelling, caught Mark's eye and gave him a wink. Turning back to his son he said, "So just how much booze is gonna get this car to Bakersfield?"

The son scratched the back of his head and looked around the area working up the correct figure. Gazing at the ground he said sheepishly, "Twenty."

"Twenty-goddamned-dollars!" Millard roared. "You fillin' up the queen-fuckin'-Mary? You don't need no twenty dollars. Here. All I got's ten. Take it and let it burn a hole in your pocket like it always does."

The son got off the hood came forward and took the crumpled bill and tried to sneak a peak into Millard's wallet. Millard yanked back the crusty billfold saying, "If I told you that's all I got, that's all I got. Now git."

The old farmer returned with the smug smile of control on his face. It faded when the boy spun a circle with the hot-rod, squealing on the hard dirt, spaying gravel against the house and another huge cloud of dust into the crack

211

between trailer and add-on. Millard glanced at Mark and shook his head silently with a look of wondering disgust.

The old man was bent at the shoulders, not from age, but more out of a purposeful bearing. He walked with his arms protruding behind him, arching the elbows high and shoving the head far out in front. Bony hips pushed in front of his sliding gait almost as far as his head causing his back to bend into a question mark. The feigned assemblage of qualities gave him the look of a comic book character, every action and stance previewed for effect rather than sincerity. But it was a good natured charade, one in which he believed he was having the desired effect of coping with the situation at hand.

He measured the bottle at eye level one more time and took a sip. Offering the slightly less voluminous contents to Mark he said, "Ten bucks'll get him to town with enough to booze a little. If I give him twenty it'll be too much and job or no he ain't goin' to Bakersfield. With twenty him and five of his deadbeat friends'll be drunk in an hour. Ten'll keep him sober enough to get there. If there ain't no job he'll be back. Mark my words, if he ain't on his way to Bakersfield, like he says, he'll be back in about four hours oiled like a whores crotch tryin' to start trouble. Don't pay him no mind. If he takes a poke at you you've got my full permission to knock his head clean off his body. You hear me? Bust him good. It can only knock sense in, there ain't none to get knocked out.

"Little, goddamned fruits of my loins, ain't they? Why them ratty little kids never did know the difference between wantin' and gettin'. Don't get me wrong, Sammy. I love my kids. They just got me backed into a corner and they know it. I give and give and give and give and they take and take and take and take. Some sort of cycle I ain't busted yet. Oh piss on it. Gimme that bottle. Ahhh. There we go.

"It just don't seem you get no sympathy from kids. Been five years since mamma died and it might as well be five-hundred as far at they's concerned. Not that they paid a lick of respect five days after it happened let alone five hours. I guess I should be thankful they held they's mouth straight five hours afterward let alone five minutes." The old farmer flapped an arm in the air, scratched at his scalp, then pulled a battered cowboy hat off the floor and put it on. He rubbed his neck and looked to the ceiling, squinting one eye completely shut. "Seems I was gonna do something . . . oh, yeah, Sammy. We were gonna look at that car of yours. Let's go take a look." Millard slapped both hands on his lap and stretched up slowly as if suddenly very tired.

"There's really no hurry," Mark said.

"Really?" the old man queried. "It's OK to fix it tomorrow?"

"Sure," Mark replied. "If you don't mind my staying another night, tomorrow would be fine."

Millard suddenly looked more spry. "Well, if there's no hurry, I guess we should go on into town to get a little more booze. I don't think it'd be proper to have my boy be the only one oiled up. Hell, it's gettin' late anyhow. Too hot to do any damn work on that car. A fellah would burn up under that hood now. My kids don't know about hard work. Hell, my damn daughter comin' here tellin' me to fix her car is the hardest work she's done in a month. She's a woman who thinks she knows every damn thing so I should let her fix it. She got no money to fix it so I got to. Stinkin' kids took damn near every penny I got. My wallet's so hungry the moths give up on it." The old man paused to look over to Mark. "Shit, Sammy," he continued, "those stinkin' kids of mine know when I got a little and just cain't wait to take it all. Every penny. If I put a little money away and right away, here they come barkin' out gimme, gimme, gimme, until there ain't nothin' left . . ." He gauged Mark one more time seeing if the comments were taking effect. Mark wasn't biting, not because he didn't want to, he just didn't know what the farmer was getting at yet. The old man continued a little more blunt. Slapping at all his pockets he said, "If my pockets were an oil drum they'd be ringin' for an hour. Yep. Empty to the last friggen drop. How the hell a man supposed to go out and have fun on nothin'?" Still no recognition by Mark. "Yep, I don't no how the hell we're supposed to get drunk when my kids took all my damn money."

Finally Mark absorbed the clue. "I am sorry. I should have offered earlier. I have plenty of money for our liquor. I should purchase something for your kindness. I do not know how long I would have been on the road if you had not stopped to help. Perhaps you would like me to buy some food also?"

The old farmer stood nearly straight and adjusted his hat with a large smile. "Praise Jesus Lord," he exclaimed, "screw food. I cain't believe you finally bit the bait. For a while there, I thought I was fishin' for the Loch Ness monster. Come on, let's go and get some real nourishment."

CHAPTER TWENTY-FIVE

"I want to thank you again for having me over Sharon," Barbara said trying to sound sincere. "It's really nice to get out of the house. It's such a nice evening too. The temperature is just about perfect outside."

Sharon pretended to be more involved in the cooking than she actually was. "Mmmm-hm," she let out disinterestedly. "Jeremy always likes to take care of his friends. He likes to cheer people up."

Barbara didn't want to get angry at Sharon but it was getting to a point where she was tempted to do so. All evening long Sharon had been treating her like toxic waste. Barbara didn't really understand why Sharon felt so threatened. She had never viewed Jeremy as anything more than a friend. Barbara felt like getting mad at Jeremy for not recognizing the situation and not putting either of them in the same circumstance again. But he seemed so genuinely removed from the little head-trip his wife was on she couldn't do that either. Outside, through the screen door, Barbara could see Jeremy rounding up his two children who were playing in the yard in order to get them to bed.

Barbara tried again to be friendly. "I just came in to get another beer," she said. "Why don't you come outside? It's a lot cooler."

Sharon gave Barbara an abbreviated smile then turned back to the mixing bowl. "I've got a lot of work to do. Thanks anyway."

Barbara retreated out the back door trying to distance her from the tension. Jeremy had both children, one under each arm. He was twisting around in circles laughing and joking. "Time to go," he said. "I got you; time for the big bed. No more excuses or I'm gonna get you; time for bed." He came to the back door and Barbara walked down the wooden steps, off the porch, to make room for Jeremy and his packages.

Jeremy paused besides her giving a wink. "Say goodnight to Barbara, now," he commanded.

The two, cute little children comically strained their heads up from their horizontal positions from under his arms to bid her good-night. "Night Baabra," they said in unison, giggling. Jeremy continued into the house.

The big mercury vapor lamp suspended over the back porch lit the yard bluish white, casting stark shadows behind the picnic table and grill. The children's toys were scattered around, a great many more toys, Barbara noticed, than she had had when she was a child. The high green fence, bordering the alley, faded colorless under the glare of the lamp. Insects began navigating the area around the light in wider and wider arcs, and in greater multitude, causing Barbara to walk further away and take a position at the table. The yard was well kept, short, and dry and firm to the touch.

The noise of the city seemed far away. Above, stars were not discernable, all of them blotted out from the city glow and porch light. A slight breeze had a refreshing chill and carried up the remnant smell of a fresh mowing from earlier in the day. Barbara kicked off her sandals and rubbed her toes in the lush turf. She dragged a hand across the rough texture of the grey, wooden planks making the table top. She tapped on one plank, and then an adjacent one, noticing each made a distinct sound. Tapping on one, then the other, then back and forth, she made a little nonsensical tune. The screen door opened then smacked shut under force of the spring. Jeremy came out to join her.

"What a beautiful night," he said as he sat down opposite her. The bench on her side rose slightly to counter-balance his weight. "I don't know what's wrong with Sharon, all of a sudden got to have the kids some cookies. Oh well. We'll enjoy without her."

Barbara shrugged her shoulders. "It was a great barbeque Jeremy. You've got some sweet kids."

"They were good tonight. But they can have their spells."

A silence fell and Barbara resumed her tapping tune. Jeremy picked at the label of his beer with a thumb-nail. "I told you they wouldn't follow you," Jeremy said referring to the reporters, "not a one."

"They seem to be thinning out quite a bit," Barbara said shaking her head. "I don't know why they should with this Josiah thing coming up." She looked Jeremy in the eye. "You think Mark did it? You think he really did it?"

Jeremy shook his head. "Don't know. Don't really have an opinion." He returned Barbara's stare. "I don't want to believe that he did."

Barbara shook her head up and down. He was hoping Mark hadn't perpetrated this heinous crime for her sake and she appreciated the show of support from Jeremy. "Me too," she said.

Inside, they could hear the doorbell ring. Jeremy looked at his watch. "Who the hell is that?" "Honey!" he yelled to his wife. "You want me to get that?"

"No," was the reply from the kitchen, "I can get it."

Barbara gave Jeremy a knowing look. "I'll bet it's for me," she said.

"No way. If they would've followed you they would've come a long time before now."

Barbara could hear Sharon's heels clicking on the kitchen linoleum. The screen door opened. "See?" Barbara said standing.

"It's somebody for you Barbara," Sharon said holding open the door, "some huge guy."

Jeremy stood up and motioned for Barbara to sit back down. "I'll handle this," he said. "I'll tell them you went home, out the back way. That OK?" He was already on his way.

Barbara acquiesced. "Sure, why not."

She looked around the yard one more time. There wasn't any back way out, really. At one point there was a latch which opened a small gate on the top half of the fence to dump the garbage but no other opening. She imagined tomorrow's headline: Crazed Cerasoli Leaps Fence to Escape Reporters; Ninja Lover Continues Mutilation Spree. Jeremy meant well, she thought, but it probably would have been better had she just gone out to face them.

Inside she could hear Jeremy's voice rising to an angry yell. Now she really felt bad. She took another swig of beer and leaned forward on the table to peer into the house through the screen. Suddenly, Jeremy's voice took on a more wild tone, Sharon screamed and she could hear the breaking of glass and furniture. Barbara jumped to her feet and started toward the house. As she came up the steps she could see a huge, black man pointing an object at Sharon who was kneeling over Jeremy, limp on the floor beside a broken lamp. The object in the massive hand sparked and hissed. Sharon gasped, then fell slack over the body of her prone husband with a tearful groan.

Everything on Barbara tingled. She felt as if her feet had grown roots. She didn't know what to do. The huge man closed the door behind him and looked around, business like, almost casually. His eyes came to the back door. Green and intense they locked in on Barbara's face as if guided by radar. Barbara found herself yelling in complete terror, "Hey! Hey! Get away from them! Stop!" The realization was relatively slow to sink in. He had been asking for her! The little man from the store came back to her mind; pictures of Josiah haunted the background; the resemblance of the huge creature to Mark was undeniable. "Hey!" Barbara screamed. In a quick motion the massive arm came level holding the small object. It sparked and hissed and, nearly simultaneously, the screen in front of her eyes lit in a brilliant flash of sparks, fire, and electrical noise.

The feet knew more than the mind at this point. They had started Barbara at full stride for an escape. She flung herself against the fence, leaping just high enough to lock her arms over the top. The rough cut top of the boards dug splinters into the soft parts of her under-arm as she struggled to kick a leg over the top. As she succeeded in getting one leg over the fence she heard the screen door slam. Looking up, she saw a huge shape, now illuminated from behind by the lamp, sprint toward her. On the edge of the back walk way the massive being grunted and flipped straight back, smacking onto the cement with an audible splat and a gasp of exiting air from deflated lungs. A toy skateboard shot out from the collapsed shape and rattled against the fence.

Barbara dropped over the barrier into the pitch-black alley. Her eyes weren't accustomed to the shadows and she promptly flew over a full garbage can smashing a knee into the pavement. She stumbled to her feet, staggering over the scattered refuse like a drunken man, ignoring the throbbing leg. In a second more of stumbling along a crash of splintered wood filled the passage behind. Light came into the alley from the porch light through a gaping hole smashed in the fence. In front of the smashed and splintered opening she could see a shape darting towards her. In total blackness she strode, terror driving her to fly blind. Her breath hissed in and out of lungs not able to sustain the adrenalin that had forced her to fly. Her bare feet tore at the asphalt, burning and scratching. She could hear footsteps behind, getting closer.

At the end of the alley a car came around with its high beams on. Barbara spun her head around as she ran. The massive man was only twenty feet behind. She heard the engine of the car roar to life toward her. The big shape lumbered on and raised an arm pointing the same object that had knocked over Sharon. Barbara stumbled then lunged into a recess in a fence on the opposite side of the alley from Jeremy's which harbored the neighbor's garbage cans, trying to get out from between the two attackers. Between the two cans she squeezed her body trying to stand in order to leap into the yard at the low spot in the fence to which they were attached. The object in the man's hand hissed and one of the garbage cans pinged, shooting off sparks that ricocheted onto Barbara's left arm. She screamed with pain. The bloodied arm twitched unnaturally, then fell numb. She kicked against the ground to push herself further into the recess screaming as loud as her winded lungs would allow. A massive hand locked onto her ankle like a vice. Kicking and screaming it started to drag her from her position when it suddenly let go.

In a roar of clatter, banging of cans and one large thud, the car had rammed into her assailant so close it came within inches of smashing her foot. A dark green car door was now blocking any exit from the recess. For a moment, all that could be heard was a garbage can lid rolling away and the purr of the engine. "Get in!" a voice screamed. "Get in goddamnit!" A head appeared out the window of the door. Barbara instantly recognized the little bald head from the man in the store. He lunged out the window, up to his waist, and grabbed Barbara by the wounded shoulder and hair. She struggled to her feet and went head-first into the window drawing her legs in behind as her torso went clear to the dirty floor mats. The engine howled into reverse and her neck and face jammed mercilessly into the wiring and vent conduit under the dash; her one good arm clutched furiously and futilely at the cloth on the seat as her legs flayed around the inside of the cabin under whim of the direction of the car. The auto bounced out of the alleyway savaging Barbara's shoulder against the floorboard and twisting her neck. In a squeal of rubber the car stopped and reversed direction. As they gained speed she felt a hand come down and grab her by the shirt. "Come on," the voice said, "you better get straight now. They'll be on their way in a moment and it's only going to get rougher."

Barbara pulled her butt onto the floor using her one good arm and the help of the man, putting her back toward the steering wheel. She crawled onto her knees then pushed herself up onto the seat gasping for air and twisting her neck around to make sure it wasn't broken. They hit a culvert at speed bouncing her clear to the ceiling, jamming her neck one more time. "Slow down damn it," she screamed, "fuck, slow down!" The small, stocky man took no notice and slid around a corner. Barbara braced herself against the dash with her one good arm to no avail, sliding almost into the lap of the driver. After two or three more harrowing slides the short man began to slow and gaze into his rearview mirror.

By the time they pulled onto a freeway they were going normal speeds. Barbara continued to check her neck and shoulder and started worrying about her paralyzed arm. There was a scratch across the top of the forearm along with what appeared to be a burn. The blood had already clotted across the sore and in streams where it had dripped down the arm. She picked it up with the good arm and let it drop into her lap.

"My arm's dead," Barbara said, finally breaking a silence between them. "Something's wrong." Tears began coming out. "Where the fuck are we going?"

As if disconnected from her line of thought, George said, "I think we lost them. We can take it easy now."

"Who are you?" Barbara growled between tears. Then, catching the nastiness in her tone, she calmed. "I guess I should say, 'thank you.' I guess."

The man gave Barbara what she thought of as a worried glance. "You were pretty lucky," he said. "That guy could snap any bone in your body with no more effort than you might break a pencil."

"Oh wonderful, as if I didn't know that. Any moose that big . . . why did he hurt my friends? What does he want?"

George didn't hear the last two questions. He was already lost in thought. He should have brought out his gun. He should have been more ready than he was. It was just so surprising to see them so soon. Killing one of those bastards would have made Frank's night. Anyway, it's for sure they're still in the city, and they haven't yet found Mark. Also, because they were after this woman, they don't have a very good idea as to where he is. Perhaps this woman will come in handy. They must still believe she knows where he is. She could prove to be powerful bait to bring them out into the open again.

The violence exhibited by the huge visitor put George's mind at rest. In the back of his mind there had always been the possibility Frank was lying in order to get an ally. He didn't know for sure which side had killed Josiah. The description given by the only eyewitness could have fit either party. Before tonight, there existed the possibility to think of Frank as the aggressor since the only direct evidence George had pointed to Frank as an assassin—Frank himself admitted he had been the rifleman. The good expert in forensics had kept his eyes open to all possibilities along the way. But tonight changed all that. He now knew, without a doubt who the bad guys were.

CHAPTER TWENTY-SIX

Across the trillions of miles of cold, dark space, in a place the aliens called home, he had seemed a specter larger than life. Behind every locked door he, or one of his agents, lurked to insure the planned outcome of every event, social, political, or individual. Each and every result wanted by the Republic was driven to fruition through any means meeting his ends. Methods which were spoken of in low tones and hushed whispers only in the light of day; procedures one dare not refer to in the uncertainty of the dark. And control, all control of every emotion which normally moved in random rhythms amongst the vox populi, sat in the palm of his hand as his weapon, puppet, or toy of whim. Power loomed in his shadow from fear and his shadow was cast across the solar system into the home and bed of every being aware of his will to control. He was more than flesh and blood; he was an incubus peering through walls, hearing the intimate talk of husband and wife, and peeling back all secrets, laying bear the soul as only an un-feeling, merciless monster might.

And yet shadows have a diminishing point. No matter how large the object, its silhouette will diminish through distance. Across the vast parsecs of space, even the darkness cast by a massive object will fade from umbra, to penumbra until it exists no longer. Such a great shadow of home did not travel the distance to earth. And an incubus is not flesh and blood with natural desires, weaknesses and shortcomings. Familiarity not only breeds contempt, but also dispels illusions. This angel of death, who had seared the mouths of billions shut with terror, was only a man, and one worthy of contempt.

Nagrom was injured and tired. He was sick of killing. He was sick of death. He longed for the simple things of home, the food, the music, the particular liquors of spice and fire homemade by the hill-folk from his region. Nothing could be the same ever again. Not one of his friends from the Trans-solar Elite was left alive. Anyway, if they had been spared a fiery death, they would have been old, unrecognizable men, who had seen at least sixty years of living, he had not, by the time he got home. And what would home bring? Matan refused to allow him to read the dispatches from home anymore; they were too depressing. Would they be heroes or strung up by the neck? The government was collapsing. For all he knew it had already collapsed; it was a suspicion ever since Matan sequestered the news from home. There was, probably, no-one to fight for anymore. Death seemed a more pleasant option to this present task, so futile, so merciless, fighting for such a coward, so far from home, in a struggle so stupidly unnecessary.

Nagrom had not been one of the ghouls who had inhabited the inner sanctum and dungeons of Intelligence. He, therefore, did not understand torture and violence for their own sake, like those brutes who found a rationale in such things. The idea of vindictiveness seemed foreign to him. In his mind there should be a plan, an objective and the two should go hand-in-hand as long as they remained congruent. A man with a bit of honor in him cannot understand one who is evil to the core. A military man knows when to cut his losses, retreat, or surrender. An ideologue, consumed with hate, must go until there is nothing left but ashes.

Nagrom was one of those beings blessed with a multiplicity of the ingredients for success beyond what should have been bestowed on any one individual. Born a great grandson of one of the founding fathers of the republic he went on to graduate first in his class at the academy among several thousand cadets. Physical size and strength matched his intellect and he became an expert in hand to hand combat, winning dozens of planetary awards. Survival tactics became his specialty and love, amazing even his instructors at his tenacity for maintenance and capacity for endurance. And now? Now he was on a planet, fifteen light-years away, with a soft bellied, craven tyrant whose only talent—beyond having milked his blood-lines to get to the top of intelligence—was an ability to instruct people on the methods of torture—Matan was above actually performing the dirty little deeds himself.

Nagrom looked at his commander, lying on the bed supine as if he were dying with nothing more than a stomachache, and felt like spitting. The former master of intelligence, prince of dread, was groaning and demanding relief for something a child should not worry about. Nagrom imagined what he would do to a child of his own if they had carried on so over a bellyache. And the Premier was demanding relief as if he were some sort of parent, or nursemaid, sent along only to hold the hand of the miserable, little wretch. Nagrom thought about the survival treks he had made through the great dessert, eating and surviving on things which would make a rodent puke. Thoughts of former accomplishments, great and varied, mixed with the present situation and made him more disgusted. He held his feelings inside, though, masking them with a bland expression he knew that was favored by the ruthless commander—the Premier preferred his men to be without opinion.

The wrist on the right hand was swollen to nearly double its normal size. A knee-cap was bruised so badly that it barely bent. The vehicle had caught him in an awkward angle and knocked him headlong into a telephone pole where it cracked his skull and left him groggy enough to allow an escape. He had assumed the car roaring down the alley was the Premier coming around to offer assistance. And why not? It was logical to think that his commander would be interested in the chase. This is why he had not jumped out of the way. When the automobile was on him Nagrom realized he had erred but it was too late. He should have known better than to believe the Premier capable of such strategy. He should have known that the Premier would not have dirtied his hands. Stumbling and staggering, blood gushing from the wound on his head, he made his way back to the car and his commander. Eyes flashed with indignation in the dark and cruel words came out of the Premier's mouth berating and demeaning him as a fool and coward for failing. The scene played over in Nagrom's mind.

Discontent had been brewing in the massive officer's sharp mind ever since the landing, eating away at and occupying his acumen. After reading the bulletins sent from home during Matan's sleep, a depression filled him to the top from his deepest recesses. The magnificent armada of Ranson had been incinerated some twenty-seven years before. Knowing that the war had already been lost sapped his resolve to continue. He, of course, had no-one to express this to. Matan dismissed the reports as if he had been reading a novel. Nagrom needed a reason, however flimsy, to fight. The Premier needed no reason but his own hatred. The reports from home did not seem to have an effect on him at all. Nothing seemed to make the soft, spoiled commander feel, least of all the opportunity to have empathy for another being.

Josiah was the first person Nagrom had ever tortured. Killing was in him, years of training saw to that. Yet, this was a sport not befitting him. Military training had taught him honor and dignity, not cruelty. He had shot prisoners without hesitation when ordered to do so. Kneeling on the ground, hands tied behind their backs, he had, without a twitch, placed the barrel of the gun to the back of their head and mercilessly flicked their life out of this existence with no more thought employed than if he had sneezed. There were pretenses given for the order. Pretenses he had not questioned. Though heartless, shooting someone was an order which seemed infinitely reasonable to creating such misery by torture. A war was on and misery oozed from the walls and welled up from the ground. No-one thought about trying to create it, to lengthen it, to extol it. Only his deep sense of duty had carried him through the experience. He could still feel the poor little thing twitching with agony. He could still hear the wails for mercy and see the eyes rolling white into the head. He, Nagrom the magnificent, top officer throughout the Trans-solar Elite, was having nightmares. This, to Nagrom, was an omen as to the evil of the event. Another war was now going on in his mind and misery could be found there as well.

"Nagrom," groaned the Premier, "is there no relief from this filth they call food? You, young and strong, are of a stouter constitution than myself. I haven't felt so ill since I was a child."

Nagrom held his dispassionate affect, not replying, though the irony of the Premier using the word 'child' played inside his head.

Matan rolled his head on the pillow until he saw the dutiful officer sitting erect at the table. "They told me you were the finest, killing machine on the planet," he continued, "not only have you not proved to be that, but you are also a pitiful conversationalist. I should have settled on someone more versed in literature and the arts. Not some huge beast—that has proved incapable anyway—that can only stare off into space when it is not given orders."

Matan raised his voice to a mocking tone to bark the order as if to some domesticated animal, "Currency, Nagrom, go and fetch some. And we will need a new vehicle. This one is too recognizable. I'm tired of your stony presence anyway."

The huge officer stood and in his deep voice said, "As commanded Premier." Then, he exited without another sound.

Nagrom did not allow himself to think at times like this. It was only important to act. Duty, instilled through years of exhaustive indoctrination, could still carry the day. If he ruminated over events, anger would fester into a space in his gut where it could not be relieved. Thought and duty, at this point, could not mix. He had been castigated by superiors before. Sometimes it was their only function, but this was somehow different. So far from home nothing seemed the same. Verbal punishment had been lavished on him throughout training and in real exercise; it was the way of the Elite to demand nothing but perfection. Yet, in such a place, after such events, he had to rely on nothing but duty or he might go mad.

It infuriated Nagrom his strategy was given no counsel. His mind was sharper than the Premier's in many ways, especially in the areas of tracking and reconnaissance. Sending the larger, more conspicuous of the two out to do menial errands made no sense for a pair that was trying to meld with the population at large. Try as he might, slumping and shuffling, the huge man, with his chiseled muscles, drew the stares of anyone walking in the night. It wasn't long before he drew the stare of a particular set of eyes he would have liked to avoid.

A policeman, driving the beat, looked at the picture on his sheet, and back to the giant. He was, perhaps, larger than the description might suggest, but it was close enough to take a look. No-one walked down the boulevard at this time of night unless they were a suspect for something anyway. The officer called in the routine stop and pulled up next to the wary suspect. The suspect stopped and refused to turn toward the officer. Then the officer approached the suspect for questioning.

CHAPTER TWENTY-SEVEN

Officer Espinoza rubbed the sleep out of his eyes with one hand while blowing into a cup of coffee held in the other. His partner, officer Jablonski, sat across from him reading a report, eyes bloody, face pale and intense. Espinoza was always willing to ameliorate his exhaustion rather than do something sensible like getting a good night's sleep; he worked better that way. A cup of coffee, a splash of cold water in the face, a long yawn and he was ready for another couple of hours. Jablonski, however, seemed to fight being drowsy all the way. The more tired he got, the longer he would stare and the harder he would have to concentrate. On one exceptionally long shift, Espinoza had seen his partner stare at the same page of a report for an entire hour, fighting the paper, the print, and the straining eyes into a dead stand-still.

Not only did Espinoza placate his exhaustion, he didn't mind looking tired either. He found it an un-written law in the precinct that you were never supposed to look tired. No matter the time or how long you had been on shift, when the captain walked into the office you were supposed to sit up, look alert, and pretend you were listening even when nothing was going into the skull. But not officer Espinoza. When he was tired he just didn't give a shit. He would place a cheek on a palm and let his eyes drift to slits as he slumped into the most comfortable position in a chair. As the captain gave briefings a dirty look was always in store for the drowsy looking detective. But Espinoza didn't care. He wasn't out to kiss anyone's behind. If he was tired, he was tired. Later, he would repeat much of what the captain had said to his rigid, wide-eyed partner who hadn't heard a word. And, of course, get no credit at all from the captain.

This morning wasn't much different. They had been drug out of bed at three o'clock in the morning to investigate another killing linked to the suspect Mark Johnson. For three hours they had combed the crime scene and asked questions. The sun was coming up and with the sun the faculties seemed to fade from the task and they were able to think of nothing but the soft, warm mattress waiting at home. Jablonski hadn't turned a page in at least thirty minutes. If it weren't for the urgency, and special circumstances of the killing, they would have already called it quits: today it had been a fellow officer.

Officer McKitrick, a fourteen year veteran of the force had been on graveyard. He was filling in for another man who was on leave. He liked to do so as he needed the extra pay to help pay for his kid's college tuition. McKitrick's last known words were a routine call-in about a suspect on foot who roughly matched the description of Mark Johnson. There had been several hundred other such sightings. There had even been sightings by fellow officers. None of them had come to anything but this one. This sighting had cost officer McKitrick his life.

Espinoza reached out and pulled the report from Jablonski's hands. Jablonski didn't move or react to the missing report and continued to stare between his two erect hands as if the report was still there. Trying to say something relevant to the missing report he said, "Let's go over this one more time."

"Not much to go over at this point," Espinoza said. "I think we need to get some sleep before we can do anything constructive."

Jablonski rolled his graveled eyes to his partner and acquiesced. "I think you're right." Then, almost as an afterthought, he asked, "Did McKitrick have any kids?"

Espinoza shook his head up and down. "Two kids." Then he added, "He and his wife were separated," as if it were some sort of consolation.

"Seems so incongruent," Jablonski went on. "A big, stout healthy guy like that getting his neck wrung like a chicken, ribs all busted to pieces right through the vest. The suspect had some help from something, a club, PCP, or something."

"I used to see McKitrick down at the gym. He was one hell of a boxer. I can't believe someone could do this alone. Not to McKitrick. Certainly not some drunk like Johnson. I gotta believe there's more than one."

Jablonski looked at his partner. "It all kind of makes you feel a little fragile, don't it?" he said. "This isn't the right kind of job to have your mortality sneaking up on you." The two officers exchanged a meaningful, but abbreviated glance.

The station was nearly empty. Only a few of the investigators were on duty. Those on duty were mostly those poor unfortunates of the night shift who kept largely to themselves. The insulation amongst grave-yarders reinforced a stereotype among day-timers that the night people were rather eccentric. When one of them actually came over to talk to the two detectives it caught them off-guard. A tall, willowy, pale Anglo detective floated over to their corner of the large room as a somnambulist might. "Call for you two on line one," he wheezed out dreamily. "Some sheriff out of Barstow, it's something about the Johnson case." The way he said 'Johnson case' showed certain irreverence at the notoriety the two officers were getting for being on it. As he breezed back to his desk the stereotype held by the two day-timers about the graveyard crew was significantly strengthened.

Officer Espinoza took the call. "Yeah?" he barked gruffly. He wasn't going to be too polite. They had answered hundreds of calls on the case and most of them were red herrings. Besides, they had more important matters at hand—like sleep.

"Hello, this is sheriff Boulding from Barstow. Is this the officer on the Johnson case?"

Due to the publicity, there was no need to describe the case further. "One of 'em" Espinoza said.

"Yeah," came back the voice a bit embarrassed sounding, "we got some information for you. It . . . uh . . . is a little late."

"Go ahead," Espinoza said impatiently, not caring what was making the voice embarrassed. He just wanted to be done with the call.

"Seems that yesterday our duty chief left a message at shift change to call you guys, about three-thirty in the afternoon. It was . . . uh . . . labeled 'urgent'. And, well, uh . . ."

"Yeah, yeah, shit happens, what's up?"

"Yesterday, during the day shift, at approximately three minutes after five, it seems that someone called in a report. Now, the duty officer usually fills out a referral before leaving. But she was called in by the captain so that he could give her results on a training sheet. So, when she left the desk the new duty officer . . ." Espinoza rolled his eyes while listening and glared in frustration at his partner who was blinking his eyes to insure that they were still open. "Was just coming in and he didn't see the note on the . . ."

"Listen man," Espinoza broke in, "I don't give a shit why it's late. Just tell me what the hell you got. OK?"

The duty officer on the other end of the line paused, then continued, sounding a little hurt. "Well, I was just trying to relay the chain of events so that you would be able to know as to why there was a delay. We don't usually operate this way out here and I wanted to let you know that we were concerned, very concerned with this delay."

Espinoza rolled his eyes one more time and took a deep breath. "Fine. We're tired. You don't operate like that. I believe you. Go. Tell me."

"Well, somebody called in and said that they had recognized your Mr. Johnson down at a local liquor store . . ." Espinoza motioned to his partner for a pen and paper . . . "It comes from a reliable person, not one of them publicity hounds. In fact, two people confirmed the sighting this morning . . . . uh, when we finally confirmed it."

Sheriff Boulding went on to relay all the relevant facts. In addition to relevant facts he also relayed a substantial detail: the local press had already been apprised of the situation, notified in advance of their report. Espinoza and Jablonski were not impressed with the handling of the case.

Espinoza finished scribbling notes and slammed down the phone. "Stupid, hayseed asshole," he spit out.

By this time Jablonski was on another line, stoically keeping his sunset red eyeballs wide open. "Yeah," he said, "I see . . . Are you sure? . . . yeah, OK thanks a lot."

"Ready to go to Barstow?" Espinoza asked. "Guess we've got a substantiated sighting. Sheriff tells me the press is going to beat us there."

"Not just yet," Jablonski said, straining to stand.

"What do you mean?"

"Looks like we might have another suspect. Last night, about ten-o'clock, seems a man close to Johnson's description knocked out two people with some sort of taser—they just came to. Then he made off with our girl Cerasoli who was over for dinner. Not too far from where they found McKitrick."

"And?" Espinosa asked while taking the seat vacated by Jablonski.

"And it wasn't Johnson."

"Are they sure?"

"Yeah," Jablonski said, and then launched into his detective mode. "The guy knocked out was Johnson's social worker prior to Cerasoli, Jeremy Brown. He's positive it wasn't Johnson. But he says the resemblance is uncanny, just bigger, lots bigger. Maybe somebody big enough to do the damage on McKitterick. This is really getting screwed up. Is this guy a copycat because he fits the description? Has Johnson been a red-herring the whole time? Why does he want Cerasoli? Is she more screwed up than we thought? Did she plan this? Had she been telling us the truth all along and then changed her story when we showed her Josiah just to please us?"

Jablonski continued stating the questions keeping tab on the number asked by extending another digit on his hand with each one listed. When both hands were full of questions, detective Espinoza took in a huge sigh and stated, "I guess this means more coffee, huh?"

CHAPTER TWENTY-EIGHT

Barbara looked down at the large man with some concern. The sweat beading up on his brow in the cool room told her he was in bad shape. The shoulder was swollen clear into the upper arm. The wound was blackened against his brown skin and puss discolored the bandage to a milky yellow. Belabored breaths came in short, weak, separated bursts. Muscles rolled into lumps, sinewy, twitching across his shirt-less torso as if contorting with each gasp of air. She had never met Mark's 'uncle' before. Before, that is, she found out he wasn't really his uncle.

It all seemed too ridiculous. This slumbering giant, looking every bit a human being—albeit an exceptionally well muscled human being—was supposed to be an alien. They were supposed to be on the earth to hide from assassins. Mark was supposed to be the king of an entire planet. That silly, polite, drunk was supposedly going to be retrieved in a couple of years by an enormous fleet of space ships. It all seemed like the seeds of a cracked-pot cult. Yet there was the physical evidence: The bizarre resemblance of the huge assailant to Mark; the strange object which had bowled over Sharon and Jeremy; Mark's sudden paranoia about being killed buttressed by the wounded uncle. She imagined herself on a hillside two years from now, with flowers in her hair, waiting for the rescue fleet. All around them reporters took pictures and editorials trumpeted their folly. In the end, they would walk back down the hill in disgrace, like so many doomsday prophets, another foolish yarn and a footnote in history. The whole premise of aliens hiding on earth seemed ridiculous; which is why she came so close to dismissing it. It seemed to Barbara a made-up story would have held together a little better. The tale George told seemed to have the missing edges so many true to life stories do. A made-up story would have had more answers to obvious questions. Simple questions like if they wanted to hide, why didn't they bring a disguise? It all seemed probable, but Barbara was reluctant to throw her complete confidence into the story.

Barbara wrung out a wash-cloth in some cool water in a bowl by her feet. She wiped the sweat from Pestia's forehead, rinsed the cloth again then placed it, neatly folded, across his brow. Barbara didn't have any medical training. She was only doing what she had seen done in movies and was trying to be useful. It was obvious, alien or not, he was in great pain. How serious this was and how far or how close to death he was she didn't have a clue. She took his pulse. It was weak and rapid, about one-hundred and ten per minute. He was cool to the touch. Were these good signs or bad signs for an alien? That is, if he really was an alien. Signs like this, she thought, would not bode well for a human being.

The hotel room was small and claustrophobic. Being cooped up with two, older and strange men was thoroughly disconcerting to Barbara. Had they acted differently she could have imagined it some sort of weird plot to sexually abuse her—such was the state of her apprehension toward strange men after three months in the social services. But they were perfect gentlemen. They went so far as to be unnaturally unaware of her sexuality. Coming from a scene where everyone was hyper-aware of her gender, this was perplexing. It wasn't as if she wanted them to be coming on to her; it was just she found it wholly odd that they did not. They both seemed so consumed with their project; legitimately consumed. Frank was preoccupied with pain and the general aspects of the problems at hand—though he did take time to act haughty. George was intensely engrossed with every detail and had no time at all. In Barbara's mind, this added to the credence of the story. Either they were both equally nuts, or this drama was real—at least real to them. Barbara peeked out the window to the sunny day and wished she was out there too.

Though she was caught in a type of veracious limbo toward the idea of aliens, yet she did know there were people out there who wanted to hurt her badly. The excitement of the previous night played over in her head. Here in the hotel, it was no longer scary. The events were now, to Barbara's embarrassment, rather exhilarating, exciting, and full of daring-do. The thought of being caught up in some sort of intrigue filled her with a type of confidence she was not used to. Being in on the inter-workings of a drama which had captured the fascination of a public greedy for information made Barbara almost proud. She had survived the hoard of the media and she was now in on the 'real' story, capturing some of the benefits of the drama after having suffered through all of its suspicions.

George had asked her to stay out of sight. He was the only one not yet searched for by the police and had gone out to get food, money and scout out the landscape. Barbara wanted to be with him, furthering her exhilaration at the intrigue, but knew he was right. After talking to him extensively the night before, Barbara had decided to stay with them rather than go to the police. It gave her comfort to know she was not, in any way, their prisoner and she concluded George would be much more sensitive than the police to the idea she was being stalked by some huge alien.

She looked into a mirror and was taken aback by what she saw. Her face was white and further bruised than before. Her black hair was everywhere and for the first time she noticed she was in the same clothes as the previous night, rumpled, torn and filthy from the flight. Not drawing attention to herself, looking like this, would be even more difficult if she were to venture out. She looked like she had just come out of a barroom brawl.

She decided showering would be silly as she would have to put back on the same clothes. Continuing along the same line she thought, what the hell am I going to do without any clothes, toiletries, blow-dryer, and all the other things I use everyday? Not even a goddamned toothbrush. The realization she hadn't brushed her teeth suddenly made her teeth feel fuzzy and thick with plaque.

Trying to take her mind off of her hygiene she began surveying the room. On the foldable luggage rack was George's suitcase. It was ancient, grandma-styled and an ugly, olive green. It was open at ninety degrees against the wall and the contents made Barbara feel odd. Old striped boxer shorts, jockey underwear, stained socks, a battered electric razor, and wrinkled pants and shirts were crammed in without a hint of order. She would have imagined a military man being more fastidious. Or at least more up to date. It looked like something her father would have packed, in form and content. A funny, old musty odor hung over the open case and she moved on to other things.

In a corner which would be behind the bathroom door when opened was Frank's backpack. It was an oddly constructed pack, not having any outside straps beside the shoulder harnesses, and they seemed to be without adjustment slack. The fabric was silvery and looked smooth. She peered closer and the fabric appeared smoother, not revealing any stitching or weave. She drug a finger across it and it felt almost plastic smooth, yet looked more dull than that in texture. She turned around and looked at the slumbering man. His breath was heavy. He was in a deep sleep. She knelt down beside the medium sized bag and decided to take an innocent peek.

The opening wasn't immediately discernable. A fine line running on three sides of the square, near the top, opened when pulled to reveal itself a flap, protecting what looked like an inner zipper. She looked one more time toward the sleeping man. His labored breathing, and the hum of the little air conditioner were the only sounds in the room. Not even a car could be heard on the road outside. She felt a twinge of guilt, paused, then continued anyway. There wasn't a head to the apparent zipper and she searched back and forth several times around the top of the bag looking for such a handle. Finally, not finding an opener to the seam, she grabbed under the line with one fist, above it with another, and yanked. Several things happened at once.

Her fists tensed up with the current flowing through them. Her fingernails felt like they were being shattered and peeled off all at once; her hair stood out from her head. A piercing whistle oscillated from low to high seeming to go painfully right through her brain on the way into the room. The whistle was shortly accompanied by her own yell of pain. "Yaaaaaaaaaaah," she screamed.

A large black hand came over the top of her to touch the bag. When it met the bag, her hands jumped free from the charge and she flopped back onto the hotel scented carpet. As soon as she caught her breath the same hand grabbed her arm and yanked her roughly to her feet.

"What are you doing in my luggage?" Pestia yelled suspiciously.

Barbara looked at the angry face and felt suddenly very, very petite and weak. Her face flushed red from embarrassment. "Nothing," Barbara gasped out, clutching one hand righteously to her chest.

"Nothing does not set off the alarm," Pestia said pulling her away from the bag. He bent over to investigate, then resealed the flap of the bag with a quick flick of a finger around the edge. He stood tall and glowered at her. "What are you up to? What are you trying to do?"

Barbara paused; eyes stretched wide toward the huge man, and then let out a flustered laugh. "You saw what I was doing: getting caught being nosey. That's one hell of an intruder alert. I'm sorry. I'm bored. I was being a snoop."

Pestia eyed the little, white thing suspiciously. Her black hair on her neck and around the little face, to him, only accented her whiteness. She looked so disgusting it was hard for him to think of her as a sentient being and not some subterranean mole-person shaken out of the bowels of the earth by some calamity.

Barbara read the repulsion on his face. "Look," she went on shrugging her shoulders and sending her hands into the air, "if I had wanted to do something bad to you I could have while you were sleeping. I didn't mean any harm." His disgusted, snarling countenance stood, so Barbara turned away, sat on the bed, took the remote control and started watching television.

Pestia was astounded at her sudden disengagement. Angered further by her indifference to his interrogation, he yelled, stamped a foot, and lapsed into a military bark. "Stand up! Answer questions! You have violated my property!"

Barbara turned off the television and stood up. This time, instead of feeling small and weak, perhaps because she had felt that way before, she threw the remote to the floor and yelled back, "I told you what I was doing! If you don't like it, tough shit. I don't particularly like the way you look at me, talk to me, or act. You can take that attitude and shove it."

Pestia's mouth dropped open. This was highly unexpected. An entire year on planet earth and this was the first person who had screamed at him. It was a healthy slap in the face for the big, injured, and vulnerable man. Barbara's face was flushed red with anger. Pestia flashed back to her embarrassed red face as she lay on the floor, then back to the present. He kind of liked the way the red looked. For the first time he saw a different kind of texture in the skin. He saw the small, white hair on the face, the pores, the interesting red lips.

Barbara saw him growing puzzled, then turn his head. "What's wrong?" she asked, none too nicely, yet worried about his sudden pallor.

Pestia felt odd, almost as odd as he was ill. He had suddenly recognized another being. Though he had been in close proximity for more than a year now, he had yet to realize the equivalence in the differences between them. Knowing he was to encounter beings on another planet, he had always expected differences. He had just assumed all the differences would be a demonstration of them being inferior. With the substandard social controls, the second-rate technology, he had just assumed the beings themselves were also inferior. The assumptions caved-in on themselves, leaving Pestia with deep introspection.

"Nothing is wrong," he said staring into the mirror. "I am sorry I yelled at you. Please do not look into my luggage until you have obtained permission."

Barbara picked up the remote and lounged back onto the bed feeling better about the situation, but still tense. She turned on the television and Pestia wandered into the restroom. He locked the door and looked into the mirror. There, he saw a man; not a general, not a highly stationed official, not a protector of the last vestiges of the empire, but only a man. A man in great pain; one whose pain was getting worse; he saw an older man with foibles, hates, likes, dislikes, and folly. The lines on the side of his eyes were more prominent than he remembered. Pestia, living through the hell of life, was feeling his impermanence. The adrenalin from hearing his alarm was wearing off. He felt weak. He did not believe there was much time now.

As his eyes clouded, memories from home came to him. Sweet, touching memories of family and pride of station. He alone had risen through the ranks to control the military. Confidant to the King he had been. Yet, it all seemed so distant, as if he were peering into someone else's life, or into a former life he had already moved beyond. As the clouds grew thicker, the pain more dominant, the figure in the mirror changed. The transposed image filled Pestia with calm. A great friend was there, the one last seen in the hall of euthanasia. He smiled at the old general and raised his hand against the glass as Pestia did too. Pestia could feel the touch of the glass all the way to his soul. The image spoke. "I forgive you my friend Pestia," the image of his gracious friend said, and then nothing more.

George pulled the old truck into the motel entrance. In through the window of the office he could see the old manager bobbing his head around, craning to get a look at the entering vehicle. George knew by the demeanor, the degree of inspection, something was wrong. He wondered if his seatbelt was dragging outside or if something was wrong with the truck. Or, at least, he hoped it was the truck. He parked and watched the old man come across the parking lot in his rearview mirror. George knew by the hustle in his step the truck was fine; there must be something wrong with the room.

Even though it was hot, the old fellow was wearing a dingy sweater over the top of his sweat stained undershirt. George decided to roll down the window and wait for him there. The old man stomped right up to the driver's side. "I want to ask you," he started, dispensing with salutations, "just how many people you registered in that room."

George felt a tinge of shame at having done something so petty as having lied about the number of people going into the room. He had registered himself only, figuring it would better cover their tracks if someone were looking. And it would save a few of what were becoming precious dollars. "Only me," he said with a smile.

The old man got a wide silly grin on his face. "That a fact?" he said sarcastically. "Well, seems like the mice are doing a fine job of making a ruckus."

George felt his face flush a little, then tried to be defensive. "I don't know what you're talking about. I'm kind of busy so . . ."

"Well now," the old man continued, breaking into a full smile, "why don't we go on up there and see. Better yet, why don't I just call the police and have them go up there with us?"

George's whole body tensed at the sound of the word 'police'. He smiled back to the inquisitive little face. "OK, I got two others. I'm sorry."

"Now, I just don't understand people like you. Is having no extra bed, towel and soap really worth that much money? You don't look like no scroungy type. Why the hell . . ." The old man went on to give George a good lecture on the perfidy of modern Americans and on how it 'used to be'. George felt positively awful about the scene, feeling as if he were an incredibly cheap bum. He let his eyes roll to the sky during the monologue. The high cirrus clouds were streaking over the dirty brown, smog laden sky, making it all a little more sticky and humid to go along with the annoyance of heat. When the old man finished, George apologized again, handed him the extra cash necessary, and grew into an awful mood.

The little, window-mounted air-conditioner made quite a racket from the outside. George rightly guessed the other two occupants of the room must have been raising quite a commotion to have drawn attention to themselves. This certainly was not going very smoothly. His last credit card was now at its limit. The lady at the bank had been rather snide about it all. An overdrawn check had been there to greet him. The last of his savings just covered the bounced check with enough to spare for a little gas, food and for what could be only a couple more days worth of cash. Thinking about the money turned his mood more sour than ever.

George flung open the door, the large, plastic room number attached to the key rattled around. He saw Barbara lying on the bed. She gave him what he thought of as a nasty look and he set his bag of groceries on the table. He just wasn't in the mood. He closed the door and turned to the little lady. "What the hell kind of noise was going on in here?"

Barbara then, by anyone's standards, did give him a nasty look. She turned off the television and, since it had worked before, stood and slung the remote to the floor. Bouncing on the floor the remote turned the television back on. "Look," she said in a muted, strained voice. "I don't know what you people think I am but I'm not going to be talked to like a child. If you can't treat me like an adult, then don't talk. And I'm out of here. Understand?"

It was the last straw. The evening before he had saved her life and now he had just spent nearly the last of his money bringing her some food. He blew. "All right," George snapped, "then get your prima donna little butt out-a here. And while your at it, say hello to your big buddy for us. Before he tortures you to death, that is. Just make sure and understand we ain't going out of our way to save you again."

Barbara saw that her little role play for respect was falling flat. She sat back down on the bed, instantly changing moods. "Well, now that you put it that way," she said with a little smile, "I guess it isn't all that bad. What's for lunch?"

George wasn't apt to change moods so suddenly. "See for yourself. You can do something, can't you? Where's Frank?"

"He's in the bathroom."

"What's he doing?"

Barbara resisted a smart-assed answer and only shook her head. "I don't know," she said, "He's been in there quite a while."

George didn't hear her. He walked past her to the television suddenly mesmerized. On the screen was a smartly dressed woman. In one corner, on an inset of the scene, was a photograph of Mark.

"Turn it up," he said to Barbara. Then louder, "Turn it up!"

Barbara bent over and fiddled with the remote as fast as possible. The sound faded in. "It is the first confirmed sighting of the Mystery Hero," the lady crooned excitedly, "since his disappearance nearly two weeks ago. Our man, Bernard Regal, is on the scene in Barstow. Bernard, what do you have for us."

The scene changed to the desert, where a curly haired man with a phony English accent stood in front of the barren landscape in desert battle fatigues. "Well Maria, San Bernardino County Sheriffs yesterday received two separate reports of having seen presumed Mystery Hero Mark Johnson at a local liquor store east of town. The liquor store is near, maybe appropriately enough, the ghost town of Calico. Unnamed sources inside the sheriff's department confirm the sightings and say that local officials are combing the area for further evidence."

"Bernard, what do police speculate as to the reason Mr. Johnson might be in the area?"

"Mr. Johnson has a history of heavy drinking and presumably he was here to buy liquor, though that has of yet not been confirmed."

"I mean, Barstow, surely there are many liquor stores in the state, but why one in Barstow? Bernard?"

"Yes, Maria, that seems to be the real mystery for the Mystery Hero right now. Why Barstow?"

"Turn it off," George said. "Goddamnit, turn it off."

George had crouched to one knee in front of the television as if before a shrine. He rose slowly. "Frank," he yelled to the bathroom. "Frank!" He started knocking on the door. "Frank!" There was no answer.

Taking his multiuse pocket knife out he pulled up a sharp dowel. He worked the dowel into the small hole on the knob until the lock clicked open. The door moved only a couple of inches before it was blocked against something. George pushed hard and poked in his head. By this time Barbara was standing over his shoulder. George stated the obvious. "Jesus, it's Frank. He's down."

George worked his way into the bathroom trying to be careful as the door was against Pestia's head and shoulder. He pulled Pestia's torso off the white linoleum far enough for the door to open fully. Dragging him by his one good arm he made his way for the bed. He struggled against his surprising weight.

George looked to Barbara who was standing silent, both hands up against her mouth. "For Christ's sakes," George snapped, "give me a hand."

Barbara bent to grab the bad arm, then thought better of it. She looked for an appropriate handle and decided to use his belt loops and drug him from there. They made it to the bed and, with substantial effort, got him on it. They both were breathing hard from the effort. They looked at the collapsed form, which was barely breathing. Their eyes met, both of them shook their heads.

"Holy shit," said Barbara, "just what the hell are we going to do now?"

CHAPTER TWENTY-NINE

"He won't get far," a chubby sheriff remarked, while wiping the sweat of his brow on his sleeve. "Not in this heat. The buzzards will lead us to him in no time at all. You get anything on that helicopter yet?"

The other sheriff, younger and much smaller, replied, "Nope. The dispatcher just started laughing. The brass don't think it's a real priority. They don't care who we're chasing. Says it's too expensive. Figure we can get him on foot. And they mean that we get him and get him right now."

The bigger sheriff took off his hat, brushed back his sweaty hair and clicked his tongue in disgust. "It ain't never a priority when they ain't the ones doin' the hiking. Jesus Christ. They tell us we got to get him now; then they tell us how we got to go and get him. Christ almighty. Well, call in for the dogs—if they'll give us that—and get your walking shoes on deputy. We're in for a long day."

The two cars were parked in front of a deep wash, with sharp banks, where a small dirt road had led them. Inside the wash, sticking nose first against the rocky bottom, was the car of their suspect, steam still hissing from the broken radiator. The man had fled on foot into the desert in the middle of the hot afternoon. As far as they could tell, he was carrying no water or supplies. The landscape undulated on sweeping hills which were covered on every square inch with rock and cactus. Some of the most foreboding parts of the Mojave desert were here. Topsoil, of a sort, could only be found in low spots like the wash. The rest was as grizzled and terrible for anything to live as any place on the planet. Both the sheriffs, especially the elder, did not relish having to hike out over the snake infested terrain.

The suspect could still be seen. Getting to him was the problem. You could see everything for miles in every direction not physically blocked by a rise. The cactus clung low to the ground and the cream-colored, squarish rocks were only large enough to make passage exceedingly difficult, ranging in size from a fist to a small file cabinet. The suspect was mounting one of the larger hills, now only the size of a speck in the distance. The dispatch office overruled the helicopter for more than the fact it was too expensive. Spotting someone in the desert was not the problem. Searching for a suspect was never a problem; it was only a matter of running him down and the helicopter would not necessarily help because it had no place to land. So, the sheriffs were required to go and get him on foot.

Had he been a lower profile supposed suspect than that of Mark Johnson himself, of television and tabloid fame, the standard procedure would have been to wait for him to come crawling back with his tongue hanging out to beg for water. They had done this passive procedure before with criminals ranging from drunk drivers to murderers. Everyone of them would, without exception, at some point, stagger or crawl back, harmless as a kitten, praying for one drop of liquid. But this one was different. This arrest was going to be made under the glare of public attention and doing something as callous as letting a man go into the desert with the possibility he might die of thirst was not something the department was willing to admit to under the glare of a television audience.

The radio in the car of the older officer sparked to life. He leaned in the window grabbing the microphone. "Yeah?" he said.

The voice on the other end was of a fellow sergeant. "Hey Pete. Thought you might want to know that the television trucks that were parked out front sped out-a here like a bat out-a hell a few minutes ago. Little more than a coincidence I think."

The sheriff clicked his tongue again. "Who the hell tipped them off?"

"I can't prove it, but you know who."

"Boulding!" yelled the chubby sheriff. "That fat mouthed son of a bitch. I'm gonna cram my fist right down his throat. That's all we need is a stinking television crew."

As if on cue, a large white van with a satellite dish on top appeared over a ridge on the highway and slowed at the opening of the dirt road. The larger sheriff pointed to the opening. "Get your unit down there and block it," he yelled to the younger man. "Don't say a damn word either. We already got one fat mouth in this department. We don't need two."

The young man jumped in his cruiser and roared down the road in reverse. As there wasn't room in between the rocks on either side to get around him it effectively blocked the road. He met the television van about seventy yards down the dirt track just in time to see another, similarly outfitted van, come off the highway.

The older sheriff threw his hat to the ground in disgust. "Shit almighty," he mumbled. "Goddamned reporters can get here before my backup. Jesus. Where's that canine unit?" He picked up his binoculars from the front seat and looked for his suspect. The large, black shape had travelled much further than expected. The sheriff just caught the last of him disappearing over the ridge, probably some three and a half miles away, still running at a good clip.

The sheriff grabbed his radio again. "Dispatch," he growled into the microphone, "where the hell's my canine?"

The dispatcher, a man familiar with the older sheriff, came on with a sarcastic tone. "Well, well, if it ain't officer tenderfoot. I didn't know you were so anxious to get on with your duty of keeping the snakes company."

"Cut the crap," the sheriff snapped. "I got two . . . now three television vans breathing down my ass and a whole parcel of movie jockeys to go with them. Get me my unit so I can get the hell out of here."

"Already on the way. By the way, should we hold the bowling for you tonight or are you going to be able to fit into your shoes?"

The sheriff didn't reply and threw the microphone back into the car. "Fuck off," he mumbled under his breath. The speaker on the radio continued without a response. "Take comfort," the voice said, "that you're going to be the most famous tenderfoot the world has ever seen."

The big man saw his backup coming over the rise in the distance and started down toward the reporters who were now overwhelming the young officer. "Get those vans out-a here," he yelled. "Let my backup through. Get those vans the hell out-a here."

The canine unit could only advance a hundred yards or so closer to the scene with the vans out of the way, but it was more important to the sheriff to occupy the reporters and crews with something other than asking questions. The vans backed up, but three reporters, one from each van, each with a camera man, stayed behind to begin the inquisition.

"Sheriff, who's your suspect? Is it Johnson?" one silly looking reporter asked.

"No comment."

"Why the dogs?" asked a reporter who the chubby sheriff recognized from newscasts.

"Lots a small crevices and holes a man can hide in out there. The dogs will take us right to him."

"So it is a male suspect," the goofy reporter opined. "Can you confirm an African-American suspect?"

"No comment." The chubby sheriff motioned to his advancing backup. "Come on. Let's go."

The sheriff ordered the younger man to stay with the reporters and to keep them from following. There were three other officers, each with one dog. The big sheriff started down into the wash sliding on the bank which broke away under his feet. By the time he came out the other side, several hundred yards along, sweat was already starting down his face and stinging his eyes. The rocks were rough going, bending his ankles back and forth despite the heavy boots. Pulling him eagerly forward, his dog sniffed judiciously over each rock, instinctively steering clear of the gnarled and stunted cactus. About thirty minutes into the chase the big, old sheriff heard a distinctive noise. It was a helicopter. He glanced around and stood still until he could make out the craft. It was coming in fairly low and made a tight circle around him and his men, who were fanned out to either side. The lettering on the side read, 'Eye-witness News 30'. The big sheriff stared for a moment, then mumbled, "Jesus Christ. This is going to be one hell of a circus."

CHAPTER THIRTY

George turned up the car radio when the news flash hit. Barbara had been dozing but was roused by the louder noise. It was very hot and everyone had a bad case of body odor. Barbara felt wretched in her dirty clothes. Wind battered her hair into knots through the open window. It was the only respite from the brutal afternoon heat. She turned around and glanced at Pestia slumbering uneasily in his cramped position in the back-seat. These were rough conditions for the healthy let alone for someone so sick.

"Shelby Benson is on the scene," the announcer on the radio said. "Shelby, what do you have for us."

"Well, Bob, it is truly an incredible scene. We're out here some thirty miles east of Barstow, just off highway forty. San Bernardino county sheriffs are believed to have cornered Mystery Hero and suspected murderer, Mark Johnson, in a parameter triangle some twenty-five to thirty square miles in area between highways fifteen and forty. The suspect was seen heading north across the rugged terrain after crashing his car into a dry creek bed while trying to elude sheriff deputies on a high speed chase. The sheriffs have called in the dogs to track Johnson and they are hoping to capture him before nightfall."

"What's the scene like currently, Shelby?"

"I'll tell you Bob, it's very rugged territory here, as many have seen on the live pictures. Just a surreal feeling watching the fugitive scramble over rocks while being tracked on the ground by sheriffs and from the air by the eye-witness news-copter. The mood of the local officers is one of confidence. They expect to get their man. They are being joined in the manhunt by Los Angeles detectives assigned to the Johnson case and they too share this confidence. With us is sergeant Espinoza of Los Angeles homicide. Sergeant Espinoza, what makes everyone so confident that you can finally pin down this elusive suspect?"

Sergeant Espinoza smoothed his hair back, stared nervously into the camera and responded, "Well, as you can see, this isn't an easy place to hide in. It's very open terrain. We have the north and western approaches covered on the roads and are extending a perimeter across the desert to the east. If he can get out of this it will be a miracle. At least very unlikely."

The studio announcer jumped back in. "Shelby," he said, "can officer Espinoza pin down a more accurate time of when they expect to have Johnson in custody."

"No, Bob, they just said before nightfall. Sources in the sheriff's department tell me that, because of the rugged terrain, it's usual to let the suspect come to them because they can't hold out long without water and supplies. So even if they miss their man tonight, they fully expect to have him incarcerated by tomorrow morning at the latest."

"What do you mean by 'letting the suspect come to them'?" the announcer went on, "Do you mean that . . ."

George flipped off the radio and shook his head. Barbara could feel the car speed up. It was still at least an hour to Barstow. Across the mountains which ring the metropolis of Los Angeles the terrain grows steadily more dry and barren. It was a hot and lazy scene not conducive to sustaining anxious circumstances. The sun and ground gave off a pummeling sort of heat far more conducive to despair. The sky, beyond the San Bernardino mountains, was now a real blue out of reach of the valley smog. The road had multiple lanes and was wide and ran straight toward the horizon. It seemed wholly incongruent to have such a wide highway running in a place so devoid of human life. Yet swarms of cars were on the road, going somewhere.

"I don't want to sound like a pain in the ass," Barbara said, "but do you know what we're going to do when we get there?"

George adjusted his grip on the steering wheel and shook his head. His mood was poor. He tried to run what the man had said over in his mind for clues as to a more exact position. He reached up and flipped the radio back on.

". . . it seems to be the case. As reported earlier on First Report, the suspect Mark Johnson is believed to be trapped in a rugged area of desert east of Barstow. After a high speed chase by sheriff deputies, Johnson reportedly wrecked his car into a dry creek bed and continued on foot. We will keep you up to date on that. In other news today . . ."

George flipped off the radio again. "Damn it," he said. "Things are just not looking too good right now."

CHAPTER THIRTY-ONE

The old pick-up truck, an oxidized blue color, with rusted cattle racks rattling loosely as the bald tires bounced over the wash-board ruts, pulled up to the dilapidated trailer. The following column of dust now washed over the top of the old machine choking the occupants, causing them to cough and irritating their eyes. Had someone been watching carefully, they would have noticed the meandering quality of the truck's advance and how it had come nearly to a halt on the highway before laboring around a turn which took it wide off the track and over several large rocks. They could have listened to the long delay between gear shifts and the grinding, retry, grinding, and retry before the next gear was found, and seen the clumsy way the vehicle lurched forward when the clutch was mishandled. From the evidence, it would not have taken long to decipher the condition of the driver.

Millard shook his old, chrome door handle back and forth, slowly at first, then with more agitation. The entire trim of the inside was gone lying bare the sheet metal and window. You could look right into the door cavity, as Millard did, as if he were going to decipher what was wrong with the interworking of his handle.

"Fuck, goddamn," he mumbled slowly, reflecting his drunkenness. "Hey Sammy. You havin' any luck with yers?"

Mark smiled at the little man and replied cordially, "What of mine should I be having luck with?"

The old man wheezed out a laugh and laid his head onto the big, hard steering wheel. "Why you natty headed, dingle ball," he gasped out between giggles, "yer door handle. Any luck with your door handle?"

Mark calmly reached behind the old farmer and pulled open the door lock. Millard craned his neck around to gaze at the lock, then back to Mark.

"Holy Christ," Millard said shaking his head. He reached up with a hand to smack the top of his crown in disbelief forgetting the battered cowboy hat already resting there. The limp hand slapped at the hat which pushed the brim down over squinting and bloodshot eyes. The mouth remaining visible under the brim first drooped open in amazement, then broke into a wide mouthed smile—showing a host of broken, yellow teeth atop receding gums. The smile was accompanied by wheezing noises that must have been a squealing giggle. "Goddamn, shit Sammy, we're drunk."

"Yes we are," Mark concurred, "I think that is readily apparent by our actions."

Millard pushed up the brim of his hat with an index finger, blinking his eyes to focus on his large, black friend, his demeanor suddenly more serious. "You know what Sammy?" he said wobbling a bit on the old spongy bench-seat. "You know what? You talk funny. Just where the hell you from anyhow?"

Mark paused before responding in order to get another gulp from the bottle first. He lifted it off the floor boards and pulled out the old wine cork which had been shoved into the screw top bottle.

Millard saw this travesty and started slapping clumsily at Mark's big hands. "No, no, damn you," he said, "use yer teeth like I taught you, ya godamned, dusty-headed, natty, dingle ball."

Mark pushed the cork back into the bottle with his teeth, smiled and returned the bottle to Millard. There had been a rather lengthy, prior discussion as to the benefits of corks over screw tops and as to how Millard always kept an extra few corks around for the current bottle. Millard believed it was more than just preference. He believed it a safety issue. A screw top required more attention than a cork and sometimes needed two hands to deal with it, thus leaving the steering wheel unattended. A cork, however, could be dealt with by a set of firm choppers and a single handed yank while the eyes never left the road. Mark debated, for a while, the safety benefits of a screw top when re-closing the container, since a cork was often lost when spit out to take a drink, but caved in gracefully to Millard's forceful debate. "No, no," Millard had protested, "Ya see. If ya ain't a ninny or a complete drunk ya don't have to spit it out. Just leave the cork between yer teeth while ya take a drink. Then you can keep track of it. Cain't do that with no screw top." Millard then took it upon himself to demonstrate the maneuver, gagged on trying to swallow, blew whiskey out of his nose and had to swerve to the shoulder for an emergency stop. Tears flew out of Millard's eyes and snot from his proboscis along with the ferociously burning liquid. Mark stayed doubled over in laughter for at least five minutes.

"See there," the old man said as if something had been proved by him using his teeth on the cork, "easy as pie. You just remember that and how to drive when yer seein' double and you won't have no problemo." He handed the bottle to Mark.

Mark took a swig then pulled the bottle back from his lips wondering about the 'seeing double' part of Millard's diatribe. He looked at Millard. "Seeing double?" he asked.

"Yer just like all them young, little farts. Don't keep good advice five seconds. Now, for the second time, when yer seein' double, ya stick yer head out the window for fresh air ta feed the brain and ya close one eye so ya don't see double no more. That's what I was doin' back there. I ain't no poodle tryin' to flap my tongue. I was just tryin' to show you how to drive straight. Is that what you think. I sa poodle?"

"These are certainly interesting safety tips. But isn't driving intoxicated itself a dangerous activity? And is it not illegal?"

Millard flapped his head up and down loosely. "Sure it is," he agreed. "But that's for them who don't know how to drive when they're drunk safe like me. Now if you learn how to drive safe when yer drunk like me—like I'm teachin' ya—then don't pay no mind to that."

Mark took a swig and handed the bottle to Millard. The old farmer took a long, slow sip, then reached up to scratch his head under his hat. The hat fell into the bench seat beside him exposing his sweaty, white hair. "Seems I was gonna ask you something," he said. "What the hell was it? You know Sammy, I like drinkin' with you. All my friends, or ex-friends, all start gettin' mean or serious or starts cryin' all over themselves when they drink anymore. I don't need no fancy house or fancy car or wine, women, or song, all I want to do is to die with peace of mind. Nobody drinks to have fun no more but me. Not even my shit-for-brains boy drinks for fun. You drink for fun, don't you Sammy?"

Mark felt funny at the question. It probed at his motives which were not secure or clear to himself. He smiled and said, "Sure, I drink for fun."

"Yeah," Millard concurred, "me too. It's fun damn it. Tomorrow ain't no fun. But that's what's so good about bein' drunk: You don't care about tomorrow." The skinny farmer slapped his dusty jeans in recognition of his humor, but the levity was quickly lost. "Seems I was goin' to ask you somethin'," he continued, scratching at his bony chest at the opening of his shirt.

Mark shook his head and pushed his dark glasses back up his nose from where they had been drooping for quite a while. "I believe you asked me something about my form of speech."

"That's it," Millard said trying to snap his fingers in recognition but failing. "You talk funny. Where the hell you from?"

Mark smiled broadly. "Why, from another planet, of course."

Millard started wheezing out a laugh which mixed with a cough turning his whole head red from the neck up. "Well," he gasped, in-between the giggles and coughs, "you sure act like yer from some other planet." He pulled open the door latch and promptly flopped down onto the hard dirt like an old sack of bones.

Somewhere in the middle of the night Mark's eyes came open abruptly with a rush of adrenalin that had finally overcome the saturation of alcohol. In his hard breathing and sweat no particular thoughts came to mind, only vague feelings of guilt and shame. He stumbled up off the cracked vinyl couch, clothes were littered everywhere. Only one thing drove him: to find a source of water to quench his thirst. He could not remember having fallen on the sofa the night before. The last events of the horrendous drunk were lost on him. He tripped over items littering the floor and made his way to the sink. He cupped his hands under the mineral crusted spigot and drank long on the rusty water. He finished by splashing the water around his face and onto the back of his neck. It was then he noticed the light. An odd, soft, whitish light coming in from every crack and window, uniform as if the entire atmosphere outside had become magical, glowing plasma.

Mark stumbled to a dirty window and looked to the heavens. Up there he found a large, white eye staring back at him. Ah yes, he thought, the moon; the wonderful orb which graces and eases the night. They had told him of the orb before coming, yet it was more beautiful than he had imagined. He imagined the hypnotizing circle as a hole in the blackness of space leading back to his home. His home for nineteen years. Friends his age were now fifty years old—at least for any who were still alive. If he could leave for a return today they would be eighty when he arrived, and he not yet twenty-one. His father was now dead. His mother had died years ago when he was still a child. He stared hard into the porthole trying to imagine his world, the friends, the foods, the familiar places which had always brought solace. He wondered what of those things still survived. He remembered how the school children had taunted him for being the prince, for sticking out, for being different. He remembered crying at his father's feet wanting to be nothing more than another normal child, un-tethered to responsibility, not having to take such a prominent position among his peers.

He felt rather immature at the moment, as if he had transported his emotions back to the earlier time. He had found in the last year he rather liked drinking, liked it too much. It was a good way to amuse himself and he rarely thought about home when was drinking. He assumed Pestia was now gone and knew he should take better care of himself. But perhaps he was drinking because Pestia was gone. He knew hundreds of thousands, perhaps millions, had died at the hands of Matan personally, yet the thought of the general, this lone, brave sentry, perishing at the Premier's hands, so far from home, was a greater travesty to the Prince than all who had perished before. The thought of going back to his home to be king was diminished because of it. For a year, as news from back home on the monitors became more cheery, he had dreamed of he and his friend going back together and not he alone.

The young man thought about his new home and felt the irony of living in a republic—it had been a republic which had driven him from his home. Yet, this was a different sort. People in this republic seemed free to speak their minds. No-one was lurking around the corner to run blasphemers into the dungeon. No-one was there to tell the press what to write, and who to hate. He had grown to loathe the very word 'Republic', but this was very different indeed. The citizens of the United States were not yet controlled by the spending habits of a super-wealthy class. The prince saw evidence of some of this happening, but the degree to which it was perpetrated was less by leaps. He wondered at the difference. What made the monarchy of Bren such a good thing and the monarchies of earth so tyrannical? What made the Republic of the United States so free and the Republic of Ranson so evil? Was it only a matter of time before one resembled the other? Did the system of government employed change the people, and were the differences in outcome, good and bad, merely logistic? Or did the people change the kind of system employed, and was the outcome predicated on the mettle of citizenry with-in it? He continued his thoughts and reminiscings until he grew very tired.

The Prince stared at the moon so long it formed a spot on his retina so its image stayed even when he closed his eyes. He dwelt on the spot, still present on his closed eyes, and grew both sad and resolved. Perhaps it would have been better to have come here by himself. He then would have had to take full responsibility for his actions. Perhaps he would not have caused such foolishness as he had done; as any young man would have; as a young man he wished he was. He pondered his state and recalled his father had not taken the throne until he was thirty-seven. His father had been well known in his youth for his lust for life and everything else within his grasp; this was expected of young men and women in Bren. He would not have the same opportunities as his father. And Pestia would have no other opportunities at all. The Prince felt very alone, flopped onto the couch, and slipped into an uneasy sleep.

CHAPTER THIRTY-TWO

"Just what the hell do you mean, 'We can't find him'?" the sheriff's superintendent said squinting his eyes and leaning close to the seated sheriff.

The larger sheriff, who had led the initial chase to the dry wash, sat with anger in his face to augment his sunburn until it reached beet red. He worked his raw toes around in his boots uneasily and licked at his chapped lips. He was disgusted with the supervisor for not having approved the helicopter to do the job right, and not allowing him the latitude to simply wait out the suspect when it wasn't approved. He was so hot, tired and disgusted the sheriff seriously considered sticking a middle finger up into the superintendent's face and walking out. Somehow, he managed a growling answer instead. "That news-copter kept pretty good track of him," he snapped in response. Though raw, he considered his smart aleck answer a vast improvement over what he wanted to say, and hence, in contrast, above insubordination. His supervisor didn't see it that way.

"That'll be all of that kind of horse-shit Pete," the supervisor said stiffening. "You know why you didn't get any chopper. If you can't do your duty, then tell me that. Then we'll find someone who can do the job. Understand?"

The big old sheriff shifted around in the wooden chair more annoyed than before, just more determined to control it. The superintendent always had a way of twisting every little outburst back toward the totality of his job. He always made it seem like any little incident, no matter how insignificant, could destroy years of hard work and discipline—under this superintendant the job always seemed on the line. Sometimes the old sheriff felt like a pressure cooker which couldn't let out any steam, the pressure just kept building and building and building.

The superintendent saw the determined man's lips press together until they turned white and decided to back off a little. "Well anyway," he said, "you're going to get your birds tomorrow. L.A. county is going to loan us two for the day. But only for one day."

On mention of the helicopters the old sheriff's jaw made an audible knock shut in disgust. Now he was really pissed off. He had to spend the whole day getting torn by cactus, scared to death by snakes, and nearly passing out from the heat to get what he had needed in the first place. He crossed his hairy, sun burned arms and stared down at the floor.

The supervisor sat down on the front of his desk and continued with his business-like tone. "You're going to have to come up with a briefing pretty soon," he continued, "the press is chomping at the bit. Don't expect them L.A. city boys to bail you out with any excuses either. They're just as mad at us as the press." The supervisor paused for just a second, then pressed on as if the sheriff had been given enough time to formulate a rejoinder. "Well?" he queried. "What the hell you going to tell them?"

The big sheriff kept his head down. I'm going to tell them, he thought, that my lazy, cheap-skate, good-for-nothin', mother fucker boss don't give me the tools to do my job then puts me on the hot seat.

"Well?" the supervisor crowed.

The sheriff swallowed hard and looked back up. "I'm gonna tell them the truth," he said. At the mention of the word 'truth' the supervisor's face took a more stern 'don't-you-dare' look to it. That particular word had long since taken on a double meaning for everyone in the department. Telling the 'truth' was often a code phrase meaning something more like, 'to hell with diplomacy, I'm out to screw you'. The sheriff took note of his boss' defensive posture, having already considered the alternate meaning of 'truth', but continued on a more career-safe course. "I'm gonna tell them that we didn't find him. That the dogs couldn't get no scent and they didn't do nothin' but howl around in circles. It's dark now and that we'll get the son of a bitch in the mornin'. How's that?"

"That'll do," the superintendent said standing, allowing his severe expression fade to something more professional. "Everything else is a great, big 'no comment'. The birds are going to be in at five a.m. Make your teams and have them ready to start in concert on the hour. You're going to need a good night's sleep. Let's go face the cameras. Ready?"

The old sheriff creaked to his feet, joints aching, feet throbbing. The thought of another day out on the desert made everything hurt just a little more, even if it might be from a helicopter. On the way out the door, toward the bright lights and flashing cameras, one might think the big, aching man, rarely under the glare of cameras, would be rehearsing his statement nervously to himself. Rather, still seething from his supervisor's reaming, he was thinking angrily, 'Birds! What a stupid thing to call a helicopter'.

George waited out the night full of anxiety. Pestia did not regain consciousness on the trip or in the transfer to the new room—a laborious effort for the two conscious members of the team—and began to look worse. He watched Barbara sleep, envious of her lack of attention to the crises at hand. Instead of being angry with her, though, he thought she looked pitiable with her bruised and scratched face. Sleeping peacefully, curled up on one side, she reminded him of his own daughter who he had not seen in nearly six months. Hair in a mess, no make-up, bruises and all she did look more like a waif than a professional woman. When she was awake he was continually annoyed by her apparent lack of devotion to him and Frank. She seemed detached, aloof, not willing to offer suggestions; much like his own daughter seemed to him. Maybe it was more his perception or maybe it was his own bull-headedness.

When morning finally came George and Barbara monitored the television for news continuously, in shifts, or together. The day before, upon first arrival in Barstow, George had gone out to the site of the crash. At the now famous wash he could get no closer than the end of the dirt road before sheriffs chased him away. He had circled around to the highway on the north and poked his way along the dusty roadside using his binoculars to scan the horizon hoping beyond all hope he would see something, anything. Later in the afternoon, however, several hundred curiosity seekers began to move in along the road in front and behind with some stopped along the shoulder. Hours drifted on toward sunset and the sheriffs began to take a dim view of the crowd, wanting to clear everyone out before dark. When George saw a sheriff he was all too familiar with—the tall, gawking man from the hospital—he retreated to the hotel in despair, not wanting to draw any sort of excess attention to himself. He didn't really know what he was doing anyway. He had hoped something would develop en route, maybe see one of the assassins, or pick up on a clue.

Barbara stood up and flapped her blouse out and in to dispel some of the odor collecting there. "I've got to take a shower," she said. "And I've got to get some clothes to change into."

As usual, George was not listening and was lost in his own line of thought—Barbara's statement acted only to trigger what was on his mind. There was quite a lot to be on the mind of the old soldier. Frank's condition not the least of it all. Although George knew that Frank tolerated him more than he liked him, in the last week George had grown a strong allegiance toward his large companion. Frank had become his sudden mentor in the domain of interstellar politics, travel, and intrigue, and George lapped it up with all speed. George knew his questions were tiresome, and often annoying, but he couldn't help himself. When would another opportunity such as this come? He even allowed himself to begin a fantasy of returning with the fleet to act as an unofficial emissary from earth; he didn't have much keeping him here anymore. Yet, fantasy made it all seem less real and this caused George to keep a tight reign on any imagination.

This next musing of the moment had to do with one item: money. He was broke. There was no more checking account, savings, or credit limits to push. The only assets legally remaining was his old, battered four-wheel drive and a handful of clothes. And his truck, at this moment, was several hundred miles away, parked on the street in front of the home of a friendly acquaintance. George had only planned to leave it there a couple of days while Frank and he consolidated their operations. Perhaps it was now impounded as derelict, taken from the street in front of the house of a now unfriendly acquaintance. He would not have blamed him much if he had the old hulk towed away. George had not felt this wretched and wanting for cash in his entire adult life.

George followed Barbara's statement with his own agenda. "I'm not proud to say this," he started, "but I'm going to need some money. We're going to need money. Is there anyway you can get a hold of some?"

Barbara at first recoiled from the suggestion, reflexively indignant at the request from a near stranger, instantly suspicious of his motives. She then tried to hold the solicitation in an objective balance. The balance not forthcoming, she opted for an easy way out. "I don't see how," she said slapping at her pockets. "I don't have my wallet, identification or anything. My purse is way back at Jeremy's."

"What about friends, relatives or parents? They could wire you the money."

Barbara hadn't expected such a quick slamming of her escape hatch. She rolled her eyes to one corner of the room, away from George, thinking fast. "Well, wouldn't you need some kind of identification to pick the money up?"

George stayed leaps ahead of her on the reasoning curve. "Not with wired money," he said efficiently. "You can pick it up with a password. You could get money from the bank by answering test questions about your accounts, but that would be too risky. Risky, that is, if you still want to be here to help."

"Oh," Barbara said shaking her head up and down trying to look relieved, thinking furiously. "What if, uh . . . what if they are, uh . . . what if the police are monitoring the phone and know where to come to."

George was feeling a mixture of anger at her elusiveness and embarrassment at having to ask. From the start he wasn't sure how to handle her. He didn't know whether to send her to the police to beg for protection or to take her under his wing. He had tended toward the former while Pestia had argued to keep her as an eventual decoy for the assassins, to draw them out. Now she knew the whole story, however, and Frank was out of the picture, so he needed her to help. To George it was a simple matter of logistics. Anyway, if she were to go to the police now it would prove damaging to their cause—the assassins, as of yet, did not know who was on their trail and in one visit to the police the press would oblige them all information. Her demeanor, though, told him she didn't really want to stay. He realized he hadn't actually asked her if she wanted to or not. Asking could either force her to commit a little more to the cause or, at worst, get someone so non-committal the hell out of the way.

"Barbara," George said, "if you don't want to stay and help, you don't have to. We thought we were helping to protect you. The assassins probably don't need you anymore anyway—now that the whole world knows where Mark is. All I ask, is that if you get picked up by the police—which you will—you don't tell them anything about us. That is, if you can stand to do so after your first experience of lying to the police."

As it put her in a quandary as he pressed for the money, it put her in a quandary he had suddenly given up. She tried to play it the other way. "Well, how am I supposed to get home?"

George was still laps ahead. "If you want to go home," he said, more businesslike than before, "Pick up the phone.

Dial nine, one, one, and say, 'my name is Barbara Cerasoli'. The police will do the rest."

The double edge to his reasonableness put Barbara into mental quicksand, stuck and sinking fast. She sat down on the foot of the bed and looked at the pale and sweating body of Pestia. "If I go," she said, "who's going to take care of him?"

George let out a disgusted groan and scratched his head. "Look, if you're going to stay," he said shaking his hands in the air for an irritated emphasis, "you're going to have to pitch in some money. If your going to go . . ."

"I know, I know," Barbara interrupted, the soft tone of her voice telling George she was surrendering. "I just meant to say I could help out by staying. I'm going to stay. I'll call my parents. They're the only people I know with any money."

George accepted her de facto apology and was already on the march. "We'll use a phone away from here just in case your parents are being monitored. We won't know it's being monitored unless they tell us. Would they tell us?"

Barbara waggled her head, got a mournful look on her face and responded, "Probably not."

George thought for a second, then asked, "Will they go to the police if it's not?"

Barbara shrugged her shoulders. "Maybe. You can never tell."

They went to a pay phone several blocks removed from the hotel. The call was humiliating for Barbara. Her buzzed father railed on one line while her fawning mother cried on the other. She told them she was fine but needed a couple of hundred dollars to get back home. They didn't believe her. Perhaps because she *was* deceiving them she was incensed by their skepticism. She checked her anger and held to the plan of getting some money. They assented only after Barbara groveled for quite sometime. The money would be wired to the local Western Union station and she could pick it up tomorrow. Barbara put down the phone, shook her head in disgust, and turned to George. "I sure hope this works," she said. "I would hate to have gone through that for nothing."

The burley, old sheriff squinted his eyes to keep the sand and dust out as he stepped off the noisy helicopter, one hand holding a handkerchief over his mouth. He could feel the noise of each blade swipe rumble right through his torso and it felt like someone was playing bongos on his ears. This continued until he was well out of range of the whirling shafts of steel. The day had been long and he had never realized before how afraid he was of flying in a helicopter. His legs shook and his shoulders were so tight from anxiety they ached almost as bad as his feet had the previous day. He was thankful to be off the precarious, unsteady platform, but mortified to see the superintendent himself waiting at the staging area. He had hoped to put off what he thought would be a dismal confrontation until he got back to the station. Behind the sheriff's supervisor, on the other side of a cordoned-off area, the crowd of reporters stood, two to three times larger than it had been for the morning's briefing. He blinked at the swirling dust and hoped the departing craft could somehow raise enough of a cloud to camouflage and allow him to disappear from the area un-accosted by the waiting hoard and pretend he hadn't seen the superintendent at all. Spinning its nose away from the crowd the spindly craft leaned forward into the setting sun and took off.

The staging area was only a flat piece of dirt near the crash sight suitable for the landing of a helicopter. It was the first thing the superintendent chewed the sheriff out for. "For Christ's sakes," he snapped at the sheriff, ignoring pleasantries, "could you have found a dustier, more god-forsaken place than this to run briefings? We're only fifteen minutes from town. What's wrong with having them land near the station?"

The big man picked some pebbles out of his eyes. There really wasn't a place near the station for a helicopter, and it was logical to be near the search. He held his tongue.

"Nothing, huh?" the supervisor continued, grilling the officer. "What the hell is going on?"

Though his supervisor had started out berating him, the big sheriff shook it off. Today he was in a vastly improved mood—being scared in a helicopter was an enormous improvement over spending the whole day on the ground. He wiped his dusty, sticky lips on his sleeve. "I wish I knew, sir," he replied. "There's not a trace of the bastard; nothing from the dogs; nothing from the air; nothing from the perimeter; nothing. In this heat, two days, I gotta believe he's dying, dead or wishin' that he was. But where?"

The sun dipped low on the horizon showing off a crimson red body and a glorious, accompanying array of orange and reddish hues. The stack of reporters, not thirty feet away, seemed beaten and subdued from having spent the day in the heat. Not one of them was yelling a question. Every bit of the scene, the people, the cactus, and the rocks themselves seemed to be begging for the cool evening for a respite from the brutal afternoon heat.

The supervisor pulled a handkerchief out of his back pocket, wiped his face, and inspected the dirt trapped therein. "I don't know what the hell's going on," he said, softening his tone, and actually looking the sheriff in the eye for guidance.

The sheriff glanced at the reporters, then turned away lowering the brim of his hat and leaned against one of the squad cars parked there. "Well," he said, relishing the new and sudden attitude of his boss, "did they get anything from the car?"

"That's another weird thing," the supervisor said, "They got two sets of prints and neither one of them is Johnson's. L.A. city doesn't even think that Johnson is out there. After all this crap, boy, oh boy are we going to have one great big egg on our face if that isn't Johnson."

The big man was beginning to see the origin of his boss's new found humility: he was worried about the politics of the thing. "Well," he said, commiserating, "you don't go running out into the desert for no reason. He was running for some reason." The sheriff looked over at the media again. "They know that yet?" he said sending a thumb in their direction.

"Not yet. They're too busy with the other big story. That Cerasoli girl resurfacing."

"Oh yeah. I heard it on the radio this morning. What's she got to say?"

"Who the hell knows? Those L.A. boys think they own the goddamned station now. They got her sequestered like she was their own property."

The sheriff had found another reason for his supervisor's new found charity: he was losing control of the situation. Though he was enjoying the palsy-walsy comportment of his boss, as compared to the usual, he realized it was temporary and felt any deeper camaraderie would prove distasteful. "Well," he asked tying up the loose ended conversation, "should I give them a briefing?"

The superintendent scratched at his nice haircut and kicked at the dirt. "Hell, almost no need. They're already tired of what we got to say."

The big sheriff adjusted the brim of his hat higher and put his hands onto his pudgy hips. "Who?" he said demanding who the new spokesman was.

"Boulding."

"Boulding?" the big sheriff snapped, the hurt apparent in his voice.

"I didn't authorize it. He did."

"Who did?" snapped the big sergeant.

"Boulding, he took the call from Cerasoli's parents, didn't tell nobody and went down there by himself to get her. He's a goddamned hero now. Got his picture on every news show."

The sheriff kicked the dirt in disgust. "Why that big, fat-assed, son of a bitch. That's the only time in the last ten years he's gotten off his big, lard butt and now he's a hero."

CHAPTER THIRTY-THREE

His body could not hold out much longer; he knew that. He had been trained to push to the limit, he knew where it was, and it was close. He was not going to panic—it would only sap needed energy—but a real assessment of possible failure was necessary. Should he give in to his pursuers? Would it be possible to surrender and make them understand who he really was? If they would not afford him the status of an extra-terrestrial, would it be better to spend a lifetime in jail, or die a more honorable, albeit miserable, death in this desolation?

He had nothing but his trousers, some broken shoes, and a pocket knife, not even a shirt on his back. His trousers below the knee were shredded from cactus and the skin underneath ripped raw and swollen. Lips no longer resembled those of a normal man. They were cracked, blistered, swollen and bloodied until they stuck out from his face like a hideous beak. Nettles from cactus lined his swollen throat making it almost impossible to swallow and difficult to breath. Injuries from previous battles were slowing him. He had found bits of plastic he had sown together with his shoe laces to act as a barrier to the sun and camouflage. He had tried to spend most of the daylight hours under rocks, but frequently had to crawl out into the heat to find a new hiding place in order to avoid detection.

It was desperate, yet he was still alive, and he hadn't given up.

Hunger was not a concern. Hunger had yet to find a way through the thirst. Moisture can be found in some ingenious ways if you are trained. The desert here, however, yielded little moisture to even the best trained; even when they had good equipment; even when they weren't being chased by a group of armed assailants. Moisture was to be had in minuscule quantities. And after three days and two nights in this hell it was what Nagrom concentrated his entire effort upon. Sucking the juices from insects, drinking the blood of small reptiles, and constantly sucking moisture out of pieces of cactus which could be gleaned from the thorns, he made it through three horrible days—the cactus leaving the tenacious, little nettles in his throat as payment for their liquid. A man, crazed with heat and thirst, will do anything for moisture.

It was a fiercer desert than the worst of his home. Or, perhaps, he only imagined it as such since he was now here. Tonight was the third night and he was in his best position yet for eluding his would be captors, though his will was now lagging. He could see a highway and the lights of police cars waiting there. The highway denoted the northern perimeter of the dragnet. Had he been the same man as he was when he first set foot upon the planet earth, he would have already been loose of their grip. Twice he had had opportunity to kill one of them and both times he had held back. His position would have been greatly improved had he done so. They were equipped with weapons and, more importantly, they were carrying water, precious water. Instead, he buried himself deeper into his crack in the rocks and let them blunder stupidly by. He was sick of killing. The torture of Josiah had planted some fundamental seeds in the back of Nagrom's mind. Repulsively, the scene of breaking the policeman's neck played over in his mind. The weaker man had no chance. His spine cracked under Nagrom's blow easily, much too easily. He was sick of killing and he would be sick of it even unto his own death.

Slithering his way out one of his many daytime hiding places, a mere crack in the rocks where he had chased away some scorpions, he prepared for one more night of collecting moisture, and attempting escape. The dark proved to be his friend just a little more than it was an enemy while there was no moon. While he could move better undetected, cactus could not be seen until it was felt, rocks gave way on treacherous slopes causing him to fall, creating unwanted noise in the silent land. He crouched low to the ground, staying in every depression possible, moving across exposed areas in quick spurts, always to a location picked beforehand never wasting a step. Had he had the luxury of time he would have waited for the moon to rise and used it and its clever shadows to aide in his movements. But time was the real enemy as his body continued to dry beyond repair. After moving another couple of hundred yards, slowly, painstakingly, with a care and purpose that belied his physical state, Nagrom sat still in a low spot and watched his friend rise in the east.

The orange glow of it rising had always been magic to his eyes, but in the last two nights, at the end of a grueling, miserable day of slithering with the snakes, the moon had risen to a more profound status. It signaled a recess in the torture, a moment of reflection, and a chance for diversion. He stared at the emerging orb. He lost track of everything around him. Memories flooded his ravaged mind pushing out the pain, the sorrow, the desperation. Simple memories of youth, warm fires on cold nights, the reassuring touch of his mother's hand, songs and games and everything good came to fill him. He stared on. Nothing so beautiful had he ever seen than this milky, sad, grey face. He sat in his low spot and crossed his legs, relaxing for the first time in three days. The great eye of the night rose to stare back. Truly, thought Nagrom, only a good and great God could have placed such a thing. Why was he here? Was the solemn recognition of this orb a sign? Was he to spend the rest of his life pursuing duty, or was he to find some greater meaning than duty in some sort of universal dignity?

The memories came, sweet memories of youth, all shed of the silly trauma every child has only the good came to him. The reminiscing was of the proper perspective to a man near death. Only the good matters. Only the good brings hope. Nothing is found in the disappointments of youth when viewed from this attitude so far away from home; all lessons to be learned from disappointment should long since have already been shifted through so even they too only seemed good. As the respite from his misery continued, Nagrom began to realize the most important memories of his life lie before his time of duty; duty which he had dedicated his life to. Even those sweet memories of his career had little to do with the objectives, medals, tasks and orders he had struggled so hard to obtain, and believed so paramount at the time. Memories which filled him with warmth, on this his darkest hour, had much more to do with the friends and people he had met to laugh with, to talk to, to walk beside. How was it he had come to this place? How was it he had forgotten all the sweetness of life until this night? This mystical sphere up in the sky was shining light into his eyes and into his soul as never before.

Change in a man is slow. It comes through sluggish, fluid movements that push against the instilled notions of a being. Imperceptible changes in your reality keep building up against your beliefs. Like a river whose motion is imperceptible, change can move you without you even knowing it. One morning you wake up and your raft is many miles from where it used to be. The landscape is now different. If you want to believe you haven't moved, you are lost. Since the movement is slow, and because it is, the realization you are changed is sometimes not readily apparent. In a seminal moment, it will hit you. It slaps you in the face. One day, at some time, you realize you are no longer the same.

Nagrom was waking up from such a journey. He had gone out into the soulful light and suddenly realized his surroundings, his demeanor, were suddenly a long way from where he had believed them to be. The light, awakening his conscious to the changes which had been moving him from his virtual course, was coming from a newfound friend in the sky. Like a mariner who had not considered a strong ocean current in his navigation towards home, Nagrom had wrecked upon an unfamiliar shore. In what could very well be his last day in the cosmos, Nagrom had become a changed man.

He rose from his seated position to stand ghostly grey in the thin white light, not letting his eyes off the moon. "Duty without reason," he whispered, his voice croaking from dryness, "is hollow. Honor is not real without scruples. Glory is a charade without a moral conclusion."

He knelt down onto one knee, closed his eyes and pondered those things he had said. It was as if someone else were speaking through him. A deeper sense of self was taking hold of his mind. It was time to forget the hatred of others. It was time to see beyond the foolishness hate brings. The reformation of Nagrom was well on its way to being complete and with it had come a new vigor. A power deep in his soul welled up to aid him in his current struggle. Tonight he would finish the escape. Tonight he would escape all things haunting him.

Slowly he worked his way toward the police cars down the moonlit slope. The static position of the officers and the delineation of the highway told him it was the northern boundary of the search area. He knew that if he could get to the other side of the highway, and find some water, he would be free of their grasp. There were two officers near the vehicle and their conduct puzzled Nagrom at first: they were very nonchalant. One was reading a paper under the interior light of the auto; another was blowing into a cup of steaming liquid. Neither seemed intent on a search. Both appeared to have given up the idea of finding the fugitive—seeing the liquid caused an angst he struggled to keep down.

After a while, Nagrom's spirits began to climb watching the two men. They must believe he was dead, he thought. They must have already given up the chase. Today they had not come with the helicopter and the number of men on foot was greatly reduced. The idea of escape became ever more real. Though deliverance was closer, he still needed to be careful. Nagrom watched the man sip gratuitously from the cup and his mouth ached for any drop.

They were parked on a high spot along the highway with a commanding view of the sweep in either direction. They had the night vision goggles, yet, to Nagrom's delight, they were no longer bothering with them. They sat unused on the hood of the car. It was hard for him to think. He was so dehydrated the cup in the officer's hand became an object of focus. He blinked his sand and salt crusted eyes and fought to regain his strength. He turned away and came upon his final plan.

He worked his battered body closer to the highway but in a direction away from the officers. About a half mile from the original police car he could make out another sheriff's vehicle in the distance. He continued until he gauged he was an equal distance between the two. Near the edge of the highway Nagrom began pulling himself along on his belly until he was nearly on the asphalt. When there was a long lull in the already sparse traffic he sprang to his feet and sprinted to the far side. Yet his quickness had left him. His legs wobbled. Trying to expend this amount of energy he felt on the verge of collapse. He flung himself to the ground on the far side and waited until his energy returned, gasping at the dry air. Precious minutes passed and with them a few, lonely autos. When his breath came back he summoned what was left of his strength and wiggled his little knife out of his pocket. Two suitable rocks lie nearby, one small and one large. He laid the blade off the end of the larger rock as it sat on the ground. Raising the second over his head he brought it down smashing the end of the blade, breaking it off. He took the small blade, which had snapped off near the handle, and waited for an opportunity.

A lone car could be seen coming in the distance. Nagrom waited until he was sure there would be a good interval between this auto and another. He crawled out into the slow lane with his blade and the smaller rock. He carefully pounded the broken knife into the soft, warm asphalt with his crude tool, point up and blade perpendicular to the direction of the traveling automobiles. As fast as his exhausted legs would allow he limped off the highway stooping as low as he could. One-hundred yards or so down the road from the planted edge he retreated into the desert scrabble, scrambling out of range of the oncoming headlights just in time.

Perhaps it was because he was so close to freedom, his will began to fade. Like a man dying of thirst might go mad seeing a glass of water he could not touch, Nagrom was fading with freedom in his grasp. He needed luck, just a little luck. And luck needed to show itself soon. Apprehension balanced his hope and the panic of failure lurked at the edge.

The lone auto approached the area where he had placed the blade. With just a little bit of luck the blade would puncture a tire. With a little more fortuity the blade, wide area facing the rubber, would snap off in the first tire and save the second, leaving the chance of vehicle repair with the one spare tire. The lone car approached. Nagrom held his breath and squinted his eyes. It did not slow and went on past. Nagrom hung his head. Providence was now in control.

Had the blade merely broken and not done its job to even one tire? Had the vehicle missed it? His breath was still heavy. He tried to pull himself up to go for an inspection but his body was failing him. Up the road, in the distance, came another set of headlights. Nagrom lowered himself again deciding to rest until this vehicle passed before trying to get up to see what the problem was. The automobile, a smallish one, came closer and closer. Nagrom lowered his head. He could not watch. In the area where the knife should have been there was a bang and the exhausted fugitive surged to life, raising his head in hope. The auto swerved slightly to the right. The single hiss of air told Nagrom he had hit his mark and only once as he had hoped. Providence had been with him.

The car slowed to a stop and pulled to the shoulder almost right in front of Nagrom, his dehydrated body tingling from the incredible fortune. The door opened and he could see from the dome light that the driver was the only occupant. Nagrom bided his time, pulling himself stealthily along the ground, inching towards his means of escape. The man pulled the spare out of the rear hatch with a slight grunt, his form outlined in a slow motion strobe from the pulsing red of his emergency flashers. After breaking the lug-nuts loose, the car went up on the jack groaning and creaking with every twist of the screw lifting it.

A few late-night travelers filed past, unconcerned with the stranded traveler, rumbling down the lonely highway while Nagrom hugged the ground. Another set of head-lights came closer and slowed. The weary outlaw wedged himself into a dip in the terrain, pressing his face flat against the dirt. The cackle of a radio told him it was a police officer. Nagrom's heart raced. Panic which was lurking on the edge pressed on him. He dare not raise his head. Casual conversation skipped over the top of his anxieties, he not hearing a word. Pleasant laughter seemed to mock him. A slamming door caused his body to twitch, and the officer moved away. Nagrom raised his head to watch the red tail lights depart, pushing his hysteria back to its place of control. The short, little human resumed his activity.

Lug-nuts rattled into the hubcap and the flat tire was pulled off and heaved into the rear hatch. The flashing lights of the car were hypnotic to one crazed with thirst, straining to concentrate, inching with the last of his might forward. The spare went on; the pudgy man struggled to get the lugs lined up properly in the dark. The last lug-nut came out of the hubcap and the man spun it gracefully into place with the spinning t-wrench. The car lowered. Nagrom raised himself off the ground. The highway was clear. The moon barely illuminated him in-between villainous splashes of red coming from the car's emergency flashers. The man leaned his full weight on each nut to give them the proper torque. As the last was tightened, from behind his unsuspecting head, a scratched, blistered, and calloused fist struck him on the temple. The man grunted, saw stars and rolled to the ground unconscious.

Though he knew the man could not hear him, Nagrom felt for some reason obliged to make an apology anyway. "Sorry my friend," Nagrom croaked. He bent over the victim pulling out his keys and wallet. As he bent over him, as if to convince himself of his new attitude, Nagrom whispered, "I'm not here to kill you."

The liberated survivor slung his unconscious victim into the passenger seat and tied his hands securely with the seat belt. To beat a column of approaching head-lights he hurried to the driver's side and opened the door. Before slipping into the car he looked once more to his guiding light in the sky. If he would have had moisture in his body, a tear would have come. He was now free. Truly free.

CHAPTER THIRTY-FOUR

Detective Espinosa saw his partner was getting a little overheated in the interrogation and stepped in to establish some semblance of control. Physically placing himself between his fellow detective and the cross examined he brought the shouting to a stop. A lot of people believe the "good cop, bad cop" routine is a well rehearsed performance designed to extract information from reluctant suspects—sometimes, maybe it is—but for these two it was much more a modus operandi of circumstance. Espinoza pushed his red-faced, screaming partner gently back by one arm motioning for him to take it easy. Jablonski sputtered a bit, then acquiesced.

Espinoza sat down on top of the table in front of Barbara taking an even tone. "You know," he said scratching at the palm of his hand, "people just don't like being lied to. And these aren't, like, no little white lies. Barbara, people are dying. Maybe you can put a stop to it. Maybe you can't. But we're never going to know until you tell us what the hell is going on."

A hand smacked down on the little table causing Barbara to jump. Jablonski had returned to follow up. "Goddamn it!" he yelled. "You have got to stop playing, playing like you're some kind of fucking spy. This isn't pretend. It's real."

"Hey, hey, hey," Espinoza said turning toward his partner. He got up and led the flush-faced man back to the corner he had been sputtering in. "Let's give her one more chance, huh?" Ever since the death of McKiterick, Jablonski had taken things a bit more personally. Perhaps it was because he was, as he said before, feeling his impermanence on this earth. Maybe he hadn't gotten enough sleep. In any case, he was feeling pretty damn hard against Barbara right now.

Returning to the table, this time Espinoza actually sat down in the chair opposite his detainee. He clasped both hands together in front of him and rested his elbows on the little brown wood table. "Listen now," he said calmly, "my friend over there is upset because you're jerking us around. You're jerking us around through the whole goddamn country. I know he's loud, but I think he has a reason to be upset. Me too, you know. I'm even getting a little pissed off. So, what's it going to be?"

This was Barbara's second day on the grill. She was tired, irritable, weak and frustrated. She had been turned in by her own parents and had spent the night in a cold, lonely cell. They said she could have a lawyer, but in her mind having one would only make it more complicated. Everything seemed more complicated now, confusing. She found it hard to focus and listen. Ever since being removed from George and Pestia it all seemed more and more ridiculous. She had promised not to talk, but it was all so futile. Aliens? Space creatures? It was a bad dream that she was waking up from. Stalling did little to placate her examiners. Stories made-up on the spot, and torn to pieces by their logic, only infuriated them. Why take this?

Barbara rubbed her temples with one hand. "If I talk," she started, catching the rapt attention of her interrogators, "can I get a couple of aspirin?"

Espinosa leaned back in his chair. "You can have four bottles of aspirin if you want," he said.

"And a glass of wine?"

Espinosa turned to motion to Jablonski but he was already out the door. The detective spun back to Barbara. "You can have the whole winery, on me," he said with a smile.

Only a few minutes later Jablonski reappeared with a huge bottle of generic aspirin in one hand, a tape recorder in the other, and an expensive bottle of red wine under an arm. When the aspirin had been taken, and the open bottle sat on the table beside a paper cup full of the scarlet liquid, Barbara started her story by saying, "You're not going to believe this."

She relayed every bit of information she knew. Names, dates, places and even her speculation. When the name of the hotel George and Pestia were staying in came up, Jablonski hastened out the door one more time. Barbara continued until everything had been poured out, not sparing any detail. She told them of the spacemen and how, for a while at least, she had believed it. She told them how two more had arrived later and how they were out to kill the earlier arrivals. She went over how George had described their arrival in the Saline Valley and of how his friend had been wounded in a confrontation there. She told them all about her near abduction at Jeremy's and about the huge man who had looked a lot like Mark. The story ended with her arrival in Barstow and her attempt at securing a little cash.

"That's it," she said in conclusion. "That's everything, all I know. I thought I was doing people favors by keeping quiet. They asked me to keep quiet. I didn't want to hurt anyone. I didn't want anybody to die. I just want this to be over."

Jablonski had returned and was listening in earnest. "Your hotel room was empty," he said. "The registration said one person only."

"George did that," she said. "He wanted to fool people. He said that if people were looking for us it would make it harder for them."

"Would he lie about the license number of his vehicle on the registration?"

Barbara shrugged her shoulders. "Probably. He was smart. He knew what he was doing. I told you, he said was a forensics expert with the military."

Jablonski nodded. "We're checking that too."

"OK Barbara," Espinoza followed up, "you told us that this Gregaris guy, George, knew all about Josiah being murdered when you first met him."

"Right."

"Do you remember what time that was?"

"Right after I left you guys. About two in the afternoon. Something like that."

Jablonski and Espinoza exchanged glances. Espinoza continued, "Well, we didn't get the connection to Mark's case to the press until almost two-thirty. That means he knew about Josiah being killed—at least as it related to Johnson—well before he should have."

Barbara stirred in her chair uneasily. "You think that George and Frank killed him?"

"We don't know what to think right now," Espinoza said. But we do want to talk to this guy. If he knows about Josiah being dead, he might, at least, know who did it.

"Anyway, Barbara, that's all for now. We got some work to do on what you've told us. Don't go anywhere where we don't know about it. We're going to need to talk again." Espinosa leaned forward and poured Barbara a little more wine. "And see?" he said. "That wasn't so bad. Now we got the whole story and everybody's happy." Barbara stared at the little paper cup wondering how happy George and Frank were going to be.

Another officer opened the door of the little windowless room. It was a local sheriff. He glared oddly at the wine bottle then motioned for both Espinosa and Jablonski to come outside. Espinosa picked up the tape recorder and took it with him for safe keeping. The three huddled near the outside of the door in the busy hallway.

"The captain said I should brief you guys," the young sheriff said keeping his voice low. "The army got back on this Gregaris guy and it's real weird."

Espinosa shrugged. "Try us."

"Yeah," the sheriff went on, "they had a Captain Gregaris and he fits the description. But that's all they would say about him. The guy asked me why I wanted to know and I told him about the investigation—about Mark, and all that . . . you know. Anyway, the guy puts me on hold for a long time and when he gets back, he tells me they're sending out a security man right away. Seems that they're already looking for him. I guess he's already wanted but they wouldn't tell me what for."

Espinosa and Jablonski exchanged glances and Jablonski asked, "When's this guy coming?"

"Tonight."

"Tonight?" Jablonski repeated and looked at his watch. It was nine o'clock. "Good god. Tonight?"

"Yep, he said he'd be here in two hours. Must be kind of important to them. Kind of makes you think we hit a nerve, huh?"

Nerves had been hit, alright, but none of the three could imagine the furor going on in the military hierarchy at the moment. Ever since the arrival of a second craft the military was scrambling for clues as to its origin. One isolated event could be overlooked as a fluke. Two similar events created a threatening trend. Work done on identifying the previous craft suddenly came out of complete obscurity into great demand. Most of the original reports, however, appeared to be doctored and some were even missing. It was proving to be a messy business opening up the Gregaris file for all those who had spent the previous year trying to bury it.

The whole affair had been swept cleanly under the carpet with surprising totality. One might believe such a suspicious craft would have stayed in the collective consciousness of the military for much longer. The general in charge of the whole mess thought the forensics expert was gone for good. Yet, the general would never have dared to have been so bold in his excoriation of the captain had he had a crystal ball. Not only was the pentagon sticking its nose back into the investigation, which was bad enough, but a congressional oversight committee had gotten wind of the cover-up and was threatening to hold hearings. Many of the good congressmen's constituents had been filled to the brim over the years with tabloid hints at pentagon attempts to conceal extra-terrestrials and some of the suspicion had rubbed off. This was a boil on the skin of the body politic no good politician was going to let slip by without a thorough lancing. Lack of information sparked curiosity; curiosity fed paranoia; and at the end of the day hoots and howls of 'cover-up', 'foul-up', and 'conspiracy' were echoing across every layer upon every echelon of military hierarchy right to the very top. The lid had been blown right off of this one and there was no going back.

Everyone who was anyone at the base had had the name Gregaris burned into their brain along with the specifics of his report. The arrival of the second craft had put him at the root of all significant scuttlebutt. When the sheriff asked about Gregaris red flags went up all around the compound. When he told them it had to do with a case involving a suspected 'spaceman', alarms all the way to Washington started screeching.

The security man being sent, post-haste, was the very same intelligence officer who had first grilled Gregaris more than a year ago. Since the time of the second craft, however, it had been his turn on the hot seat. All sorts of difficult questions were being asked: Why had Gregaris not been taken more seriously? Where was he now, when they could use his experience on the second craft?—and probably the most difficult question—Why had the report been re-written to suit the conclusions of people who had never been to the crash site? It was this intelligence officers' turn to have his butt in the fire. The second crash was being investigated by a much larger team than the first and preliminary indications did not bode well for the Major: they seemed to agree with Gregaris' original account. Nightmares had happier conclusions.

The man sent, Major Barton, sat glumly in the civilian transport he was driving to Barstow, watching the dim world go by in the moonlight. Word gets around a military base much like gossip gets around a small town. If anyone is under scrutiny and being looked down on by the brass the whole base knows about it just about the same time the person under scrutiny knows. Everyone on the base knew Barton was being grilled like a sausage over a camp fire. Everyone wanted to keep the 'guilty by association' to a minimum and went to great lengths to not be seen with him. There were a large number who avoided the Major who had participated in the ridicule of Gregaris and knew the 'guilt by association' had a grain or two of truth to it. The driver who took him to the car pool didn't even say 'good evening major' until they were well out of sight of staff headquarters. The major checked out a car, only silence transpiring between himself and the clerk and was on his way. Arrogant individuals find eating crow much less palatable than ordinary people, and Major Barton found it less appetizing than all but the most arrogant.

Though things looked bad for the Major at first, the phone call from the top brass had been a Godsend. He could have, after all, been taken off the case—which would have meant he was completely written off. Going to Barstow might prove his road to rehabilitation. It was his chance to locate Gregaris, find some way to get on his good side and convince him to come help with the current investigation. Much had been made of the fact Gregaris' original draft had been shredded and rumors were flying in the absence of detail. Rumors linking the Major to such unsavory terms as 'foul-up', 'cover-up', and 'conspiracy' were wholly unsavory to the Major. Barton knew that it would be a hard sell to get help from Gregaris if and when he was found, but it was worth a try and anything beat sitting back in the dust bowl getting evil stares.

Like most people haughty beyond reason, Barton had no idea how deeply offended Captain Gregaris had been, and of the 'snowball's chance in hell' he had of getting George to co-operate. The wheels in the mind of the cynical Major turned during the entire trip intent on a clear strategy for placating Gregaris. None was immediately hatched. As he walked into the police station and identified himself, he still didn't know how he would try and leverage the forensic expert's help. It was only after the officers there told him that Gregaris was wanted for questioning in the death of Josiah, and fellow officer McKitrick, did the Major realize his plan of attack: He would get Gregaris out of the hands of the police in exchange for his full cooperation in the investigation of the second craft. Barton might also hold out for a good word put in on his behalf, but he would wait and observe Gregaris' demeanor before slipping that one in.

The sheriffs on the swing shift were not particularly polite to the Major. Much to Barton's consternation he was just one more pain in the ass to the local authorities—it was reminiscent of the attitude he had been encountering on the base. They had been overrun by reporters and Los Angeles city police and were not in a conciliatory mood toward another agency butting into what they thought of as their business. They did spend enough time, however, to get him up to date.

Though they did not have Gregaris they had a description of his vehicle, a probable license number, and the fact he had been in the area in the last twenty-four hours. Also, as far as they knew, Gregaris did not know he himself was being pursued and therefore should have little reason to flee the area. The sheriffs gave the broad picture, but it was the Los Angeles detectives who filled him in on the specifics. Major Barton found the Los Angeles city police much more congenial—both parties commiserated on how they were being mistreated by the locals. Not long after his arrival, now past eleven-thirty, the shift commander got the heads of the three agencies represented together for a meeting.

Outside the interrogation room, where they had spent most of the day and night grilling Barbara, Jablonski and Espinoza waited for the conference along with the dapper Major. The young sheriff who had made the phone call to the military base led them to a briefing room where there was an older man in a suit standing with a briefcase beside the Sheriff's superintendent. The superintendent looked sleepy, eyes puffy and red, as if he had just been drug out of bed; pressure from the eminence of the investigation was obviously getting to him. The older man was introduced by the young sheriff to the other three as the blood specialist of the local laboratory where the department sent all their work. The drowsy superintendent plopped down without a word. The other four followed, arranging themselves around a large, shiny, wooden briefing table; minus the young sheriff who knew his place and retreated deferentially.

"Gentlemen," the older scientist started in a slow, careful, deliberate manner, "I was the one who asked Bill here, the superintendent, to call together the heads of the various agencies. What I have, I think, concerns you all. I have found something rather curious concerning this case that might tie up some loose ends or, perhaps, create some." The old man adjusted his reading glasses and flipped through some papers. "I am the same technician who handled the Gregaris case of a few weeks ago. If you aren't aware, Mr. Gregaris was detained here on suspicion of cruelty to animals. They thought he was the one who had kidnapped a baby gorilla from the Los Angeles zoo since they had found what appeared to be animal blood in his truck. Well, it didn't stick because it wasn't gorilla blood they found on the seat of his truck. Anyway, I happened to be the one who determined that it was not gorilla blood on the seat. However, I never did determine what kind of blood it was. Just that it wasn't human or gorilla. Because of that, out of a professional curiosity, I preserved some of the samples until such a time that I could get around to figuring out exactly what kind of blood it was. Now, yesterday I was brought several small blood samples taken from the car that the suspect Mark Johnson was in."

"We're pretty sure it ain't Johnson," interrupted the superintendent, showing a certain amount of irritation at the fact. The others nodded in agreement.

"Well, whoever it is, or was, as the case may be," the scientist continued, "I tried to determine his blood type also, and ran into a funny thing. Seems that this blood sample didn't type very well and, as a matter of fact, it wasn't human blood at all."

With the words, 'wasn't human blood', an electricity charged the air. The old man ran his eyes around the room to each person there, then continued. "Now, just as a hunch I went back to the samples from a couple of weeks ago. I realized the time pressures of this thing and decided to stay late tonight. And I'm glad I did because of what I was able to find." The old scientist let his eyes connect with every occupant of the room over his reading glasses, taking a deep breath. All were suddenly in rapt attention, even the sleepy superintendent. "Whoever that is out there, he seems to have blood very similar to whatever it was that bled all over Mr. Gregaris' truck."

The silence was deafening as each individual tried to process what had just been said. The superintendent suddenly stirred more awake. A few glances of recognition were exchanged. The old man continued, repeating himself for emphasis, "Because I had determined that it wasn't human blood that they had brought me from the wreck, I compared them to frozen samples from the Gregaris case. And, if not identical, then they are very close. At least from the same species."

The stunned silence of the others was finally broken by the superintendent. "That might not be the blood of our suspect. I mean, nobody actually saw him bleed there. I mean . . ." he drifted off to stillness as his own explanation did not convince himself.

"That may be the case," the old scientist retorted. "But, if it is, then whatever the animal was that bled on the seat of this car was also the same type of animal that bled on the seat of Gregaris' truck. An event I consider highly unlikely. And if it is . . ." The old man swept the room with his gaze in dramatic fashion. "And if it is, the blood of our suspect then the person seen running out into the desert is not human."

CHAPTER THIRTY-FIVE

Barbara would never forgive herself. One long, lonely night after she had definitively swum to the top of her cauldron of confusion and self-doubt and turned over all evidence against George and the huge, wounded man, she found out all the stories she had been told were definitively true. The headlines, even those of respectable papers, screamed the fact. Mark was, indeed, an alien. The information of the meeting from the previous night was supposed to have remained confidential until further specialists had time to analyze the samples and data, but trying to contain such a volatile report was like trying to dam up a tsunami with a toy shovel and pail of sand. If she had only held her tongue one more night. If she had just believed them an iota further. The inauspiciousness of the timing weighed on her and ate into her sensibilities.

Sounds of the office chatter and clatter, low in the early hours of the morning, all seemed pronounced. The click of heels on the tile, the rap of an occasional typewriter and murmur of voices all seemed to invade her head to remind her of the present reality and the painfully slow passing of time which would, someday, separate her from her actions of the previous night. Lights above, soft and neon, seemed stark and harsh, illuminating everything she didn't want to see. Time was moving slow now and everything reminded her of that fact. Reality has cruel ways of imposing the present and shielding the idea of a future.

Barbara sat in one corner of the station free to go but unwilling to move. Life had been drained from her body as surely as if someone had opened a tap at the bottom of the heel and forgotten to shut it. She ruminated over betraying the two desperate men and felt like doing something drastic, but didn't have the energy. She had betrayed a real alien. She could now be the villainess of two planets and not only one. Though she had felt the eyes of the world upon her, there were relatively few people noticing her now. Though reporters still came around, the throngs were gone. There was bigger news elsewhere. Barbara had come to the point more depressing than being despised: she was now irrelevant.

She realized the danger of torturing assassins was now more real to her. It had been crystallized rock solid in the form of a blood test. Everything had been true. She realized the danger but almost welcomed it, as if some suffering on her part could undo the damage she had done to George and Frank in their quest. The police were suddenly sure it was not Mark out in the desert. It meant one of the assassins, if the police conclusion was correct, one assassin was now still lost in the desert continuing his search to kill Mark. That being true, Barbara knew she had just contributed to the murderer's cause and putting Frank and George behind the eight-ball with the police. The very-terrestrial police were not the least concerned with her relaying the account of the extra-terrestrial squabbles. To them, Mark, Frank and George were the major suspects. No-one else had yet implicated themselves and if assassins existed, the police would worry about these facts when they caught the other three. In Barbara's mind, it was a painfully slow unfolding of a Greek tragedy. Yet, Barbara could not have known the drama being played out in the desert at this very moment and how irrelevant, she as a protagonist, in this act of life had actually become.

Somewhere to the east of town, at that very moment, George was watching the sunrise. He had always endeared himself to the clarity of the morning light, no haze, no smog, only sharp focused vistas ready to please the finest eyes. He was at the age when the clarity of the morning reflected his lucidity of thought after a night of rest. When he was fresh at the beginning of a new day he felt spry. And George needed a clear head today. Things were getting confusing very fast.

His brow was covered with dust and sweat; his breath was heavy and his limbs weak. Exertion seemed to extract a heavier toll with every passing year. Though the sun was still low in the sky it was already warm enough to be uncomfortable, and his weariness amplified the discomfort. His hissing breath, heavy from the effort, was the only sound on the great desolation. The silence and vast expanse emptied him of feeling, dissipating it as if emotion were radiating off of him into the quiet along with his heat. Life seemed to drain with it and when his breathing quieted he bent over in the silence feeling crumpled and old.

The tired soldier squatted to the ground and patted the loose soil tenderly as if reliving the final touch of his friend's lifeless brow. He remembered how he had pushed the eyes closed; how the rich, walnut-brown skin had faded to an ashen grey and from warm to cold. Both hands smeared the dirt level like a finger painter trying to remove all traces of the hands that had smoothed the canvass. The dirt was warm and dry and bereft of life. George stood and watched a handful of the dusty, pale soil drain from his hand.

It seemed so ironic to George that life was still going on around him. Undisturbed throughout the world, human beings carried on their normal routine. People were drinking coffee, driving to work, watching the television. Politicians blustered, industrialists made millions, scientists pondered the universe and he was the only cognizant piece of creation to witness this horrible event. A being, upon whom the history of the planet should be hinged, passing without a sound.

The hard, military man felt weak and stupid. Should he have gotten a doctor beyond the advice of Frank? Could he have done more? Would going to the authorities have saved him? Tears rolled down the tan and leathery cheeks. George lowered onto both knees and continued smoothing out the shallow grave.

Would the soul know where to go? Thought George whimsically, is there a place that connects us to these people beyond our physical world? Could he go there now? There was no ignominy in this burial, George thought. Nature was beyond the magnificence of any mausoleum devised by man and if there was a connection between the two places then nature surely held the key of commonality.

There had been so little time spent between the two yet George felt a great loss. Suddenly he was disconnected from the titanic events playing out around him. What had been a handicap in looking for Mark, let alone protecting him, suddenly became remote possibility. George lovingly arranged the rocks to look undisturbed. Who would ever appreciate the hallowed nature of this ground? He replaced a small creosote bush in a depression scraped with his hand then scattered a few pieces of dead, grey and twisted mesquite across the area. No-one would ever know. Frank would not be a laboratory specimen for the tabloids.

Perhaps, George thought, it wasn't important for anyone to know. If nature was the key then let it be the only harbinger. Let it be the one to hallow the ground out of reach of the dabbling fingers of those so far removed from it.

"I'll never let them have you," George promised to the ruffled desert scrabble, the small plot that held Pestia. "You won't have to go through that."

George slung the shovel into the back window of the car. He would find a more circuitous route home, wherever home might prove to be this day. He knew the authorities were looking for him. The media was almost as fast as having a direct link to the police, though not quite. He needed to get another vehicle. But how? He was out of money and nearly out of desire. Was he really a suspect as an accessory to murder as the papers had said? What would they do with him if he were apprehended? Was it true they no longer believed it was Mark out in the desert? Was it an alien? Had he been dragging Frank, in his last desperate days, around on a wild goose chase? Reality and tabloid gossip seemed melded into one and George unable to determine which held grains of truth. He leaned against the car pulling his large, straw sunhat low. He looked at his hands which were good and blistered from battering the shovel into the un-giving landscape. George looked at the grave. He had done a fine job in covering it up. He picked up several small pebbles and near where the head of his friend had been laid he formed a small cross, small enough to not be noticed but large enough for him to know it was there. It was a fitting gesture but something was still missing. Deep down inside something about the whole scene just wasn't right.

Pestia never regained full consciousness, sometimes coming to in a sort of delirium. George couldn't help but think his large companion had sensed the air of hopelessness around him and chosen not to come back. As he knew, Mark was lost in the desert; the hope of getting to him dimming; the hope he was alive waning. Somehow, thought George, Pestia had absorbed the misery of his surroundings, felt it, and lost hope. Despondency had soaked into the being he knew as Frank as surely as it was dripping from George. Yet, in and around all these feelings George, could sense something was wrong. Or, at least, something wasn't right. Underneath all the pain of the moment there was the feeling there was some fundamental fact he was overlooking.

Sweat dripping from his face, George swung his tired legs into Frank's old automobile. There, sitting on the filthy mats of the floor was Frank's silver backpack. George was startled by its sight. He had originally planned on burying it with Pestia, to let all secrets of this man and his charge pass into the great beyond together. He picked it up still curious as to why it had shocked Barbara when she touched it and not himself. Perhaps, he would eventually find a separate burial spot for the mysterious bag. It would make the probability of people finding both more remote. George pondered reopening the grave and burying it in the same spot but then decided to keep it, for a while anyway. George felt he had fulfilled his moral duty by not letting his friend, Frank, end up in a bell jar in the Smithsonian.

George wondered about his responsibility towards those aliens en-route to the planet to retrieve the deceased. He wondered what he would tell them when they finished their thirty year journey. How would he relay the facts? What would they think when they found out our police might have chased their prince into the desert to face a miserable death of dehydration? He wondered how he could possibly contact them. Perhaps the bag held a communications device of sorts. One could only hope, George thought, if

Mark was dead the aliens were more understanding to harsh circumstance than earthlings were.

George never looked into the sack while Pestia was alive. He didn't know a lot about its contents. He did know it held Frank's meager selection of clothes and that it must hold a device which received information from the home planet. From time to time Frank would excitedly update George as to messages sent about news from his home. He would be excited even though he knew the information was at least fifteen years old. George was hoping the receiving device might also be a transmitter. Though Frank had never indicated he had such a device, the forensics man found it logical that he should. How else would he contact the arriving fleet as to their location? The only other possibility, to the analytical captain, was that the receiver also acted as a sort of homing device.

By and large, George found Frank very lean on devices. He would have imagined an alien advanced enough for interstellar travel having come with a whole host of little gizmos ready to figure out and solve a large array of problems. He often wondered if Frank was hiding the existence of many other items in the sack besides the receiver. The original thought was to bury the bag, secrets intact. Yet, as he pondered the situation, he fought to find a real motive for wanting it open, trying to balance the need for such an intrusive, immoral act against a fierce, professional curiosity. Was it honorable to let the dead man's belongings go into the ground without being disturbed? Or was there some legitimate reason to need to explore the contents? George rubbed his forehead and bit his lip. It just might have a way to contact the arriving fleet, he thought. Maybe it would do some good. Maybe it would help him out of this desperate situation. He would now find out.

Before inspecting the sack, George decided to drive for a while on the small track to distance himself from the secrecy of the grave. Rocks thumped against the undercarriage—George was not used to driving something other than his truck in the desert. He drove slow to minimize the cloud of dust he was leaving behind. People could spot a trail of dust behind a vehicle well before the vehicle itself; which could be spotted miles away on the flat surroundings. After another four or five miles, at a point where George was sure even he himself would have had a hard time relocating the shallow grave, he stopped the car.

So it was, thought George. Another hero had passed into the great beyond without fanfare, recognition, or appropriate ceremony. George had imagined his huge friend succeeding in his task. One day he would see him fly off in a cloud of glory, his task finished. It wasn't supposed to end this way. Heroes were always supposed to triumph. Perhaps it was just a flaw of his own mythology which caused him to believe heroes should be the ones triumphant. Maybe he was using the wrong characterization of the word 'hero'. In either case, his friend Frank was dead.

Silence seemed to swallow him. It exaggerated every motion. Leaning back caused his clothes to rustle against the vinyl seat. Moving his feet caused a scraping of boots against a dirty floor. Every motion described a sound which entered his ears to describe it again for his mind. George opened the door—the clicking latch pronouncing itself to the envelope of silence. He got out to sit on the hood. The little turn in his guts was the only thing surviving the silence. Suspicion, trained by years of experience, held out against the anguish and loneliness of the silence and fought for his attention. Something basic was wrong. The whole scene was wrong.

Facts lined up in the mind of the forensics specialist one by one for chronological review. He went back to the very beginning and the images and associated data of each scene progressed from the earliest days he had met the man he knew as Frank. Along the review the deep seated suspicion grew more frustrating. George rubbed his forehead. What was wrong, the feeling told him, was wrong with the recent past and not the entire past. He began the review again, this time moving backward from the burial. As he moved backwards his suspicion grew more excited to a point, then less excited as he progressed as if playing a game of mental 'hot and cold' as to the location of the errant analysis. Slowly the time frame became more specific. There was something wrong with the very first news reports about Mark being chased into the desert. In the time line, before this event the suspicion grew cold. After the chase and hyperbole of the desert search had begun, the feeling grew even colder. Somewhere in-between the suspicion grew hot and anxious and danced excitedly as one would when a player of the game kept stumbling back and forth across the object being searched for.

George scooted off the hood and leaned into the vehicle. He pulled out his canteen and took a long drink allowing some to spill into his hand which he washed across his face. He returned to the hood and fell on it with both elbows. The feeling inside was screaming at him. It was right there. Right there. Right here, George thought and patted the hood of the old car; right here, a car. George snapped to attention with the realization and the relief the solving of a puzzle brings: It had been the wrong car.

The first news reports had shown the wrecked automobile. The backend could be seen plainly sticking out of the ravine. Though he could not have known what kind of car Mark was driving, he knew Mark could not have been driving this car. He knew who's car this was. He had seen it once before, parked in front of Jeremy's house. It was the car of the assassins.

George's whole body tingled with hope. Mark might very well still be alive and, in news to him almost as good, at least one of the assassins was now presumed dead. He kicked himself over and over for not having recognized it before as if recognizing the fact would have prevented Pestia's death. George found himself pacing in a small circle, his heart racing. Mark was alive, he thought. He must be. There was still hope. With one of the assassins out of the way hope shown even stronger. What he needed now was a lead. What he needed now was a little bit of luck. It was time to review the whole thing. If he had missed such a glaring and simple fact as the identity of the car, then there surely must be other things he was overlooking.

George took off his hat and waved it into the silence. "Ya-ha," he yelled filling the void with his voice. "Frank, my friend, it isn't over yet."

CHAPTER THIRTY-SIX

Harold Bates had been one of the finest beat reporters for the Los Angeles times. He had worked his way up from being an office gopher—back in the days when they still had a budget for such things—to doing spot pieces, to doing regular assignments on some of the biggest stories of the year. Though, as the years went by, the time between big assignments became longer and longer. Younger, brighter, and better looking reporters pushed into his territory. Harold didn't blame the youngsters. He was sure he had probably done the same to someone else earlier. Management had wanted to give him an office position rather than see him suffer the stain of having to begin taking entertainment pieces, but Harold preferred being in the field. He didn't like the office, the politics, or the ego charged atmosphere in it.

Many younger souls at the paper would have sold chunks of their anatomy for this story. It was consoling the management threw him the best of the entertainment stories. Still, had he had his druthers, he would rather be doing serious journalism than this 'quasi-tabloid shit'. It was a sign of the times for Harold so many young and bright reporters saw this as one of the 'big stories'. Everything he valued to have real meaning seemed to have less and less meaning these days to everyone else. And everything which used to have little to no meaning seemed to be an object of obsession for the young people now. Who would have guessed twenty-five years ago, when Harold had just finished his first writing assignment, that the most coveted position on staff would be head of 'Life Styles'.

Harold took a long sip of his straight-up whiskey and shook his head. He didn't believe for an instant this Mark Johnson was an alien. Probably no more than some freak who liked rolling around in exotic animal blood. He felt it was only another 'cold water fusion' story staying in the headlines just long enough to be debunked. Sip after thoughtful sip the tumbler went dry and Harold waved at the bartender. The pudgy bartender gave him a tired look and waddled down to see him.

Fucking hick, Harold thought, he hasn't figured out yet my money is green. He was the only one in the bar and couldn't get any service. It was typical, though, every time he went out to the sticks the locals had it in for him. They were invariably insular, rude and never responded well to Harold's 'gimme now', big-city body language.

"What now?" the bartender asked as if he had been disturbed in the middle of something important. The bartender was used to people who said things like 'excuse me' and 'please' and wasn't impressed by this big, sour city fart in his tie and jacket. He had been putting up with dozens of them every night for almost a week now and wished their business and attitude would find another roost. And they could take their big tips and ram them right up their asses. This sort of 'come-here-with-a-flick-of-the-finger-or-whistle' abuse wasn't worth any amount of money.

Harold and the other reporters didn't see themselves as rude. They weren't acting any different than they did to long time bartenders back home and were dismayed at the surliness of the waitresses and bartenders here in Barstow. They, in fact, felt their hand was being forced and were compelled to start acting rude.

Harold leaned forward towards the bartender with a smirk. "Could you find it in your heart of hearts to possibly refill my glass."

The bartender's lips puckered up in a scowl. "Now you listen here. I don't have to take that kind of crap."

Harold put both hands on the bar and pushed himself back with an odd, sarcastic smile. "And what kind of 'crap' is that? Having to serve patrons? What exactly did I do to piss you off besides ask for a refill?"

The bartender replayed the scene in his mind looking for the adjectives to portray his case. When the 'what' and 'how' of his aggravation proved too elusive for words he blurted out, "You know what the hell I mean."

Harold leaned forward again. "No, I don't. And I don't care what you mean. All I want to do is drink a little whiskey. Or is that considered discourteous in these parts."

The bartender snatched up the glass. "I'll fill up your whiskey, damn it. But I don't have to take any crap."

"Looky here," Harold said with a smile. "If I dish out any crap, I'll let you know just so there isn't any misunderstanding. All-right?"

Harold's sarcasm left the bartender, intentionally and ironically, a touch confused. Rather than respond he went about getting some more whiskey.

Behind the lone patron a door opened to the bright summer scene and another reporter from a rival paper came in and sat beside Harold.

"Hey Bud," Harold said moving his suit jacket from the adjacent stool for his companion to sit.

"Hey Harold," said the reporter of equal age, but less hair, "anything new today?"

"Yeah," he said, lowering his voice and sending a subtle finger toward the pouting bartender, "old Bubba here is having a meltdown."

Harold's friend shook his head. "That isn't anything new. We had him so pissed off last night I thought he was going to take a swing at someone. For a while I thought he was going to break down and cry."

"And your crime?" Harold asked, thrilled to hear the bartender had had a rough time.

"Ordering drinks."

"Don't you just love service out in the sticks? Hey, someone told me you interviewed the Cerasoli woman today. How'd it go?"

The door opened again and another reporter came in. It was that time of day for them to start arriving. Harold and his friend didn't take much notice of the new arrival, since he was a standoffish guy with a funny accent who never said much. The lone reporter took a seat near the door not bothering to acknowledge the other two.

"Well, I'd like to do Cerasoli," Harold's friend responded, "but I only talked to her, which wasn't pleasant at all. What a steely little princess that is. I think she's as nucking futs as Johnson. This story has more squirrels than a walnut grove."

"Isn't that always the case?" said Harold. "Crazy people are the only ones who want to work with crazy people. I haven't met a psychologist or social worker yet who could lick a stamp without shoving a thumb up his ass. Speaking of squirrels, have you talked to that sheriff Boulding yet?"

"You mean the one man band? Yeah. Are you kidding me? Is there somebody he hasn't talked to yet? And I mean talked to, talked to, and talked to."

"Yeah, you've talked to him." Harold laughed and then took a sip. He turned to look at the large, black reporter sitting by himself.

The bartender returned with Harold's whiskey and turned to the other reporter. "Yeah?" he asked gruffly.

"I'll have the usual," Harold's friend said with false sincerity.

"Usual what?" the bartender demanded.

"Oh, you don't remember? Well, I'm kind of hurt. It's a vodka soda with a twist. Please." The friend exaggerated the 'Please' in a way that almost tipped the inimical bartender off as to the sarcasm used. It went by him, however, leaving only a vague feeling of increased hostility in its wake.

The bright light entered the bar from behind again and both heads at the bar turned to see who was coming in. The silhouette faded into a body and face as the door shut revealing a thin, long-haired, scrappy-looking local boy with red eyes. The skinny young man rubbed a hand through his hair and shuffled toward the two reporters, wobbling a bit, noticeably drunk.

"Hey Russell!" yelled the bartender at the local. "I told you to get your drunk ass out-a here. Go on. Git!"

The words from the bartender had no more effect on the young man than to have him give the bartender a dirty look. "I ain't talkin' to you," he drawled.

"You ain't talkin' to nobody. Get out-a here before I call the cops." The young man continued advancing on Harold and his friend causing the bartender to retreat to the phone. "That's it," the bartender yelled, "I'm calling the sheriff."

Unfazed, the tough looking young man continued until he was facing Harold and his friend. He stood there with his arms hanging loose, both hands instinctively held in fists looking like two balls of rough hewn wood swinging on the end of a thick rope.

Harold gave his friend a sidelong look and decided to take the initiative. "What's up?" he asked the young, inebriated man.

The local boy rubbed his hand through his long, dirty hair again. "You guys reporters?" he asked hooking one thumb into his dusty jeans and weaving around.

Harold thought about saying something smart like, 'No, we're the asshole patrol and it looks like we just got our limit', but decided the kid looked too tough and responded sensibly. "Sure kid. We're reporters. What do you need?"

The wobbling young man rubbed a hand through his greasy scalp again and looked around as if for secrecy's sake. He leaned forward almost whispering. "You guys want to know where the hell that spaceman is?" The two reporters exchanged glances one more time. "Huh? You guys want to know?"

"Sure we want to know kid," Harold said, letting a smile creep onto his face.

"I ain't no kid and I ain't fuckin' with you," the drunken boy said. "I know where he is."

"OK," Harold's friend said. "So why don't you tell us?"

The boy licked his red, chapped lips and looked around once more to insure privacy. "I'll tell you," drawled the wiry, young man. "But I want somethin' first."

"Somethin'?" Harold asked imitating the boy's country twang. "What somethin'?"

"You know what I mean."

"Everybody in this town thinks we know what they mean, son," Harold's friend said. "Come right on out with it. What do you want?"

"I ain't yer son," he snarled at Harold's friend. Then back to Harold, "A hundred. Gimme a hundred and I'll take you to him."

"Oh, is that all," Harold said sarcastically. "Look friend, no offense, but even if we had one hundred dollars we probably wouldn't give it to you. Alright?"

"I just got off the phone, Russell," yelled the bartender from the far end of the bar, pointing an accusatory finger. "The sheriff's on his way."

The young man turned to the bartender. "Shut-up you fat pussy," he snarled through a drunken drawl, then faced the reporters one more time. "Suit yerself. I'll go find me someone else who wants to know."

Harold's friend shrugged and turned back to his drink. Harold, however, kept his eyes on the retreating drunk. The way the boy had so easily backed away from the offer raised Harold's suspicion. Lack of resolve in the selling of the case told him that the drunken kid might actually have something to offer. Harold, from experience, knew a real moocher was usually much more persistent. He thought about trailing the young drunk out to follow up on the hunch. It would only take a minute or two and he could always sneak a hundred extra bucks onto the expense report. He was about to stand but changed his mind when the big, hefty, black reporter, with the bad accent and attitude to match, got up to do the same. Let him waste the one hundred dollars, Harold thought and turned back to his cocktail.

CHAPTER THIRTY-SEVEN

Nagrom had done his duty well. Prior to his being chased into the desert, he had brought back a suitcase full of money, close to one hundred thousand dollars. The Premier had even complemented the stout warrior on a job well done. Money was something which brought out the very best in the Premier—he knowing the power it wielded no matter the place or time.

Matan, whose expensive tastes translated across the galaxy, would have no trouble spending thousands of dollars. He would stay only in the nicest hotels. He would drink only the most expensive wines even though he found all earth wines putrid—though more palatable than the 'carbonated urine' of earth beer. A fancy car would carry him in his search. Currency aided him in all physical facets of his new life. But having the money was a great advantage beyond the luxuries it brought. It did much more for his morale and mood. A mood which was contingent upon his place in society.

People stopped asking questions of an obviously different person when he arrived in a Mercedes. Money smoothed people's nerves over those eccentricities Matan would, from time to time, display. Police no longer stared at a black man when he changed in his rags for a thousand dollar suit. The same people who had offered nothing more than a sneer suddenly became doting vassals. Currency was power on any planet and Matan knew how to exploit the Achilles heel of all good people: greed.

Matan knew the police were looking for a person of his description and took on a rudimentary disguise. A hair permanent did not exactly imitate the African-American look but was close enough to one of their styles to pass. It was certainly less conspicuous than his previous flat, shiny top. Colored contact lenses masked, to a degree, his other conspicuous trait. The dark brown lenses mixed with the sharp green to create an odd, dull, dirty green color—unnatural to earthlings still, yet much less noticeable than the energetic, bright green of his countrymen. Even so, sunglasses were used whenever possible. Matan was thankful he was hiding from such a primitive and fractured force as the earth police, rather than his own, unified, secret police. No-one hid from them for very long.

Nagrom's death, reasoned Matan, had been a blessing in disguise. Nagrom had served his purpose in doing the dirty work then had drawn all the attention away from anyone else by his spectacular demise in the desert. He found travelling alone, now loaded with cash, a more pleasurable and much less conspicuous event anyway. Besides, since coming to the planet, Matan was not all that sure as to the loyalty of his subaltern. Sociopaths like Matan hold onto power by being able to sense such things or, at least, forcing themselves to think it possible of any trusted friend. The Premier felt the shift in the demeanor of his huge ally after the extermination of the first earth creature. There was something different in the way he held his eyes, a slight change in the timing between orders given and the obligatory 'yes sir'. Nagrom had served his purpose and had died the way a soldier should, thought Matan, before he had a chance to disgrace himself with any idea of mutiny.

Matan despised earthlings. He found them dull, simple and weak willed. They were easier for him to manipulate than people of his own planet—to persuade to do most anything; and especially with money. It was the main reason why he despised them: A manipulator never respects anyone easily manipulated. He attributed part of the ease of exploitation to the nature of the paper currency itself. On his own planet they used debit cards which looked just the same regardless of spending limit. Being able to hold the different denominations in his hand, however, and see the size of the stack, made for a more powerful draw; a draw which had a strong effect even on the Premier himself. He liked the way the paper felt in his hands as he snapped out bill after bill from the large roll. People always stared, envy pouring from their eyes. Though he despised earthlings, he was intrigued by their loyalty to the green paper when a deal was wrought. Matan promised himself he would remember the allure actual cash offered if he were ever to return home again. Any extra added control would be welcome to reign in his more wily countrymen.

This was how he had imagined it all: wielding power, prestige, and dominating. The first week on Earth had been horrible for the pampered leader; sleeping on worn mattresses; eating what one could find; and suffering the disgrace of having people stare at him because he was different in a lowly sort of way. But now he was in his element, landing on his feet in a stance ready for aggression. He had found the key that unlocked these creatures and was quick to use it to get whatever he wanted in terms of materials, physical pleasure, or logistic support. Machiavellians were that way throughout the galaxy. Those poised to exploit always seemed to find their bearings the fastest.

As news from home was fairly bleak for the Premier the idea of setting up permanent residence grew more palatable. News had not only grown bad but his homeland had been taken over by his enemies. Local transmissions from Ranson, since the fall of forces on Bren, were being jammed and the only updates were from his adversaries—updates which varied from general information to direct threat. As a consequence of the menacing tone from home one day he casually tossed the receiver into an incinerator. Who needed news from home anymore when it was all bad? Besides, Matan figured in a few years he could be ruling this planet. Then he would build a new receiver and a huge transmitter as well to send back his own messages to those still loyal to the oligarchy.

Logic for such a takeover was sound enough to the Premier. The industrial base of Earth was primitive enough to pay a king's ransom for his knowledge. Experience in developing microprocessors for his spy network would be valuable enough. But his school training in super-composite materials would make him invaluable to the highest bidder—country or company. Though the United States was the most logical choice, having the most sophisticated military and largest economy, he had no specific allegiance. Any country willing to help him rule the world would be his friend. After all, a country like the United States, with all its affinity for individual rights, might prove systemically a harder nut to crack than others. He felt he shouldn't limit his options.

After gaining control of the industrial base he would use the manipulative techniques learned at home and take control of the political base. Advertising and innuendo swayed these dullards much more thoroughly than the people of Ranson. What had required months of careful, non-contradictory deception at home seemed to be accomplished in a single sentence here. People were moved to believe most anything bad about anyone or anything they saw on their television screens and showed little to no faith in their institutions. Matan remembered the riots he inspired the first time he publicly renounced the King. And that was after months of propaganda laid as ground work. There would be no riots on earth, however. From religion, to politics, to science, earthlings lacked a strong core of beliefs, and seemed to lack faith in what beliefs they had. Matan even had gone so far as to fantasize about using the earthlings for an eventual return to home. After bringing their industry up to appropriate levels, he could create a massive fleet armed with these lowly droids to take the home planet back by storm. There would be, however, plenty of time for making fantasies come true after the present task was complete. Yet, then there was the problem of the rescue fleet.

The only substantial deadline for the masterful Premier was the arrival of the fleet some three years hence. They would surely be spoiling to put his head on a pole. They would be awakening with the horror of battle fresh in their minds and bent on revenge. The only way to turn them back without them ripping apart the planet to get at him would be to show them the futility of doing so. Matan understood the weaknesses of the Monarchy and one of their main weaknesses was compassion. He would have to kill the prince then find some way to prove it to the fleet without revealing himself. The conquerors would not ruin the lives of a few billion creatures for only revenge—as the good Premier would have done without hesitation. Yet, they might risk it in order to get to their Prince, and find Matan for a bonus.

He was not in a great hurry to get the job done, but in enough of a hurry to not want to lose the scent of the trail. Luck had been on his side to a great degree so far and he could not count on it always being so. The earthlings were doing much of the work in finding the Prince and he must seize the initiative while the short attention span of these brutes continued to do so. This led to a quick strategy of masquerade. There were several groups looking for the Prince; two of which were the police, who would be hard and dangerous to imitate, and the press. The latter fit him like a glove.

All Matan needed to do was act natural. Act pretentious, pompous and pushy, scribble a few notes into a pad, and no-one at all would check his credentials. The charade worked wonderfully and was the best gamble for picking up leads. It gave him access to information at the instant events were taking place. Without any work at all he could sit back, listen, and move when the rest of the pack did. Matan was hopeful, but not in his wildest dreams did he expect it to work out like it did; sitting in a bar, in walks a drunken fool to deliver the prince on a platter.

The rest of the pack of journalists would not know. He could go alone. This was good fortune beyond reason. He tested the drunken fool with several questions on the sidewalk in front of the bar and it convinced the Premier he might be onto something. He could almost smell the trail of his victim. Keeping his growing exuberance well hidden, he insisted the young fool come along for the ride to show him the exact location. He did not want the boy to tip such a rumor to others if it was true, and he wanted to exact a toll if it were not. Besides, the drunken fool had sold himself and the Premier had paid. For one hundred dollars, Matan now felt as if he owned the boy's soul.

As he continued to examine the young fellow during the ride answers to questions convinced Matan more and more it was for real. The drawling beast came up with details Matan knew he was incapable of manufacturing. Past the physical description, which everyone who had seen the pictures could detail, the boy described the Prince's erect, 'prissy', way of sitting; he identified Matan's accent as being very similar; he gave a name that the Prince was using. Matan could barely keep his excitement under control. The Premier found it amusing the drunken creature had no idea as to the treachery he was conducting. One young, ignorant, and angry man possessed with the hatred of prejudice was selling out the hopes of an entire planet for one-hundred increments of paper. It engrossed Matan the way the drunken fool would forego his bigotry and talk to a dark skinned man like him when money was involved. Delighted, the evil Premier soaked in the irony and marveled at the simplicity of the events being played out. The little fool suspected nothing, being greatly impressed with the vehicle he was riding in. The greasy haired youth said he had never been in one so fancy and wished he could buy one himself one day. Matan thanked the young man and told him this was indeed the land of opportunity.

It was only about fifteen miles from the center of town to where the drowsy boy said he lived. He pointed out the road and described the trailer. He said he did not want to go in because of what his father would say. Matan, to be true to his sense of history, thanked the boy hardily, had him get out of the car, then shot him between the eyes. Thanking someone for such treachery with anything less than death, thought Matan, would be missing the true understanding as to the value and reward of treachery itself. For good measure he retrieved the one-hundred dollar bill from the dusty pocket; he had purchased the soul and now the soul was gone. Using the hair of the soulless entity for a handle, he drug the body to a culvert which stood over a nearby wash and slung it casually into the shadows.

Matan found himself humming a cheery, military tune from home. He dabbed at his forehead and the corners of his mouth with his handkerchief. He adjusted his jacket and cuffs, noticing the sparkle in his diamond cufflinks. Everything was perfect. No-one else had come along. The area was deserted. The only witness dead. He could feel his power growing. He could sense the magnitude of the moment. The only heir and hope of four billion adversaries was within his grasp, sitting in his palm to crush at his whim.

Red sunlight filled the west, toward the victim, with a light of ceremonial blood. Revenge was hanging over the head of the Premier, sitting on his back, watching over him to guide his every step. It filled his arms with vigor. Strength flowed down from his vengeful ego into his limbs, into his finger tips causing them to tingle with anticipation. Hatred was not enough. Being feared was not enough. The spiteful coward would not be satisfied until the nemesis was dead. Not until he saw the prince cry out and quake at his feet. Not until blood ran and it caked sticky, and purple onto the feet of the avenger would Matan be satisfied.

Fate was on his side. Providence had led him to this place. Blind with the ambition hate brings, and drunk with the intoxication which is power, he let himself feel. He felt the position of himself between the triad of worlds upon which this story was written. Upon which this story will finish. Since learning of the turning of the tide of the revolution he had not felt a single thing. Feelings, for the power hungry, can only be felt in the context of power gained. Letting themselves feel anything else is admitting loss, damning ambition, and tacit recognition of a universe in which the power of beings crawling on the surface of a planet means nothing at all. But feelings were his friend now and, for a person such as this, friends were meant to be worked and milked until they had no further use. Feelings of vindictiveness, which masquerade in the minds of the power hungry as joy, roared through every artery and vein sending a tingle to every hair on his head.

Surely fortune had led him here. Surely his success would be a lesson to the weak. If one rumor had destroyed an empire, so too could one well-placed bullet. His name would be on the lips of every man, woman and child; if not to praise him, then to curse him. Curses, which would come from his enemies, meaning more to the venomous spirit than praise from his allies. A curse from an adversary is recognition of a formidable foe. The worst imaginable fate for the Premier would be for people to forget him. Now, no-one would ever forget.

Matan fancied himself poetic, and an intellectual. He disdained what he perceived as the frail jabbering of effete professors who condemned his philosophy of dominance. They were some of the first to go to the dungeons during the purges. Ideas had always been his only true enemy, ideas with the association of conviction. They were something he could not destroy. They seemed to follow him everywhere. No satisfaction had come from crushing them physically. Bloody tables of philosophical adversaries, tongues ripped from their faces, only brought a brief rush of masquerading joy then returned to continuing frustration. It was the ideas of the intellectuals, wrapped in the armor of impenetrable rationalizations, forged in those despicable ivory towers which haunted him. They haunted Matan long after the quivering corpses had gurgled their last bubbles of blood.

What philosophical treatise would these intellectuals offer up to him now? Was success proof enough the strong survive for these twiddling, pretentious fools? Or would they still fight him, wag their fingers as if they owned his mind and try and steer it with their impotent deliberations? Triumph would surely put the specter of his enemies to rest. It would undoubtedly lock them into a hell of failure. Triumph was the only rationalization to Matan and he would carry any failure to his death—death being his only avenue for admitting he could be wrong.

Sanctioned by his own evil philosophies, shrouded in a cloak formed by being insulated from any other opinion, holding up a shield of self-righteousness impervious to reason, Matan stood at the intersection of history, the crossing of worlds filled to bursting with pride at what he was about to do. Truly, here was the victor. Certainly this was the vindication for every evil he had perpetrated upon his people. Power had won, won over the hackneyed gabbling of ivory-towered jack-asses. Matan, in his mind, was now vindicated, adjudicated positively in his universe of one.

The sun grew more reddish and distorted as it approached the horizon. Shadows from scant shrubs, and dead tumbleweed lengthened and crept toward the feet of the lone, figure standing outside the trailer. Darkness rolled in from the west chasing the light over the horizon. Standing straight and strong, watching the dilapidated trailer like a vulture, the Premier waited for the blackness to come.

C HAPTER THIRTY-EIGHT

Ever since speculating that Mark must still be alive a new energy and resourcefulness came over George. Problems which seemed insurmountable only a day ago had been gobbled up and digested in innovation after innovation. Chief among these concerns had been his mode of transportation, which George knew had been identified by the authorities. This had caused George much hand wringing. He had been locked into the absurd idea of coming up with cash to buy another vehicle. Since his new found ray of hope, however, the problem was solved with a two pronged, divergent effort. A suitable wreck was found and the plates exchanged with the dilapidated vehicle he was using. Various solvents were tried and finger nail polish from Barbara's leftovers came out the clear winner in lifting the current tags and re-gluing them onto the wrecked car's plates. After that, for good measure in further disguising the identity of the auto, he took the old battery out of the wreck and poured the acid into a jar. He took the acid and, using a piece of rubber for spreading, smeared the acid over large sections of the paint job. The next morning revealed a mottled mess of blistered paint and jellied goo which rinsed off with a hose borrowed from a gas station to leave a mixture of primer, bare metal and original color. Cover the ugly mess with a good layer of dust and the thing would be unrecognizable.

Passing a few bad checks, unthinkable to the despondent George, but not to the newly driven George, solved temporarily the money crisis. And the problem of being identified, now that he was becoming a renowned outlaw thanks to Ms. Cerasoli, was solved with a razor which shaved his head—an act George would have thought unthinkable under any other circumstance. With sunglasses, a good start on a goatee and transportation, George was ready for taking on the trouble at hand: where was Mark?

George was hoping Frank's mysterious silver sack might hold a little help in his quest. He realized it wouldn't lead the way directly. He knew if it could Frank would not have hesitated using it to guide the way. What George was hoping for was a clue, something to guide himself by. Besides, he was damn curious as to what might be inside.

Parked off the road, in a fairly remote location, George set about opening the sack. The nearly seamless rim shielding the inner connection flipped up easily. George was very interested in the way the material felt, almost metallic. He carefully inspected the inner seam and underwent the same befuddlement Barbara had at the lack of an apparent entry point. He put one hand on top and the other just below the seam and yanked. His fingers instantly felt like they were being chewed on by a hundred little rodents. A siren blew into one ear and out the other, screeching from low to high, feeling as if his cranial cavity was expanding and contracting in rhythm to the pitch. Suddenly the realization as to why the bag had shocked Barbara and not him came to his mind in a mocking tone: he hadn't yet tried to get into it.

George growled at the sack and raised his heavy boot off the floorboard to pin the bag against the passenger door.

Using his foot to hold the sack he pulled his hands free with a gasp. He shook the vibrating fingers in the air to dissipate the pain. The siren continued to wail. As his fingers regained their ability to open and close on command, George stared at the silver sack wondering how he would shut it up. The sound was piercing and George suspected it was more than just noise the way it hurt the ears and disoriented his thoughts. Just when he was getting ready to jump out of the car the alarm went silent.

George blinked, rubbed at the outside of his ringing ears and turned to his little, silver nemesis. George, to his pleasure, saw he had succeeded in getting the top of the bag open. He rubbed his eyes as if not believing them, still trying to reorient himself, and looked again. The entire upper seam had come apart and was gaping about an inch. Fumbling in the glove box George found a long, insulated screwdriver. He took it and poked the sack cautiously, then flipped open the top all the way. He pulled himself up putting a knee onto the bench seat so he could peer inside the silver bag. Using the screw-driver he poked at the clothes lying on top. Getting up his courage again, he tapped the sack gingerly with an index finger. Nothing happened. He did it again and still nothing. Growing in confidence he pulled the sack over for inspection with both hands.

Pestia's clothes were well known to George since he only had a few. They were on top. Below the stained and torn clothing there was a jumble of thin wires which came out in one mass, not attached to anything. On the bottom was a grey cylinder, looking as if it were made of plastic. George retrieved the cylinder and held it up for inspection. On one half of the cylinder, a long square section running along the tube, seemed to be a segment of a different make-up than the other half and the two ends. There was no button, switch or anything else suggesting apparent operation. George found that either end of the thing rotated when given a bit of pressure. The rotation of the side to his left did nothing, but when he rotated the side to his right he heard a 'click' and lettering appeared on the square. The lettering resembled something like hieroglyphics to George. They were a collection of lines and dashes arranged at differing angles. Rotating the side to his left caused a procession of the markings in whichever direction he was turning the end. As he rotated the end away from himself the markings appeared from the bottom. And, as he rotated the cylinder towards himself, the markings appeared from the top.

George rightly guessed this odd little tube was the receiver and complained out loud, "Too bad you don't speak English." As soon as George finished his sentence the word 'English' appeared in large type across the little square screen then faded into a smaller print of English sentences. "Yes," George hissed with a smile.

Hardly able to believe his good fortune, George looked around the vehicle to insure no-one had been attracted by the siren. It was easy to check, there was no-one or no thing within miles save a dusty bush or two and a million rocks. George could be forgiven, however, for the attack of paranoia. This was one of those moments in time where good fortune just seemed too good. Since he had begun this project it had gone from valley to peak, and peak to valley, in such a capricious manner he didn't know what to expect around the next corner. Here he was about to read the news of another planet, the first of his species in recorded history to do so, and he fully expected something to bring him crashing back to earth. He held in his hand a receiver from another place, an object which was about to enlighten him about the doings of another planet in the universe.

It was another time in a series of times he was feeling the significance of events, and they left him breathless.

In the top corner of the small screen there was a number. The number changed in no immediately apparent fashion as he scrolled up or down. George assumed, from his own earthly bearings, scrolling down meant he was coming to more recent messages. With one complete rotation of the left end of the cylinder the screen stopped scrolling. He figured this was the last entry. The number in the corner of this entry was 011180. The entry was short and didn't seem all that important, at least any significance was lost to George. It read:

Power flux success continues. Fleet com. transfer 11895, monitoring 610kHz.

George reached up to scratch his head while thinking, surprising himself with the feel of his bald scalp—it felt unnaturally smooth. The word and number "monitoring 610kHz" seemed the most significant item since he assumed he understood it. Someone was monitoring the AM frequency of 610kHz, but for what reason? He rotated the cylinder slowly backward and began to see the pattern involving the numbers. It would have been easier to see had they sent a message every day. Then the first two digits would have cycled down from thirty or thirty one, and the third digit changing as to the corresponding month adding a forth when necessary. Instead they jumped around and delayed his correct analysis: The number was a date, the first two digits the day, the third and sometimes forth the month. The 80 must be the year, the earth year, the message had been sent, corresponding to the fifteen year delay as indicated by Frank. It was the date, in earth terms, of when the message was sent. He had correctly assumed the entry read was the last sent; or at least the last to have arrived.

Not feeling any sense of time, or the heat which began to engulf him, George read entry after entry. He started out by greedily scanning all he could, then returned to his investigator's sensibilities and began taking notes bent on deciphering every cryptic statement. As he read he became more and more engrossed and a picture, an exhilarating scenario, began to take shape.

About six months prior to the last message received by the little tube, there began the mention of this Power Flux. From what George could make of it, it seemed to be referring to some sort of engine modification in the oncoming rescue fleet. Deciphering the exact nature of each message was hard in as much as the translation was spotty in points deferring often to vague words like 'thing' or 'that'. George postulated there was probably no English equivalent for and words that fit were inserted assuming Frank would know what they were talking about, or just have him read the original translation. A typical entry was:

15580 Remodification continues. Thing machined, power test proves rating. 15% enhancement test complete. It holds and improves. Will update rate.

Not something which made sense in and of itself, but when strung together with dozens of other entries a story began to emerge.

Scientists on Frank's home planet had designed engine improvements for interstellar travel. Since the rescue fleet was not travelling at the speed of light there was room for improvement and apparently some great breakthrough in speed enhancement had occurred after their departure.

Engineers had woken the crew from their state of suspended animation and set them to work on installing these design improvements en route. The messages sent to Frank were telling him about the improvements and as to their significance. When the significance hit George, he dropped his pen and stared off toward the horizon.

"The date," he said out loud. "What's the date today?. It's the ninth. Oh my sweet Jesus."

Design improvements had bolstered the interstellar speed by nearly fifty percent. Had they made the modifications prior to take off this would have cut the time of travel by one third, to about ten years. Since, however, they had done the modifications en route it would decrease the total travel time by somewhat less—to about twelve years. Or, to just about the time it was now.

It was the ninth of August, 1995, or 09895. The fleet communications transfer, fleet com., translated by George to mean the estimated arrival time to be 11895, or August 11, 1995; they would be monitoring the AM frequency 610.

CHAPTER THIRTY-NINE

Captain Barton ran his eyes across the headlines oblivious to the irony of an intelligence officer gathering information from newspapers. In the convenience store where he was browsing there was an ample supply of all sorts of chronicles ranging from screaming tabloid to relatively sedate. "Alien Invasion!" screamed one headline, "Johnson Rescued By Fleet of Giants!" bellowed one more. Another, a more responsible journal, read: "Still No Trace of Johnson." He picked up one edition which had a map on the front showing the location staked out by police for the previous three days and the last known sightings of the presumed alien. "Blood Checked By Experts, Confirms Alien" yet another headline said. Barton cocked his head and squinted at the large letters. He knew the definitive blood test results wouldn't be back for several days yet; the map, however, was what he wanted as it also had a summery of events to catch him up to date.

"You gonna buy one of them," the clerk snapped leaning over his counter to glare at the jaunty major. The flood of outsiders was taxing the cordiality of the good people of Barstow, right down to the lowly convenience clerk.

The indignant Barton gave the young man as demeaning a stare as possible and said, "Of course," and went back to his reading.

The young clerk, undeterred or unaware of the Major's haughtiness followed up his first rude comment. "Well?" he said looking back and forth between the paper and the Major's face. "There ain't no free reading. Not in this store mister."

Now completely flabbergasted at the pugnacious young man, Barton tucked the paper under his arm and made a stiff and quick march to the counter. Reaching into a pocket he flung a dollar onto the stand. "Keep the change," he snorted and walked toward the door.

Upon exiting the establishment the little door buzzer went off, followed by another series of beep, beep, beeps, which seemed more familiar. The beeps continued until the major, still steamed at being treated like a freeloader, realized it was his personal pager going off. He pulled it loose from its belt clip and read the LC display across the top of it. There was the number of the person paging, a number he recognized as coming from the base headquarters, and a one word message: NOW!!!!!!!!

The dapper and arrogant major was now in a complete state of humiliation. He felt he deserved better than a single word even if it was urgent; and all those exclamation points. They were acting like he was some sort of grunt ready to jump whenever they happened to snap their fingers. Perhaps he had made a few mistakes with the Gregaris file, but this was too much. At this distance from his supervisors Major Barton felt compelled toward subtle insubordination and pondered the idea of ignoring the message.

The late afternoon heat was oppressive. The cogitating major stood weighing his options and squinted toward the sun as it made its way toward the horizon. He glanced at his watch. Before coming to the desert he would not have believed seven-thirty in the evening could be a continuation of the hottest part of the day. He slipped on his smart looking sunglasses and looked at the pager once again. All right, he thought, I'll call.

There was a phone booth across the street in the shade of a short mulberry tree in front of a filthy looking gas station. Crossing the street he met eye to eye with a couple of men in suits—sweating worse than he was—who he recognized as reporters from the police station. He acknowledged them politely with a dip of the head. Reporters were everywhere and the good major was more than disappointed none of them were the slightest bit interested in talking to him. He felt like letting a few juicy tidbits slip about his mission in order to catch their attention, but knew it would only eventually backfire with his butt in a bigger sling than it already was. He dialed the number collect.

"Yeah, this is Barton . . . Major Barton, I've been paged." Barton stewed on the purposeful un-recognition of his voice; obviously some underling with an axe to grind. He wiped his dripping forehead with a handkerchief, tapped a foot, and glanced at his watch again. "Hello? Hello?" He was cut off.

Major Barton leaned over the top of the phone with his hand and let his head droop down onto his forearm. This too will pass, he thought. The indignation of having to suffer through a snotty operator, who was certain there would be no reprisal from a wounded duck like the major, made the heat all that much more unbearable. Sultry stuffiness clouded his lungs and raised his irritability. He dialed one more time.

"Yeah, this is Barton, again . . . Major Barton. I'm responding to a priority page. Yeah, yeah, I'll hold."

The major tried to reign in his temper. He tried to bide his time by looking around his surroundings. About one hundred feet down the side walk there was a local bar where he had seen the reporters dip into. The door of the establishment opened again and, this time a young, long haired, man with a loose swagger came out. He was quickly followed by a large man who Barton recognized as another reporter, one with an exceptionally bad attitude. The two men he observed talked for a moment then walked across the street to a fancy car. The incident was inconsequential to Barton and he went back to fuming at the receiver.

Bam, bam, bam. In frustration Barton hammered the handle against the phone. "Damn it," he hissed bringing it back to his ear. He leaned back onto the phone resting his head so that it was turned and looking down the street. There he saw someone else hustling toward the bar. He looked out of place since he didn't look like a local, not with the shaved head, and he definitely was not a reporter in his grubby clothes—at times it seemed the reporters outnumbered the locals. Behind the goatee and dark glasses there was something familiar about the stocky little man. He had a rigid walk and military gait, so un-like his appearance. And the expression, his brow was knit, worried like, worried like someone . . .

"Hello Barton?" the phone cackled to life. "This is General Trembath."

But Barton did not hear. He lowered the phone and set it slowly on the hook moving carefully now like a lion stalking prey. He knew the worried looking little man. He could be buried behind a stack of Hollywood makeup and he would have recognized him. Walking into a bar, not one-hundred feet away was Barton's ticket out of the doghouse. Right there in front of him was his career salvation; General and snotty operator be damned. This was going to be his finest hour. The little pigeon had flown right back into the cage for him to lock the door. It was Gregaris.

George had nailed down the problems affecting him just in time. Somehow his sub-conscious mind sensed the inconsistencies in his thinking and forced him to review the situation and find a ray of hope. He had found hope and used it to drive away the 'cant's', 'shouldn't', and 'won't' always associated with getting something difficult accomplished. With a little money, a different looking car, and new identity, hope flourished. With the hope came the huge influx of energy associated with the idea planet earth was not going to be alone come tomorrow. George had not slept since.

He rented a hotel room and did what he does best: plan. He studied maps, facts, locations, watched news reports, listened to the radio and tried to think of anything that might help. But nothing seemed to crack the solid wall keeping him from the rest of the protagonists in this little drama. There was no seam, soft spot, or end to be flanked. One assassin was out there, so was Mark, and nothing he could think of could link himself to either. In desperation he spent a good chunk of an evening cruising the roads near the police dragnet, then the rest of the night looking through bars and restaurants. For all he knew, however, both Mark and the assassin could be a thousand miles away by now. And, furthermore, there was no definitive proof Mark ever was here other than the assumption the location of the assassin would be associated with the location of Mark. The idea the assassin had been successful in killing Mark prior to his being chased out into the desert crossed George's mind, but he did his best to reject the thought. In his mind, Mark was alive and that was that.

It was midmorning when George returned to his hotel. He had purchased some cheap and awful Chinese food to stuff his face—the first food in two days—while he picked up on the news from a local radio station. About half way through a box of congealing noodles, news on the situation at hand came on with a live interview. With chow mien hanging from his bulging cheeks, sitting close enough on the end of the bed to kiss the screen, George reached out and turned it up.

It was a news conference with, as usual, dozens of reporters, lights, cameras and microphones crammed into an undersized room. The focus of the conference caught George a little off guard. A little cleaner and paler than last time he had seen her, it was Barbara, standing with a tired expression behind a wooden podium. George bit off the noodles hanging from his face, tossed his plastic fork into the box and the box onto a nearby dresser. "backstabbing bitch," he let out around the half chewed noodles.

"When and at what time did you become aware that Mark Johnson was an alien?" one reporter asked, the camera panning to him, then back to Barbara.

"For sure, I didn't really know until you did," Barbara replied. "It was, as you might sympathize, very confusing. Sometimes I believed it. Other times I just thought I was going crazy. I wanted to believe the people I was with, since they were very nice people. But I . . . well it was very unbelievable."

George could see the hurt in her face. She seemed very sincere. He waggled his head and made a cynical smirk of tacit recognition to the television.

"To follow up," the reporter continued, the camera panning back to him, "could you please clear up the . . ."

As the reporter spoke his voice faded from George's ears. His eyes had drifted off the reporter to the crowded wall behind him. Among the microphones, bodies and cameras was an exceptionally tall reporter, a black man. George rubbed his eyes and leaned forward until his face was nearly touching the screen. His mouth drooped open. He couldn't believe his eyes. The camera switched back to the young, tired woman. George's heart was pounding. He could feel a crack in the solid wall of separation. An illusion it might have been, yet it was a lead necessitating further investigation.

As fast as he could drive without attracting unwanted attention, George made his way down to the sheriff's department. He drove past the front of the building in order to size up the situation. There were news vans of every stripe all disgorging wads of cable. He parked near the end of the block and made his way back. Some of the first newsmen were coming out of the building on their way to their respective van or vehicle. On the front yard of the old, brick courthouse there were a handful of curiosity seekers and George took his place among them. Before he could look around or feel too hot, coming down the steps of the building, he saw a pair of fancy shoes. He followed the shoes up the long thick legs, covered with fine cloth, to the rotund center. The large hands, the color of a peach pit, swung confidently. The hair was different, the eyes not green, but it was him. It was the same assassin he had seen in the car out in front of Jeremy's house.

Sirens and flares were going off inside George's head. He felt as if his feet had become cement and his body a bright green roman candle of recognition. The big man slipped on sunglasses and walked down the stairs. George slipped his hands into his pockets and lowered his head, making himself more conspicuous than if he had followed the rest of the crowd into pushing closer. Though it was supposed to make him less recognizable, George had never been comfortable with his shaved head. Because it was so different from how he had ever looked before, and a more radical departure than ever from his conservative style, he felt as if it made him stand out from the crowd like a flashing, beacon. And now, face to face with his adversary, knowing this enemy, masquerading as a reporter, surely had seen his picture, George broke out in a cold sweat. The big head of the assassin swung from side to side, and George could feel a glance bounce off the top of his bald pate. The large man, to George's relief, moved on by.

Excitement was not a word for what George felt. It was an exhilaration beyond words. He had not been recognized and the hunter had no idea he was now the hunted. A quick walk to the car and the chase was on. He followed the huge man who was driving in a car more expensive than George's house had been. They ended up at the best hotel in town. Later, George followed him to the fanciest restaurant. George knew, at some time, he must kill this wretch. If Mark was alive, which George believed Mark was with all his heart, this fellow had to go to insure it stay that way. What he wanted first, however, was to know what the assassin knew. Was the other assassin really dead? Or had he escaped? It would be foolish to rush, show his hand, and let the other get away if he was still alive. Furthermore, George wanted to get away with it. He wasn't about to rely on the sensibilities of a jury believing the necessity of killing someone because he was trying to kill someone else and trying to explain the person he killed was from a different planet. George knew the vox populi had all the alacrity and acumen of a bridge abutment and would turn whichever way the wind was blowing and continue through brick walls of reason. He would do this in a way where he could go free, unworried about the possibilities of lynch mobs. Barbara would have felt better, he thought, knowing she had indirectly helped his search. Perhaps, when this was all over, he would try and let her know.

It was late afternoon, early evening before George followed Matan to a local bar. He waited in his car, feeling the sweat dribble freely down his head; no hair was there to absorb it. Not three minutes later a staggering boy appeared from across the street and entered. Not three minutes later Matan and the drunken boy came out, crossed the street and got into the assassin's fine automobile.

Who the hell was this kid? George thought. He watched the car go down the ruler-straight road for a while then got out to enter the bar. He wasn't going to lose him, George reasoned. He knew where he was staying and he hadn't seen him pack a thing out of the hotel. He would first try to pump some information out of the bar patrons as to the 'who' and 'what' then get back on his trail.

George entered the dark bar. He was hesitant to remove his sunglasses but had to in order to see. He walked up to the bartender trying to avoid the stares of the others which he knew must be reporters. "Hey ya," George said to the bartender, trying to sound as folksy as possible.

"Howzitgoin'?" the bartender replied, thankful as hell to have someone other than a reporter in his bar.

"Well," George continued leaning onto the counter, "I just saw some drunk kid come out-a here and I think I know this guy."

The bartender didn't like the inquisitiveness in George's voice. With all these reporters around he was instantly suspicious. "And?" he said.

The tone of the 'and' told George to take it easy. "Well partner," he went on in folksy talk, "that there boy, I believe owes me some money. Now, the funny thing is, is I can't remember his name. Bet you wonder how that is, don't ya?"

The bartender was still suspicious, yet a little curious as to how someone could be owed money and not know who it was doing the owing. Besides, this fellow had such a friendly smile. "How's that?" the bartender said, beginning to soften a little.

George's mind was racing: How was that? "Well," he started not knowing what to say until his mouth said it, "I was out drinking with that boy the other night and uh . . ." George thought as fast as he could, "and uh . . . the police came along and picked him up for being stupid. Seems that boy has a talent for it."

"He sure does," the bartender concurred now completely softened to the countryfied stranger.

"Yeah, he do. Anyway, I felt bad for him so I went down there to bail him out. You know. Somebody my age shouldn't be drinkin' with kids. So I loaned him the money to get out. Well, this kid just takes off. Don't say 'thank-you' or nothin'. The police won't tell me his name. Tell me it's none of my business. Well, I just wanted to find out where he lives, and maybe . . ."

"Beat the shit out-a him?" the bartender roared with delight at the thought.

George could feel the eyes in the bar crawling all over him. "Shhhh," he motioned, "now I don't want to hurt nobody. Maybe I could talk to his dad or something. You know. Set him straight."

"Good luck," the bartender laughed. "His dad is a bigger drunk than he is."

"So, you know where I could get a hold of him?"

"Sure, if you want to try."

"Yeah. Hey, what did he come in here for anyway? I saw him leave with some big, uh . . ."

"Nigger?" the bartender crassly filled in. George could now really feel the eyes on him.

"Yeah, that big guy."

"Oh, he's one of them asshole reporters," the bartender said, loud enough for the prying eyes and ears. He then snuck a glance around to gauge the effect of the phrase. "This kid—by the way, his name's Russell, Paul Russell—says he knows where the space man is. If you ask me he's tryin' to get money for booze. The boy's a complete scrounge. His daddy too. Both of 'em ain't worth the skin that covers 'em."

George left the bar, address in hand. He shoved it into his pocket but he needn't have kept the paper; he would remember something so important. The notion rattled around in his head: Just what if this drunken kid actually knew? If he did, he was leading the king's assassin right to him. In any case, if the assassin thought it an important enough of a lead of follow up on, so should he. He hurried to his car.

Perhaps it was because he hadn't slept. Perhaps it was the excitement and apprehension of his new lead, but George didn't notice a person following close behind. He didn't hear the characteristic click of military shoes on the sidewalk. In fact, he didn't notice the man at all until he sat down in the car and closed the door. Before he could make out the face, the body of the follower took a couple of long strides and bent down into George's open driver's side window.

344

"Why, it's captain Gregaris, isn't it?" Major Barton said, grabbing George by his dirty t-shirt and pushing his face close through the opening.

George instantly recognized the arrogant pretty boy who, only one year ago, had helped ruin his military career. A heightened state of awareness came over him. There was no time to think, he had to get away. "Don't know who your talking about," George mumbled, "get your hands off of me." The frantic captain tried to put the key into the old dash but the young major leaned inside to stop his hand.

"Oh, you know what I'm talking about," the major said, "and there's a couple of ways we can do this." George said nothing, thinking, thinking, straining for an idea. "We can either fight it out—I jump into this window, we scream and wrestle until the police get here, and they take you away. Or . . . or maybe you could come with me back to the base instead. Back to the base where you wouldn't have to worry about certain things: like a murder charge. You know what Gregaris? Bald is kind of becoming on you."

George heard the change of momentum in the aggressive conversation. This bastard wanted to deal and George had a good idea as to 'why' after the coming of the second ship. The arrogant asshole would be answering a lot of untidy questions about having buried the last report. "What do you need me for?" George asked, stalling for time to think.

"So many different reasons, George. Firstly, you can clear up all those misunderstandings about me and your report. Secondly, you can help all those good people figure out why we got aliens running amok. Seems a lot of people back at HQ actually think I was against your first report. I'm sure I could get you loose from the local authorities. That is, if you can get me loose from the headhunters back at the base."

The good captain cringed at the thought of cow-towing to such a slime as Barton. Now he understood the major's tactics. Though he gleefully would have gone to prison rather than cooperate, he pretended to ponder the options given in order gain some more time. "Can't go," he said at last.

"George," the major said with the confidence of a man in control, believing he sensed desperation in the captain's voice, "either we go to the base, or you go to jail. It's kind of simple."

"You don't understand," George said, pleading. "You don't understand. If I leave now, it'll all be lost. Here, I can prove it."

George started to reach under the seat but the major pulled him back up by his shirt. "Hey, hey, hey, no funny stuff. Keys. Give me your keys."

"Alright," George said handing over the keys. "No funny stuff. If you see this you'll know we have to stay. You can even help."

Major Barton was skeptical, but wrapped in the intrigue of the moment and flattered the captain was trying to squirm out of the ultimatum. It caused his ego to glow. He watched warily as the little captain reached under the seat. "Slow, slow," the major commanded holding onto the shirt.

George complied and pulled out, very slowly, the silver backpack. "Here," he said. "If what you see in here doesn't convince you that I need to stay, for just a little while longer, then I'll go quietly right back to the base and gladly clear up anything you want."

The major shoved George's keys into his pocket and took the silver sack. The words 'gladly clear up anything you want' resonated in his head. Freedom is mine, he thought and felt utter rapture at his apparent, impending absolution. "No funny stuff captain," the major said as he let go of George's shirt. "No funny stuff," he repeated. He inspected the sack for a moment, thinking more about his new state of power than the sack; feeling enhanced George had caved in so easily to his demands. "All right, how do you get in?"

"Just grab that flap and pull."

"Just grab this flap and . . . ." the major let out a scream. His voice was drowned by the piercing siren.

George fired open his driver's door bouncing the corner of the window guide off the stooping major's forehead. He got out of the car and lined himself up in front of the gyrating man. Barton was shaking back and forth trying to dislodge the attacking pack as if he were doing a hyperactive dance with it. George timed his kick as the major spun his direction and nearly lifted him off the ground by his crotch. As the major gasped and groaned under the severity of the kick, shock, and shriek of the siren, he fell to the ground. George pulled his keys free from the pocket and jumped back into the car. Squealing tires sounded his retreat as he sped away from the growing crowd; reporters had disgorged from the nearby cantina and were, as expected, noting the entire incident. He was sad to have to leave the bag, but it had done its job well. It was empty anyway. He wasn't about to put anything he might need back into a sack he hadn't figured out how to open without alerting the entire county first. Relieved as he was to be free of the major, George knew he was running out of time. He couldn't have picked a worse audience to escape in front of. The police might not be far behind. Maybe it would be good to have them following. Maybe he was headed for a show down.

CHAPTER FORTY

Millard pulled his craning, skinny neck back from the filthy window. "Hell, fuck-fire," he said shaking his head, "I swear I heard a gunshot. Wonder if that fool boy of mine tried to get him a gun so's he could come back here to scare you off. Hope that was him blowin' his foot off tryin' to load it." Millard looked down at the large, mildly inebriated young man who was sitting placidly on his couch. "You should've knocked the livin' shit out-a that asshole."

Mark shrugged his shoulders and let a smile add to his relaxed appearance. "I do not want to bother your child. You have been a good friend of mine."

"Yeah, well, if I could I would've knocked that un-flushed turd right out the door. He's too damn big for me now. Come in here spewin' crap out-a his mouth. Drunk off his ass. You should-a knocked him into tomorrow." He leaned to the window again. "Swear that was a gunshot."

"Your son, he does not like black men."

"Ain't like a man can like somethin' less. Stupid asshole. Just like his grand-pa. Head harder and thicker than a rock. Got no sense but bad sense."

"That's funny," Mark replied raising the bottle they were sharing. "I know people from my home who would not like him because he is white."

"Well there's a hell of a lot more to not like about that retarded monkey of a half wit than his skin."

Conversation between the two fell as the awkwardness of race rose between them. Replaying the events from earlier in the day was still a touchy matter. Paul had come into the home demanding that Mark leave. Millard had refused and Paul had caused quite a scene leaving the scar of racial hatred and epithets across their collective experience.

Besides the hatred of prejudice, Paul had also sown the seeds of innuendo. Since Mark had brought it up, talking about his home, Millard decided to follow along those lines of just where his visitor was from.

"Ya know Sammy," Millard said in between short gulps. "I've been meaning to ask you. Well, don't consider it impolite, but I've got to . . . well, you talked about people from your home. Just where the hell is home?"

Mark measured his response by looking the old man in the eye. "Do you believe what your son has said?" he asked.

Millard stalked across the floor with his odd gait, pulling off his hat. Spinning around at the other end of the dirty room he said, "Sammy, I seen some pictures in the paper. I know they look like you. But I want to believe you. Tell me and that's that."

Mark lowered his head trying to clear it of some of the alcohol and find the most ethical thing to say to his friend. He did not want to lie, but he did not want to have to run again either. "I do not think that I know what you mean. If I tell you that I am not, what will you believe?"

"That'll settle it."

"And what if you suspect what I tell you is a lie?"

"I'll still believe it," the old man said putting his battered hat back on.

Mark laughed. "You will believe me even if you know what I say is a lie?"

"It ain't for me to decide. That's for you."

"What will you do if I tell you that it is true?"

Millard shook his head and snatched the bottle out of Mark's hand. "I knew it," he gasped in frustration. "I knew I shouldn't-a brought it up. Now yer questioning me. Hell with it, I don't care. Don't give a sweet goddamn in a rhino's ass."

"In that case," Mark said laughing again, "let me tell you that I told you once before."

"Yeah, but I thought you was jokin' then."

"In a way, I was. It was funny to say so. You laughed very hard."

"Yeah. I laughed. But it ain't funny now. And not for the reasons yer thinkin'. It's that fool boy of mine. That fool boy that keeps goin' around pretendin' he's a walkin', talkin' butt-hole stick. By god, one day I'm gonna . . . Guess I should-a beat off that day when momma come around. Well, Sammy, bein' hows it's true—least wise you say so—we gotta get you gone. If yer the boy they lookin' for then they're on their way. That goddamned, belchin', droolin', empty-headed, scum-cravin', fart-smellin', greedy bastard boy of mine is gonna try and get rich off-a sellin' you out. We gotta get you somewhere else and pronto."

Mark suddenly felt more awake than he had been. It had been naive of him to not have guessed it. It had been more than naive. It had been just plain stupid. If the boy suspected he was who he was, he must believe he would tell friends, who would tell other friends, who would eventually lead the authorities to him. Mark should have known better but was blinded by his alcohol and, to a further extent, his unwillingness to leave a place where he felt so secure. Here, among the wreck and filth of a house ready to fall down, accompanied by a man who was certainly an outcast among his own people, Mark had felt a companionship he had not known in years. Here was someone willing, for no other reason than the fact he was in need, to house him, feed him, fix his car and share his last drink with him. The old, musty eyes looked at him without the pretention and judgement he had felt around him for the last year. Nor were they filled with the awe and distance felt from all of those well meaning subjects back home. Instead, they were filled with messages linking them together. A little sparkle detected in the old man's eyes connected with something behind the orbs themselves. A willingness to be open, honest and even disgusting in his presence. For all the respect and love he had felt for his faithful general, in some ways he felt closer to this gyrating little man, though it was a different sort of thing he felt for Millard. Certainly on a scale the weight of feeling would tip toward his fellow space traveler, from common experience and loyalties. But this wasn't something for a scale. It was a connection with another being that stood out from being reasonable or rational. It was an understanding which made Mark happy, and that was all.

Millard watched the large, young man pondering his options until he felt the urgency implied in what he was sure had been a gunshot. "Get up! Come on now. We gotta get you out-a here."

Mark stood up and gave Millard a forlorn look. "Where should I go?"

"Don't get pitiful on me now," Millard chastised sensing the sudden depression. "We'll worry about where yer goin' when you get there."

"Millard?"

"What?"

"Why do you not go and get the money of giving me up for yourself? It would be a very substantial sum."

The old, dusty farmer spit on the filthy carpet. "Oh shit, now yer really gettin' pitiful. Get yer goddamned bag and let's get out-a here."

Creaking down into the cluttered garage portion of the house Millard lead the way. Mark shoved his sparse number of dirty clothes into his gym bag and followed. Moving outside into the dimming light the old farmer suddenly tensed up. Sensing the little, crooked man's sudden change in demeanor Mark, half way across the garage, stopped and even backed up a couple of steps. Though it wasn't necessary, Millard motioned with his hand low and behind him for Mark to stop. Something wasn't right. It came to him just as soon as he walked outside. Nothing ever changed on the outside of his house. This was a constant view. Yet this evening something was different. The only thing immediately obvious was that 'something' was different. What it was he didn't know right away. His suspicions had been aroused by what he was sure had been a gun shot. The solution to his suspicion came more slowly than the suspicion itself.

Low and toward the wash to the far left side of his vision it came. A bit of red shone through some of the crouching creosote bushes down the road. Sunlight was dipping level behind the house and was illuminating something along the long drive-way, nearly, but not completely, out of sight from his perspective. Subtle as it was, dim to a point where it was almost not observable, it was there. No doubt about it, there was a reflector. It was the kind of reflector characteristic of the tail light of a car.

No-one ever parked in his driveway. No-one had reason to stop only half-way up the road. From the direction of the glitter it was either pointed out the driveway—an even more curious event, for someone to have come in then turn around to park—or it was across the road, blocking the exit, with the backend pointed toward the house in a cockeyed way. Millard figured the latter and this fact, coupled with the gunshot, perked up all of his sensibilities. Someone was blocking the exit. Someone had fired a shot—he was sure of it. It certainly wasn't his boy's modus operandi to be so subtle. Perhaps if someone had fired a gun right through the window to scare the shit out of him Millard would have known 'who' and 'how drunk'. But this was queer; totally unexpected.

Clouded as his faculties were with alcohol it would surprise people how sharp the wily old man could be. He noticed the light but refrained from glaring or staring at it. And a characteristic feeling was on him. Eyes were illuminating and tingling every bit of his flesh just as surely as if they were physically rolling around on the back of his neck. Someone was out there and not with the car. They were in the bushes, hiding themselves, watching. Rotating his head around he pretended to take in the sunset and nonchalantly reached inside the truck to pretend to rummage for something, thereby giving an excuse for having come outside. Then he stretched and nonchalantly sauntered back inside. Once through the battered entry he tried to push the door casually shut. It stuck, as it hadn't been closed for months, forcing Millard to give it a kick.

"Goddamned door," Millard grunted as he forced it to.

Mark looked around suddenly more suspicious of his surroundings. Staring at the old man he wondered at the pause outside, "What?"

"Somebody's out there," Millard responded in an anxious whisper. "Don't know who or why but it ain't that boy of mine."

"Who do you believe that it is?"

"It ain't the police. They don't worry about waitin' for nobody to come to them. Might be one of them reporters that's been pokin' around town. One thing's for sure. We gotta wait 'til dark to get you out-a here."

Plans had to be made. Neither of their vehicles were capable of traversing the desert cross-country and the only exit was blocked. They would have to leave on foot. If it could be assumed the person doing the spying was waiting for them to come to him down the road then it would be safer to exit the rear of the house. Millard knew every square inch of dirt in every direction within miles of his place and was confident he could navigate in the dark back to the main road. Water and a little food were gathered, enough for one night and the most of another day if it was needed. Millard dusted off his shotgun and searched around for the newest looking shells. His rifle would have been better in such open country but there was no ammunition to be found.

Mark stayed low and away from the windows growing more resolved for the task at hand. Responsibilities to his home were beginning to take their rightful place at the top of his agenda once again. Instinctively, Mark began to realize who was out there. As if he could feel the malice and evil crawling across the dusty rocks and into his heart he became more and more convinced Matan had found him. He wanted to be sure, though. He felt ill at ease simply running out into the desert to hide. He, as all people of Bren, felt a great compunction to try and kill him first. What would people of home think of him if he did not try? Would they expect him to save himself first? Would they forgive his drunkenness which had got him into the situation in the first place?

Millard scanned the outside in the last of the day's light by squeezing close to several cracks in the garage. Nothing in his field of view told him anything more than he had seen in his earlier trip out the door. There were two ways to play it, Millard figured, and both ways depended on what the person out there was up to. If the person was content to wait for them to come to him, it would be safer to wait until it was very dark and late and sneak out then. But if the person was waiting for dark to come in close, it would be much safer to get going right when the light was confused about whether it was day or night. Millard thought about it, pondering the best strategy, until he saw a movement.

Between the house and the wash, toward the beginning of the road, the land humped up a little bit, the residue of some ancient flood. On this little, rounded ridge the low bushes were thin and the rocks thicker. Tumbleweed tended to collect in front of it in bunches, the closest of which were not fifty feet from the house. Over the ridge he came, crawling, almost seeming to slither between the creosote bushes. He had picked the lowest point in the hump, a little crease no deeper than a foot or two. Over the hillock he came not making a noise until he disappeared behind one of the further bunches of tumbleweed. He had been exposed for no longer than ten or twelve seconds but it was long enough for Millard. His hand was now being forced. It was time to run. Millard slapped at his leg to get Mark's attention from inside the house. Mark appeared at the step to the garage kneeling on his haunches, supporting himself with a hand on the door.

Millard glanced away from the scene only in short bursts to whisper his orders. His fingers kneaded at the barrel of the shotgun as if working a lump of dough. "Time to git," he hissed lower than before. "I see our friend. He's sneakin' up to the house. Go on out the back. Git. Be damn quiet. Go out a hundred yards or so and wait. If I don't come in an hour keep on goin'. Just remember which way that road is or they'll find you by the buzzards circlin' overhead. I got ol' sneaky out there in my sights and I'll make sure he don't follow."

Mark shook his head. "What if he causes you trouble? I should be here to help you."

"Look son," Millard said rolling his eyes, "I ain't no hero and I cain't raise my voice to yell at you now. Git. One thing I do know is that he wouldn't be here if he didn't think you was here. So, if he's lookin' for you, he won't find ya. If he's lookin' for trouble, then he'll find it." The crooked old man patted at the shotgun for emphasis. "Either way I'll be fine. Now git. We know where he is now. That's our advantage. Got to grab what they give you boy. Now git."

Mark gripped his sack and double checked for his water. He was obeying orders but not liking them a bit. The back door had been cleared earlier of clutter, stacks of ancient magazines and buckets of paint. It had not been checked, however, for its ability to squeak, which it did no matter how careful Mark was. There were no steps and Mark used his long legs to ease himself onto the dirt from the height of the trailer. He took long careful strides not looking back. Using the route prescribed by Millard he made for a propane tank. Then, using it for cover, made toward an old abandoned pick-up. Behind what was left of the old machine Mark peaked back toward the trailer. He had not closed the door. He knocked the side of his head with the heel of his hand for having been so stupid. If someone were watching it was an instant tip off someone had indeed exited. Mark knew he could not risk going back but he stayed and stared at the door as if he could somehow will it shut by a contrite stare. He bent down and smacked himself one more time. Then he heard voices.

He was probably only one hundred feet out the back door and in the quiet of the dessert he could hear Millard's voice. It wasn't loud enough to make out what he was saying but the caution in it carried with the tone. It was like a warning, or an ultimatum. Silence fell again followed one more time by the anxious voice. Then a gunshot. Mark quivered as if the shot had gone right through him. It hadn't been Millard's shotgun. He knew it must have been the assailant firing the shot. Mark found himself panting, wanting horribly to run back to the aid of his friend. He peeked around the corner of the truck and the open door gaped at him like a black wound, now the most prominent feature of the house. He wanted to lunge at it, rip the door from its hinges and break it across the fiend on the other side. Impulses began running over logic. He actually twitched in a motion toward the trailer then pulled himself back.

Suddenly the roar of a shotgun was heard, once, twice and hope burst on him for a moment. Millard was, for the moment, alive. One more gunshot came and with it, almost simultaneously, a wail of pain. Had that been his friend? Now several more shots, in quick succession which brought another ray of hope: the fiend must be shooting at someone still alive. Mark turned and ran. What else could he do? His vision blurred through tears. Sounds of the battle tore at him. Scenes of his friend bloodied and dying filled his mind. Then it was him, the assailant. Like a swooping bird of prey his shadow swept on him and the vision of his face sank its talons into his soul. Matan was a demon, a specter of evil that had followed him across the expanse of space. As one might carry the memory of some great trauma inseparable from their being, Matan had become inseparable from his existence. Mark wiped his eyes and strained into the darkness. One more gunshot and he stopped.

Stuck between the want of valor, the duty of friendship, and the notion of saving himself for the greater good he froze and stared back at the barely visible house. He was to wait one hour for his friend. Or should he even bother? If the evil one had been dispatched, then Millard would come right away. If Millard was dead he was only wasting time. But what if Millard was wounded? What if his friend needed assistance? He stared at the house begging for some sort of clue.

CHAPTER FORTY-ONE

Pain always seems to peak just after the source is removed. When burning a hand leaves a hot piece of metal the hurt inevitably reaches its zenith in the instant after the metal is removed. Perhaps the mind is able to concentrate more fully on the pain once the urgency of getting rid of its origin passes. Perhaps the pain takes a little bit of time to travel the length of the arm and the worst of it is still coming once the hand lets go. In any instance, however, the pain climaxes after the fact.

It was just this climax that Major Barton was feeling after peeling the bag off of his fingers. He had succeeded in removing it by pulling it against the bumper of a nearby truck. He had rolled over to the old silver fender, gasping for air, grunting for strength against his battered testes, and hooked one strap frantically over the corner, yanked as hard as he could and rolled free. Laying on his back in the middle of the street he felt as if his fingers were going to explode or had already done so. The pain in his throbbing digits almost superseded the nauseating tidal wave emanating from his crotch, but not quite. Up through the mist of his bleary eyes and dulled senses were faces crowding close. Their mouths were opening and closing but nothing was getting past the sirens ringing in his ears, ringing as if a piccolo had been blasted through his ears with a shotgun. Lips were moving and they could be read as saying, "Are you all right?" His head rested flat on the hot asphalt, not noticing what it was doing to the back of his scalp. He brought both hands up so that he could see his fingers in his peripheral vision. As he stared into the sky, he flexed them to make sure they were still there and still worked. As the explosion of nerve impulses going on between his ears began to expand and dissipate, sending bits of his faculties off into oblivion, he gulped for some more air and reached out to some of the faces standing around him.

"Call . . . police," he gasped as helpful hands came down to pull him to a seated position. "Hurry. Call the police. I found him. I found Gregaris."

One of the men standing near, which had turned from a face to a pair of knees as he sat upright, spoke up. "Police are on their way."

The group conferred and several confirmed the fact the police had been called. But the group continued to talk and what they were saying, those bits beginning to filter into the mind of the Major, were upsetting. The group was wondering if anyone would show up. They were wondering if every cop in the county, let alone state, was now on its way to where they had trapped the spaceman.

"Help," commanded the Major breathlessly, "help me up."

Helpful hands came down and pulled under his arms raising the shaky man to his feet. Nearly sinking back when the pressure was let loose the hands came back to pull him over to the hood of a car for support.

"What spaceman?" the major asked. "Where? When?"

One of the helpful hands responded. "They say he's holed up in a house down near Adelante. They say it's the same one that was hiding in the desert."

The major tried to clear his head and respond. But on the verge of retching from his penalty kick, he could only gasp out, "What?"

Still another voice behind him followed up. "Yeah, I heard it on the radio not two minutes ago."

Continuing his recuperation the nauseous man wheezed out, "Where?"

A voice in front of him answered, "Hell, you could just follow the train of cars."

As if to punctuate what had just been said a news van roared by barely missing some of those who had gathered in the street. The major looked around him and noticed there wasn't a tie to be seen; a sure clue that the reporters had indeed made a hasty departure. If he had been more conscious of events as he was agonizing, he would have noticed the disgorging of the bar. Some of the reporters had to literally run around his writhing body in order to get to their cars. Pagers all over town had lit up and every phone line into the area was jammed. The electronic age has not only brought information faster but also in tidal-waves of saturation. Mankind, as a creature of flesh and blood, was having to physically jump and run to the next spot. None of those doing the running thought about the impossibility of keeping up with electronic pulses and wireless transmissions traveling at near the speed of light. All of them were on their way as the electronic pulses which had sent the crowd scrambling had already faded from terrestrial memory and a thousand more filled the air with new and different messages. The electronic age has great advantages of efficiency. But, as early users of the computer found out, and reporters have yet failed to realize with their own machines, if you put garbage in you get garbage out. The rallying call to the town of Adelante was urgent, yet without reason. It was full of importance, yet without merit. Much nearer, at an old trailer, events infinitely more meaningful to the universe were being played out.

In a small house in Adelante, the police had truly trapped one of the aliens. They had followed a tip from a petrified young Hispanic man whose car had been abducted right under the nose of a sheriff. The man had escaped while the alien slept and run to a neighbor's house nearly a mile down the road to phone the authorities. Less than a minute after the phone call the electronic hurricane began and not a minute after that the entire population of hotel occupants in Barstow, California was on the move.

Nagrom was exhausted and seriously dehydrated. He had fainted more than fallen asleep. Once he had filled himself with liquid, whatever energy that was left in his system went to processing the restoring fluids. Normally, in the past, he would have fought the urge to lay down. He now, however, gladly let the swoon come upon him. Prior to his reformation he might actually had found the energy to fight it. But not now, the will to fight had been taken out of him. Happiness and contentment were now his goals. Peace, of mind and planet, was now his marching order. When the bullhorn woke him from his deep slumber he was not surprised. He was, in many ways, relieved. He could now pay for his sins. He could now shed the demons of the past and walk to his future gladly paying any penance required.

Looking outside the kitchen window toward the front of the house, Nagrom saw the sun setting behind the police cars parked there. Men, of a different color than he, and yet men, crouched behind their cars pointing their weapons. Ironies of all kinds filed through his mind. Ironies of a hunter being trapped by his game and one of the finest soldiers of

Ranson refusing a fight, willing to face judgment for a crime he was ordered to commit. He bent down into the kitchen sink and washed his face. Cool water would be one thing he would never take for granted again. Splashing the water into his countenance, using his huge hands, he pretended it a baptism of sorts. He knew of the Christian religion. He had studied it as part of his pre-mission collection of facts. Since he was on planet earth, he reasoned, let this now be my own revision. Let this cool water symbolize the cooling of hate, the gelling of hostility and the washing away of old sins.

One can only imagine the astonishment on the faces of the sheriffs present when a man described as armed and dangerous, who had eluded a dragnet of unprecedented scrutiny for three days surviving the desert heat, and who was supposed to be an alien of immense power, simply walked out the front door to offer himself for arrest. Nagrom complied to their every wish with a pleasant docility, even with a serene smile on his cracked and mutilated lips. He laid down, put his huge arms behind his back and gave no resistance to the placing on of handcuffs. It took some time before the deputies watching the scene lowered their weapons and relaxed. They kept waiting for this being from another planet to pull some sort of trick, to spit out a death ray or to simply vanish. But nothing of the sort happened. So total was their bewilderment they completely lost their sense of protocol. They didn't know whether to put him into the back of their police car or wait for some special vehicle. Should they read an alien his rights? With mouths gaping, many sheriffs simply stared at the tremendous physique, circumnavigating the huge man in wide, slow circles. As the television crews began to swarm in, however, they decided to go with convention and put him in the back of a unit to drive him to the station.

The officers had been confused by Nagrom's actions only because they did not know their captive's demeanor. They did not realize, yet, their prisoner was glad to be in their possession. They did not know that by being caught Nagrom had finally set himself free.

C HAPTER FORTY-TWO

By the time Captain Gregaris had deciphered the bartender's confused directions and reached the house it was nearly dark. Several wrong turns and dead ends aggravated the exacting captain to no end. He half expected the entire police force to have beat him there by having taken a more direct route. He would have thought himself at the wrong location because their absence had he not seen the name on the mailbox. Rusted and dented, the remains of a mailbox, leaning sorely on its rotted post, proclaimed the residence with the barely-visible, handwritten name 'Russell'. Up the dusty track, leading to no house he could see from the road, he saw the fancy car parked sideways, blocking any entry, but no driver. George passed the track until the view of his car was blocked from the showy vehicle by the dip of the highway and parked.

George figured that if someone in the driveway had been listening carefully they would have heard him cruise past and park. He could have gone further down the road in order to insure a more clandestine arrival, yet his sense of urgency told him to work more with speed and less with caution. It was George's hope whoever was there was not being so careful. He pulled his little twenty-two pistol out of its holster wishing he had something much larger and more accurate. Through the dimming light he started off the shoulder of the road into the desert, back toward the driveway.

Widely spaced, low bushes among the rocks gave just enough cover to keep from being seen but did not impede his progress. He crouched low and kept a brisk walk across the desert scrabble, zigzagging between bushes. Plans began to formulate in his brain. Going down onto one knee he craned his neck up to scout the horizon. He could just see the roof of the shack and its proximity to the assassin's parked car. There was no sign of the murderer himself. What would be the strategy?

Should he assume Mark was still inside and make haste? Should he assume the drunk kid was probably no more than just making drunken boasts and take a 'wait and see' approach? How much time would he have before the authorities did arrive? They surely must be on their way. The trail could easily have been followed. He was seen coming out of the bar, they would question the bartender, and the bartender would tell them he wanted directions to Paul's house. Had they already arrived and, seeing their suspect wasn't there and left? Not likely. They probably would have had it staked out just in case. Despite an impending arrest, George wished the authorities were already there—the security in numbers against a formidable assassin outweighed George's fear of going to jail.

Then another twist to his strategy: Was this the opportunity to kill the assassin? Could he kill him, leave the weapon behind, and assume the police would treat the drunken boy as a suspect? Not likely and drunk boy or not it was beyond George's ethics to implicate someone else in a crime he had committed.

He continued to creep forward while doing his strategic planning, proceeding until he heard voices, then there was the first gunshot. George was startled but went right into action. On a quicker pace, he continued his stooped run to the house until he came to the top of the slight rise overlooking the ramshackle domicile, gun in hand.

There he was: The assassin, Maybe ninety feet away from him, he was bent behind the back of an old pick-up. Inside the door of the dilapidated place he could see an old wiry man moving cautiously out the door holding a shot gun. In the hand of the assassin, George could make out a long barrel of a hand gun, maybe a forty-four. The quick thinking military man put the puzzle together quickly. The noise had not been a shotgun. The old man was not hit. The assassin must have missed his mark and was now taking cover.

As the little man came out of the house George was in a quandary. Should he try and yell at the man to warn him of his assailant's position, or should he make a run at the bastard and try to kill him? Yelling would give away his position and ruin any possible surprise. George would have to be much closer for any semblance of accuracy with his small weapon. The longer barreled gun of the assassin was much more accurate than George's weapon. If he were seen, George could be picked off much easier than he could do any picking. George lost the debate when he found his feet moving toward the crouching assassin. Inherently it was his attitude to force the fight.

He ran low and fast feeling horribly exposed, though neither of the two protagonists noticed him at the moment. Fear and adrenalin pulsed through his veins. It was a gamble, but George now had his fig-leaf of self defense in a court of law to kill the assassin. Though the events seemed a long, drawn out period of time to George, the occurrences came and went very fast.

Matan leaned to near the edge of the truck to spy where the old man was. Millard saw the corner of his head but his old reflexes were too slow. He fired once sending out a flash of light, pumped and fired a second shot out of frustration at having missed the first, succeeding only in blowing into splinters the corner of his truck's old sideboards. Matan turned away quickly from the blast doing a spin toward the hood of the truck. As he spun he saw George rushing at him from behind, through the gloom. He raised his small cannon and fired just high of George's diving body to keep George in the dirt. Matan sprinted to the front bumper to find a more defensible line of fire.

Noticing George, and being startled by another person in his front yard with a gun, Millard stopped his advance on the truck and raised his shotgun reflexively at the prone military man. George was trying to get a clean shot at the retreating assassin when he saw the barrel of the shotgun swing his way. He yelled intending to indicate that he was a friend, but only came out with "Hey!" and dropped his head as flat to the earth as possible expecting a shower of pellets. Instead, he heard the boom of the forty-four and, almost simultaneously, the old man wail in pain. George brought his head up to see Millard clutch at his shoulder and stagger back until he fell hard against the weathered boards of his garage, falling propped-up in a seated position, blood pouring down his shirt. Matan had put the poor old farmer out of action. George now had no ally in the field.

The captain let go a quick couple of shots as the large target darted behind the far side of the vehicle. The large, dark shape disappeared for a second, only to only to reappear on the bulbous hood of the battered, oxidized truck, leveling his ordinance at George. George could feel his sudden vulnerability crawl over his skin, tingling his scalp and widening his eyes. A nakedness of exposure lit every pore on his body. Wide open as a barn door he might as well have had a target painted on his forehead.

As the gun came down to rest on the hood, giving the evil Premier a perfect platform on which to steady and aim his gun, everything seemed to slow even further. George was thinking ten thoughts at once. He damned his small gun and poor aim. He wondered how he should tempt fate. Should he pray for a lucky shot at the better covered, better armed enemy? Or should he make toward the bunch of old tumbleweed, save his ammunition, and try to gain some tactical advantage in position? Perhaps he could make it to the fancy car, render it unusable, and close off the assassin's escape. In that millisecond, when thoughts were spewing into George's brain from many avenues to intersect at that one point, one thought took precedent. Run!

George fired one shot at the hood trying to force down the head of the attacker to gain some breathing room. He then rolled over and over until he gained enough momentum to leap to his feet, pressing both hands on the rocky, warm earth. He heard the thunder of one shot, then another. He swung his gun wildly toward the truck for another cover shot as he ran. Ten feet before the tumbleweed the thunder of another shot came and this time the thunder had lightning; lightning which gave searing agony through the upper part of his left leg and knocking his feet out from under him. Suddenly the world was sideways, the pain clouded his urgency for a crucial second. He had fallen hard enough onto his elbow to wrench his shoulder and cause him to let loose of his little twenty-two. George rolled onto his belly and scanned for the weapon. In that instant, the amount of time to fall, drop something and regain it, the large man was on him.

George's eyes came to focus toward the vehicle just in time to see the foot coming. Matan kicked the little man in the face with all his considerable might. Gregaris' whole body spun on the impact, which nearly knocked him unconscious. In a wholly instinctual move at preservation, fighting through incredible pain, George rolled onto his stomach and tried to get to his feet. A large, heavy foot came down on his head pushing it sideways to the stinging earth and holding it helpless.

George heard the hammer cock on the forty-four. Time froze as the stalwart captain waited for it to go off. The delay seemed interminable. Mouth pressed against the earth, his sharp, panting breath blew dust into his eyes. He was now less scared than disappointed. Though fear was one of the many things he was feeling, he was more disturbed by the fact he had failed; first his friend Frank, then himself. The pause in his execution continued. The adrenalin pouring through his veins drove out the pain and gave him thoughts. Think, think, he told himself. Don't give up yet. There must be a way out.

Matan looked down at the battered little man and took stock of things. First the wretched, little creature in the house tried to ambush him, now this savage. These filthy, little animals were ruining his plans. All of his glorious schemes were coming unglued. He had put this one in the bag a little too soon and it infuriated him. Vindication would have to wait one more day. Those who had delayed it would pay.

Matan took heart in the fact he had recognized this second one from his picture in the paper. He was deemed by the media as being an accomplice to the earthling wench Nagrom had let slip between his fingers. He surely must know something about the Prince. And if he didn't,

Matan would make him wish he had known. Extracting any usable information would only take time. He would make the wretch pay for ruining his plans and delaying his grand absolution. He would make George reimburse him for every hour of deferral through an hour of agony in interrogation.

And the plans were truly ruined, thought the Premier. If the Prince had been there, as he truly believed he had been, the little scared rodent would be long gone by now. Maybe this was just a trap gone awry? If it was, then the foul, little inferior would know where the prize was hiding. He would talk. He would tell the Premier.

As Matan considered the foiling of his master plan he started grinding his foot against the cheek as immediate punishment. Gregaris groaned and tried, futilely to grab at and stop the pressure of the shoe. Matan leaned his full weight onto the head then jumped off only to send George's body sliding against the ground with a massive kick to the ribs. All air left George's body. He rolled onto his back convulsing for the lost air. Through the pain and sand in his eyes he saw the massive foot come down again, this time onto his throat.

"Well, well, little pig," Matan said in his cool, pleasant voice he reserved for such times of his pleasure, "it is time for you to tell me where I might find a friend of yours."

George shook his head in response, gasping to get a little oxygen down the pinched esophagus. The huge gun was close to his face and aimed between his eyes. Though it was nowhere touching him, he could feel the spot where it was being aimed, just above his nose. Pressure increased very slowly until foot was completely choking him. In a final act of preservation George swung up as hard as he could at the testicles of the huge man, but his arm was well too short to meet its mark. The pressure increased sharply on his esophagus until George thought it was crushed.

As the smaller, wounded man began to pass out, Matan expertly let off the pressure just enough for him to get adequate air to come to. "Yes, good soldier, fight," the pleasantly vicious man crooned. "All good soldiers must fight. And yet, all good soldiers know when to surrender. You will surrender. You will tell me what you know. I have hours and hours of plans for you my good soldier. You will have days to contemplate surrender, to beg for it. You will beg for me to let you surrender."

The foot came down hard again and with it a roaring thunder. A thunder that, instead of the pain of lightning, came with a rain. It spattered onto George's face as the foot came off of him. He rolled over and opened his eyes, coughing, gagging for breath and clutching at his throat. He saw his hands covered in blood. He wiped his face with the other hand and it became stained with more blood. He quickly and nonsensically felt for the spot between his eyes, just above his nose, his quivering hand expecting to find a hole. But there was none. In front of him was a pair of shoes. They were not the same pair of shoes which had kicked and choked him. Following up the long legs he saw it was Mark, looking skyward with both arms held high, one of them holding Millard's shotgun.

Then came the roar of triumph George Gregaris will never forget. It was a scream dredged up from the soles of the feet right up to the outer most hair on the head and it filled the air and soared to heaven. No triumphant howl of any being throughout all of history could have matched this triumphant howl. It was a screech which melded with all the release and triumph available in all of nature which had spawned such an urge to bellow. The ground seemed to tremble under its might. It would be a roar carried heavenward at the speed of light until it lit up every window of every house throughout an entire planet. The echo would be heard in cheers and songs and sonnets over drinks in feasts and in parades and festivals for a thousand years hence: Matan was dead.

CHAPTER FORTY-THREE

The world would never quite look at itself the same again. As one's actions are influenced when one knows they are being watched, the citizens of earth were now influenced every day with the knowledge they were no longer alone in the universe. A planet, alone, can have illusions of grandeur the universe was created only for them. One small speck of dust, on the corner of a hundred-billion stared galaxy, amongst an expanse of a billion more such galaxies, carried such arrogance as long as it was isolated. Yet, when there was definitive proof that across the expanse of space there existed another culture, from another root, having differing ideas as to why the universe was created and such grandeur was shattered and arrogance withered with the shattered remains.

A lone, huge man, or rather being, sitting serenely in a cell out in the desert, had altered the planet's perception of itself. Scientific analysis on his genetic and chemical makeup proved he was different beyond a shadow of a doubt. To those who held out the belief he might only be a freak of our own nature, Nagrom offered scientific information which dwarfed their own, and glimpses of worlds beyond imagination. Finally, in the coup de grace of proof, he gave coordinates of his home planet's position and frequencies of appropriate communication in order for them to establish contact. This final step of connection might prove extra-terrestrial existence to the last, paranoid, person who still clung futilely to the pomposity of the Homo sapiens having the exalted place in all of creation, but probably not. One annoying character flaw found in Homo sapiens is the ability to maintain belief independent of fact.

National leaders would clamor for his attention. The focus of six billion people would be his when he spoke. World organizations would follow his advice. And yet, for now, Nagrom's only request was he has a window where he could see the night sky and have further communion with the celestial partner which had changed his life.

On such a humble request, the sheriffs quickly complied. Even in this time of skeptics, prior to definitive, scientific proof he was alien the guards were enamored with their well spoken prisoner. Though he admitted it, they had a difficult time matching this well mannered and pleasant man with the pitiless, torture-murder of a pitiful, homeless bum. Yet details he gave about the gruesome murder told the Los Angeles detectives he was too accurate to not have been there. He also told them of the evil accomplice; the one who had ordered the killing; one which must be hunted to the death before he spread his remorseless terror further. The police would eventually find and have Nagrom identify Matan's body. The knowledge the Premier had met an appropriate fate brought Nagrom great satisfaction.

Enamored as they were with their guest the earnest, country sheriffs were more enamored with the attention he was bringing them. Outside the humble little station, not much bigger than a suburban home, hundreds of cars and vans jammed the streets in every direction. Where there had been grass on a front walk there was now thick lumps of cables going to lights and television crews jockeying for position. Authority upon authority upon authority all came together at the spot to screech for their right of jurisdiction. Jablonski and Espinoza were there arguing for the city of Los Angeles. Major Barton was there insisting an alien was an issue of national security—let alone his job security. The San Bernardino County Sheriff's Supervisor was there mostly drowned out by the others. And it was not long before the F.B.I. was there. Each and every one of them argued their case as to why this prisoner was actually their prisoner.

The great eye of society was now upon the little town of Adelante. It leered close in tunnel vision to a being who had already forfeited his role in titanic events, intent on nothing else than in finding insouciant, inner calm, and the righting of past wrongs. Not far away from the focus of that great electronic eye, which perceives itself as all-seeing through its myopia, was the real story for the ages, going on completely out of sight of the all seeing eye. Twenty miles away a Prince and his two recuperating friends were set to be written into the history books of worlds beyond. As they hobbled around cheering their success and mourning their loss no-one, other than they, on the three planets concerned knew what was going on. The presumptive focus of all of mankind was, typically, on a mere sideline.

Though he could not have known what had just transpired twenty miles to the north-east, Nagrom was aware what his capture had done to the focus of the electronic eye. Therefore, when the question came, "So is this Mark Johnson one of you?" Nagrom did his part. Through the question Nagrom saw the vision of the rising moon in the desert. He could remember his contrition and vow of change. Pale colors from the scene filled his mind along with the tranquility which was inspired by them. In that instant he knew he held the keys to all his fellow beings light-years away. Flashes of battle, flags, fallen comrades, and loyalties that seemed farther away than his home charged one side of his mind. On the other was only a belief. In this speck of time Nagrom clung to his new belief. The belief he had been wrong. And in the pursuit of righting these wrongs, he felt that the shield of righteousness was now his. And now, in this instant, the response to set it all right. Nagrom replied looking puzzled, "I have seen his picture in your papers and know of him." As a pause rested in the packed chamber, a feeling of freedom and release washed through his entire soul. "But he is not one of us. You need not seek him." Nagrom would hold onto this one lie until he had knowledge the Prince had safely departed.

Unbeknownst to the Prince and his devoted, ragtag sentinels, their former enemy had now released them from the dragnet threatening their capture and a possible ruination of a King's return. And unbeknownst to Nagrom, the return of the King was at hand.

It was the grave-yard shift and Carl 'The Alley Cat' Jones was reading one of the many articles in the L.A. times about the capture of the spaceman the previous evening. Daytime personnel were fast asleep at their homes; the janitors had gone away. He was the now the lone inhabitant of the little radio station. Sometimes, when he was tired, he didn't care too much for the night shift. But usually he liked it. Nobody cared how he dressed. Nobody much cared what he said on the air. He could be as un-kept and rude as he felt and nary a complaint came across his desk.

The building he was in, with its tall transmitter blinking a red light on and off to ward off phantom planes, was on the outskirts of town. Essentially a plain, square box, it was built by a cost-conscious owner without heed to location or style. The nearest neighbor was almost a half mile away. Outside, the courtyard was lit with a pair of old-fashioned incandescent spotlights. The wide, graveled yard around the station was empty tonight save for the big four wheel drive of the lone occupant. It was one of those hot summer nights having a sort of electricity in the air.

The bearded, spectacled and corpulent Mr. Jones stretched and scratched at his belly. He had no idea as to what was about to happen. There was no window in the broadcast booth to the outside where the disk jockey could have seen him coming. Carl would not have been alarmed if he had. Weird things happened on the graveyard and he would have just told him to come back in the morning if he wanted to talk to someone. If it had been the old rock station he had worked at back in L.A. he would have been more concerned. Rock stations were more prone to having weird things happen to them than country stations and in Los Angeles weird was becoming the norm. And more often, anymore, weird was accompanied by dangerous. But not out in Victorville. A lone stranger appearing in a parking lot hobbling along would not by itself make alarms go off in anybody's head. Even a person as beat-up and scroungy looking as the one getting out of the old car.

Most everything at KVAH was preprogrammed and Alley Cat only got on the air when the coffee could no longer do its job. It had been an uneventful night and the weary disc-jockey was having to go to the mike more than usual to keep awake. "Hey everybody out there," Carl said trying to sound enthusiastic about the just finished song. "If that last one don't get yer blood pumpin' then yer already asleep. Alley Cat Jones here, and don't you-all forget that yer listenin' to K-Country KVAH, six ten on your AM dial.

Now let's scoot a little boot to the fine beat of our next little ditty while the Alley Cat howls." The tired young man turned the appropriate dial then let his headset drop onto the table. He groaned, rubbed his eyes while yawning, and stretched out on his chair again. When he opened his eyes the hobbling little man was there.

The door to the broadcasting booth was open and there stood George. The sight of anyone standing unexpectedly in a doorway at three A.M. would have been startling enough to the drowsy Mr. Jones, but seeing a person as battered as George was truly frightening. Eyes puffed and purple, both lips cracked and swollen, scratches and scrapes from the chin down to the neck. The poor captain was a terrible sight.

Carl jumped to his feet yelling, "Hey, you, what the hell? What the hell you doin' in here man? You don't belong in here." He took a couple of steps toward the pummeled, worried looking, little man to scold him further and escort him out the door. He stopped and recoiled when George raised a forty-four.

"Well Alley Cat," George said with a smile that revealed a freshly broken front tooth, "you wouldn't believe it but I do have a reason for being here."

Carl 'Alley Cat' Jones, after viewing the huge gun, was more than amenable to show the wounded captain how things worked in the station. He showed him how he could shut off the music; how to tell when he was on the air; and how to broadcast live. Then he obligingly crawled under a table and sat with his back toward the big gun.

George was tired and in pain, yet the enormity of events were carrying him on a cloud. He looked around the silly little broadcasting booth and tried to get a grip on the magnitude of what he was about to do. He pulled the piece of paper out of his pocket on which Mark had written the message. It was spelled out phonetically for him to read. Though the coming armada surely would have a capable linguist aboard, they figured a message in the home language would insure results. George practiced it until Mark was sure of its comprehensibility. In a few minutes, from such a homely and humble place, he would return a King to his throne.

The wounded and weary captain had precious little time to ask Mark questions. Only twenty-four hours after the shooting they needed to be ready and there was much to be done. Millard was in serious shape and needed a hospital. The captain's wounds, though throbbing, could wait for more extensive treatment; more than the field dressing and a couple of belts of Millard's whiskey. Mark talked while dressing the captain's wounds and dabbling alcohol at his many scrapes.

He told George, politely, he thought many of his questions irrelevant. Many of the little gadgets he presumed that a "spaceman" would have simply did not exist on his home planet. Gadgets, Mark explained, were created for reasons. On his planet, until very recently, there was no need to have all sorts of sneaky little devices which killed, maimed or spied on people. Efforts of intelligent, creative people had gone into advancing medicine, science, engineering, and the arts. All of these areas were vastly advanced over those of this planet. He found it incredible George was not interested in these things. He further explained he and Pestia wanted to bring as little as possible which would identify themselves as different. The only 'gadgets' they had brought were the receiver, and an interesting array of wires which, when used in conjunction with the receiver, could act as a sophisticated radar device. It was brought along to monitor the intentions of air traffic in case Ranson had sent a fleet after them. Furthermore, the array could, when modified, act as a sounding board of friendly radar to notify an advancing fleet as to their location. Monitoring the 610kHz was only a backup to the array and for any special instructions which might arise. George sheepishly told him he had discarded the jumble of wires. Mark laughed out-loud and pointed out the irony of George discarding one of the objects he had been searching for. "Obviously, my friend," the Prince had said while tying a bandage to George's leg, "our peoples are very different." George sat in an embarrassed silence, wondering why he had not asked more important questions first.

Mark told George it didn't matter where he was to be picked up. The fleet, with its larger, more powerful and more sophisticated ships could pluck him from most anywhere on the planet without fear of interception. George thought, true to his sense of humor, Mark should be picked up in the same spot where the other two crafts had landed. Mark did not understand the significance and considered hiking out into the desert to be retrieved an unnecessary burden when they could come and get him right where he was standing. But he wanted to follow George's wishes to help repay his help and loyalty to Pestia. George was ecstatic. What would the old brass think, George thought, having a third extra-terrestrial land in the saline valley?

Mark thanked George for his courage and George thanked Mark for the experience. And just that quick he was gone, driving north for his rendezvous with destiny. George worried something might happen to him along the way. Though alien, George mused, he was just as human and prone to failing as he was.

Not wanting to wait too long, and fearing he might get too wrapped up in reminiscing, the ever efficient captain grabbed the microphone, shut off the music and read the little paper. On it was a message telling the oncoming fleet in their language to 'listen and come to this place'. "Juju imp Rye-eel-tock imp ron-jock-ee," George spoke carefully into the large, fuzzy microphone. This was followed by the latitude and longitude of the landing site, right down to the minute and second. George repeated the message perhaps three-dozen times, waited a bit, then did it again.

After several more minutes, George leaned up to the microphone to try it one more time. As he leaned forward, in a quick pulse, the station lights dimmed and every needle on the panel went crazy. A few seconds later another pulse, then nothing more. He could not prove it, but George was sure it was their way of telling him the message had been received. As he leaned back into the soft, leather chair a feeling of satisfaction came over him like he had never known.

Terrified as he was, the big man under the table began probing his captor for motives. "What's all that shit you sayin' over the air?" Carl said. George didn't answer. Trying to find a way to reason with him, Carl pursued, "Now, you must know, that when people heard all that stuff that you said on the radio they probably called the cops. Somebody's bound to be comin' to check on what's goin' on. So you better not shoot or nothin'. I mean, they only got you on a few felonies now. You don't want to go up for murder."

George let his cracked-tooth grin grow again. "Just stay put and nothing is going to go wrong."

The speculating Mr. Jones continued, "You know, I bet them cops is already on the way. You probably only got a little time to get out-a here. And, hey, I didn't see nothin' if you know what I mean." The pained captain was getting tired of the conversation and didn't respond.

As if to fulfill Alley Cat's prophecy George heard a car pull up outside. He got up to lean out the open door of the booth. It was, indeed, a sheriff's car coming across the gravel courtyard toward the front door. George casually walked down the hall and locked the outside door, returned to the sound booth and locked it also. George, for some reason, felt compelled to buy a little time. Maybe he just wanted to savor the moment. Maybe he wanted to collect his thoughts. Would they understand what he had really done? Would they consider them mitigating circumstances even if they did? How much of what was past would they continue to hold against him? George had never been in a jail cell and wondered how it would feel. George, from the papers, knew that Nagrom was now in custody. How would he correlate George's events? Would he at all? Would George become famous? Despised? Loved? Revered? Forgotten?

Moments after he had returned to his seat the phone in the booth rang. It was the sheriff. George told them who he was and told them he had taken over the station for a little while. He said he would be coming out in a minute or so. They seemed surprised to have a hostage taker so amicable to surrender.

George put down the phone relishing the irony of the moment. Very soon they would be singing the praises of his name on a planet across the galaxy and he would be in handcuffs. He pushed the appropriate switch on the panel, leaned up to the microphone and, just for good measure, repeated his message one last time. He needn't have. The transport was already descending. Sensors had followed the progress of both previous ships and the advancing fleet knew the landing site well. In a matter of minutes, the good Prince would be in the welcoming arms of his countrymen and the American military offered another lesson in humility.

"Hey buddy," George said to Alley Cat. "You guys got anything to drink in here?"

Alley Cat responded, eager to please, still showing George his back. "Sure friend, look in that little refrigerator under the sound board. We got beer and everything."

George bent down and pulled open the door selecting a beer. He pulled the tab and took a long draught. The cold liquid stung his broken tooth. The weary captain looked to the ceiling, raised his beer and said out loud, "The King is dead. Long live the King."

After hearing George's side of the conversation with the sheriff, the scared Mr. Jones became a little more confident he wasn't about to be shot. "I told you the sheriff was comin'," he said. "Just what the hell are you doin' anyway?"

George laughed and took another long drink. "Why? Can't you tell?" he asked. "Can't you tell that I've just become an interstellar hero?"

THE END